This is a work of fiction. Names, characters, orga...   ...places, events and incidents are either products of the author's imagina...   ...ly resemblance to actual persons, living or dead, or

Regrets by M J Tennant

Published by M J Tennant

Barnsley, S71 5SH

https://mjtennant.weebly.com/

eBook formatting by KDP

ISBN: 978-1-3999-4623-0

Dedicated to those of us who live in the past. It is human nature to make mistakes, learn from them and move on. Life is too short for regrets.

Live life to the fullest xxx

Contents

One

Regret

noun

a feeling of sadness, repentance, or disappointment over an occurrence or something that one has done or failed to do.

Fuck my life.

Have you ever thought back to that one moment when everything turned to shit?

That impulsive decision you made to 'seize the day', only to have it bite you on the arse the morning after?

Yes? Well, join the club; almost one year later, and I'm still dealing with the fallout.

I'd made a mistake, screwed up in the worst possible way, and now said 'mistake' had just sauntered into the bar like a reoccurring nightmare. His unexpected appearance was like a heavy chain being draped across my shoulders.

The moment I noticed him almost forced my heart to stall; if only time travel were possible, I would *literally* sell my organs to go back and change things, but of course, reality bites. Life has no undo button.

He was here, in the flesh, and totally unavoidable.

I took a deep breath, mentally coaching myself to remain calm, that feeling of needing to escape was almost consuming; reality crashing into my lap.

I was sitting in the local pub catching up with my friend Connor, who *must* have noticed my look of panic, as he twisted to shoot a bored glance over his shoulder.

Luckily, my 'reoccurring nightmare' hadn't seen me yet, and I shrank against my seat, trying to look as small as possible. Maybe if I kept going, I could disappear entirely. That would have been so much better than having to deal with the shitstorm that was fast approaching.

The name of that storm; Hurricane Nathan, aka Nate Lane (a fucking category five). Raw panic started to burn the back of my throat.

Connor viewed my wilting body with an unsympathetic expression before rolling his eyes.

"You'll have to see him at some point, Ella—you both live in the same fucking village. You can't be a pussy forever," he announced, stating the bloody obvious. There was no in-between with Connor. It was either black or white, and he usually backed the black team; this guy was all about the darkness.

My lips suddenly felt dry as I sucked in another anxious breath before leaning across the table, my body language on full attack mode.

"I thought you said he was in London?" I whispered sharply, unable to hide the accusatory element from my tone.

Connor rolled his insanely broad shoulders, totally indifferent as he quirked his head to one side. "He was. It appears he's back now," he pointed out flatly.

I grunted and pushed back into my seat, huffing. "No shit—tosser."

He shot me a lopsided smile and flipped me the finger. He didn't give a rat's arse that trouble could be brewing. Connor embraced conflict like it was the closest of friends.

Personally, I *hated* drama and avoided it at all costs. To provide you with more understanding as to how far I'd go to escape it; I'd spent the best part of the year in America, *thousands* of miles away. Hiding.

Now I was back and had to deal with this perfect storm that was homing in on me like a missile. Why did I suddenly feel as guilty as fuck? Connor was right, I *was* a pussy.

My brother Tom came back from the bar, dragging out a chair and plonking himself into it.

"Sup?" he questioned, flicking a glance between us whilst placing his pint on the table. Connor took a swig of his beer, watching me intently over the rim of the bottle. He shrugged.

"Nathan's here and Ella is shitting in her pants, bout sums it up," he replied drily. I wanted to punch him in his condescending God-like face, even though I'd probably dislocate my wrist. The guy was as solid as a rock.

Tom looked uncomfortable and he swung a veiled glance around the room before saying, "I'm sure it'll be fine, it's been ages. I thought everyone had moved on?"

I shot Connor a cautious look. Tom didn't know the full story.

My brother was always the positive one, the saviour. It was in his nature to attempt to put things right. That's why he was training to become a vet. Well, that and the incessant need to climb further up our father's arse; brown-nosing little git.

Our dad owned a veterinary practice and was proud that at least *one* of his children had decided to follow in his footsteps. I was the screw-up; Tom was the prince. That's just the way it was in our house.

I didn't feel guilty that Tom was still in the dark about my secret. My 'mistake' was *far* too delicate for a girl to share with her *brother*, the only person I had told was Connor. My confession had of course been partly alcohol induced. I wasn't a sharer by any means and most of my friends were boys, it would have been weird. At the end of the day, when it comes to female issues, some things are better left unsaid.

Nate turned away from the bar and our eyes locked. His reaction to seeing me was mixed. Shocked at first, to the point where he almost did a double-take and then a strange expression set in; inquisitive I would go for.

A boulder the size of Yorkshire settled in the pit of my stomach.

He smiled shyly and I returned it; not wanting to embarrass him. Kyle and Max, two non-identical twin brothers were with him and they also paid for their drinks before heading toward us.

I swallowed as they approached our table and shifted my chair to provide more space.

Connor shot me an eyebrow that stated 'good luck, there's no way I'm tangling myself up in *that* web of bullshit'. Now being Mr. Unsupportive and all that. He could be such a difficult sod.

Tom stood, also moving his chair, and then the boys did the usual fist bump, man hug shit as they greeted each other. Connor of course, remained *exactly* where he was. His hello came with a flick of the beer bottle he cradled against his chest.

Not wanting it to appear awkward, I too stood and dished out some huggage, I'd not seen anyone for a while and so remaining seated would have looked odd. No one batted an eyelid about Connor's unaccommodating behaviour of course. It was well known in the village that the guy had a mile-wide streak of stubbornness and played by his own rules.

As I got to Nathan, I smiled up at him. Yes, I was bricking it, but I was also pleased to see him (sort of). We'd been friends once, good friends. Before 'it' had happened that is. It's amazing how something so normal can taint things.

We embraced briefly. His scent brought unclear images of 'that night' into my thoughts and the arguments that had followed for weeks afterward. The whole situation was bathed in regret; for me anyway. I pushed those thoughts aside as I felt meltdown-mode fast approaching.

"How have you been?" he asked, looking down into my upturned face; I could see he was nervous.

"Good, you?" I replied as brightly as I could manage before drawing back, and putting more space between our bodies.

His eyes roamed over my features like he'd not seen me in a decade. "Not great," Nathan began in a sad voice, "I'm not going to lie."

Fortunately, the others were too busy fumbling to get their chairs under the table. I certainly wasn't intending to hold our unavoidable discussion in front of an audience. Connor just remained sat where he was in brooding silence.

"We can talk later, OK? When we're on our own?"

He nodded, and my pulse twitched with relief.

We took our seats and the banter started to flow. There was a definite hint of awkwardness from the get-go, but as the hour ticked by, this thankfully lifted.

I spoke about my time in the States with my auntie and the places I'd visited in New York. Nathan hung on my every word like he was taking notes at a meeting. He even asked me to repeat certain bits; so, he didn't miss anything.

Connor watched him silently, buried amusement in his dark gaze, but I could see it. Trust Connor to find joy in my pain, I swear the guy got his kicks from seeing other people suffer.

Kyle and Max started to co-tell a story about the police raiding an abandoned farm in the next village and Connor, now looking bored shitless, stood and went to the bar.

Once he was out of earshot, Tom came to life like a caricature of himself beside me. It was almost as if he had been waiting for that perfect moment to offload, and spill his guts. I was thankful, as his timing couldn't have been better. It distracted Nathan, who shifted his gaze and stopped staring at me like I was his next meal.

"So, Harlow's arrived. Met her this morning and my God," he began, almost dribbling, "she's gorgeous." He was such a bellend.

I frowned, confused as to the 'her' he was talking about. When it came to my brother, I rarely understood what he was saying. He was the most cryptic person I knew, like a Rubik's cube with the stickers moved around; un-fucking-solvable.

Nathan beat me to it. "Who the fuck are you on about Wade?" he asked, calling Tom by our surname.

My brother drained the rest of his pint. "Harlow, Mike's daughter. She's here and pardon my French but fuck me, she's so cute."

I sat upright in my seat, surprised; Tom knew the word fuck?

All the guys suddenly stood to attention as if he'd just announced the arrival of an underwear model. Here we go. I had seen this sex-starved guy's response before. It was severely pathetic to watch.

Unfortunately for the boys in the village, there was a definite female totty drought in our part of Yorkshire. Luckily dad's practice ran an apprenticeship program for student vets and vet nurses. This meant that young, pretty girls would study at the surgery occasionally. Not that they were *all* pretty, but they still had breasts and vaginas; two major preferences when considering the tastes of the hormonal imbeciles sat around me.

Nathan also appeared interested and I wasn't sure how I felt about that.

When he wasn't watching me, I allowed my gaze to roam over him. The guy was good-looking, I'm not going to lie; dark hair, olive skin, and a proper boyband-worthy face; he just wasn't the one for me.

My deadbeat brother was still *rambling* on like he'd found the love of his life. "She's small and pretty, a definite natural blonde with bright blue eyes. Killer body, I couldn't stop staring— even Marcus commented."

I almost threw up in my mouth. Marcus? The thought was *so* gross; the guy had to be pushing sixty. Dirty old sod.

"You planning on tapping that?" Kyle questioned with a dirty grin to which an unfazed Tom jabbered.

"Maybe, but after a few dates, so we can get to know each other better. We're not all perverts you know."

I snorted and pinned Tom with a look that said it all. "You know it doesn't count if you have to drug them, right?"

My words caused the others to laugh and my brother shot me a fake smile and the two-finger salute. The guy didn't stand a chance if Connor's stepsister was as hot as he was making her out to be. There was an ongoing debate within our friendship group that the deodorant Tom wore, contained woman repellent. He had as much luck with girls as I did with impressing our parents.

More chatter about the *angel sent from heaven* spewed forth. You'd think they'd all been *starved* of female company when I was sitting *right there*. OK, I knew I wasn't God's gift to men, but I wasn't a total hog, surely? Maybe I needed to start wearing makeup?

I suddenly felt small and insignificant, ironic considering that is *exactly* what I had wanted to be when Nate first appeared.

Feeling subconscious in my oversized hoody, I knew I was seen as 'one of the lads', having known most of these guys for years. However, they could have toned it down a touch. Even Nathan had jumped on board, and I was suddenly invisible. Fickle twat. My eyes narrowed in on him with renewed curiosity. He was probably trying to make me jealous.

"So, you're thinking of asking her out? Like on an actual date?" Nathan chimed in with a curl to his lip, the shape more of a jeer than a smile. Any awkwardness he'd felt when he first saw me was gone now, and he was happily back on his throne. Not a throne made from iron, like the one from Game of Thrones, Nathan's seat was made from the rotting bones of past shit-stirrers.

Tom shuffled uncomfortably in his seat before muttering a quiet, "maybe."

Nathan scoffed. "Good luck with that one bro. You'd better run it by Connor."

"Run what by Connor?" Connor's voice suddenly bled into the mix like a sliced artery as he appeared back from the bar with two beers. He handed me one, his face unreadable.

Tom cleared his throat noisily and shuffled nervously in his chair. Talk about being caught with your pants down.

An amused, knowing look circled the table as Connor straddled his seat. "Well?" he repeated, his eyebrows arched in question.

There was a beat of silence and I decided to fill it; having no shame in throwing my brother under the bus.

"Tom met your new stepsister today and he can't get rid of his hard-on. He reckons the collar definitely matches the cuffs," I replied crudely with a chuckle, taking a sip of beer with a forced innocent expression.

Even after I attempted to lighten the mood, the atmosphere was still rather tense.

Connor took his time to reply and a petrified Tom quickly blurted. "There was no talk about hard-ons or anything else actually. But yeah man, Marcus and I bumped into her earlier, she seems all right," he back-pedalled. He was *such* a vagina, but I suppose who wasn't when it came to dealing with someone as unpredictable as Connor. The guy was a ticking time bomb.

The whole village seemed to have been waiting for the arrival of Mike's daughter like she was a fucking movie star attending the Oscars. I'd been in another country for weeks and *nobody* apart from Nate seemed overly bothered that I was back. Where the hell was *my* red carpet? A renewed rush of annoyance pumped through my veins. It appeared I needed some new friends. Harlow this and Harlow that. Connor had also been banging on about her for days. Although not in a good way. He spoke about her arrival like she was a new strain of COVID.

Connor had offloaded one night having met her at his mother and stepdad's anniversary party. After what he'd shared, I'd concluded that she sounded like a proper stuck-up bitch. She lived in Surrey in a *massive* house with her mother, yet still sponged off her father whenever she needed something. It was textbook stuff. She was probably one of those girls that looked good, but had *nothing* interesting to say. Like the type of girls who timed their life around the latest season of Love Island. Nice and shiny on the outside, but on the inside, dull as shit.

Connor leaned back in his chair and glanced around the table with a hooded expression, giving nothing away; not to the others anyway. Only I could see the lurking danger. We wound each other up, but we were close. Con and I had shared our demons one night after getting blotto on Absinthe on the beach last year. I grimaced at the memory as I still couldn't stomach the stuff. And by that, I meant both the drink *and* Connor's demons.

Tom took Connor's silence as a green light to carry the hell on and that sense of doom continued to pulsate in my gut.

"She seemed cool; great sense of humour, and easy to talk to. Only arrived this morning." He directed these facts *at* Connor as if he was telling him something that he didn't already know. Yep, if there was a king of the twats; my brother would be it.

The muscle in Connor's jaw started to tick, which was not a good sign.

"Tom told us she has nice tits," Nathan lied with a toothy grin, his ability to needle Connor impressive. The two guys were usually OK, although they weren't the closest of friends. Nathan still bore Connor's mark, a slim white scar on his right eyebrow. A reminder of a past fuck-up.

Tom rolled his eyes and was just about to chip in but thought better and knocked back his pint, even though the glass was empty. He was such a twit.

There was a beat of silence before Connor replied in a bored voice, "can't say I've noticed." He then lifted his own drink slowly to his lips. He was probably silently counting to ten. His counsellor had taught him this trick as a calming method during a crap anger management course.

My brother, who could not take a hint, carried on regardless. Go ahead, Thomas. It's your funeral.

"I thought I'd give her a tour of the village and stuff, once she's settled—if you're cool with that of course Con?"

In unison, all the others turned slowly to Connor for his answer, almost holding their breath. Like that pinnacle moment at the end of the movie when the big reveal occurs. It was comical really, but I hid my smile.

I felt Nathan's foot move against mine like he was trying to send me a message, but I purposefully ignored him and concentrated on watching the brewing storm before us. As I mentioned earlier, Connor was so unpredictable, there was just no way of knowing how it would go.

The big guy was now sprawled in his seat, taking *ages* to reply, his eyes laced with scorn. The quiet treatment was possibly a tactic he used to intimidate his prey, like a tiger in the grass before it pounced.

Connor suddenly cleared his throat which caused everyone to jump and Max almost knocked over his beer.

"I doubt there's any point, Tom. Once the novelty has worn off, Barbie will piss off back to London. Without your or anyone else's tail between her legs, I might add. Not that any of you twats would stand a chance. She's too squeaky clean to bother with farm scum."

Everyone laughed nervously at his words, which held a blatant 'stay the fuck away' message.

His reply intrigued me. If the girl was so amazing to look at, Connor would surely be the first one to get in there, irrespective of whether she annoyed him or not. He enjoyed angry sex as a coping method, my friend Natalie had explained one night.

Connor slowly ran his gaze around the table, taking in everyone's expressions, before simplifying his message for those that were not-so-bright. "To put it into words that you pricks understand. She's fucking off limits."

There was another moment of silence around the table. Usually, burly village boys didn't take too kindly to being called names, but if Connor Barratt was the one doing the calling; they let it slide. A disgruntled look circled the table as he unashamedly cockblocked his friends.

"Interesting warning. I'd say you want to bang her yourself," Nathan suddenly announced, crossing his arms over his chest. He was definitely the bravest and, at times, the stupidest of us all; Max being the one who currently held that title.

Leaning back in his seat, he continued with his goading.

"Sounds like you're definitely after that pussy yourself, Barratt."

Connor suddenly straightened and rolled his shoulders before cracking his neck from side to side. A gesture he did when he was pissed off.

"Sounds like you're after a broken nose, Lane," he drawled as he put his beer down, linking his fingers and placing his elbows on the table in front of him. The guy had big fists, and let's face it, everything about him was *huge*. And yes, I mean everything, so Natalie informed me. I certainly didn't know first-hand.

Like persistently farting in Church, Nathan didn't know when to stop. He unfolded his arms and necked his beer before stating.

"I don't hear you *denying* it, especially if she's anything like Wade described. Which I will take with a pinch of salt, Tom being Tom. I remember that receptionist that he went on and on about for days; absolute munter."

I watched Nathan thoughtfully. So far, I was impressed by his fairly calm attitude toward seeing me again, but where Connor was concerned, he reverted to type. The two boys humoured each other and that was it. They both knew that if it ever came to physical blows again (a story for another time), it would end their part-truce for good.

Connor's expression was pensive as he stared across the table, without turning his head in Nathan's direction.

"Kind of weird really, her now being your little sister," Nate prodded again. He really was a proper tool, if only the guy had a mute button.

Connor flicked him a glance.

"She's not my sister, shit for brains."

Nathan pulled a face, undeterred.

"But surely, she's family now and you'll be living together. That's just my opinion of course."

"And since when did I give two shits about your opinion dickhead?" Con sliced back.

Nathan just sat there wearing a shit eating grin, brazenly enjoying provoking the beast. He was nuts, *everyone* in the village knew the guy he was baiting was a loaded gun.

Connor was definitely ruffled, but his icy control was still intact, partly due to the medication he was taking I imagined, otherwise the table would have been thrown over by now. The guy took prescription antidepressants. They helped him keep his shit together, *most* of the time.

"Have *you* seen this centerfold Ella?" Kyle put in from my left, blatantly not wanting to be left out of the drama. "It would be interesting to get a female's opinion."

I shook my head and took another sip of beer.

"Nope, but I'm gonna and I'll let you know right," I responded with a playful grin and a wiggle of my eyebrows. I too enjoyed a wind-up.

Connor un-steepled his fingers and grabbed his beer, snorting as he continued to eyeball me over the rim of the bottle. I could see that he was now mildly curious at my decision to join in the poking. He saw what we were doing and that this was a 'ganging up' type of scenario. It did happen on occasion, but it was *always* Connor who came out on top.

"And why would you want to do that, Ella?" Connor drawled out slowly, leaning back in his seat, those dark penetrating eyes never leaving my face.

My reply was immediate as I volleyed back. "To check out the competition, of course." It wasn't a total lie as if she was as stunning as Tom was making out, she may threaten the one thing I truly wanted. Let's face it, Barbie, I was not.

Connor smiled wolfishly as Nathan then cast a suspicious look between us. He was probably jealous, but he had *nothing* to worry about. Where Connor was concerned most girls wanted to climb that like a tree, but not me. The headache that was Connor Barratt was not what I wanted at all. We had only known each other for a couple of years, but we were more like brother and sister. I was probably closer to Connor than Tom. He certainly knew more about my life.

Connor stared at me for a long icy heartbeat.

"I wouldn't upset yourself, Ella. There is no competition. Tom's right; she is quite the sight with the face and body of a porn star but nice and pure, unlike some, that's for fucking sure."

That was some slap-worthy shit right there. Any other girl would probably have burst into a full-on strop at Connor's words, but not me. Nope, I had been trading insults with this guy since the day we met.

"So, you admit she's fuckable. With your track record, I can't imagine you keeping it in your pants for long. Shall we place bets gentleman, oh and Ella of course."

14

There was a burst of supporting banter that whizzed around the table. Excited chatter about the newcomer and how this would affect Connor's constant thirst for sex. I wrinkled my nose at the thought. Yes, he was my friend but the guy was probably riddled.

And just like that, the atmosphere shifted as the object of our playful teasing decided he had had enough. We all knew the guy blew hot and cold at the drop of a hat and was, at times, unhinged. It was a well-known fact to most people from the village that he had issues. I, of course, knew the background behind those issues. 'Screwed up' didn't even touch the sides.

Connor rose to his feet, larger than life, shooting a glower at all our faces. A 'dismembering stare' I would say, holding a definite message. I just grinned back, but Kyle and Max dropped their heads as if scrambling to hide from the sudden heat of the fallout. What did they say about the heat and the kitchen? Well, times that by a fucking million.

Nathan's stance remained unchanged, but he'd wisely dropped his gaze. I'd met some obnoxious personalities in my time, but Nate had the ability to top them all.

Connor's tone was biting and he spoke down at us like a teacher telling off a bunch of naughty kids.

"Maybe I won't control myself; we all know I usually don't. Maybe I'll see if Harlow does taste as pure as she looks. Let's see, shall we? But I tell you here and now that the rest of you fuckers better keep it in your pants, unless you want to lose it. And that goes for you too, Ella. Just in case you do bat for the same team. God knows you dress like you do."

After what was his parting message, Connor necked his beer and *slammed* the bottle on the table *hard*, making everyone jump. The guy had attitude in fucking spades.

Nate turned to watch his departure with a mocking expression before spinning back. "Well, that went well," he chimed brightly with a cheeky grin, over-fucking flowing in his own self-worth.

Kyle tutted over Nathan's sarcasm. "Are you fucking high? You don't know when to leave it, *nothing* good ever comes out of riling the fucker."

"He's right Nate, you should have shut that shit down sooner. It's like you want him to deck you again," I cautioned jumping on board. Nathan Lane had always had a wicked sense of humour.

Nate's eyes were now assessing my face with a look that said he liked what he saw. Butterflies started to flutter in my stomach; a fucking zoo of them. I preferred it when he was ignoring me.

Swirling his beer around the bottle, he replied.

"I can take him," with a cocky smile. His words were firm, but they lacked confidence.

Puffing out a breath, I ran a hand through the wispy curls of my cropped hair.

Kyle and Max exchanged worried glances and Tom… well, I don't know what he did. To be honest, he'd been so quiet, I had forgotten he was there.

"Did Connor just call you a dyke?" Max suddenly reflected with his stupid face on. He wore this at least once a day. Pigeon's grasped things quicker than Max. The clown was a total school drop-out, but fun to be around; *most* of the time. Unfortunately, brains and Max didn't share the same fucking planet.

I barked out a laugh at Max's comment and lifted my eyes to the door that Connor had left through. I didn't feel fazed by his lesbian remark; he knew there was no truth in that after I'd confessed my 'mistake' and who it was that my heart truly desired. I also knew he'd be fine with me, there was never any grudge-bearing between me and Connor.

Pushing my thoughts aside, I responded to the dope sitting across from me. "You can't say that these days dipshit, you have to say gay. Political correctness and all that." Like he would know what *that* meant. Too many syllables for dear old Max to handle. I corrected him on purpose to help him, the guy wasn't homophobic, he was just as thick as shit. He'd have used the word not realising that it wasn't something that was accepted in today's society, where everyone should be allowed to be whoever and whatever they wanted to be.

There were deep grooves in Max's brow as he attempted to compute what I'd said.

"I suggest you google it," I advised in a bland voice.

We all concentrated on our beverages in silence. I could feel Nathan's eyes drilling into me and at that point, I refused to make eye contact. I couldn't be dealing with deflecting any more silent messages.

The distraction that was Connor's stepsister had now left the building and my having-it-out-with-Nate-chat was speeding toward me like a race car.

I decided to break the tension. "So, anybody watched that new series on Netflix, The Watcher?"

The chatter recommenced, and it flowed OK, with Tom *attempting* to change the subject back to Pickering's new shiny treasure, Harlow fucking Williams. Had the guy not heard a word Connor had said? He should have been fitted with an off button at birth. Part of me hoped he asked her out. The guy so deserved Connor's foot up his arse.

I purposefully checked my watch to signal it was time to leave.

"We'd better head back Tom," I suggested.

"I know it may come as a shock, but I've only had one beer, so I'll drive you home in mine if you'd prefer, Ella? I know you don't like riding in Tom's car with all the dog hair and shit," Nathan put in with impressive speed as I necked the rest of my drink. Part of me wanted to scream no and run for the hills, but I accepted that the time had come.

Tom was looking at me with concern while Nathan took our empties over to the bar. "Will you be, OK? The car's not that bad actually. Marcus helped me clean it out the other day. You can come back with me if you want?"

I shook my head, eyeing Nathan's back. "No, it's fine. He's sober. I can deal with him when he's like this. Tell mum I'll be home before ten."

He pulled me in for a hug which wasn't totally unwelcome. Tom was a nobhead, but he was still my brother.

"See you later dickhead," I quipped grinning.

"Will do shit-face," Tom volleyed back in an amused tone.

I said goodbye to Max, Kyle, and Tom as Nathan came back from the bar.

As we left the pub, two things happened and I wasn't ready to deal with either.

We walked into the car park and Nathan turned toward me, looking down into my face with a longing expression. It appeared our time apart had not changed anything, for *him* anyway.

17

He was standing way too close and he shot a quick look around the area, scanning to check we were alone. The guys must have left through the other exit.

Facing me, he mumbled, "It feels like you were gone ages during your last trip. It felt like I'd never see you again," Nate whispered. He meant it too, it was written along every pained groove on his face.

I could see the intent in his eyes and he leaned down and planted a quick kiss on my lips. My tummy flipped-flopped as the contact still took me by surprise; but I felt *nothing.* No fireworks; nada.

Nate was standing too close really; he needed a lesson on boundaries and I stamped down the unfair urge to kick him in the nuts.

The only thing the kiss did was remind me even more of my colossal mistake; the drunken night we had shared when I'd slept with this boy and had given him my virginity, something I had regretted every day since. Tortured myself over.

Nathan's phone suddenly rang out and he took a step back and held up a 'one-minute' finger as he took the call. As he moved away, I lifted my fingers to my lips; they felt numb and there was no tingle, no fire, nothing. Not like when 'he' kissed me.

Nathan motioned toward his car as he spoke to the caller and I zoned out as I approached the passenger side.

Leaving him alone to continue his conversation, I lowered myself into the entitled A-hole's Porsche. The obscenely expensive, probably hand stitched leather, creaked against my backside.

My heart was like a crazy person trying to escape behind the prison bars that were my ribs, as Nathan ended his call and eyed me through the windscreen. His shoulders were set in a hard line and I wondered who he had been talking to.

After a brief smile, he joined me in the front, moving to start the car, sharing the identity of the caller with me. I took it like a bullet.

"That was Ryan. He's back from Scotland," he mentioned drily.

It felt like a firework had gone off in the car; *Ryan was home*?

For all that is Holy. I sure hoped my fake smile didn't break my face.

You see, that was the problem, the 'complication'.

Ryan Lane was Nathan's older brother. He also happened to be the guy I thought I was falling for.

Yep, I had shagged the object of my affection's *younger* brother in one moment of drunken madness. Proper seedy I know.

And then comes the fun part.

Neither brother knew about the other; Nate didn't know I had feelings for Ryan, and Ryan wasn't aware I had slept with Nate. To put it bluntly, it's a bitch of a situation, hence…

Fuck my life!

Two

Nathan fired-up the engine and it growled to life. Said vehicle was a limited-edition Porsche 911 GTS in python green with black leather seats; a twenty-first birthday present from earlier that year. What could I say? Nathan Lane got a hard-on for all things fast and flashy. The car he'd driven last year, a Range Rover Sport, had been just as ostentatious, but he'd wrapped that one around a tree one night after a few too many Bacardi's.

He'd gotten away with it, of course he had; he was Nathan Lane, a member of the Lane Elite. Un-fucking-touchable. The Lane family lorded their privilege like the world owed them one.

I eyed his profile warily as he pulled out of the car park, wondering if I had the guts to take the initiative and start the conversation. I wasn't sure what to expect, his calmness had an alarming quality to it, as 'Hurricane' Nathan was rarely calm.

He beat me to the punch.

"So, how does it feel, being back?" he began, darting a glance toward me before refocusing on the road. He sounded so relaxed, unfazed even. I knew it was a façade, the guy should be awarded a fucking BAFTA for his performance so far.

I remained silent, slightly worried about what was to come. I suddenly felt that need to hide inside my oversized hoodie again.

Nathan's foot pumped the accelerator, swiftly overtaking a tractor in front of us. The vehicle shot forward and I flattened my hand against the leather dash to steady myself.

I so hoped he didn't lose his shit whilst driving as that would *not* go well for either of us. I needed to ensure that any possibility of a potentially boiling temper was carefully reduced to a simmer.

I jump-started my tongue. "It feels strange but good. Travelling was starting to give me whiplash and so it's good to be back. And of course, it's great to see everyone together again."

He snorted. It wasn't a pleasant sound. Apprehension slithered in my stomach like a snake.

"*Everyone*?"

He delivered his comment in a tone of stark disbelief as if he didn't believe he'd be in that group. I took this with a pinch of salt, the guy thought *everything* was about him. Although undiagnosed, everyone knew that Nathan Lane was a first-class narcissist.

I pushed my hands into the pouch of my top so I didn't start biting my nails; a nasty habit of mine.

"Yes, *everyone*. Even you Nathan, in fact, *especially* you."

There, it was said, and it was true. I *had* missed him, just not in the way he wanted me to. I started to chew the inside of my cheek.

His death grip on the steering wheel appeared to relax, his knuckles changing from white to pink and I almost sighed out loud with relief.

"I don't get why you didn't come and see me so we could talk after your first trip away. I came to the house but Tom told me you'd already left. You must have only been back for a couple of hours. What was the point?"

"I was *travelling* Nathan and my head was focused on fitting in all the places I wanted to see," I lied. "And anyway, we always ended up fighting and I just couldn't do it anymore. I needed the time apart." I could only see the side of his face so it made it difficult to gauge his full reaction to my words.

I wasn't that afraid of 'getting in the ring' with this guy and would not pull my punches easily, but I certainly didn't want to do it when we were travelling at almost sixty miles an hour. Every tree we passed seemed to have my name on it.

He carried on regardless, like a wounded soul.

"I texted you several times last week and you didn't reply to one," Nathan delivered moodily. He was pissed off and I suppose he had every right to be. I thanked the heavenly stars looking down on us that his tone at least lacked aggression.

This was moody-arsed 'sober' Nathan. This version, I could deal with.

"I also sent you messages on Facebook."

I made a point after he admitted to overloading me with messages. "Exactly, you were coming on too strong and it was stifling. That was one of the reasons

I went away to start with." Well, that and to clear my head about the Ryan thing. I kept that bit to myself of course.

"I didn't mean to push you into leaving, I just wanted you to know how I felt, how I still feel," Nathan went on in a strained voice. I sure hoped he didn't start going over old ground again. My jaw tensed.

I withdrew my hands from my hoodie and started fiddling with one of the rips in my jeans as another distraction.

"It was for the best Nate, I needed time. After everything that happened, my head was a shed and I felt like such a fuck up."

His brow creased. "*You* felt like a fuck up? You didn't do anything wrong for fucks sake. *I was the fuck up*," he barked out.

I lost count of how many 'fucks' were flying around us as I almost choked on my tongue. Nathan hardly *ever* admitted to being in the wrong, in all the six years I had known him, not once. This was new.

I opened my mouth but nothing came out.

Nathan shuffled in his seat, appearing uncomfortable before shooting me a half-smile.

"You don't want to know about the rumours floating around when you *first* left. There was some right shit going around the village. I almost knocked Noah Savvas out for banging on about it."

I buried the looming smile, imagining Nathan knocking out someone like Noah was like surviving a bullet to the brain, pretty impossible. The guy was bigger and meaner than Connor, a walking, talking steroid. No one messed with Noah.

I pursed my lips thoughtfully; I'd heard all the pregnancy shit. "Yes, Connor told me."

"I thought he would have. He wasn't impressed either. They had him pinned as the father, which pissed me off. Why was Connor the dad and not me? Surely, *we* were seen as the closest?" he hissed out. Motioning between our bodies with his hand.

Pulling a face, I scoffed. "Nathan, we're talking about a non-existent baby here. Who gives a shit?" The topic was bizarre in the extreme and heat stung my cheeks.

He shrugged like a moody little boy. "It just fucking bugged me." He then sighed, saying. "Look, let's go back to mine so we can talk properly, and not while I'm driving."

I must admit, his suggestion of having this out in some place *other* than his car was welcome, but *not* at his place; no thank you. Ryan could be there and if he saw us in the car together, I'd be mortified. Not that Ryan knew anything about Nathan and me. As far as he was aware, Nate and I were just friends. I imagined that was still the case as I had sworn Nathan to secrecy about our sleeping together. Yes, the guy was a drunken mess, but he wasn't totally untrustworthy. This discussion, which I admit was long overdue, needed to take place somewhere neutral.

I cleared my throat, thinking up a plausible excuse. "It's late Nathan. I think it's best if you drop me at mine and we meet up tomorrow. I've had a couple of beers tonight and I'm tired. I think we need to tackle this with clearer heads." My God how grown up I sounded.

From his body language, he took my suggestion like an actual hole in the head but after a few beats of quiet, he nodded and agreed with me. "OK, if that's what you want."

What the actual hell? Again, I was stunned by how quickly he conceded, it was so out of character. Nathan always fought his corner to get his own way.

He indicated and took the A-road which led to my house.

"Probably better to talk about us somewhere else, I get it," Nate rationalised, partly to himself. I inwardly cringed that he used the word 'us'; a sure-fire sign that the guy still *wasn't* getting the message.

It was an odd one really as we'd been friends for such a long time. I still hadn't seen it coming; the attraction thing. It was like he'd woke up one-morning last year and thought, I fancy Ella.

I continued to hold in the sigh of frustration, Ryan seemed to be getting further away with each sentence his brother uttered, and that deep-rooted feeling of disappointment started to gnaw at me, like a massive dog with a never-ending bone.

I decided against unpicking what he had divulged and smiled. It took a huge effort but I managed to make it appear sincere.

He ruined my attempt to look undaunted when he recited his earlier comment, this time in a small pained voice. "I just missed you Ella every day, so *fucking* much. I checked you out on Facebook all the time and saw all the places you'd been. It sucked shit without you."

Batting off a looming stalker comment, my heart squeezed, I *hated* that he had been hurting and that I was the cause. I loved him, of course, I did. I just wasn't *in* love with him; a gargantuan fucking difference. My feelings for Ryan were so very different, my body literally ached *twenty-four-seven* for the man.

My gaze swept over him. Nate needed reassurance. "I know and I missed you too Nate, you *know* that," I put in quietly. I restrained myself from giving him a friendly pat on the leg, the gesture may have been misread and I *certainly* didn't want to give out any more mixed messages; the situation was complicated enough already. It may also have seemed a bit patronising under the circumstances.

I closed my eyes and pushed my head back against the headrest, taking in that new car smell. The scent gave me an idea of how to possibly change the subject.

Opening my eyes, I twisted to face him. "So, cracking wheels. I got your texts with the photos and so I knew she was a stunner, unique colour too." I purposefully switched the subject to cars, one of Nathan's favourite subjects, other than himself of course. The guy was a proper petrolhead.

He initially beamed in response but then his face turned thoughtful. "I remember the day well. I got the best birthday gift a guy could ask for," he shared, darting me a look. He had extremely long eye-lashes for a boy.

My smile widened. "I'll bet. I know how much they cost."

He shook his head as if I had misunderstood him.

"Not because of the car. Because *that* was the morning that I heard from you. The first text I'd had in weeks. You wished me a happy birthday, with three kisses. As I said, best gift ever."

So, my text was better than his one-hundred-and-thirty-grand motor? Coming from someone as materialistic as Nathan, if I had cared for him in *that* way, those words would have been a dream come true.

At that point, I felt like the biggest bitch on the planet and some of my past resentment melted away.

"Look, I'm sorry for the radio silence Nathan, I didn't mean to make you feel like shit."

Nathan drove the car in through the gates leading up to my house, remaining silent whilst he parked in his usual spot. Our house had a double garage, separate from the main building, and was out of sight. He'd always dropped me off there as it was the only place on our estate where my parents wouldn't see us.

The Lane boys had a rep and my parents would flip out if they knew I was involved with either of them. This, of course, only added to the torment as I hated the cloak-and-dagger stuff. It just made things more difficult. And of course, as well as the age difference between Ryan and me, there was also the fact that I'd shagged his brother to contend with.

Nathan turned off the ignition and twisted towards me.

"You don't have to be sorry and anyway, it's over now. You're back. We can talk about it tomorrow when we've recovered from the shock of seeing each other again. It isn't my intention to smoother you Ella. That's not what I want at all. I just want to talk, like we *used* to. And I have stuff to say, shit you *need* to know."

His 'shit you need to know' comment worried me but I pushed the feeling aside. Nathan's words sounded way too mature for his mouth, I now felt thoroughly confused. Had the guy had a complete personality transplant over the last few months? I was almost speechless.

We stared at each other for a moment longer and it was like I was seeing him for the first time.

Unbuckling my seatbelt, I leaned over and curled my fingers over his thigh in a reassuring gesture, it now felt like the right thing to do.

Nathan placed his hand over my fingers and squeezed, his usually drawn expression now appearing much more boyish.

Confusion flooded my brain like a tsunami, but I dragged myself out of the storm before allowing it to swallow me whole.

"I'll text you in the morning and arrange a time to meet and we can talk then. At the minute, my head is still in two different time zones though, so please don't expect too much of me."

He released my hand, a flicker of something I wasn't quite sure I liked skittering across his features. "I stopped doing that months ago."

Before I could ask him what he meant, he smiled, his relaxed expression back in place and he peered across at me.

"Anyway, go on fuck off. Sleep well. And I'll see you tomorrow."

I nodded and turned away, uncurling myself from his sports car with a million questions swimming around my head.

It appeared the Hurricane may have run its course and instead of leaving behind the usual devastation, the actual aftermath was hope.

Hope that one overindulged, chaotic, and at times twisted bad boy, had actually changed his ways.

Of course, at that point, I had no way of knowing if that was a reality, and would only know with time.

I watched him pull away in his ridiculously green car, my mind a maelstrom of emotion.

I knew that coming back would not be easy, but could I really have predicted that it would be this hard? I also hadn't heard back from Ryan after I'd texted him to say I was home; what the heck was that about? Especially now I knew he'd returned from Scotland.

Making my way into the house, I briefly checked my phone to see it was well after ten o'clock.

It was so quiet. My folks and Tom were obviously in bed which was mildly irritating. So much for waiting up to ensure their youngest returned home safely!

I released a pent-up breath of frustration and re-pocketed my phone moodily. Sometimes it was like I didn't exist. There was absolutely no equality in how our parents treated me and my brother. My mother had probably tucked Tom up in bed when he'd got back and thrown in a bedtime story for old times' sale. At almost twenty-two, he was still mollycoddled to fuck.

Grunting, I locked the front door and threw my keys onto the side table.

The hallway was large like the rest of the house and was always cold. At least mum had left the standing lamp on in the corner, so I could actually see when I came in. She probably did this to ensure I didn't bump into stuff and wake everyone up. I doubted it would have been solely for my benefit.

Glancing around the area with fondness, I felt a thump of contentment, I was home. No more toing and froing around America, living out of a suitcase; home was familiar and I *liked* familiar. I enjoyed my time in the States although I'm not sure it broadened my mind like they say travel does. If anything, the only thing it had done was allow me to hide from my problems, instead of dealing with them.

I dashed away that particular thought before it could mature, it was too late to be going over past mistakes. That could wait until tomorrow.

The main stairs in our house were grand and situated in the middle of a large marble-floored hallway. They ran straight up the centre of the house and then branched off on each side like a letter T, leading to a variety of bedrooms and bathrooms. My brother and I used to have so much fun zooming down those banisters.

I'd been born in this house; it was part of me. Leaving it, albeit temporarily had been difficult. But I'd had to do it. I'd needed the time alone to get my head in order; maybe spend some time 'soul searching', whatever *that* meant.

I numbly started to tackle the stairs to my bedroom, my mind a mush of self-serving thoughts.

The truth of it is, no one sees me; not really. Most days I'm not even sure I see myself. I don't know who I am, or what I'm *supposed* to be. Tom had a plan, a mapped-out pathway. Apart from my *blossoming* gardening business (no pun intended), I had nothing.

I'd spent most of my life feeling ordinary. Even to my parents, I'm considered the weak one, the underachiever. Tom is the child to stand out in their eyes. He was the one to be proud of; I was just someone lurking in the background. Doubt and disapproval hammered through me on a daily basis.

It was the same at school, where I'd also been invisible. The last two years had been the hardest, but I'd managed to carve my way as the 'funny one'. 'Class clown' was better than being ignored right?

To look at me from the outside, no one would ever have guessed that on the inside, I was such an insecure mess.

Looking back, it feels like I'd slept walked through most of high school. No subjects were of interest to me and I excelled at nothing. I just got on with it, turned up, and made a fool of myself occasionally, but mostly kept my head down.

My teachers used to view me like I had something mildly contagious most of the time. Forget motivation and encouragement, they made me feel as thick as shit on a regular basis.

I remember my last class with my least favourite teacher, that pinnacle where I had given up on school, realising that it just wasn't going to work for me.

My history teacher, Mr. McNerney had stared down at me, assessing my vacant expression with shrewd eyes before wearily uttering. "The wheel is turning, but the hamster is dead."

I hadn't a clue what he'd meant until Jonathan Bell, the nerd who sat in front of me, climbed out of our teacher's arse, turned in his seat, and translated, in patronisingly slow diction. "The lights are on," he explained, "but nobody's home." It eventually clicked of course, and I'd silently agreed with him. I'd still felt like a loser of course.

Jonathan Bell, now there's a guy from the past. I smiled as I moved across the landing. Everyone used to send him Christmas cards with bells on them. Teenagers can be so cruel, can't they?

I got through my exams with some grades, but nothing to shout about, my talents leaning more toward the creative side. Once I left school, I slowly started to get it. That's why I'd started with garden design and landscaping, I was 'green fingered' my mother once said. I worked well with my hands and was definitely an outdoor girl.

Once I had realised this and embraced it, I started to find my feet. I loved being surrounded by nature (no matter the weather) and I was also good at flower arranging. I'd designed my Cousin Becky's flowers for her wedding last year and they had been illustrated in a local village rag

Before my decision to go away, I had managed to secure some other wedding work and a couple of gardening jobs.

Then on that trip back home from America, I'd bumped into Ryan at the station, shared a taxi, and BOOM. The dots in my life had started to align; my whole being had screamed 'meant to be'.

During that journey, we'd hit it off, sharing an instant connection. Our banter had been so natural and unforced, we fed off each other. Filled the silence. An electric type charge had skittered across my skin during every accidental touch of our bodies. A tap on the knee, hands occasionally colliding as we chatted, joked, and pretty much put the world to rights. We spoke about each other, our families, and our pasts; we were greedy for information, and keen to get to know each other more.

Each time we met after that initial meeting, the bond between us had become stronger. After the second time I'd seen him, he'd kissed me. The attraction was instantaneous, but there was no nonsense that comes with being in the company of a crush (which is what Ryan had been to me for several years prior). That part where you feel nervous and tongue-tied in case you say something foolish. I hardly *ever* felt unsure in his company, he lit me up. I could be one hundred percent myself with him. I didn't even show my friends that side of me; the whole package. With Ryan, there was no need to hide. He got me.

It's strange really, we are so different in so many ways but we just seemed to complement each other.

I was funny to his serious. My personality lightened him up and he brought me back to earth when I need to be grounded (you can't joke your entire way through life and end up expecting to achieve something.)

It felt like Ryan and I were the real deal. Of course, as with all new relationships, I was still insecure and suffered from the occasional wobble. We hadn't put a label on 'us' yes, and this had played on my mind whilst I'd been away. Our 'relationship' or whatever it was, had also been going on in private. We were at that early stage where we wanted to keep things quiet and block out any negativity from external influences. As well as the age difference, my parents would not have been overly thrilled at the thought of me dating one of the Lanes.

Almost sleepwalking to my bedroom, I plopped myself on the bed and eyed my luggage moodily. I hated unpacking, most of it was wardrobe and I wasn't one to care about fashion really. If only my mother would allow me to live in my boyfriend jeans and a hoodie, I would happily do so.

Fashion, make-up, and girlie shit, just wasn't me. I'd met my mother halfway in respect of clothing, it was way too much of a headache to do anything else. Jenna Wade was one determined lady, it just wasn't worth the effort. I'd probably go full-on Emo if I had it entirely my own way.

Pulling my favourite blue hoody over my head and throwing it on the chair of my dressing table, I discarded my socks and tackled my jeans, pulling them off my legs and standing in just my underwear. I was wearing a pretty, lilac lace matching bra and knickers set. My underwear was probably the only feminine thing about me. I did girlie where no one would see it; just for me; my little secret. Ryan had of course had a sneaky peek, but that was it. We were taking things slow. I'd bleached the thought of Nathan seeing me in my underwear from my mind.

After brushing my teeth and washing my face, I peeled back the covers of my bed. The hairs on the back of my neck prickled, it was the strangest of sensations and I rubbed my hands up and down my arms to suppress a shiver.

My curtains were still open and I darted across to close them, realising that I was still in my underwear. Not that anyone would have been able to see me, our nearest neighbours were not that close and their house was located on the same side of the road.

Directly across from our house were rolling fields that belonged to Two Oaks Farm, the place owned by Connor's stepdad Mike and his mother, Rachel. The location the 'fitty' Harlow Williams would be spending the summer.

From Connor's remarks, I couldn't imagine her sticking it on a farm either. She certainly didn't sound like an outdoor girl.

Maybe I'd meet her and she'd be really nice. I certainly welcomed the thought of more female friends. I just hoped she wasn't that amazing that she turned Ryan's head. I'd be lying if I said that hadn't been playing on my mind.

I briefly checked my phone, still no message from Ryan. I eyed the screen moodily, seeing my '**I'm home, can I see you**' message, sitting there all on its own which made me feel like a bit of a saddo.

Placing my phone onto the bedside table, I climbed under my duck feather duvet, the covers gladly enveloped my frame, as if they too had been awaiting my return.

Staring up at the cobwebbed ceiling, I recalled the madness that was my life after that one night I had spent with Nathan Lane. The night it all went wrong.

I had relived this night in my head more times than I can remember.

So, in a nutshell…

Three

Nathan and Ryan's parents ran their own business selling farming equipment and they always took their holidays at the same time each year during the summer. The busier period for orders fell in autumn/winter during the off-season, as this was the time when most farmers focused on servicing/replacing engineering vehicles or equipment.

Both sons worked for their parents, with Nathan occasionally helping with deliveries and Ryan travelling the country attending farming conferences and trade shows. Ryan was a salesman, the glorified frontman, and Nathan the dogsbody. This was the hierarchy in all areas of their lives. Nathan had always walked in the shadow of the brilliance that was the elder Lane; an unbearable detail he resented; hence his rebellious ways and bad attitude.

Usually, Sally and Adam Lane *never* left Nathan home alone and always ensured Ryan was around to keep an eye on things. Any trust they'd had in Nathan ended abruptly when Nate burned down one of the barns holding over one hundred thousand pounds worth of farming equipment. They had been insured, but that of course hadn't been the point.

During last year's holiday trip to Cyprus, Sally and Adam left Nathan and Ryan to look after the estate and to keep things ticking over business-wise.

And by estate, I *mean* 'estate', the Lanes were one of the wealthiest families in our part of Yorkshire. For the last twenty years, they had been the top supplier of agricultural equipment in the whole of the UK.

Sally and Adam were well respected in the community but their children were not. And by this, I meant *both* brothers, Nathan's wild-child ways having tarnished the reputation of his older brother, not significantly, but it was there.

So, back to Nathan and being 'home alone'.

Every year, since his sixteenth birthday, Nathan would throw a huge party at his house whilst his parents were away. Ryan usually agreed to it as long as he kept the numbers and noise down, ensured nothing got stolen, damaged (or burned to the ground), and that any mess caused would be cleared up the next day.

Last year, the party had taken place as usual, but Ryan hadn't been there to oversee, having been called away last minute to 'help out a friend'.

To say the party was eventful was the understatement of the year.

Last year, July...Nate's House

"Please tell me you're not arguing already?" I put in sharply; my voice purposefully raised to be heard above the music. It wasn't even seven and the party was already relentlessly full-on.

There were bodies everywhere; noisy banter, laughter, people smoking and drinking and a handful of girls dancing, which was new. Groups of friends were scattered all over the house and there were a few couples making out. It was probably the most crowded party I'd ever been to.

At that point there was a healthy vibe in the air. It was definitely the place to be and I embraced the buzz I felt by being there. That however, was about to change.

After ditching Max, who suddenly decided to join a game of beer pong with Natalie in the kitchen, I'd spied Connor and Nathan at the far end of the living room and from their body language, I knew they were fighting.

Connor leaned his head toward my voice as I spoke, but his eyes were glued to Nathan's face. My stomach turned over. Connor and Nate falling out was usually a sickening combination.

"Well, what's going on?" I prompted.

Nathan replied. "Grandpa here's trying to ruin my buzz."

Connor wasn't impressed. "Dickhead here thought he'd spice things up by allowing a group of fucking strangers into his house," he complained, his temper simmering as he continued to glare at the other boy.

"Really, who?" My brow threaded as I glanced around the room, my gaze coming to rest on a group of older guys standing in a huddle by the fireplace. I must admit, I hadn't noticed them when I'd first arrived. They definitely weren't from the village and stood out a mile from everyone else. Forget sore thumb, more like a woman performing a lap dance in church. They just looked wrong.

I felt my own buzz dip at the thought of trouble. The police had been called to last year's party and I didn't want to go through that shit again. I had been grounded for a month. If my mother knew I was here this time, she'd shit enough bricks to build a wall.

My trepidation spiked in my chest as I noted Connor's hands were curled into fists, again not a good sign.

Swinging me a warning glare, he bit out fiercely. "And fucking Moses Wallis, are you on glue? I swear to God Nathan, what were you thinking? You know the guy's trouble." His words were terse.

Nathan released a breath that whistled through his clenched teeth. "You don't have to be a cock about it. Whatever happened to the more the merrier?" he put in with a mask of careless indifference.

Moses Wallis? Shit. I suddenly felt tongue-tied, I'd heard that name before and not in a good sentence. Didn't he run some type of gang in Scarborough or something? Either way, the dude was bad news.

Connor dashed a hand through his hair, turning to glance rudely at the group before shooting Nathan another pointed look, more intense than the first. "You don't know these people is the point dumbass."

Nathan jumped to his defence. "And you do?"

"No, I don't. That's my point dickhead. I don't associate with fucking criminals," Connor returned.

"Look, are we done now?" Nathan questioned, obviously tired of Connor's roasting.

"No, we are not fucking done!"

Realisation hit me. Connor was expecting trouble, and in these types of scenarios, he was usually always right. The guy was a beacon for the dark shit. The enormity of the situation suddenly hit me and my lungs almost seized up.

How the hell had a bunch of lowlife city boys even heard about the party anyway? I relaxed my shoulders and took another sneaky look, not wanting them to know we were talking about them. From the cagey way they lazily surveyed the area; they were more than aware that people were watching them.

It struck me forcibly at that moment that we may be in over our heads. And why the hell wasn't Nathan's older brother Ryan back yet? After the shit that went down last year, he was supposed to stick around to keep an eye on things. The guy was a walking book of common sense. Nathan didn't even know the word 'sense' existed.

"Chill for God's sake, if they get out of hand, we can handle it," Nathan shot out thinly; his voice lacking that quality that we now needed; confidence. When would the guy learn that arguing with Connor was a pointless exercise?

Connor cursed at that one, clearly unimpressed.

"If it gets out of hand, you can handle it. You're not dragging me into another shit storm," he bit out tightly with a penetrating look. "You're on your own tosser," he added before placing his bottle of beer on the windowsill.

Adrenaline pumped through my veins like liquid fire at the thought of Connor abandoning us. Out of everyone I knew, he was probably the only guy who could handle himself if the situation did become toxic. Of course, Nathan's brother Ryan wouldn't do so bad either, being as tall and almost as broad as Connor, but the guy was nowhere to be seen. I racked my brains, wondering if I'd seen Natalie's brother, Noah there. He was also a well-built fucker with an attitude the size of The Hulk.

I refocussed my attention. Nathan was obviously taken aback as he glanced at Connor's rejected bottle of Bud, which was still half-full and he twisted his head back, now looking pale. "So, you're saying you won't have my back if anything kicks off? What the fuck bruv?"

Connor leaned in and slapped Nathan across the chest with the bank of his hand. "You better pray it doesn't Nate, as if I do have to get involved, once it's done, I'll be coming for you." At the word 'you', he drew back his hand and shoved a finger into Nathan's chest. Nate grunted from the impact and it pushed him back a step.

I watched Connor stride away with a sinking feeling of despair. Surely, he wasn't really going to bail on us?

"That's fucking loyalty for you," Nathan called after him as Connor headed toward the kitchen.

Connor's uncharacteristic about-face was like a fist in the stomach and I shuffled closer to Nathan, mirroring his drawn expression.

With a flick of his head, he huffed. "Some fucking friend."

I ignored him, my throat suddenly felt dry and scratchy.

Attempting to rationalise my mind, I weighed up the possibility that we could have been misjudging this group of people. Yes, Wallis and his buddies had a bit of a rep, but that didn't mean they would necessarily cause trouble here.

My eyes narrowed as I shot Nathan a withering look. How on earth had they found out about the fucking party? It's not like they would have been passing and had been drawn in by the lights, Nathan's house was in the middle of nowhere.

Shaking my head, slightly annoyed that Nathan had once again screwed up by letting these unsavoury people into his house, I questioned in a harsh voice, my inner bitch screaming to come out. "Which one of your moronic friends invited them?"

Nathan dashed a hand across the stubble on his jaw before hastily discarding his own beer, which was of course empty. Nate never wasted a drop of alcohol.

The atmosphere in the room behind us was charged and not out of the ordinary but who knew what would happen if one of the outsiders started to throw their weight around.

I raised my eyebrows, prompting an explanation.

Nate moved his back to the wall behind him by the window and leaned against it. Crossing his arms over his chest as he divulged why we now had six rather beefy strangers at the party and one skanky looking female one.

"I was out of weed and Max said he got his last batch off a friend of Wallis's. I bumped into them when I was clubbing at the weekend and one thing led to another."

I rolled my eyes so hard it hurt. "And how the hell did your dealer get a fricking invitation here?"

His look said it all. "Connor's right, you are mental," I puffed, starting to lose my shit with him.

He pushed off the wall, unfolding his arms, and started to pace. Blatantly agitated, he turned to me with an exasperated look. "I get it, I fucked up. Moses asked me to join them in their booth at the club and we got talking is all. I was stoned. I invited him and his mate on a whim. I didn't expect the whole fucking gang to turn up."

I drank in the information, racking my brain for a possible solution and coming up with zilch. We needed to get them to drink up and leave, hopefully without anything kicking off.

Our eyes tangled. "This is a mess. What are we going to do?" I fought the urge to go after Connor.

"Fuck knows, I could just ask them to leave?"

The incredulous laugh burst out of my mouth like gunfire and I couldn't stop myself from snapping at him. "Yeah right, like that's a good idea. You have heard of Moses Wallis right, he's part of some fighting syndicate I heard. Do you not like your teeth? There are also six of them. Seven if you count the hoe."

I gave the group another glance; they looked rougher than sandpaper and appeared totally content where they were. Why wouldn't they be, free booze and drugs and plenty of half-naked totty to feast their eyes upon. Fucking freeloaders. They were currently sprawled over by the sofas, the biggest of them stood with his back against the fireplace. The other guests gave them a wide berth as they passed.

The big one was saying something that amused the rest. He was the one to worry about, the 'leader'. He had to be Wallis. His friends were either hung on his every word or focused on a couple of girls who were dancing close by, unaware that there could be danger lurking.

Nathan shifted to the side of me as we both now stood gawping at the group. "Maybe it'll be OK if we just leave them to it," he uttered with a slice of hope.

I blinked my eyes, the stress of the situation causing my head to ache. God knows why I had been friends with this boy for so long.

"Let's just pray that they don't start to enjoy themselves too much," I added as the female in the group got up and started to gyrate in front of one of her male buddies. She was wearing skinny jeans with massive rips in and a scarlet top that slid off one shoulder. Her hair was jet-black like Nathan's. Ironically their colouring was similar, they could have been related. I batted off the unhelpful thought.

Nathan hopped from foot-to-foot, before saying on an exhale. "Fuck me. Why the hell did I mention the party in the first place?"

"Yep, that's my question," I nodded and folded my own arms, wondering if I had the balls to speak to them, maybe share some jokes to get them onside. In the past, I'd managed to joke my way out of several tricky situations. I pushed the circling thought of gang rape aside. When the hell had I become so dramatic?

One feasible solution dawned on me. There was no other way, sticking my tongue into gear again, I suggested. "You're going to have to call Ryan, get him to come back now."

Nathan physically recoiled and he grabbed me, separating my arms, and dragging me out into the conservatory. "You are joking? How in the hell is that a good idea?" he spat into my ear before yanking me around to face him. He wasn't that gentle either, my arms were like twigs in his hard grip. I was fairly tall but unfortunately on the scrawny side.

I yanked my arm away, now determined to make the guy see sense. "He'll know what to do to get us out of this shit. I mean it Nathan, the big guy with the nose almost squashed flat against his face, reeks of trouble. I imagine that's Wallis. Ryan has friends, safety in numbers, and all that."

His eyes drilled so hard into mine like he was trying to tunnel into my head. Nathan battled with my suggestion for around a minute longer, before he slid his iPhone from his jeans.

"Fine," he spat, his shoulders sagging as he turned away and went out into the garden away from the noise. No doubt so Ryan could actually hear what he was saying.

Something in me eased and I left the conservatory and set off toward the kitchen where I had left Max and Natalie. Time to round up the troops.

My thoughts drifted to Ryan and how he'd react when he learned about the group Nate had decided to add to the guest list. Would the guy lose his cool or would he manage to maintain that icy calmness that surrounded him? There wasn't a problem he couldn't un-pick, his eyes were bright with intelligence. He was definitely the best-looking guy in the village and so worth an ogle; which I partook in whenever I had the chance.

Over the last six years since I'd known Nathan, Ryan had been a secret crush of mine for at least two of those. He was gorgeous; tall, dark, and handsome with a rangy, athletic build. He took himself a little bit too seriously and didn't smile much, but he was masculine perfection at its best. He was also around seven years older than me, a proper grown-up, but he was cool. I couldn't cope with overly temperamental guys my age and had always been attracted to older men. My high school teacher, Mr. Haswell had been my first crush during puberty.

Ryan also dressed immaculately; usually in tailored suits, which made him stand out against the rougher-looking local boys. A true success, in my opinion, having managed to work off that stigma of the 'typical boy from the village'.

Nathan complained that Ryan was an extreme control freak, but that hadn't put me off either. I knew Nate was secretly jealous of his brother. There had been a variety of issues between them growing up.

My thoughts raced back to said nightmare, Hurricane Nathan and the penis picture he'd sent me on WhatsApp by mistake last week. Although similar in appearance, Nate and Ryan were very different as people. I couldn't imagine Ryan sending anyone a shot of his cock, it was so tacky. I had not welcomed the image; willies were ugly things at the end of the day; even if there was an actual point to them.

I moved through the throng of people, chatting along the way. I needed to get the thought of Nathan's penis out of my head. So gross. I'd been shocked at first and hadn't known how to take it. When I'd first established what it was, alarm bells had kicked off in my head as Nate had been acting strange over the last few weeks. He'd been so much more touchy-feely and I had caught him staring at me with a strange, almost pained expression. It certainly wasn't a vibe I had encouraged.

To my relief, the dick pic was actually meant for Ellie, one of my dad's student vet nurses who was working at his practice. I'd spent a good week winding Nathan up about it in order to clear the air and hopefully bat his strange behaviour away. The lingering looks had continued, but I'd just started to ignore them. Working out what was going on in Nathan's head would be like taking an exam you would never pass.

"You fancy giving me a tour of the palace gorgeous?" a voice suddenly chimed in, cutting into my thoughts. My pulse sped up.

I stopped just before the double doorway to the kitchen and turned toward the deep sound. It belonged to him, the smashed nose guy, and my guts felt like lead in my stomach.

Oh my God. Play it cool, and don't show your fear, guys like that can smell fear!

I smiled, attempting to scramble a reply before he took offence. My mother told me that smiling was a natural medicine for your health, but I had a feeling it wasn't going to help me in this particular situation.

Where the hell was Connor? Although we'd only known each other a short period of time, the guy had definitely grown on me, we sort of saved each other, like having another brother, but one that could actually look out for you. My real brother Tom was a complete wimp.

"I'm just looking for my friends, sorry," I replied with a ragged breath, giving him my full attention. If I came across as rude, it would not go well. This guy was the shark and I was that unfortunate person in the water, telling myself to keep still. It was all about self-preservation.

"I was just wondering what the bedrooms look like?" he put in with a cheeky grin before taking a drag on his cigarette. One of his buddies joined us and I could sense a shift in the air from those who were within earshot. None of them came to my rescue though, useless twats.

Panic started swirling in my stomach as they leered at me. There was a pregnant pause.

"You going to introduce us, Moses?" his tattooed friend questioned with a slow, lazy smile. So, I was right, the big one was Moses Wallis. And what type of name was that? The guy couldn't have looked less biblical if he'd tried.

I shot a glance between the two men and pushed a curling tuft of hair behind my ear, needing something to do with my hands.

"Was that your boyfriend?"

"Who?" I replied without thinking.

"That big fucker that stormed off," he drawled, his mouth at my ear. I noted he was missing two front teeth. I totally didn't want to know how he'd lost them.

I shook my head. "No, he's just a friend."

What had started off as a great party was turning into my worst nightmare. I silently prayed to God for some reprieve.

Replaying my reply, I could have slapped myself, why the hell hadn't I said yes?

I'd started to lose feeling in my legs, they didn't appear to be moving even though I was sure that's what my head was telling them to do.

Both guys exchanged a look before I blurted. "The other guy with the black hair, that's my boyfriend," I lied and they raised their eyebrows, totally undaunted.

"What you doing Moses, don't think I won't tell Kezia that you've been hitting on the locals," the girl who was with them began, sashaying over. Even through the fog of my fear, I noted she had massive boobs. That name Kezia suggested that the girl she spoke about would be as rough as fuck.

"Kezia isn't here is she, and we're just fucking talking, piss off Laney," he replied with a grunt, clearly not happy at 'Laney's' interruption. She moved away and went to sit on one of the other guy's laps. He too was watching us with idle fascination until 'Laney' leaned in and started to suck face. How vile.

As I made to move away, my eyes fell on Kyle who had just come in from the hallway, clutching a red solo cup. He took one look at the three of us standing together before setting off with a determined stride toward the kitchen. Hopefully, he'd seen my silent SOS message that must have been punched into my forehead.

"Anyway, I'd better find my friends. Enjoy your drinks," I replied in a fairly even voice, considering there were all sorts of crazy going off inside me.

'Moses', moved to block my path. He didn't necessarily do it in an aggressive way, more of a, 'stay and play with us' manoeuvre. They were the cats and I was the mouse.

"Stay and have a drink with us. You don't want to be rude when we don't really know anyone do you?"

As I went to move around him again, he put out an arm to stop me and I noticed his skin around his knuckles was badly scarred. We're they scratch marks of some kind?

I shook off the thought as I shit you not, Connor suddenly appeared like my prayers had been answered by my side, and even though I should have been relieved, I wasn't. The thought of it turning nasty, terrified me like the thought of death. My heart was beating so loudly in my chest I was surprised no one could hear it.

"What's going on?" Connor questioned, his height almost matching that of the guy called Moses and easily topping the others. As if on cue at his appearance, the other four guys materialised at the sides of the other two. It was suddenly a 'them and us' squaring-up situation

I peeled my tongue off the roof of my mouth in an attempt to try and stop it from kicking off. My insides turned cold.

The strangers remained silent, their focus on Connor. Weighing up the threat I imagined, and he was certainly that. The guy was big, all towering aggression at the end of the day, and enjoyed confrontation like it was a fucking aphrodisiac. In a nutshell, Connor usually got off on knocking the shit out of stuff.

Moses took a step back and I turned to Connor.

"We were just talking. I was on my way to find you?" I put in before the others could make a comment that pushed Connor into lamping one of them. I noted his hands were already fisted at his sides; he was as aggressive as an abused stray dog.

A couple of other guys from the village and Kyle and Max also appeared by our sides, obviously sensing something was about to go down.

"Yeah, as she said. Just talking, not that it's any of your fucking business," Moses replied without a trace of fear.

"So, you were talking," Connor began, his eyes never leaving the big one's face, his body poised for action. "And now you're done."

They weighed each other up for a few more beats.

"You're a big fucker, aren't you?" Moses observed, turning to grin at his buddies, who all copied him like fucking mimes. They obviously couldn't think for themselves. The girl called Laney, also stepped into the huddle, her eyes wide as they took in Connor like he'd be the perfect father to her kids. She probably had several already.

Connor didn't answer straight away, as if he was trying to ensure he read the situation right before making any moves. And the guy was well known for making the 'first' move. Especially when he was off his medication.

He shrugged. "So? You scared, pussy?" He pushed his head closer to Wallis's face on the word 'pussy'.

Moses took a step back and viewed Connor with a skewed type of fascination.

"Just an observation mate. We were just asking curly here for a tour."

Curly? He was talking about me. What the fuck type of nickname was that?

"Not going to happen," Connor concluded flatly.

"I can ask for nothing, can't I? We're here by invitation if you must know. Ask your fucking buddy."

Connor ignored him. "Why don't you do your self-respect a favour and walk away? I'll allow you to finish your drinks before you leave." His patience was wearing thin and he appeared larger than life. Connor's existence was just so much louder than everyone else's. He literally sucked the energy from the room.

"Will you now, that's good of you. Cocky fucker, aren't you? So, this your house?"

"No, it's mine."

I suddenly felt Nathan's hard chest push into my back and Connor shot him a look over my head, or should I say glower.

There was now a definite circle around us but the music was still blaring away, as was the chatter from those corners where people were either too stoned or pissed to know or care about what was going on.

"Aren't you the guy that asked us to come and pump some life into your shit little party?" one of the other guys said. He was stoned and was probably the one Nathan had bought the weed off. He then clarified this was the case. "And to think I gave you the last of my stash, you ungrateful cunt."

I found his language offensive which was a surprise, even to me. I was one of the biggest potty mouths in the village.

I moved in between Nathan and Connor.

"I threw that shit down the toilet. As my friend just told you, it's time to leave," Nate echoed.

Moses got in Nathan's face, obviously feeling he would be easier to take on than Connor. "Witty fucker, aren't you? You thinking you're big enough to throw us out?"

"No, but I am," Connor shot out before making his move.

It all happened so fast, Connor lunged forward and grabbed Moses by the scruff of his tee, ramming him back against the fireplace. One of his buddies, a lanky skinny guy made a move towards Connor, who now had his forearm over Wallis's throat, blocking his airway. Nathan shifted and grabbed the skinny one's arms and shoved him back, shaking his head as if to say, 'don't do it'. His movements were agile considering the amount of liquor he'd already sunk.

As the group surged forward and a scuffle broke out, I fell sideways, landing against someone's body and pain exploded in my cheek. I didn't know if someone had hit me or not and I struggled for coherence, my head swimming. All I could hear were shouts and thuds, as chaos erupted. A table went over and there was a fair bit of swearing, but mostly shoving and angry words.

Hearing glass smashing, I pushed against the bodies crowding me and saw Connor and Noah 'escorting' a thrashing Moses out through the hallway, the guests parting like the sea. It appeared the guy was down with the biblical thing after all.

The whole episode was over fairly quickly, and I wasn't sure if any major punches were thrown. It appeared it was more of a shoving-them-out-the-door situation, thank Christ. Max appeared at my side to help me up and the party carried on again, almost as if nothing had happened.

"Are you OK Ella, you hit the floor fast, I thought I'd knocked you out," Kyle suddenly announced, with a hand to my face, checking my cheek. So, Kyle had punched me, fan-fucking-tastic.

"You hit me?" I bit out, thoroughly exasperated.

Kyle's face dropped. "Sorry, you kind of fell on my elbow as I moved to grab one of them," he confessed, looking extremely guilty.

At that point, I felt like bursting into tears. My heart was like a monster trying to punch out of my ribcage and my cheek was throbbing like a bastard.

Kyle put his hand around my shoulders and led me to the kitchen as I clung onto his shirtsleeve, Max following behind. I suddenly felt quite fragile, a side of myself I rarely revealed.

"Come on, show's over. It didn't get too messy thank fuck. Always feels worse at the time. Adrenalin rush and all that. Con, Nathan, and Noah are making sure they leave without doing any damage to the cars."

So, Noah was at the party.

"What if they come back?" I groaned fearfully.

"Not going to happen. They don't like the ones that fight back Ella, too much of a ball-ache. They're gone. Come on, you need a drink. It's a party and you're way too sober."

And he was right, I certainly was. I needed my buzz back.

I spent the next half an hour sitting with Kyle and Max, drinking neat Bacardi and laughing at pretty much anything they said. They were like a comedy double act.

Connor and Nathan had not appeared back yet and I wondered fleetingly if everything was OK.

Natalie's brother Noah, who was also like a giant, was now in the process of trying to coax her to leave the party, she appeared to be almost dry-humping one of the younger lads who worked in the village shop. I was surprised as she'd been shagging Connor for the last couple of months.

Some other friends joined us and we started to play truth or dare. We sat around the main kitchen table which looked out into the garden. I noticed a few couples were making out, nothing heavy, just kissing, although there appeared to be one girl with her hand down a guy's jeans and boxers. The faint glow from the fairy lights in the trees partially highlighted them. I wrinkled my nose and turned away. Public displays of intimacy were so tacky.

Nathan eventually joined us, but there was no sign of Connor. He'd probably gone to walk off some steam. Something he did when he'd opened up a can of crazy.

As Nate straddled a spare chair with half a bottle of Bacardi in one hand, I noticed a cut and a red section on his forehead. What the hell? It was threaded through one eyebrow and looked fairly deep. His eye was also slightly swollen.

I glanced at Kyle and then back at Nathan with a confused expression.

"I thought no punches were thrown?" I questioned in a slightly slurred voice. My God, I was drunker than I thought. The pain in the side of my face had lessened with every mouthful but if I left it too long in-between sips, that throbbing sensation came back. I knocked back a tequila slammer which Max had poured me, not bothering with the salt and lemon shit.

Nathan leaned back looking sorry for himself and my heart squeezed that he'd been hurt. Even though the whole thing was his bloody fault in the first place.

"What we playing?"

"Truth or dare," Max blurted with a toothy grin. "But you're fucked as you don't have any secrets to share, so dare it is. I dare you to make out with Ella for one minute," grinning like an idiot and glancing between us.

Nathan's face lit up like a petrol infused bonfire at the suggestion, but I put a hand on his chest and pushed him back into his seat. We'd made out a few times in the past, but it had always been based on a dare. He reeked of Bacardi and bad fucking decisions, there was no way I was snogging that.

"Not going to happen, we're done with those days." Nathan's recent interest in me was another reason to bring those types of shenanigans to a halt. "So, what did happen to your face, Nathan?" I drawled out through the haze of my stupor.

"Connor happened?" he huffed, leaning back again, pressing a finger to his head before studying the blood on his fingers with a grimace.

His comment almost gave me whiplash. "What?"

Nathan flicked his head toward the door. "When we got rid of those arseholes, he fucking hit me. Hard. Hurts like a motherfucker. He definitely didn't pull his punch like he usually does. Got me right in the fucking eye too, talking about a poor fucking shot."

I processed his reply before shrugging, suddenly not really that bothered. Alcohol had a habit of taking your worries away.

"He did warn you," I pointed out.

"If this fucker leaves a scar, I'm done with him for good, fricking psycho. What about your face?" he observed, concern cutting through his puzzled features.

I pointed to my attacker. "Kyle the twatbag elbowed me in the face."

Kyle jumped to his own defence, looking downright indignant. *"I did not, you fell into it you clumsy bitch."*

"Fuck you. Whatever. Either way, it won't be happening again. I think this is my last appearance at one of your parties, Nathan Edmund Lane."

That got Nate's attention. *"Don't say that,"* he mewed miserably, looking like I had just drained away all his joy.

Present

Cracking my eyes open, I dragged my thoughts back, turning onto my front. A small group of us had spent the rest of the night drinking into the early hours until there was only Nathan and I left. I remembered Kyle offering to walk me home at one point which had been brave, considering my house was over a mile away. How I wished I'd taken him up on his offer now. In the end, I decided to stay over, intending on sleeping in one of the many guest rooms at Nate's house. My parents had been away and Tom would have been in bed. I hadn't fancied my chances of being allowed in a taxi, having probably reeked like I'd bathed in spirits.

Nathan hadn't been able to get hold of Ryan, hence the no-show before the incident with Wallis and so I'd tipsily agreed to stick around and help tidy up after we'd slept off our approaching hangovers. The house had been pretty trashed.

Like a totally naïve idiot, I'd joined Nathan in his room for a while and we'd sat on the bed talking; trying not to pass out, the dick pic coming up again. And oh, how we laughed. I remember being totally shitfaced and really enjoying Nate's company. I couldn't be certain, but I was sure we'd also taken a dip in Nate's indoor swimming pool at one point. My memories of that night were so alcohol-infused, everything was still so fragmented.

I do remember part of a heart-to-heart, and a moment where I was sure Nathan had traces of tears in his eyes. He'd said something about feeling worthless all the time and that he couldn't do anything right. He'd also explained how much I meant to him and how he felt our friendship had grown. I had blamed it on the booze at the time of course.

I remember garbled feelings of wanting to make him feel better, even soothing the cut on his face, kissing the wound and then…

Then I'd woken up later that day with my 'friend', completely naked, curled against his hard body, one leg draped over his with an almighty hangover and absolute horror at what we'd both done. My head only contained flickering images of Nathan and I together, and I didn't appear to be fighting him off.

And I'd lived with the twisted guilt ever since. It was dark, muddy, deep and all too consuming.

Four

The memory of the night I slept with Nathan Lane was still hazy at best, but I remember the smug look he'd worn days afterward. This *still* resonated with me. Unadulterated shame and regret also made a regular appearance. If I hadn't wanted Ryan so much, I may have been able to move past it quicker, put it down to teenage sexual experimentation; part of growing up.

As I'd dragged on my clothes with my cheeks burning from embarrassment, Nate had laid there in his boxers, hands behind his head, without a care in the world. If anything, he seemed amused by the encounter and I wasn't sure how to take that.

Our brief discussion a day or two later had been surprisingly reasonable, with us both agreeing that it should never have happened and that it was a silly, drunken mistake. For me, it had been a bigger deal. I had been a virgin, although Nathan hadn't mentioned anything about him noticing, thank God. After that follow-up, *necessary* conversation, Nathan had also given his word that he wouldn't say anything to the others and I'd believed him. Our friendship would certainly not have lasted if he'd gone back on that particular promise. I just wanted the whole thing dead and buried. Forgotten. What a naive idiot I was.

The real problems started to develop around a week later. Nathan's clingy behaviour prior to that night together then started to make sense.

At first, it was fairly playful stuff. During moments when we were on our own, Nathan would wind me up, dropping hints about 'how I was the one who instigated that night' by grabbing his junk and 'how I wouldn't take no for an answer'. I took his words with a pinch of salt as Nathan loved to joke at other people's expense. I just hadn't been able to imagine myself making the first move at all; even the drunk version of myself.

I exhaled as my mind started to wander down that bitter, twisted path, I could still only write what I knew about sex on a napkin. I was sexually clueless. Looking back, shouldn't I have ached down there or have had some type of sex' glow? My body hadn't even felt any different, weren't you supposed to be sore after your first time?

I'd been way too embarrassed to ask Nathan for any details, especially when he made me feel like a panting-for-it tart with his 'you were all over me' gibes. It was just my luck that Nate appeared to have a full recollection, but of course he would, being more used to alcohol than me.

It took a few weeks, but Nate *eventually* stopped the sex-shaming thing. Unfortunately, the behaviour that followed, was so much worse.

The humour, I could deal with, it took the edge off the embarrassment about him seeing me naked, among other things. However, as the weeks passed by, our relationship changed completely and Nathan became a different person, obsessive, clingy and less of a friend I could talk to. It was as if our being together had tainted the friendship we'd once shared and the 'sex thing' had gotten in the way. He started texting me all the time and turning up unexpectedly when I was out with my friend Natalie, like a proper stalker.

As the weeks went by, we started to have these huge fights; even in front of the others, which cast a negative atmosphere whenever we all met up. Like an elephant-in-the-room scenario, everyone knew something was off, but no one wanted to speak about it. Nathan made suggestive hints but, being true to his word, didn't tell the others what happened. I imagined they'd guessed, to be honest. Apart from Max, our friends were fairly astute and Nate's behaviour towards me was borderline 'possessive boyfriend'.

Nathan even blurted out that he loved me one evening. He turned up at my house half-pissed and Tom had answered the door, meaning I had to bring my brother up to speed with the shit that had been going on. Tom had been so focused on his studies that he'd thankfully missed most of the explosive moments. My explanation was of course the half-baked version. I explained briefly that we'd started to argue after Nathan had shown interest in me but couldn't take no for an answer. I'd left out the sex bit of course. Sharing that piece of information with my *brother* would have been way too personal.

It also drove an even bigger wedge between Nathan and Connor as Nate would fly into jealous rages if Connor and I hung out. The injury on Nathan's face caused by Connor also scarred, which added another beef to their failing relationship.

One night at the pub, it had almost come to blows again. I'd been on my way back from the ladies toilet when Nathan had cornered me in the corridor, his huge body blocking my way. He'd been drinking, we all had.

He'd asked me what was so special about Connor, the awful darkness in his voice wrapping around me, sinking its teeth in. I'd smiled and rolled my eyes in an attempt to make light of it, and tried to move past him but he'd blocked my path with his arm. It shit-me-up a bit, I'm not going to lie. I knew he'd never *physically* harm me, Nathan could be a monster, but he wasn't *that* guy. It was just intimidating, having someone restrict your movements like that.

I'd politely suggested he let me past, but his lip curled into that sneer I hated so much. After a second attempt to get by, he'd caught my arm and dragged me against him. He wasn't that much taller than me, but I still had to crane my neck to face him. A slither of panic had slid down my spine at that point and he'd held tight, stopping me from pulling away, his eyes on my mouth like he wanted to drink from it. Like a thirsty person who'd had no water for weeks. Every last nerve in my body had been shrieking; my limbs were heavy and uncertain.

"No Nathan."

Before Nathan could kiss me, Connor appeared with a firm hand on his shoulder and pulled him off me, causing Nate to release me. I'd scuttled back, terrified of a looming fight.

Connor had basically pinned Nathan against the wall, angry hands wrapped in his T-shirt, getting in his face.

"No, means no dipshit," he'd growled down into the slightly shorter man's face. Nathan had the sense to look ashamed at that point. Connor's entire body was lit with rage which wasn't good, he was a well-built man who was unpredictable most days. I hadn't known about the darkness of his childhood in detail at that point but that was part of the reason the guy was downright dangerous. Fright had gripped me hard and I'd placed a gentle hand on Connor's shirtsleeve in an attempt to calm him, saying I was fine and that he needed to let Nate go. It had taken a while, but he'd eventually released the death grip on Nathan, Nate having raised his arms in surrender with a back-off expression. There was a decent person in there, he'd just lost his way; I knew that now. Nathan had so

51

many repressed feelings he bottled up and they constantly fed into the bad decisions he made. A chip on his shoulder the size of a small island I would say. But who didn't have problems, we were all at that awkward, approaching twenty or travelling toward the twenty-somethings age. That pinnacle stage where life just got serious and the days of just playing at it were rapidly fading away into the distance.

After that last night when Nathan lost his shit, Connor had taken my hand and we'd left together. Craving fresh air, we'd driven to the beach to watch the sunrise. He too had been going through his own struggles and it had nothing to do with Nathan.

That was the night Connor and I had shared our deepest secrets and I'd told him how I'd lost my virginity to Nathan. He listened intently and didn't appear overly shocked; not that the guy really showed much emotion anyway but as we'd sunk that bottle of spirits between us, sprawled before the crashing sea; he'd revealed his own demons. And as I said, they were much worse than *anything* I could have anticipated. I found out the real reason Connor Barratt was so severely fucked up. It was the type of stuff that kept you awake at night and it *still* turned my stomach. He also showed me some of the damage his dad did to him, stuff that had scarred which he'd attempted to cover with his tattoos and explained about the poor hearing he had in one ear. Again, due to the abuse he'd suffered years before.

Con had also spoken about his mother's marriage to Mike and how difficult he'd found adapting. Rachel Williams, *née* Barratt, had been through her own nightmare during the years she had been with Connor's father. A guy who basically dished out years of abuse to both of them.

Connor also fleetingly mentioned Harlow at that point, the unwanted stepsister he had acquired, and who was due to stay on the farm that following summer. Something he wasn't particularly looking forward to.

We'd slept in Connor's car and in the morning as he'd driven us back to Pickering, I told him about my crush on Ryan. His reaction was mixed, I could see he clearly didn't think it a good idea. He commented both on the age difference and my history with Nathan. The parting message he gave me was that I needed to deal with Nathan *before* I could ever consider anything with

Ryan, and of course in true Ella fashion, I had done the opposite. I'd run away, gone into hiding without sorting out anything.

Christmas had passed by and I had seen the New Year in with my family, staying away from local parties for fear of bumping into Nathan. I started to ignore his texts and took myself off the grid. At the end of January, I was offered the opportunity to go travelling in the USA. My dad's sister had an apartment in New York City and she said I could use her place as a base. My emotions had been mixed, but it had provided me with the opportunity of seeing America and had also given me time away from the village *and* the toxic situation between my friends. I had needed something else to focus on; to breathe me back to life.

During my time in America, I travelled home again four times over a six-month period when my auntie had to go away for work. I hadn't really felt comfortable staying at her house when she wasn't there, her being based in the big bad city.

It was during that first trip back that I met Ryan at the station and we'd hit it off. My time with Ryan had been fragmented, but I had savoured every experience so far. A couple of times I'd almost cut my trip short and returned from America early, but I'd stayed strong and Ryan had encouraged me to get the most out of it before coming back.

For our first official date, Ryan had picked me up from the corner of the lane near my house and we'd gone to the pub, just the two of us. It didn't feel weird or forced, even though I had that secret history with his brother. It just felt right. The fact that he was so much more worldly and sophisticated than me; hadn't mattered one iota.

It had been amazing and the connection had been so strong. I was so in awe of him and he was so smart and good-looking. A girl could melt into a puddle at the sight of him.

At the end of that first planned night out together, he'd kissed me and he was such a good kisser; not too much tongue. Like Baby Bear's bed, just right. One touch of his mouth against mine and everything had jumped up a notch. I hadn't wanted to go back to the states at all after that, but of course, I'd had plans in place.

Now I was back for good and over the past week, I hadn't heard much from Ryan, which was why a bit of doubt had kicked back in. To be fair, he'd never been that great at returning my texts and so I batted off that reoccurring concern that something was off. I hadn't attempted to call him from the states due to the time difference and I didn't want to come across as clingy when we were still at that fun stage.

I rolled onto my back and closed my eyes, pushing thoughts of annoying men out of my mind.

Now I was home, I had two main objectives. I would fix things with Nathan and go after the one thing that I wanted the most.

A real relationship with Ryan Christopher Lane.

That haunting thought that I would probably have to tell Ryan about Nathan soon continued to circle me like a shark's fin. As did the worry about how Nate would react when he learned about Ryan and me.

As with most things in my life, nothing was ever straightforward.

The next morning, I dragged my tired body out of bed and briefly checked my phone to see if I'd had a reply from Ryan. My heart plummeted, I hadn't. My text, still sat there taunting me.

After showering, pulling on fresh underwear, and dressing in a grey oversized hoodie and baggy jeans, I texted Nathan to say that I'd meet him that afternoon at Martha's Tearooms, a quaint café in Pickering. It had a room at the back that was usually fairly quiet. It wasn't my intention to tell him that I liked Ryan just yet, the most important thing was getting our friendship back on track and making sure he got the message that that's all we'd ever be.

At the end of the day, I didn't really know one hundred percent where things stood with Ryan at that moment, not really. We hadn't actually discussed it. Yes, we'd seen each other a few times and kissed, but nothing major. I knew I needed to play it cool as I was falling fast. Although my experience with relationships was limited, I knew that guys ran a mile from overly keen girls and preferred to carry out the chasing themselves. That's what Natalie had taught me anyway.

I tied the annoying come-undone-all-the-time laces on my trainers and pocketed my phone, deciding on crossing the road and walking over to the

Williams' farm. My curiosity about Harlow Williams was well and truly stoked and I had time to kill. It would also be good to catch up with Connor and check he'd mellowed after storming out of the pub last night. His mood swings had become much more volatile lately and this suggested he was off the meds as Tom had suggested.

Making my way down the stairs I pushed thoughts of Connor and his tragic childhood from my mind, it was still too upsetting to think about. Connor's father Carter could rot forever in prison as far as I was concerned. I'd still never understand how a parent could treat their child in that way. Yes, I felt invisible and had little affection from my folks but at least they weren't abusive toward me. Silver linings and all that.

Talking of parents, Mum was sitting at the kitchen table when I entered the breakfast room, tucking into a plate of fruit. She raised her eyes when I walked in, disapproval about my attire written along every crease on her face. My mother once commented that I dressed like a homeless person. Nice one. There was no sign of my father, but of course, he'd be at the surgery by now. Dad went on his rounds, visiting a selection of farms in the area to check on their livestock. He was a five-am riser. Getting up at that time would be my worst nightmare, hence my decision against any vet-related profession, not that I would have been clever enough anyway.

"That thing swamps you, Ella, you look twice the size," she enlightened me as to her opinion on my jumper, picking at her breakfast. It was fruit and so mega health but she still glanced down at it like she was calculating the calories with each mouth full. Mum was constantly on a diet even though she was as thin as a reed. I had mom's chestnut brown hair, dark eyes, and skinny build, unfortunately.

I shot her my couldn't-care-less-face before approaching her and planting a kiss on her cheek. Pinching a strawberry, I popped it between my lips, savouring the sweetness.

"What are you up to today? Dad says he's done you those flyers for your gardening business. I heard Mr. Haunch is pleased with what you've done so far."

I nodded, digesting her words about Bob Haunch and the flyers. Mr. Haunch had employed me to revamp a flower bed for his wife as a surprise. I swallowed, resting my back against the wall as I watched her with a blank expression. Tom was treated like royalty by this woman. He, was the prince and I was the burden, but I loved her. And I knew she loved me. She just had a strange way of showing it.

I shrugged. "I'll start to post the flyers at the weekend—Natalie said she'd help. Fingers crossed it generates more work."

Mum swallowed a fork full of fruit before she asked again. "So, are you going to tell me what you are doing with your day or not?" Like she really gave a shit.

I pursed my lips, I felt like saying, 'nothing, like you'. Mum was a housewife, she did the gym and home, and that was it. Dad was the grafter.

"Not much. I thought I'd just nip over to Mike's to check out the new arrival. His daughter arrived yesterday. Heard she's going to stir up trouble in the village."

Always one for gossip, mum placed her fork down and took a sip of juice before lowing the glass and eyeing me over the rim. "Yes, Thomas told us when he got back from the pub last night. He's impressed, although when it comes to girls, he's fairly easy to please. I wonder if he'll have any luck with this one."

I smiled. Yes, Tom was the fave but mum was unashamedly aware that the guy literally repelled females. He was too much of a nice guy. Country girls didn't usually dig nice out here, in the middle of nowhere, it was 'bad boy all the way'. Farmers worked with their hands and everything was so physical. The country wasn't for pussies, you grew up fast living in the thick of the elements.

"Course he did, the prince thinks he's met his princess. Let's see, shall we?" I shot back with a wiggle of my eyebrows.

I left my mum grinning into her fruit like she was sharing a silent secret with it.

Much to my annoyance, *everything* Tom had said about the Harlow girl was right. I was surprised I hadn't turned green with envy on the spot. She reminded me of the musical ballerina which popped up when you opened my mother's old jewellery box.

She was stunning; *ridiculously* pretty with perfect unblemished pale skin (not a mole in sight), clear blue eyes, and long wavy blond hair. She had obviously just stepped out of the shower as her hair was wet. She'd tied it up in a girly ponytail, revealing the cutest of ears.

A petite thing yet with soft feminine curves in all the right places. Her voice was also sugar-sweet, the type to give you a toothache.

I'd been tying my shoe laces when she'd appeared above me in all her womanly glory and had mistaken me for the hired help. I didn't blame her, compared to the cute camisole, ripped jeans, and pink converse she wore, I looked like a sack of shit.

I'd introduced myself as Tom's sister and she'd assumed that I was looking for him. She seemed to jump to conclusions pretty quickly and I couldn't blame her really, my introduction had been a bit all over the place. It was the shock, I think. You just didn't see girls that looked like that in the country. She stood out a fricking mile! Like she'd walked off the page of a glossy magazine and no, not Farmers Weekly! I'm talking, Cosmo, or Vogue.

Everything about her screamed *love me*, *cherish me*, and above all else, *protect me*. She had that fragile, female quality that made guys puff up their chests or beat at it with their fists like Tarzan. She'd attract the dominant male of the species like a magnet to metal and from her looks and body alone, the rough macho guys from the village would swarm around her like bees to the sweetest of flowers.

She wasn't impressed with my colourful language, each time I swore, she blinked, almost like she had a tick or something. Even *that* was cute.

I struggled to stop my mouth from blurting out what had been said in the pub but before I could stop it, Connor's Barbie comment was out there. She took it on the chin and didn't flinch, having obviously heard of herself referred to in this way before.

Woman to woman, it being my duty, I warned her about the louts from the village. Giving her the watch-your-back advice. I also dropped it in there that Tom fancied her, purely to see her reaction. She gave nothing away.

Our chat flowed fairly well and I almost mentioned Ryan a couple of times but chickened out, going with 'it's complicated'. I could probably have told her everything, she had one of those faces that screamed 'you can trust me'.

To be honest, taking control of my bitch gene had been relatively easy. As far as first impressions go, the girl was *really* nice, so I couldn't really hate her.

With my short, curling brown hair and thin body, I'd felt like a scrawny boy next to her dainty frame and womanly softness. I felt stressed at the thought of how Ryan would react when he saw her. She really was perfect in every way.

I also thought about Connor and his initial unpleasant, angry reaction toward her. It was an odd one really as I couldn't imagine anyone wanting to be mean to someone so angelic.

But Connor was Connor, a law unto himself. Unpredictable and as hard as nails, the guy didn't do soft. He could probably be moody toward a fluffy abandoned kitten. He was angst-encapsulated. Harlow Williams had *nothing* out of place and Connor being the dick of the century would mess with that if he could. It was a shame really as the two of them together would make an amazing-looking couple. They were complete polar opposites in appearance and personality. A manly man and a girly girl, surely that had to work somehow?

My mouth spread into a knowing smile. The super sweet Harlow Williams was going to have to grow a backbone if she was to cope here all summer, especially living with a bossy fucker such as Connor.

The more we chatted, the more I warmed to her presence and a thought occurred to me. Harlow may actually manage to draw Nate's attention *off* me which wasn't a total unpalatable consideration. She declared outright that she didn't fancy Connor, although I found the way she worded her reply hard to swallow. I think she thought all my questions were because I fancied him. Which was of course, rather far from the truth.

The girl definitely knocked me out of my comfort zone and brought out the goofy Ella. She'd also been so genuine and interested in what I had to say. It had felt refreshing. Most of my girlfriends (and I didn't have many) were great active listeners, the type that were just basically waiting for their turn to speak and didn't really give a shit about what you were saying. Maybe with Harlow, I could actually participate in some girl talk and get another perspective. I didn't intend to show my cards too soon, though. I needed to establish her intentions during her stay.

Thinking back to her reaction to my Connor-related comments, I'd decided to watch that particular space. At the end of the day, if Connor turned on the charm, and yes, he did have some when he needed to get laid, Harlow would be doomed. This thought didn't worry me, if anything it was the best outcome. This would take any attention off Ryan. As you can imagine, I so didn't care for that scenario.

Ryan was exclusively mine. He just didn't know it yet.

Five

As I ambled back to my house from Mike's place, the sun was high in the sky and I welcomed the warmth against my face. I *loved* the summer and the fresh air of the countryside. I also embraced that familiar sound of farming machinery which echoed around the fields surrounding me. This was home and I was so glad to be back.

I began to replay the script I had decided to stick to when speaking with Nathan that afternoon. I would be firm but fair. To be honest, I was so done with Nate and his un-relentless attention, the guy needed to get over himself.

Suddenly my phone vibrated in my pocket to say I had a text, and I pulled it out to check. I'd given my number to Harlow so she could message me with hers.

As I swiped the screen, my heart did a dance as I saw the message was actually from Ryan. After having spent the last twenty minutes in the company of the perfect Harlow feeling thoroughly insignificant, my day appeared to be looking up.

You should close your curtains before getting undressed, Ella.

A spicy wave of lust crashed against my pelvis as I thought about last night and that strange sensation I'd felt after I'd removed my jeans. Ryan *must* have seen me, which meant he had been outside my house. I so hoped he liked what he saw.

My brow creased as I wondered why he hadn't messaged so I could have gone out to see him. Maybe he hadn't, thinking my parents had still been up. Ryan Lane wasn't a risk-taker. He was far too careful and controlled for that.

I keyed in my response with a mischievous grin.

And you shouldn't be watching my house like a stalker.

I added a LOL emoji, I didn't want to make him feel like a creep.

I continued walking, watching the buffering icon, holding my phone in the air, trying to improve the connection. The signal near Mike's place was shit.

The degree of pleasure I felt at that moment was almost off the chart. I honestly hadn't felt this giddy for weeks. The quiet period had been like torture.

It wasn't the house I was watching Ella.

Even his texts were direct and bossy. Adrenalin surged in my chest as his reply boggled my mind. Was he being cute? Before my face could explode into a full-on blush, his next message dropped in under the last and I realised I'd misunderstood his reply. Slow down, girl. A hint of disappointment twanged my nerves like the strings on a guitar. **And no, I'm not referring to the pink little number you were wearing.** My underwear had been lilac actually, but he'd be viewing me from a distance and so I let him off.

I see. You should have texted me and I would have come out. I keyed in.

His reply was immediate. **I wanted to make sure Nathan dropped you off and then left like a good boy**.

At that point, I wasn't overly concerned about his words. I imagined Nathan had mentioned that we were together when he took the call from Ryan last night. As far as Ryan was concerned, Nate and I were just friends.

I thought back, searching my memory to check that Nathan hadn't attempted to kiss me before I left the car. The image of Nathan pecking me on the mouth returned. This had happened outside the pub and *before* Ryan's call and so he wouldn't have seen anything.

I wasn't intending on hiding the truth from Ryan about what had happened with Nathan forever, but it wasn't something to share just yet. Sleeping with Nathan was a silly, drunken mistake and that was it. That's what I kept telling myself anyway.

I thumbed in my reply; keeping it brief, and adding an eye-rolling emoji.

Whatever Lane, bet you were spying on me you perv?

His next text sent a rush of excitement through my abdomen.

I think you need a lesson on the more useful things you can do with that smart mouth, he replied, and my nipples pebbled against my bra. I was so hot for this guy, even his fricking text messages did something to my sex. To say I was inexperienced, the fantasies I'd had about us together, would probably have been X-rated.

The gates of my property came into view and the low grumble of a vehicle suddenly idled beside me. I pushed my phone into the pocket of my jeans before turning to see if someone needed directions.

I immediately recognised the black shiny surface of Ryan's sports car. It was sexy and sleek, a mirror of the man it belonged to.

He lowered the window and pulled off the aviator sunglasses he was wearing; our gazes tangling. His appearance snagged my breath and my heart went bat-shit crazy at the sight of his gorgeous, chiselled face. Anyone would be seduced by his charisma, blatant masculinity that just oozed from him.

His eyes were so dark they were almost black and his hair which had grown since I last saw him, flicked forward against his forehead. It made me want to lean over and push it back. It was really thick and I loved the feel of it against my fingers.

"Hi stranger," he drawled, with a flash of even white teeth. His voice wrapped around my body.

"Hi yourself," I returned with a grin, placing my fingers on the open window and dipping my head forward to drink him in.

Searching his face, my lip curled and I cocked my head, studying him. "You can add curb crawling to the list too," I pointed out with a wiggle of my eyebrows. I loved our playful banter.

Ryan shot me a 'behave yourself' look whilst trying not to smile and replied. "Nice. Get your pretty bottom in the car Ella." His voice was deep and commanding and the tone did funny things to my insides.

"I take it you're heading back from Connor's?"

I nodded.

"You know, if you put in for your test as I suggested, it would make your life so much easier," Ryan stated with *that* look. My not driving was a bugbear, he hated the thought of me walking around alone at night.

"I will do, eventually. Just haven't got around to it yet."

"In," he reiterated with a flick of his head. His sexuality made me catch my breath.

That assessing gaze of his roamed over me like a sensual caress and I moved to open the passenger door. Ryan's lips were curled in the semblance of a smile, but his expression was fairly staid. I wasn't overly concerned about that, serious was his signature look. When he did smile, the intensity of it almost made my knees wobble, clichéd I know but true nonetheless. That smile was a secret weapon in itself.

Ryan was magnificent in his navy pinstriped suit with the sharp grey tie; the white of his shirt appeared bright against the tanned column of his throat. A place I had pressed my mouth against the last time I had seen him. His jacket was hung neatly in the back, forever being Mr. Pristine. I glanced down at my rumpled clothing, the difference between us was a mile-wide but I didn't care, I was just so pleased to see him.

I almost purred with satisfaction, taking in a lungful of his heady scent as I lowered myself into the sleek interior of the car. Ryan was always well-groomed and immaculate and he only ever wore a hint of aftershave, it was subtle but one I'd recognise anywhere.

Once I pulled the door closed, Ryan pumped the accelerator and steered the car into the road. His strong tanned fingers were curled tightly around the steering wheel; even the chunky Rolex watch on his wrist added to that sexy, capable vibe. The guy could give that chap out of Fifty Shades a run for his money. Not that Ryan had a torture chamber or anything. At least I hoped not. I certainly wasn't for the rough stuff. I had little to no muscle and bruised really easily.

"Put your seatbelt on," he instructed with a flick of his head and I automatically complied.

"Has anyone ever said that you're a bossy sod?" I questioned.

He cocked a brow. "Frequently." A muscle in his jaw flexed and I wanted to trace it with my fingertips. He had such a firm, strong jaw that always looked so determined, and capable.

"So, where have you been? I thought you'd fallen out with me," I began as I readjusted my hoodie under the tightness of the belt. It sliced in a vee across my chest and actually made me look like I had boobs, which wasn't a bad thing.

There was a moment of tense silence. "Why would you think that?" he questioned absently. Was there a 'tone' to his voice or was I being paranoid? Maybe it felt a bit awkward as we'd not seen each other in a while. It certainly didn't feel as normal as it had during my last visit. I shook off the thought and replied. "Just that I haven't heard from you is all. Cold feet?" The guy was a definite cards-close-to-the-chest type.

He dashed a hand across his jaw as he drove past my house. Not dropping me home then.

"Of course not. I've been busy with work, you know how it is," he explained, a little abruptly.

I decided to leave it. "That's fine, I'll let you off. Don't worry, I'm not going to go all bunny boiler on your arse, like in that movie, Lethal Attraction."

Mischief danced in my eyes as I shot him a look to gauge his reaction before he returned quite dryly. "Fatal Attraction Ella, and are you even old enough to watch that movie?"

The banter started to flow again and I felt a jet of relief wash away my doubts. "So, you *do* have a sense of humour?" I exclaimed cheekily.

Ryan's mouth curled in his version of a smile, obviously also entertained by our horseplay.

He flexed his broad shoulders appearing larger than life in the small space of the car, almost unintentionally crowding my personal space. I wondered how he'd have responded if he'd had his hands free. Several possibilities swept through my mind like wildfire. Ryan was usually always the one in control of everything and that usually included the direction of the dialogue. I enjoyed messing with him, pushing him to lose that tight grasp he had on himself. I'd managed to make him lose his cool a couple of times, but it was a rare occurrence.

"So, are you definitely back for good now? No more trips?" he questioned.

"Why, do you miss me when I'm away?" I crooned in my sweetest voice.

Ryan rolled his eyes before shooting me a knowing expression.

I changed the subject. "So, how's it all going with you? Sell many tractors over the last month?"

"I'm not having a discussion about work with you Ella," he fired back, overtaking said vehicle.

I pouted playfully. Ryan never spoke about work or money with me, they were two topics that were off the menu. Which was of course fine by me as I couldn't think of anything more boring than what he did for a living. I wanted Ryan the man, I didn't care about his money or how he earned it.

The need for an answer to my earlier question chewed into me. "Yes, I'm back for good. So, *did* you miss me?"

He exhaled, now amused again. "Yes, actually. A little."

"A little?" I raised a questioning eyebrow. "Please don't lay it on too thick, will you? My ego will explode," I put out sarcastically. Ryan was not a guy to dish out compliments easily.

I turned to blatantly check him out, my confidence growing with every second that I spent in his company.

"You look good."

He shot me a fleeting glance. "So do you."

"I do?"

When this guy, who looked like a male God informed me that I looked good, it always amazed me. I was skinny, ordinary Ella Wade; simple and kind of plain and so not used to male appreciation of my appearance. Nate didn't count as he was more focused on the magic I must have created with my vagina.

I pushed away the mortifying thought and watched Ryan's hand as he changed gear and the car sprang forward. Like Nathan, Ryan was also a petrolhead, and he enjoyed embracing speed. I watched him handle the powerful vehicle in mute fascination.

"Well?" I prompted, when he didn't answer.

"Stop finishing Ella," he scolded, his deep voice rolling pleasantly across my skin, like a sensual current running through me. I loved it when he told me off. Winding him up always ended up with the best reactions. He also hated the fact that I swore so much. Said it wasn't ladylike and of course, I was more than aware of that. I didn't give a shit. I was the polar opposite of a fucking lady.

I curled my fingers in my lap to appear calm and relaxed when all I really wanted to do was run my fingers up his mouth-watering leg. Ryan's strong thighs were thickly corded with muscle.

"It must be a relief to be back. Travelling can be so monotonous." Ryan went away with work all the time.

"Totally. It was great seeing the sights, but it was starting to do my head in. Packing and re-packing and all that shit." Plus, I'd wanted to come back to be with Ryan.

He flicked me a warning look, possibly due to my language before saying. "Tell me about it."

I blew out a breath. "So, where are we going? Not to mine I take it?"

He directed an 'as if' type of expression at me. "Not a good idea, I saw your mother's car there earlier." His tone suggested he was amused.

He paused momentarily, turning on the air-con. "Maybe I've decided to kidnap you, steal you away and keep you to myself?" he retorted, surprisingly playful; his eyebrows now raised with mocking humour. I embraced his remark as he rarely made jokes. My thoughts shifted back to Fifty Shades again and the torture room, or whatever it was. The thought of this guy doing things he shouldn't to me was getting more appealing by the second.

I relaxed against the leather of the seat and briefly traced his leg with my fingertip before declaring. "You wouldn't need to kidnap me, Ryan, I'd be a willing victim I think."

He turned off the main strip onto a narrow single-track dirt road. I had passed this road many times in my life but had never driven down it. My level of excitement jumped up a notch as he whispered. "Are you sure? You don't know what I've got in mind."

I didn't even give it a beat to think about my reply. "Oh, I'm *definitely* sure."

My voice was low and sultry, I was thoroughly enjoying our verbal sparring.

"It's amazing how easily you bait me whilst I'm driving. Would you be as sure of yourself if my hands were free?"

The veiled threat in his words sent my pulse into overdrive as did his next ones, but not for the same reason. Lust twisted my chest and blood pumped into my temples. I wanted this guy with every thread of my being.

"Sally and Adam are away again and so I thought we'd go back to mine for a change?" Ryan hinted in a thick voice. He always called his parents by their names. I'd never heard him address them as mum and dad.

I almost choked on my breath. He was planning on taking me to his place when Nathan would be lurking there. No fucking way!

66

"Won't N-Nathan be there?" I stuttered, trying to sound unaffected by his so not a good suggestion. I could just imagine Nathan's face if I turned up at his house in his brother's car. Especially when I'd batted off seeing him until that afternoon. Talk about a snub.

He dashed a hand across his strong jaw before replying. "Possibly. So what?" My jaw was clenched so hard I could probably crack a tooth. If only we were in a 'so what' situation.

I was surprised that he suddenly appeared to not care about Nathan, he'd been so cagey about us being seen together by anyone so far.

Shit. I hadn't factored in things being tricky so quickly; this being our first conversation in over a week. I felt unable to answer as my mind raced. His proposal was like a fucking bombshell that had just gone off unexpectedly and my head was running for cover. During our on-and-off thing between us, Ryan had *never* suggested going to his house *ever*. We usually went to another village, far away where no one would recognise us.

"Well, surely, we don't want him to know anything about us?" I put in apprehensively. Realising after that I shouldn't have used the word 'us'. Ryan could be very particular about how I spoke about whatever this thing was between us. Our hooking up.

His jaw twitched.

"Ella, I could turn up at the house with you straddling me and he wouldn't think anything of it," he oozed with confidence. Oh my God, why the hell did he have to pop that image in my head?

I felt like a proper scaredy-cat as I muttered, "well, I don't think I'll be comfortable with him being there." I sounded like a little girl and mentally kicked myself. Due to our age difference, I always tried to appear as grown up as possible during our chats.

"It's Nate Ella, no big deal. Honestly, it's not a problem. He won't give a shit. He has his own stuff going on," he began as he pulled into a passing point to allow a van to get by us. The three guys that were sat in the other vehicle, eyed Ryan's wheels with envy. "Besides we'll be at my place in my annex, it's separate from the main house. He doesn't need to know we're there and it's none of his fucking business anyway." He puffed, now quite cross. Ryan was suddenly like a steamroller that refused to be redirected. It was a bit out of character. The thudding of my heart as it galloped in my chest must surely be reverberating around the car.

I paused for thought. Was he talking about taking me to his bedroom now? I batted the unhelpful picture of his massive king-sized bed, which I knew he slept in aside. This Intel came from Nathan who had moaned once about how much it cost. A wave of guilt engulfed me, the unspoken truth now weighing on me like a big fat lie. I so wanted to tell Ryan about Nate, but things needed to be said in the right order. At the end of the day, I'd slept with Nathan *before* this thing had started up with Ryan and it was one silly mistake. It was in the past and I wouldn't allow it to affect what I had with this guy.

I sighed and re-attacked the subject, ignoring the trickle of unease that was working its way down my spine. "Please, can't we just go for a walk?"

He must have misunderstood me as he shot me a fleeting glance before locking his eyes back on the road. His expression suggested he thought I'd assumed he wanted to have sex.

He indicated and I felt a whoosh of relief as he steered the car out of the dirt track which must have been a shortcut to his parent's estate. I made a mental note, after all these years, I hadn't realised where that particular road led.

"You don't have to clam up, I wasn't suggesting we go to mine so I can jump on you or anything," he put in, his perfect eyebrows sky high.

I felt a cocktail of disappointment and relief. An odd combination.

"Why not?" I put in hurriedly, partly offended. I was a girl and he was a guy. Surely, he'd relish the opportunity to jump my bones.

"Ella, we agreed on taking things slow, I'd hardly demand sex when you've only just got back. I do have some level of restraint."

And there it was, the control thing. Of course, Mr. Spontaneity, he was not.

"Well, I hope when the time's right you're not *that* restrained. I'll think I'm doing something wrong," I replied. Again, annoyed at how childish my words sounded when they were out there.

He refrained from answering, his mouth curling at one corner to show he was amused. Making this guy smile made me happy.

"Sorry," I gritted out, the heat in my cheeks reducing a fraction.

Ryan dashed a hand down his suit-encased thigh stating. "Women. You always want it both ways, we can't win."

I grinned. "It keeps you on your toes. Stops you getting bored."

"I doubt you could ever bore me. Frustrate the living shit out of me possibly, maybe talk me to death? But I'd never be bored. You're too unpredictable."

I smacked his leg playfully. "Oy, that's a bit below the belt." God the thing was solid. All muscle.

Ryan smiled and pulled the car into a National Trust car park.

"I'm not really dressed for the outdoors," he pointed out.

"That's fine. Wanna make out instead?" I suggested, biting my lower lip in earnest.

He turned the engine off and twisted his large frame toward me with a brooding expression.

"Now you're showing your age. I don't 'make out', especially in the car. This isn't high school Ella."

His tone was fairly serious but his words were complete rubbish and I told him so. "You're such a liar. The first time you kissed me was in a car," I pointed out.

He already had his answer. Of course, he did. Ryan Lane always got the last word. Nathan hated that too. "That was different. That was an experiment."

I exhaled, turning further toward him which pushed one jean-clad knee near his own. "To test what? You're so full of shit."

My phone vibrated in my pocket to say I had a text and I ignored it. Ryan's brow furrowed at my actions. Why did I suddenly feel so nervous? He was watching me so intently. I could tell he was thinking about my 'making out' comment and our first kiss. Which had by the way been up there with the most exhilarating sexual experience of my life so far. I'd lit up inside, my whole body on fire. His mouth had been strong and masterful. My limbs had felt gooey from the way he had coaxed my lips open; his tongue was amazing. Sexual bliss.

"You've got a message," he pointed out as if I hadn't heard or felt it.

"It's fine. I'll read it later," I replied with a shrug. "It's probably just from Harlow," I put in without thinking. Shit, why had I brought *her* name into it?

His now hooded gaze lifted with curiosity. "Harlow?"

Shit and double shit. Me and my fucking mouth! I felt a jolt of panic.

I almost didn't reply but he raised his eyebrows as if to say 'well'?

Tilting my chin, I adopted the most mundane tone of voice ever. I certainly didn't want to pique his interest so he'd want to check her out for himself. Hopefully, they never met. "Yes, Mike's daughter. She's come down from London for the summer."

Creases appeared against his forehead. "Oh yeah, Nathan was going on about her. The bane of Connor's life?"

Relief that that's all he'd heard whooshed around my gut like a tsunami. "That's her. Pain in the arse I heard, so you'll want to stay away from that one."

His eyes narrowed further, now in amusement and I wasn't surprised, you could almost taste my jealousy in the tight space of the car. "I'll do that," he began flatly. "One pain in the arse is enough."

I took it on the chin. He was right. I was a pain in the arse. I steered the subject away from God's actual gift to mankind. "So, what did you get up to on your last trip? Meet anyone interesting?" I probed, not sure I wanted to hear the reply. The thought of this guy touching anyone other than me almost encouraged a tantrum and I wasn't a tantrum girl. I was usually way too chilled for that nonsense.

"If you're asking me if I slept with anyone, then the answer is no." His eyes roamed over me, checking out my body language, and noting my arms. I unfolded them and pushed my hands under my bottom. I could feel that need to nibble my fingers coming on.

"How about you?" he echoed with relaxed indifference and I toyed with saying I had met someone to see how he reacted. I decided against making our situation any more complicated.

"If you're asking if I got off with anyone whilst I was away, then that's a big fat no."

A content expression flashed across his face. It was so fast I almost missed it.

He leaned one large palm on the shiny dash before pushing himself further around so we were closer. His dark head came forward, his gaze now piercing. I felt my nipples tighten against the lace of my bra at his closeness.

"I did say that you should let your hair down and experience all life has to offer," Ryan announced, slicing deeply into the atmosphere.

We'd had that *annoying* talk about it being 'early days' and not putting a label on 'us' yet. That's why he didn't like me using the term 'us'. I must admit to being pissed off at the time as I knew what I wanted and "he' was sat before me in all his male glory.

I puffed out a breath before replying.

"And I did, to a certain extent. I remember our chat well."

I had wanted to erase the words from my memory at the time as they'd made me feel that he didn't care if I did sleep with someone whilst I was away. Ryan of course didn't know that I'd only slept with one person or his identity, which was, of course, a monster truth waiting to pounce.

I pushed back against the door, needing a bit of space. Ryan now had his serious hat back on and he eyed the stiff set of my shoulders.

"I just didn't want you to hold back because of me," he responded dryly with a slightly guarded, yet composed expression.

"So, you would have been OK if I'd gone away and shagged some random guy in America, is that what you're saying," the volume of my voice increased as I felt a thread of temper snap. Just the one though, I wasn't going to go too ballistic on his arse, just yet. I'd give too much away in respect of my aching heart. And guys were great at squishing that particular organ when they were aware you were ready to hand it to them.

He tilted his head with an unimpressed glare. Ryan did not tolerate temper, from anyone. He rarely showed his own. Just disapproving looks and comments. "No, not exactly but if you had, that would have been your choice. You don't exclusively belong to me. Not yet, anyway."

A sigh of frustration burst between my now tight lips. Sometimes I wondered how far I could push him before he'd stop guarding his thoughts so much.

"You're talking in fucking riddles again Ryan," I bit out in annoyance.

"Language," he chided and I wanted to hit him. "We agreed we'd take things one step at a time is all I mean."

It suddenly felt like I'd overstepped some unwritten mark and had gone too far. I dragged my hands out from under my bottom and jammed them into the large pocket of my hoodie.

"Is this your way of telling me you're seeing other people?" I challenged with a pointed look.

Ryan rocked back against his seat; his stare unflinching. "No, Ella. I'm just pointing out that it's early days."

I tried to follow his logic; my hands fisted within the cotton which hid them. 'Act indifferent' my self-respect screamed.

"I know and I get that. I know you're not my boyfriend or anything," I agreed tartly. I so wanted to chew my nails which would provide me with a physical outlet for the wrath now bubbling inside me.

His next words took the edge off my temper.

"I feel too old to be anyone's boyfriend," he returned with a twist of his lips.

My foot started to tap in frustration. I so wanted to call this guy my boyfriend. To be able to say I had a boyfriend would be great. It would make me feel less weird and more normal, like a regular girl and not 'one of the lads'.

"You're twenty-six Ryan, not fifty." I managed to make my tone even, almost like I was telling him off. His expression twisted, maybe out of respect, as I sort of managed to swap our roles. I was now the adult and he was the youngster. My one victory didn't last long.

Ryan rubbed the back of his neck before threading his long fingers on his lap, stating. "I just want to make sure that we're on the same page. I like you, Ella, you know I do, but we need to tread carefully. Especially considering your parents and our friends. The gap between our ages doesn't worry me significantly, but you can't pretend it isn't there and that it isn't going to be an issue for some people."

"I don't give a shit about 'some people'." I whooshed out on an exhale. We'd had this conversation before.

"Me neither, when it concerns *regular* people, but we don't want to upset our family and friends."

Fuck them I thought, leaning my head back against the cold glass of the window, the whole car was starting to steam up and not just figuratively. "I get that and I agree. Honestly Ryan, we don't need to have this 'serious' type of conversation. I know you haven't made me any promises or anything. I'm happy to spend time with you and we'll see how it goes. As I pointed out before, I'm no bunny boiler."

His lips twisted thoughtfully and there was a cold silence before he replied. I sure hoped I hadn't damaged anything. At times I felt like this guy could walk away from me at any minute and never look back.

"OK, that's good then. I want you Ella, but if we're to be together, we have to do it my way. You know me, I don't approach anything in a haphazard way, that's not who I am."

"I get it, I quite like the control freak in you, to be honest," I crooned.

"It's the only way I know how to be."

I took a slow, calming breath before lifting my head from the door and shooting him a suggestive look; a getting down-to-business expression.

"So, *now* do you want to make out?"

Ryan drew in a breath and arched one sexy eyebrow, regarding me with a predatory look. My pulse raced as he unclipped his seatbelt and turned toward me; the leather of his seat creaking slightly. The atmosphere in the car became charged with sexual tension.

"When you look at me like that, how can I say no? I'm not a saint," he replied in a heavy, passion-infused tone.

Ryan's gaze was bold and unapologetic, full of promise. No one looked at me like this man. It was a look that said he wanted to punish me in some dark, exciting way. I'd always had to fight for any scrap of attention from my family, this guy made me feel wanted, desired.

His scent teased my nostrils as he leaned over my body, his arm brushing against my breasts as he released my seatbelt. Ryan's chin was set at a determined angle and I pushed back into my seat to ease the friction of his strong shoulder rubbing against my nipples.

After he'd finished freeing us both, Ryan turned his head and the dark pools of his eyes caught mine, our lips were close but not touching. A silent message passed between us before he shifted back into his own seat; our gazes remaining locked the whole time. Ryan was all serious as he patted his lap and crooked his finger, instructing me to come to him.

I pushed out of my seat and moved over, sliding carefully over the central console. The movement should have been awkward, but I easily managed to lift and slide one leg over him. Ryan helped me by placing strong hands under my arms and lifting me so I straddled the lower section of his body. Settling down against his strength, I was very aware of where the apex between my thighs touched. The sensation of his hardness was thrilling.

Once I was comfortably positioned across his thighs, he moved his hands to cradle my face before slowly drawing me down toward him. My breasts pushed against his rock-hard chest and my arms slid to his shoulders. Our bodies were angled fairly awkwardly in the small space, but when his lips met mine, I lost all rational thought, heat jetting through me. My pulse skyrocketed, my entire body igniting with delight.

Ryan's mouth met mine with a demanding pressure, his tongue driving between my lips and my back arched, pressing me further against him. I opened myself up to him, giving him *everything*. The pleasure I felt was breath-taking, all-consuming and blood pounded in my veins as my whole being raced with excitement.

He angled my head to delve deeper into my mouth. This wasn't like the kisses we had shared in the past, coaxing and sweet, this was savage and hungry.

A persuasive heat fell between my legs and I shuddered, he tasted of man and unadulterated lust. A riot of chills pulsated across my nerve endings. His mouth was insistent and demanding and I *loved* it.

Smashing into the sexual chaos, my phone started to continuously vibrate in my pocket which intruded into the moment and I groaned against his mouth as he drew back. The clouds of passion receded dramatically as I settled against his powerful thighs. Ryan dropped his hands to my waist and looked at me with a curious expression. Desire was evident in every part of his perfect face.

He must have been able to see inside my soul and pinpricks of heat crawled up my arms. There was nowhere to hide, it was out there in the car, crackling between our two bodies. Naked lust entwined with sexual frustration.

I exhaled sharply, attempting to gather control of my reaction to Ryan's invasion of my senses. "That's probably my mother. I only popped to Mike's place this morning and didn't take my keys. If she needs to go out, I'll be locked out of the house," I drew out, in a heavy, breathless voice.

Ryan nodded in understanding, before helping me back into my seat.

"I must admit, getting a call from your mother is a definite passion killer," he remarked with a tight smile. I embraced that look, as he rarely smiled.

"We could still go back to mine?" Ryan put in with a risqué twist of his mouth. My breath hitched at those sexy words and the steamy images they evoked.

I quirked an eyebrow. "What happened to taking things slow?"

There was a beat of silence. The car was thick with sexual tension.

"Fuck it," he grinned at me with veiled satisfaction. He was as attracted to me as I was to him. In that we were equal, I knew that then. My breath hitched, I just had to keep telling myself to be confident. This guy liked me, the real me; warts and all as they say. Ella Wade, ordinary, not so little me.

I smiled back at him as he started the car before pointing out, "Even you don't have the balls to deal with my mother when she's having a strop."

I clipped my belt back on.

"Good point," he chuckled, mirroring my actions.

We travelled back in silence, my lips still tingling from the taste of Ryan's mouth. That lingering feeling was delicious.

"So, Nathan's holding his usual piss up next week and so maybe we could do something? Unless you want to go to the party with Connor, which I can't say I'll be happy about but of course, it's your choice," Ryan stated with an edge to his tone. I identified the hint of jealousy.

I didn't even give it a second to think about my reply. "I don't even think Connor will go this year. I told Nathan last year that I was done with his parties. The elbow in the face kind of cemented that decision," I pointed out. This being only one of the reasons, of course, the other being the mortifying thing that had happened at the end of that night.

Ryan nodded his head in understanding. "Ah yes, I remember it well. You had a shiner if I remember."

"So, you noticed? We weren't actually into each other at that stage. I didn't think you ever saw me, not really. I was just your younger brother's friend."

Ryan changed gear and shot me a serious look. "I saw you. I noticed you years ago Ella, but the timing wasn't right, you were too young. Finishing high school and stuff."

My tummy flip-flopped at what he had just confessed. He spoke as if he too had battled with some type of crush, but due to the age difference had held back. The knowledge of this gave me a giddy feeling. The thought that we had both noticed each other screamed meant to be.

I decided to make a confession of my own. "I've liked you for ages too, you know," I put in quietly. Trying not to divulge too much and make myself appear overly smitten and pathetic.

His mouth curled into a sexy grin before he arrogantly replied. "I know, I've been batting off your come-to-bed-eyes for a least the last two years Ella. I remember you calling for Nathan and looking all gangly and awkward; watching me when you thought I wasn't looking. It was cute."

My own mouth curled at his words. "All right, big head."

He laughed, his eyes creasing and he looked quite boyish.

"So, if you're done with Nate's parties, we'll do something then. I'll text you. There's a new Italian I fancy trying."

I smiled and nodded. "Definitely up for that." I liked dining out, to be honest, I liked *everything* I did with this guy.

Ryan dropped me off at the edge of the lane near my house so we wouldn't be seen. He pecked me on the lips and I unclipped my seatbelt and left the car, feeling thoroughly content. Excitement bubbled at the thought of our pending date, I just wished it was sooner. Whether I saw him beforehand would depend on his work. He didn't like to put too many plans in place, just in case something came up. Ryan was solid, he wasn't the type that would like to let anyone down.

As I walked along the pathway to our estate, I checked my phone to see if Nathan had texted me back to confirm he'd be there for our catch-up. He had.

A sinking feeling started to overtake my feeling of happiness and the thought of the looming conversation with Nathan, created a drowning sensation like nothing I'd ever experienced.

It was time to take the bull by the horns. Nathan Lane would realise that there was not and never would be *anything* between us but friendship.

I just sure hoped he took it like a man. I of course, had major doubts about that one.

Six

I met Nathan as planned at Martha's Tearooms. I'd dressed in pale blue skinny jeans and a large sweater; nice and clean and free from any scent of Ryan. I couldn't imagine Nathan recognising his brother's aftershave, but I wasn't taking any chances.

When I arrived at the café, Nathan was sitting at one of the tables in the back room, playing with his phone. We were alone apart from an elderly couple who sat at the opposite end of the room. As I approached, he looked up and grinned at me, pocketing his iPhone, all eyes on me.

"About time—I thought you were going to ditch me again," he began. "I ordered you a coffee." Nate motioned towards the cup of steaming liquid in front of me as I slid into the seat. We'd been friends for years and yet he still didn't know me, not really. I didn't drink coffee.

His eyes were guarded and his first words were not what I expected. I had thought he'd dive in headfirst with the non-existent matter of 'us' but he didn't.

"So, Ryan told me he saw you on your way back from Connor's this morning?"

I digested his words before nodding. "Yes, I popped over first thing, I said I would last night."

His gaze narrowed. "What is it with you guys? You seemed to have been inseparable since you got back. Is there something I should know?"

The trace of jealousy was slight, but it was there. A flutter of annoyance circulated inside me. He was also wrong as I'd hardly seen Connor.

I placed my hands on the table beside the mug of coffee. I even abhorred the smell of the stuff. I was more of a tea girl and it had to be Yorkshire Tea. If it wasn't *Yorkshire* Tea, it wasn't tea.

Pursing my lips thoughtfully I replied. "I wasn't there to see Connor."

His brow creased further before I pointed out, "I went to see Harlow. To check her out, *remember*?"

My response was well received and his face lifted in understanding. He'd probably missed what I'd said in the pub, too busy directing his energy into assessing whether there was something going on between Connor and me.

Nate's body language became more settled.

"So, what did you think?" he questioned, his voice much brighter; shifting in his seat. He'd obviously been sat stewing, thinking I'd spent the morning with another boy.

"Tom's right, she's a head turner."

Nate's gaze glittered with keen interest and that thought reoccurred. Maybe Harlow *was* the perfect distraction. Take the heat off me?

My mind spun like a roulette table; could I really foist the train wreck that was this guy off on someone so sweet and innocent; *and* only sixteen? Was I *that* twisted and careless toward a member of my sex? After a beat or two of silence, I decided I was. Connor would kick off, but Nathan would have to handle it, I was done with the soft-touch approach and trying not to upset everyone all the time.

I decided to encourage the 'Harlow' direction of the conversation.

"Yes, she's stunning. She'll definitely stir up some trouble in the village."

Nate grinned and leaned forward with a pointed look. "I knew she'd be attractive. You could tell by Connor's overreaction."

Smiling, I bulldozed on without shame. Not caring that I was probably being too obvious.

"You should check her out. Pop around with the guys and give her a proper Pickering welcome. Connor's being a twat to her and she doesn't know anyone. Felt a bit sorry for her really. Maybe you could cheer her up?"

My words made Nathan crunch his face up. He wasn't stupid, I should have been more subtle in my tactics.

"Don't do that," he put in with a knowing smile. I was a bit surprised he'd caught on to my ploy so quickly, he wasn't usually that on the ball with things like that.

"What?" I bit back as innocently as I could beneath that shrewd stare.

"You *know* what Ella—don't try and throw other girls at me to get yourself off the hook."

I played with the coffee mug, allowing it to warm my hands, eyeing him warily. "I wouldn't have said I was ever *on* a 'hook' with you Nathan, not really," I put in bluntly. The gloves were off.

A mixture of emotions flickered across his face. He looked good in black jeans, a black tee, and a leather jacket. One I'd seen Ryan wear. But his looks had never been the problem. The chemistry just wasn't there for me. Not romantically anyway.

"Isn't that your brother's jacket?" I murmured with a flick of my head. Shit. How the hell would revealing my superior knowledge of his brother's wardrobe help my cause? I quickly moved that shit on.

"Anyway, back to the miracle that is Connor's stepsister. I wasn't *throwing* her at you, not necessarily. I'm not her bloody pimp. I'm just saying that she's hot and seems like a lovely girl. Go meet her, you know, don't put all your eggs in one basket." My comeback was severely on the shitty side.

He rolled his eyes before saying with a flick of his wrist. "And you're the basket in this scenario I take it?"

Pursing my lips in reflection I replied. "I didn't mean that. You're young and single, you should play the field. You always used to," I pointed out, leaning back in my chair.

He didn't like my words but I powered on, determined not to get side-tracked.

"Bottom line. I care about you Nathan; you *know* that, but we're *friends* and that's it. *Just friends.*" If I had written this sentence down, the 'just friends' section would have been underlined with a thick red marker pen. The statement came out of my mouth like Churchill declaring War on Nazi Germany. Big and bold and not to be messed with.

My words fell onto the table like a fucking death sentence. At least it was out there and there were now no minced words.

Nathan rolled his shoulders before casting a quick glance around the room.

"So, same old shit then; you're 'friend zoning' me again?"

I straighten and cocked my head with a puzzled look. "I'm not friend zoning you *'again'* Nathan. That's all there has *ever* been between us, friendship," I pointed out wearily, certain I was going to get a headache.

He cleared his throat noisily and took a drink from his own mug. There was a moment of silence, which I welcomed.

"What about when we used to make out at parties and you had your tongue down my throat? You must have wanted it then. I remember you used to be all

80

over me," he replied with a cocky tone, his face fairly blank considering his words. Like he'd pulled a mask of self-preservation in place or something.

I rolled my eyes so hard I thought they'd fall out of the back of my head.

"What the *actual* hell Nate? Those were *dares* and shit. Messing about, *not* to be taken seriously." My throat almost closed off.

His next words were like a kick in the teeth.

"Really. And what about when you let me fuck you?"

OMG he actually *said* it, and *very* loudly. His words fell into the quiet room like a fucking echo. The couple sat at the other table shifted uncomfortably in their seats and I wanted to die.

A cocktail of tempered emotion channelled through me and I leaned over the table, my eyes locked onto my target.

"Keep your voice down," I bit out in a gruff whisper, shooting a quick glance at the old man and woman. They had clearly heard and were now stuffing their faces with scone, probably to make a quick exit. I was mortified. Thank God, I didn't recognise them as being from my village.

The atmosphere became charged.

"Well, that's what happened," he voiced moodily.

Nathan dashed a hand across his jaw in frustration but thankfully lowered his tone. He appeared to have grown in his seat, all bristling male with a bullet hole in his gargantuan ego that I had just put there.

"It was *one* night Nathan and a drunken mistake. We *both* agreed at the time, so I don't really get where you're coming from."

He pushed his mug to one side and drummed his fingers on the table in front of him. I could clearly see he was getting more and more worked up. The guy needed to chill his shit.

"What if I don't agree? What if I want more?" he probed with a tilt of his dark head.

I went for the throat punch; it was now or never. I *refused* to carry on with the backward-and-forward bullshit.

"You're screwed—as *I don't want more* and I've told you that a million times. I don't see you that way. We're friends and you just need to accept that."

He shook his head, in denial mode again. "Why? Why can't we just try it and see how it goes?" He now looked like a kicked puppy and I felt like a bitch again.

Exhaling, I circled the tip of my finger around the rim of the mug before sadly saying.

"I'm not repeating myself over and over Nathan. I've had *enough*." I shot a cagey glance at the other couple, before facing him again.

Nathan shuffled further forward in his seat, directing all his energy on me. "What if I don't want to be 'just' friends? What then?" he whispered, as if only *just* realising that we weren't alone.

I chewed the inside of my cheek to the point where I tasted blood. The thought of my next words coming to fruition, made me feel as miserable as hell.

"Then we can't see each other anymore."

This statement was met by cold silence, the type that chilled you to the bone and that no number of woolly layers could ward away.

The only sound in the room was that of a chair scraping along the floor as the two old people started to put on their coats, preparing to leave. I caught the woman's eye and she gave me a brief woman-to-woman look.

Smiling tightly, I twisted back to Nathan, awaiting his decision like a criminal in the dock, crossing my arms over my chest.

He glared across the table like he *hated* me. It was horrible, but I had to stay strong. If I had a chance of *anything* with Ryan, this guy needed to get the message. The looming doom of how much worse things would be when he found out about Ryan, felt like an approaching disease, but what could I do? I *had* to follow my heart.

"This is *bullshit*." Nathan stood, his own chair scraping angrily against the floor, echoing his stormy mood.

"I'm sorry—I really am," I blurted out, trying to reason with him one last time.

He came to his feet and stared down at me glassy-eyed.

"So am I."

And with those words, the storm that was Nathan Lane, swirled out of the café, leaving devastation and grief in his wake.

My heart felt like it had shattered into a thousand tiny pieces. I had lost my friend for good.

I spent most of the next day feeling miserable about my fight with Nathan.

After a much-needed shower to refresh myself, I padded from the bathroom and checked my phone. It was almost five. I'd spent the day rattling around the house and had accomplished nothing. It was so frustrating that I couldn't just go and see Ryan, turn up out of the blue. I wondered if Nathan would say anything about our fight to him. Hopefully not, the two brothers were not really the sharing type. Old animosity and all that.

I decided to text Connor to see if he was in. Maybe I'd pop over and see Harlow again.

What you up to. I messaged.

I started to search my wardrobe to find something to wear whilst waiting for my friend to respond. **Fuck all. Why?**

Thought I'd come over for a chat.

Surprise shot through me as Connor sent me an eye-rolling emoji. That was a first. **You not with lover boy tonight?**

No. I think he's out with his mates tonight.

I toyed with how amazing it would feel to meet some of Ryan's friends, he spoke about them all the time. I wondered if he'd told them about me. I filed the thought and glanced down as my phone buzzed.

I was due to play pool with Noah, but he's blown me off. You fancy it?

The amount of games of pool I'd had I could count on one hand and so I replied. **I can't play pool.**

Connor replied. **I'll teach you.**

Sighing, I considered it for a beat or two before replying. **OK. When?** It would be better than staying in and feeling stressed about the Nathan thing.

I'll pick you up in thirty.

K.

Q's was a snooker and pool club in Scalby, a village just north of Scarborough. It was a small venue, with one main room for snooker and two smaller rooms used for pool. The more advanced players usually booked one of serval snooker tables and those less experienced played pool.

I'd dressed for comfort in the tightest skinny jeans I owned and a black top with spaghetti straps. Connor had collected me in his piece of shit Ford Ranger and we pulled up at the club just before six.

The place was dimly lit and the majority of people in there were male. Connor had booked one of the pool tables, and I went to the bar as he started to organise the balls.

I'd played pool before with my brother when we were on holiday, but I wasn't any good. Connor showed me how to hold the cue better and gave me tips, but I really was quite useless. The female bar staff kept sauntering past, unnecessarily collecting glasses so they could ogle Connor. He wore baggy jeans and a button down tee, revealing his tanned muscular arms, his sleeve of tats screaming bad boy.

I purposefully steered away from love interest type conversations and kept our chat either pool related or movies. Connor and I could talk about films all night.

Connor was focused on the shot I was about to take, gipping his pool cue, his eyes narrowed.

"This way a bit, lean into it more and lift your thumb," he suggested. Coaching me. I bent further over the table, my backside to the door when a voice said.

"Now that's a view you'd pay for." The voice wasn't familiar and I turned my head, my arms and fingers still poised to take the shot.

My heart skipped a beat; the voice belonged to a stranger. I didn't really care about him. It was who he was with that caught my attention. Ryan stood just behind him in the doorway with a beer in his hand. His deep eyes watching me. He looked uber-league hot, all in black, black jeans, a tee, and his leather jacket. I was surprised my tongue wasn't hanging out.

I grinned before turning back and taking the shot.

Thwack! I sunk a ball into a pocket and uncurled myself from the table, almost giddy with glee. Connor smiled lazily, giving me a clap for my efforts and I turned to see the two guys moving into the room.

"Connor," Ryan greeted, with a tilt of his beer. Con nodded his 'hi' and moved forward to shake the hand of the other guy. I'd never seen him before.

"Long time," the stranger said.

The guy's name was Dane Burrows. He was an associate of Ryan's that Connor had also had business dealings with. Farm-related ones of course.

I was now the only female in a room of smoking hot men, it was like a female's heaven surely. Of course, the only guy I really had eyes for was Ryan.

"Nice shot Ella," Ryan complimented as he came to stand before me. I felt a frisson shoot up my spine, knowing Connor was watching us. He and Dane had started a 'catch up' type of conversation, but they were both looking in our direction. I felt exposed. Of course, Con knew about Ryan and me but Ryan didn't know that, yet.

"It's the first one I've potted," I replied, a ghost of a smile still in place. He stood a respectable distance away but close enough for me to take in his heady male scent.

My mind started to race and it felt a little awkward, so I decided to play neutral. Ryan wasn't being overly familiar at that point. I leaned against the pool table and eyed him thoughtfully.

"I was going to say, do you come here often, but that sounds way too much like a pickup line," I beamed in a bright voice. We'd lost the other two's attention now and they were deep in conversation about cars.

"I didn't know you played pool," Ryan replied, taking a step further toward me, the table was cool against my denim-encased bottom. I was so pleased to see him and I longed to put my arms around his neck, or just touch him anywhere to be honest. I was, of course, way too aware of our audience.

I replayed his question. "I don't really, Connor was teaching me," I declared, darting a glance toward the two guys at the other side of the table.

Ryan's look darkened. "Was he."

Did I imagine the slight undertone of 'not happy' in those two short words? My brow creased. He certainly didn't say it like it was a question.

I batted off the thought. "Yes. I'm not picking it up very quickly though."

Ryan took a drink from his beer, before watching me intently over the rim.

"You have another shot," he pointed out with a flick of his head. My hand was still curled around the pool cue and I stepped away from the table and turned.

Eyeing the balls. Ryan deposited his beer on a side table and moved around me, also viewing the table.

My tummy flipped as he took control away from Connor. Ryan was the teacher now.

He pointed to a ball that sat near one of the pockets. "This one," he asserted, stretching out one lean finger as he stood beside me. His scent teased my senses and the atmosphere in the room crackled. He was so close now, a swirling coil of need circled in my abdomen.

I positioned myself, lifting the cue, preparing for my shot. Ryan moved to stand directly behind me, tall and commanding and I glanced fleetingly up at him. His body was pressed into mine and he gently pressed his chest forward which slowly bent my upper body over the table, my cue in position. Ryan ran his hands down my arms, moulding his body behind me, helping me position the cue. His breath fanned my neck and heat flooded into me as my backside pushed against the v between his hard thighs.

He released my shooting arm and slid his hand back up to my backside, nudging my legs apart. "Open your legs," he whispered and I almost melting into a girly pool of heat on the floor. I did as he instructed and widened my stance. "Better balance, better shot," he explained in a gruff voice. Heat pooled between my legs, the intenseness of it, shocking my inexperienced senses. My body was heading toward a fever pitch.

Connor and Dane stopped talking and shot each other a knowing look. They both had their arms crossed over their chests. They were similar in appearance like bookends, although Dane had sun-kissed brown hair, almost blonde.

Ryan's hand moved to my waist. "That's it, line it up and take the shot."

I felt thoroughly turned on, I didn't care that we had two guys looking on. As far as they knew, Ryan was helping me with my shot, in a flirty way but still fairly innocent. Yeah right, if only they could see what was going on with my body. I must have looked flushed, would Connor notice? Probably, he knew how I felt about Ryan.

I pulled back the cue and, BANG. The sound of Connor placing his beer on the table made me jump and I missed, the cue scuffing the white ball off centre. Ryan stepped away from me and I turned to look at Connor with a 'you made me miss' look. His face was guarded and I glanced briefly down at the beer he had discarded with a fair amount of force.

He wasn't happy with Ryan's behaviour but at that point, I didn't care. He could mind his own fucking business. If he said anything, I'd kill him.

Ryan cleared his throat as the two men, stared each other down. To the point where Dane looked back and forth with a grimace. Tension crackled between them. God, I hated this testosterone thing guys did.

Before I could speak Dane cut in, in a poor attempt to clear the air as the two men bristled like angry jungle cats. The face-off continued with the pool table between us. I rubbed chalk on my cue pretending not to notice the shift in the atmosphere.

"Fancy a game of doubles?" Dane suggested.

My eyes flickered between Connor and Ryan. "I'm up for it," I put in, my voice still uneven after Ryan's closeness.

"How about, Connor and Ella against me and Ry?"

"You're on." Connor pronounced firmly, before grabbing his beer off the pool table and placing it on the windowsill out of the way. Dane moved and pushed the remaining balls into the pockets to reset the game. Connor took a couple of pound coins that we'd stacked on the table earlier and pushed them into the money slot of the table. As Dane and Connor concentrated on setting up the game, Ryan's fingers slid to my arm and he herded me out and into the room with the bar. I followed his lead, loving the feel of his hand against my skin.

"Drink?" he questioned in my ear as he led me toward the bar. His dark eyes gave nothing away, but I could see he was both surprised and pleased to see me.

I stared up, a smile curling my lips. He was jealous. Jealous I was there with Connor and I loved knowing that. So much for Mr. Cool.

"Yes, please. I'll have a rum and coke if you're buying."

He arched an eyebrow. "Bit strong. I didn't have you pegged as a spirits girl, I'll have to remember that," he drawled as he lifted a hand to push my hair back from my forehead. It was a tender gesture but was done in a way that suggested ownership in some way like he was letting those around us know I was his. Excitement rippled through me.

Connor and Dane wouldn't have been able to see us from the pool room, but I didn't care anyway. The familiar way Ryan had touched my body by the pool table was definitely making a statement like he was branding me in front of the other two men.

I savoured his words. 'I didn't have you pegged as a spirits girl.'

"There's a lot about me you don't know Mr. Lane," I replied in a sultry voice, watching him from beneath my lashes.

"Really. Not for long I hope," he returned with a devilish light in his eyes.

He gave me a dark and promising smile before turning to the bar and ordering our drinks. Ryan also opted for a rum and coke.

The chemistry between us was amazing, so natural and unforced. The air just fizzed.

After Ryan paid for our drinks, we made our way slowly back to the pool room.

"Your arse looks amazing in those jeans," Ryan approved in a whisper, directly into my ear as he wrapped his hand around mine. OMG, we were actually holding hands, like proper couples did, and I think my heart almost stalled. His fingers were firm as they threaded through mine. I felt so special and safe and extra feminine.

"You wearing your usual scrap of nothing under them?" he said, running one firm hand over my butt cheeks.

I exhaled slowly, stopping just before the entrance to the room where Connor and Dane would be waiting. "No, *nothing* actually. You've seen how tight they are. No room."

I heard Ryan's breath catch in his throat, and he stared down at me with eyes heavy with desire. The fact that I had spoken such provocative words when he couldn't do anything about it, reverberated between us like a declaration of war.

"You'll pay for that one," he whispered sexily in my ear. His fingers then tightened on mine but I quirked him a look, my mouth curling before I pulled my hand from his, turned my back, and walked into the room. Ready for all-out war.

The guys had just set up the table, and Dane was in the process of adding chalk to his cue. Ryan came into the room a beat or two after me and took the pool cue offered by Connor. The brief glance they exchanged was respectful enough, but not overly friendly.

Ryan was the one to break. He had removed his jacked and his arm muscles flexed with power as the balls scattered around the table, two going into pockets. Dane and Ryan were stripes and Connor and I were spots.

The game, if you can call it that was a full-on battle for supremacy, a proper pissing contest, with Ryan and Connor taking turns to be close to me during my shots. Ryan was worse as you can imagine, almost like a dog marking its territory. I saw Connor watching Ryan's body language toward me during the game, his gaze hooded and slightly amused. He was in full-on protective big brother mode.

Connor was hands down the superior player and the other two guys were evenly matched. I was the hindrance, I kept missing which resulted in Ryan and Dane getting two shots each time. Hence Connor and I lost. I could see he wasn't happy about it but he stomached it, just.

At the end of the game, we all shook hands. Ryan and Connor gripped each other a little longer than was necessary. The look they exchanged was hard to read.

To be honest, having the attention of two guys such as these felt great.

We finished our drinks and all left the club together, Dane and Connor walked ahead with Ryan and me trailing behind.

Dane's car was parked next to Connor's, its shining paintwork gleaming in the dark and Connor went to admire it. It was a Ford Ranger, the same as Con's but a much newer model. The two guys walked around the vehicle, touching the paintwork and saying something about 'a raptor pack' for the bodywork.

Ryan and I stood side-by-side, watching them before he said. "I meant what I said Ella. You will pay for that comment," referencing my suggestion I was underwear-less.

I raised my eyebrows. "I sincerely hope so."

Ryan's mouth curled in the hint of a smile. "When you get home, text me."

I returned his smile. "Will do."

We all said our goodbyes and Connor and I got in his Ranger. The thing looked even dustier next to Dane's gleaming wheels.

As we travelled back to my house, Connor didn't mention the Ryan situation. The unspoken words still laid heavily between us. He spoke briefly about Dane and how he'd helped with a missing order of feed. Mind-numbingly boring farm stuff.

Just before I climbed out of the cab I shot a gibe at Connor, knowing it would piss him off. In our usual trading insults way, knowing his come-back would beat mine.

"You going to have a cold shower now? You know, to get rid of that hard-on you got from Dane's car?" I questioned with a raised brow. Pursing my lips as I pushed open the door.

Connor arched a brow and shot me a look. "I'd say that's exactly what you need right now, and we both know your boner has got nothing to do with a fucking car," he drew back, tilting his head toward me.

I smiled my reply before jumping down and heading into the house. Warmth bubbling in my belly. What a great end to shitty day.

Seven

I spent the next few days, busying myself with our garden; ear pods in, angry music blaring away. I didn't care that the work wasn't that creative, I just needed something to do. All I could think about was Ryan at the pool club and how much I couldn't wait to see him again.

Natalie had helped me post a handful of flyers advertising that I was available for work and they had slowly started to generate interest. The next plan of action was to do a good job, be reliable and hopefully secure some more work. Putting in for my driving theory test should also have been on the list, but I couldn't face it. I hated exams, they reminded me of school.

I'd spoken to Ryan on the phone and we'd texted, but he was *always* working. When his parents were away, he'd purposefully use that time to 'prove' himself. Show them he could manage things on his own. I imagine he'd want to take over eventually.

On Thursday, I received a message from Ryan, asking me if I wanted to go to a beach party and meet his friends. I'd almost shot to my feet and clapped my hands with glee. The fact that he wanted to introduce me to his friends was surely a step in the right direction relationship-wise.

Anticipation had thudded through my bloodstream as I'd waited for him in our usual spot. As far as my parents and Tom were aware, I was over at Connor's house for the evening.

The journey over to Scarborough just felt so right. I told Ryan about the work I'd secured and he was so encouraging. He made me feel good about myself, asked questions, and really listened. By the time we arrived, I was on cloud nine.

Ryan parked the car and turned off the engine before turning to face me. "Ready?"

I nodded, a cocktail of excitement and anxiety swirling in my stomach at the thought of meeting his friends. "Absolutely," I replied with more confidence than I felt, my hands suddenly clammy.

"You don't need to be nervous: I've known these guys most of my life and they're all relatively normal. Well, apart from Boyd. The jury's still out on that one."

"Will they like me?" I questioned in a hopeful voice.

Ryan's speared a hand through his hair, "Of course, what's not to like?" His gaze roamed my worried features before his mouth broke out into a smile. "Actually, don't answer that. I can think of a few things."

I tutted and shot him an interrogatory eyebrow. "Such as?" My voice was purposefully laced with mock indignation as I challenged him.

There were creases at the corners of his eyes, those deep dark pools that were usually so mysterious now danced with mischief. He seemed different tonight, more relaxed and playful and my earlier nervousness started to drift away.

"Well?" I prompted, folding my arms across my chest.

The usual dominant angles of his face had softened and he looked younger. Don't get me wrong, I didn't have a problem with his serious side, but this light-hearted version of Ryan was irresistible.

"You sing out of tune," he coughed out.

"What? I do not." I laughed. He was right of course, I loved singing but was *literally*, tone-deaf.

"Your singing voice is distinctive. I'll give you that."

"Distinctive, *that's* what you're going with?"

"How to describe it. I'd say your singing voice is what it would sound like if someone tried to play a cat."

I full-on belly laughed, my shoulders shaking. Ryan's own grin was now full and wide.

Eventually, he sobered, his eyes finding mine again and the intensity of that look was deep and meaningful. There was a long breathless moment before he suggested, "Come on, let's go and meet the riff-raff."

Nodding, I unfolded my arms and we both climbed out of the car and went to the boot to collect our bags. We'd purchased a few beers from the off-license and a huge bag of cheese puffs. Ryan had previously told me to dress warm and to bring something to sit on. I'd managed to forage a large tartan picnic blanket from a cupboard in our utility room.

As we set off down the concrete ramp onto the beach, I could see flames licking the sky from a large oil drum fire pit.

There was around thirty-odd people dotted in huddles on the sand. Some were in couples and others in clusters, everyone appeared high-on-life, drinking and laughing and some were even dancing. A surge of giddy adrenaline fizzed into me. I'd lived here my entire life and yet I'd *never* been to a party on the beach before.

I shot a glance at Ryan as we approached. "Are these all your friends?"

He shifted the rolled-up blanket more firmly under his arm and cast me an amused look. "Of course not, not all of them," he began before pointing to a smaller group that was sitting the closest to the fire. "Over there, that should be Nixon, Boyd, and Charlie. The smaller guy looks like Alex, but I can't really tell from here and he isn't a friend, not really. We tolerate him from time to time."

"Isn't he very nice?"

He gave me a lopsided smile. "You'll get it when you meet the little shit. Oh, and that looks like Melanie next to Nixon. She's OK, doesn't say much."

I nodded, switching the carrier bag to my other hand.

"You OK with that?" Ryan questioned, noticing I still held the bag of beers we'd bought. I smiled my reply and shook my head.

The sun was well and truly on its way out, but the clouds themselves cast shadows around the partygoers. I could smell the salt in the sea air. We were on the North Shore and the breeze wasn't overly intense but the temperature was much cooler. I'd worn skinny jeans, a black tee, and my signature hoody. Ryan was also dressed in jeans and a dark grey jumper and I was thoroughly enjoying watching his denim-encased backside as he walked just ahead of me.

As we approached, everyone rose to their feet to greet us, and introductions were made. The guy called Charlie took the beers from my hand and placed them in a cooler that was sitting on the sand. There were no chairs, everyone was on the floor, and some didn't even have blankets. Ryan grabbed us both a chilled beer and we settled ourselves in the circle of his friends around the fire.

Everyone was really welcoming. I'd been worried that Ryan's friends would think me immature, but after around half an hour in their company, I accepted that they were all normal and not *that* much different from my own friends. They still larked about and took the piss out of each other, the most serious person appeared to be Ryan. Although there was a definite sense of fun about him that evening.

Charlie was an accountant, with brown curly hair and shrewd blue eyes, he gave me advice in respect of my prospective gardening business and told me to keep receipts for *everything*. Boyd, appeared to be the joker of the group with a sharp wit, the Kyle / Max equivalent from my circle of friends; although he possessed far more intelligence than Max, of course. He managed a small chain of 'amusement' arcades, the news of this made me smile; how fitting.

Nixon, as he'd been introduced, was a good-looking guy with tanned skin and dark blonde hair. It was bleached on the ends from the sun and it was long, almost to his shoulders. He was wearing lime green board shorts, a black hoody, and battered white Vans. He had a tall, athletic build and was a fanatic for water sports. Pastimes such as bodyboarding and surfing were popular on the East Coast; even during the colder months. The quiet girl beside him was called Melanie.

"So, how long have you guys been together?" Nixon questioned with an inquisitive stare. He reminded me of your clichéd beach bum.

I leaned back into the warmth of Ryan's body and cleared my throat. "I'm not sure we are together officially. What says you Mr. Lane?" shooting the latter part of my reply behind me. My tone was playfully goading on purpose. It was my turn to play it cool.

"We're together. In a fashion." Ryan batted back over my shoulder. This caused Nixon's grin to widen.

"Ryan holds his cards close to his chest Ella. I imagine you've noticed?"

"No, not really," I deadpanned, attempting to hold back my smile.

"Doesn't it do your head in? Not knowing where you stand all the time? He was the same when we were kids," Nixon explained, strumming his free hand across his nose.

"Maybe I like a bit of mystery?"

Nixon snorted and his date jumped. "Fuck that, sounds too much like hard work to me."

"Everything sounds like too much hard work to you Nix. You should quit the beach and get a real job," Ryan commented from over my shoulder, purposefully baiting his friend. "How many times have you seen Point Break?"

"Fuck off. You just hate the fact that I spend most of my days surrounded by hot girls with hardly any clothes on instead of JCBs."

Nixon's gravelly voice was in full wind-up mode. At least I wasn't alone in my mission to attempt to force Ryan to lose his cool.

"Do you fall asleep when he tells you about his day?" Nixon slurred, twisting his head toward me.

I chuckled before saying, "No, we don't talk about work."

Nixon' breath whistled through his teeth, "That's probably for the best. I'd rather have a stroke than listen to that shit."

I shot a glance over my shoulder. I was sitting on the sand in between Ryan's legs with my back against his chest. His chin was resting on my shoulder, his body relaxed and totally unfazed by his friend's comments.

"What car do you drive again?" Ryan suddenly drawled from beside me, his tone amused. Guys from the village seemed to measure success by the car they drove. Nixon rolled his shoulders and attempted to look haughty.

"There's nothing wrong with my Micra."

My laugh burst from my lips like gunfire, I certainly hadn't expected that. Nixon oozed cool dude. I so couldn't imagine him driving a Nissan Micra. My Nan used to drive one.

"What about you Ella, what's your choice of wheels?" Nixon suddenly questioned.

"I don't drive."

My answer surprised him and his blonde brows rose. "Really, well if you need lessons, I'd be happy to teach you," he shot in quickly, before winking at Ryan whose head still lingered over my shoulder.

"I think if anyone is going to teach Ella anything, it will be me", Ryan stated flatly. My pulse suddenly jolted as he kissed the bare flesh of my shoulder where my hoody had slouched down.

"Nah, Ry, you drive like an old lady," Nixon hooted playfully.

"As I said, Ella only needs one teacher," Ryan began again before his voice dipped suggestively and he added, "and that's for all areas in her life." The sexual undertone could not be missed and even though a crackling fire sat between us, Nixon heard. Even his date grinned. So, she *was* awake? Her face looked very angular and sharp with her hair scraped back so severely.

Nixon raised his eyebrows. "Heard you do *that* like an old lady too," was his comeback.

"All right dickhead, you win," Ryan replied with a laugh, conceding to his friend.

There was a moment's silence and Nixon whispered something into his date's ear which made her smile widen. She appeared to be drinking neat Vodka.

Whilst Nixon's attention was diverted, I whispered, "I hope that's not true," behind me in a mock horrified voice.

Ryan moved his arms further around my body.

"You'll just have to wait and see," he whispered in my ear. I felt like shooting to my feet and doing cartwheels of joy around the fire. I *loved* this version of Ryan, so fun and flirty, it was refreshing. *This* was the Ryan I'd shared the taxi with.

The fire crackled and hissed into the night.

"So, you two bumped uglies yet?" Nixon started up again and his girlfriend moved her hand from his leg to shoulder him in the ribs.

"What?" he muttered down at her with an even toothier grin. "I can ask, can't I?"

I knew he was being cheeky on purpose; Ryan's friends seemed to be as ballsy as my own. I didn't reply, I was too busy enjoying the feel of Ryan's mouth against my skin.

"Well Ry?"

He exhaled noisily and shifted behind me; his breath warm against the back of my neck. His strong arms were now around my waist; the sensation making me tingle. "Shut it, Nixon," he replied in a half-pained voice as he continued to nuzzle my neck. The gesture was so intimate, Ryan had totally dropped his guard, blatantly comfortable in the presence of his own friends.

96

Unperturbed, his friend shrugged carelessly, taking a mouthful of beer before tipping it in our direction, pointing to us with the bottle. From his position on the opposite side of the fire, the flames highlighted his sun-weathered face.

"You know he talks about you all the time," Nixon divulged like it was the biggest secret ever and I felt another whoosh of pleasure at the revelation.

Ryan ignored him and continued to concentrate on the skin of my neck. I leaned further back against him.

"Really?" I exclaimed, twisting my head to catch a glance at Ryan as he settled his chin on my shoulder again. He was wearing a lopsided smile and he narrowed his eyes in a teasing way.

The tide was out but the waves could still be heard through the music coming from a wireless speaker in the middle of one of the other groups.

Nixon's grin was playful as he wiggled his eyebrows and saluted Ryan with his beer bottle.

"Yeah. Totally fucking smitten," Boyd chimed in, tilting his head to the side as he drank in Ryan's expression behind me. "And you can wipe that 'say any more and I'll kick your arse' look, right off your face Ry. You couldn't if you tried, fucking pen pusher." His voice was so much louder than it needed to be and his words encouraged a guffaw from Charlie and Nixon. Dominic Boyd, he'd been introduced as but they seconded named him. Both Boyd and Charlie then went back to their murmured discussion. Something about Lady Lamb Farm, a derelict piece of land in Sinnington.

Ryan released a throaty chuckle, "Cheeky little git. Pen pusher." he repeated with a roll of his eyes.

I pulled my gaze away as Nixon belched noisily and Ryan released a sigh of exasperation before suggesting, "Why don't you go and take a long walk Nixon, the sea is that way. Just keep going."

His friend pulled a face of mock horror at what Ryan had suggested before giving him the finger and tugging his girlfriend into his side. "I can't at the moment, I'm busy."

Ryan raised his own drink to his mouth before suggesting in a firmer voice.

"Then can I suggest you concentrate on your date instead of mine?"

Dimples appeared on his red cheeks as Nixon suddenly moved and dragged a startled 'date' across his legs, settling her at an awkward angle on his lap, "Point taken," he shot back, now almost wearing the girl like a shield. He started to mumble something too low for me to hear and nuzzle her neck. She leaned into him, her mouth curling at his words.

The banter felt quite familiar, the needling, that playful sparing. As I said, it wasn't *that* much different from how it was between my friends. Just a bit more sophisticated. There would definitely be no fighting at this party. I so preferred this scene to the nightmare of Nathan's annual piss-ups, where *everything* was so fraught and full of drama.

I turned my attention away as Nixon and the girl started to play tongue tennis, flicking my legs over Ryan's thigh so I was sideways. Looking at him beneath my lashes, his face looked so beautiful in the soft glow of light from the fire.

"So, I'm your date?" I taunted.

Ryan looked down into my eyes, slowly shaking his head. Looking delicious.

"You know I don't like labels, Ella," he chided softly.

"*You* were the one that said it," I pointed out, cheekily plucking Ryan's beer from his free hand and taking a sip. His other hand sat on one of my thighs.

"Yes, to get dickhead off my case," Ryan replied with a flick of his head toward Nix.

I nudged him with my elbow and leaned in toward him, resting the side of my face on his chest, his chin above my head.

"So, you talk about me to your friends?"

Ryan sniffed, probably stalling for time, and he took his beer back, before pushing my legs from their position over his thigh. I watched as he shoved the bottle into the sand so it didn't fall over and then rose to his feet; leaving me sitting on the ground, staring up at him.

"I think the time for talking is done. Come for a walk with me," he said, straightening his clothes before offering me his hand. His palm was outstretched.

I didn't need him to ask me twice and I shuffled against the sand, placing my hand in his and allowing him to pull me to my feet. He released me and I dusted some sandy grains from my jeans, before raising my head to look at him inquisitively.

The air was colder whilst standing and I smiled, taking in Ryan's masculine glory. Silently watching me down that perfect nose, he lifted a hand and traced a finger across the skin of my exposed shoulder where my hoody remained slouched. As well as being a bum man, he also appeared to be a shoulder man and I mentally filed this detail away. My black bra strap was on show, but I didn't pull the garment back into place, his expression saying he more than liked what he saw. I felt so sexy. I wasn't 'one of the boys' anymore. Not with Ryan.

His voice was a deep, husky timber.

"I like this. The whole bare shoulder thing, it totally works on you, *and* me for that matter." Thick emotion outlined his words.

"Really?" I uttered shyly.

He slowly nodded his head in response, his eyes moving from said area, back to my eyes.

"Absolutely. It makes me want to put my mouth there. And here," he said, his thumb now caressing the pulse on my neck. As he touched that sensitive area, it leapt to attention and drummed a tattoo, almost clogging my breathing.

Ryan noted my reaction and took my hand, steering me away from the group. "We're going for a walk," he informed his friends and they shot out a variety of K's.

We walked beyond the partygoers and toward a line of beach huts that were closed up. It must have been after ten and the darkness was closing in. We stopped beside one of the huts, the sound of the ocean was much louder there.

Ryan turned to stare down at me. "Are you enjoying yourself?"

Pleasure flooded my senses. "Yes, you?" I batted back.

He ran a finger down my cheek, his expression intense. "Very much so."

The heat between our charged bodies gave me the courage and I moved forward and looped my arms around his neck. The soft music in the background faded away. No one else mattered. All I could hear in my ears was the rush of desire and my heartbeat.

Ryan placed his hands on my waist and lowered his head to kiss my neck again. "I like kissing you here," he whispered as he raised his head.

I gave him my best sexy, suggestive smile, raising a brow. "Really, *just* there? Anywhere else?"

He quirked his head thoughtfully, his gaze briefly running down my body before he replied, "*Everywhere* else."

I exhaled, my chest rising and falling against the heat of his hard body.

"Does that shock you?" he questioned.

My smile widened and I tilted my head further back. "It doesn't *shock* me but it definitely does something."

Ryan lowered his head again, his lips skimming the top of my ear.

"Does it make you wet?"

My breath caught in my throat. "Ryan!" I shot out with a half-laugh. I felt a mix of thrilled and shocked at his choice of words.

He shrugged those perfect shoulders of his. "What?" he said innocently.

I shook my head, in a tut-tut motion and dropped my arms from around his neck.

"I think the booze is going to your head, you're usually *way* too reserved to say something like that," I pointed out.

An expression I didn't recognise skittered across his features, before he quickly masked the emotion.

"Reserved is *definitely* not something I'm feeling right now," Ryan growled in a throaty voice, his watchful gaze now quite predatory.

"What do you mean?" I questioned breathlessly, my words at war with the awareness exploding through me.

"And that reminds me," he began, ignoring my question, his dark eyes penetrating. "You have a debt to settle with that smart mouth of yours." I knew he was referring to the way I had goaded him at the pool club. And pay I did.

I took a step back but Ryan reached for me, taking me by the upper arms, his fingers so sure against my skin. Our gazes were locked and he started to walk me slowly backward. His eyes were on my face and I could feel my shoes sinking into the sand as I moved, following where he directed. My mouth parted, like an automatic invitation, and a shiver started to tickle up my spine.

The solid surface of a beach hut touched my back, and Ryan released his grip and slid his hands to circle my wrists. He rubbed his thumbs across the pressure points there as he lifted my arms above my head and he held them against the hut; excited butterflies kicked off behind my ribs; a fucking zoo of them.

My palms felt hot, and I stared up into his dark features, his infamous control had gone. Need began to crash through my body. That look in his eyes kept me captive, as well as his hold.

Feeling helpless and *loving* it, Ryan transferred my wrists to one hand, holding me a prisoner against the hut. I was *totally* getting off on that feeling of vulnerability that he could do whatever he wanted to me. His free hand ran down my face and then his fingers traced my collarbone. Our eyes remained locked; tangled like the entwined limbs of two people that were starved for each other.

Goosebumps exploded on every inch of my skin as the fingers of his free hand gently encircled my throat, and he lowered his head and covered my mouth with his. My eyes drifted closed as the moment wrapped around me. I felt so small next to his large, strong body.

Savouring his taste and the way his lips moved against mine, so experienced; all male, *demanding*. His tongue drove into my mouth and it felt amazing as it slid against my own. I opened for him like a flower, drinking in the rain. Ryan's face was rough from not shaving and the friction of it against my skin created a jelly-like feeling in my legs. He growled with pleasure against my mouth and leaned further into me, his hard chest pushing against my breasts; my nipples beading at the sensation.

I was lost, I wanted this guy like an addict to the harshest drug and I struggled against his hold, needing to touch him, revelling in his strength. As he released my wrists, I pushed myself onto my toes and shoved my hands up into his hair, feeling him as hard as a rock against my stomach. Desire raged through my core. I needed this so much, this closeness. For the first time in years, I didn't feel alone.

"Fuck me guys. Get a room,"

With a tortured moan, Ryan dragged his mouth from mine and I felt like a non-swimmer in the middle of the sea; a ragged breath leaving my body. My eyes searched his face but his gaze was hooded. He twisted his head to one side, without actually looking over his shoulder. My breath left my body in uneven pants.

"Piss off Alex, you fucking letch."

'Alex', he called him, snorted; loudly. So, this was the 'little shit' Ryan had mentioned earlier. His timing could have been better.

"Well, what do you expect? If you put on a show, you got to expect an audience. You guys are so hot, you're giving me a stiffy."

I dropped my arms and Ryan tugged me around so my back was pressed against his chest. His fingers slid over my stomach and he moved his head to rest it on my shoulder again. We stood facing his annoying fucking non-friend. One he tolerated.

"A stiffy, Alex. I heard you couldn't get it up?"

I almost sniggered and I wasn't the sniggering sort. I *loved* the filthy version of Ryan; it was like being around his friends had forced him out of his shell and I was seeing another side of him.

Alex scrunched his nose up and crossed his arms across his narrow chest; he was tall and skinny like a beanpole. He held an almost empty vodka bottle in his hand.

"Oh yeah, and who told you that?"

Ryan rocked me in his arms.

"Noah Savvas. You're still his bitch, right?"

Alex dropped his arms and took a swig from the bottle before stabbing a finger at us.

"Ha ha, you fucking comedian," he barked, coughing out a laugh. He then turned on his heel and flipped us the finger over his shoulder as he strode away.

My brow creased as I watched his exit thoughtfully. "So *that's* Alex. He doesn't look like the type that hangs around with Noah."

Ryan released his hold on me and moved to my side, taking my hand in his.

As we walked back, he explained that Alex worked as an apprentice at the garage where Noah worked and that he was basically his dogs-body.

When we arrived back to the others, the fire was burning less brightly and everyone was well on the way. Ryan had only had one beer as he was driving but he poured me a rum and coke which had been pre-made in a large coke bottle.

Boyd and Charlie moved to sit at our side of the fire. They explained that Moses Wallis was back in town and that he'd been seen driving back and forth to Lady Lamb Farm.

The place used to be a cattle farm but went out of business years ago. An added plus for Connor's stepdad's farm, as he managed to pick up a portion of their business. It used to be owned by Mr. and Mrs. Crabtree but as they became too old to manage, they moved into a small bungalow, and the guy they'd employed to oversee things had allowed the place to go to rack and ruin.

After around another hour of chatting in our huddle, people started to drift away and head back to their cars. It was quite chilly and there were only embers left in the fire pit.

Ryan drove me home and we listened to Cold Play and spoke about the differences *and* similarities between our friends.

As I walked up my driveway, my feet crunching against the gravel, I felt happy.

Over the weekend, I met up with Natalie, who was again inconsolable about Connor. Since Harlow's arrival, he'd shown her zero attention. I felt a bit sorry for her. She wasn't as tough as she made out.

The night of Nathan's party eventually came and as I was deciding what to wear for our date, there was a sharp knock on my bedroom door. The sound jerked me from my thoughts, and then Tom ambled in with a carefree trot.

What the actual fuck? Was the dude in a trance and had walked into the wrong bedroom by mistake? He *never* came into my room without my permission.

I eyed him curiously as he sat on my bed, his face bright; boyish brown eyes glittering. It had been a while since I had felt annoyance at my brother's actions kick in that hard.

"Have you been smoking weed?" I accused from beside the wardrobe; my arms folded accusingly. It wasn't really a question, as I knew Tom would never touch drugs. Too much of a square.

He shook his head as if he'd been lost in a daydream. "What?"

My eyebrows shot toward the ceiling. "What the fuck do you want?" I put in, unclear as to why the tool thought he could just barge into my room.

"Did you hear me say come in?" My tone meant business.

He grimaced at my pinched look, as if I'd physically slapped him. "Who crawled up your arse?" he grumbled, partly to himself.

I answered his question with a flick of my palm. "You. What do you want Tom? I think our days of sitting and chatting on each other's beds is fucking long gone." The guy seemed determined to piss me off.

He shuffled further back against the bottom of my bed but didn't get up to leave. I sure hoped he didn't contaminate my covers with his boy smell.

It was obvious from his wounded expression that I wasn't going to get rid of him any time soon. Talking about wounded, I could see a bandage peeking out from under his shirt.

"What did you do to your wrist?" I questioned, flicking a head towards the trace of white gauze as Tom glanced down.

"Dog bite. Hurts like a bastard," he whimpered, suddenly feeling thoroughly sorry for himself.

My face broke out into a grin. "That explains it then," I replied without a smidge of sympathy.

Tom's brows creased in silent question. "Explains what?"

I cleared my throat. He was such a dumbass. "You barging into my room,"

He continued to look at me with a clueless expression. "I don't get you."

"The dog," I began, my face now dancing with mischief. "You've got rabies. Come on Tom, you're the vet. Rabies, it's a *brain* infection. That must be why you thought you could just plant your arse in here."

He rolled his eyes and shuffled from his position, with a 'be serious' expression and I relented.

Pulling my dressing table chair over, spinning it around, and straddling it I said, "Spill? You've got five minutes," offering him the audience he so obviously needed.

He shot me an uncomfortable smile before blurting out his fucking revelation.

"I have a date with Harlow."

I almost swallowed my tongue. My brother, Thomas Andrew Wade actually had a backbone. He'd decided to go against Connor's not-so-gentle advice about Harlow being 'off-limits'. I was shocked, it appeared the guy had balls of steel, if I hadn't been annoyed at the intrusion, I'd have expressed how impressed I was. I must admit, I was thoroughly intrigued by his rebellious act.

"Cool," I replied more breezily than I felt. Slightly worried that Connor may chew him out when he found out. What he announced next, was much worse.

"I'm taking her to the party," he blurted.

I worried my lip, feeling totally short-changed by his news. I didn't put two-and-two together straight away. "What party?"

He dashed a hand through his mop-like hair, looking like a little boy that had just opened his Christmas present to find out he'd gotten *exactly* what he wanted. Which of course, was a reality that happened every December for this guy.

His now wary eyes met mine. "I'm taking her to Nathan's party."

My face couldn't have looked more aghast if I had tried. "You've got to be fucking kidding me. You're taking Connor's stepsister to Nathan's annual orgy, a sixteen-year-old girl?" My words dripped purposefully with blatant disdain, I just needed to give him a taste of how bad a decision that was.

He nodded, taking a deep swallow. At least the fucker was aware of how dangerously he was treading. "Yes, I know. Bit bonkers. What do you think?"

I laughed but there was little humour in it. My brother pissed me off, but I kind of liked having him around, well, most of the time.

I asked the question that I already knew the answer to. "Is Connor OK with it?"

He chewed on a thumb, something he never did. It was a fairly girlie thing to do but it looked fine on Tom. The guy totally embraced his feminine side.

I rocked back in my seat and shot him an inquisitive stare. "Well?"

He cleared his throat. "Not exactly."

BOOM! "What the fuck does *that* mean?"

Tom almost went into panic mode before me. "I know, I was going to ask him about it as the guys and I were over there today but Connor showed up in a foul mood and I chickened out. We mentioned the party to Harlow but Connor ordered her into the house before she answered. She must have heard as she just called me to say that she wants to go with me. I felt on the spot, I had to say yes."

I closed my eyes as I took in his words. Stupid fucker. I swear to God, what with the Nate thing and now this, the chance of our friendship group remaining intact this summer was heading down the absolutely no-chance path.

"I thought I'd just drop by with her, you know. Show our faces and then take her to The Crown."

Tom's plan B still sounded retarded.

I tapped my fingers against my lips, deep in thought. I was partly pissed off that he'd chosen tonight of all nights to make his move. Now I'd be worrying about my fucking brother when I should be enjoying my time with Ryan. Yet again, Tom had managed to steal my thunder. And he'd done so without even trying to.

His next words were classic Tom. "Maybe you could come too? Safety in numbers. You said you got on OK with her? Natalie's going with Noah and we could all go in one car?"

I narrowed my eyes at his stupid-ass suggestion. I was no one's fucking gooseberry!

"I don't want to go, Tom, we told you what happened last year with that guy Wallis and all that shit. And anyway, I have plans of my own," I put out there moodily. I was starting to think that my friends thought that for me, the sun rose and set with the fuckers. I hated the fact that they probably weren't that far wrong. Which I know made me a huge loser.

"What you thinking sis? Tell me what to do?"

Instead of saying what I really wanted to say, I bit my tongue and went with, "Stop trying to be Ken to her Barbie would be my fricking advice." Shooting him a wistful glance.

Tom suddenly looked miserable and I annoyingly felt a wave of sympathy. He really liked the girl from the sounds of things and rarely got any action from the other girls in the village. I needed to harness my inner bitch.

Shaking off the thought of just how useless Tom was with members of my sex, I changed tack. I knew I needed to be more supportive.

"If you have to take her, just drop by. Don't stay long and definitely not after nine when the shit usually kicks off."

He looked at me with a relieved expression, although his shoulders were still slumped in defeat. Like I was the authority on whether or not he could take Harlow there. Like it was anything to do with me.

"You think it will be, OK? With Connor I mean?" Hope lit up his face.

I didn't sugarcoat my reply. "Absolutely not, you're likely to get your face kicked in," I began but then put in quickly as his face dropped again. "But what he doesn't know can't hurt, right? I won't say anything and we've never had this conversation, OK?"

He bobbed his head in agreement, happy that I'd told him what he wanted to hear, even though we both knew it didn't necessarily stop things from going arse-over-tit if Connor *did* find out.

His eyes searched my face, looking for more reassurance but I had none to give before he said, "Right. You're a star Ella. I'm just so buzzed. I know we literally just met, but I really like her."

I smiled warmly enough considering the circumstances. "I know bro, but please be aware that you may not be the only one who does, *like* her I mean."

He misunderstood my meaning and his brow knotted. "Nate isn't bothered, yes he flirted today but we both know he's too wrapped up in you."

I was shocked that my brother just put it out there. I knew the others weren't fucking stupid and that they knew something had gone on between Nate and me, but no one spoke about it. It felt weird hearing it from my brother's lips, even though he'd witnessed Nate's 'I love you' visit to our house.

Trust Tom to misunderstand who I was talking about, as it certainly wasn't Nathan.

I hated to be the bearer of more bad news, but I had to put it out there. Women's intuition and all that.

"I don't mean Nathan, Tom."

His look became even more puzzled, it crunched most of his face up before the truth hit him, right between the eyes.

"Oh, fuck really? But I thought he *hated* her?"

"Yes, a bit too much if you get my meaning?" Men were so thick at times!

"Shit," Tom puffed, now looking like he'd just been told he was terminally ill.

We both sat there in silence for a moment.

"Do you think she likes *him*?" he questioned in a raw voice. I had to be honest.

"Yes, probably. Look, I don't know for sure. Sorry, Tom. She says the opposite but I think she's lying to herself. There's something there. I saw it a mile off."

My brother looked like he swallowed a mouthful of saltwater before he recovered saying. "Well, it doesn't stop me trying."

How brave his words were in the scheme of things.

"No it doesn't stop you trying, but Connor breaking every bone in your hand might. You need to be careful Tom. He's your friend and he does care about you; but the guy has something inside him that cannot be tamed. When we have more time, I'll tell you what I know and it isn't very nice. Connor has been through some proper heavy shit."

We shared a secret look. Tom knew Connor had confided in me that night at the beach last year. But so far, he only knew about the anger management meds.

"Thanks. Look, I'll be careful. I just have to try. It feels so right with Harlow. The pull is stronger than anything I've felt before."

I almost released a full-on belly laugh at that one. Tom fell hard fast; there was *nothing* different this time.

"Well, fuck off now so I can get ready," I ejected dismissively, then added, "and keep an eye on Nate for me. Tell him I'm sorry I couldn't make it."

He smiled warmly. "Will do. Where did you say you were going again?"

I cocked my head, unimpressed. "I didn't. Now piss off."

As my brother left my room, I continued to ready myself for my date with Ryan, a million worries circling my head.

Eight

The song Creep by Radiohead started to play again from the confines of my bag. This was the ringtone I'd set specifically for my twit of a brother's calls.

Ryan stopped talking and placed his fork down on the table, but I ignored the sound (on principle) and continued to battle with the food in front of me. Why on earth I had chosen spag bol was anyone's guess. I probably had half of it smeared across my face.

After what felt like forever, the noise stopped and I raised my eyes back to Ryan who looked unimpressed. Great, it appeared Tom had now successfully interrupted my date the persistent little git, and now I would be forced (out of guilt) to call him back. Pretty shitty of me I know, bearing in mind he could have been calling from a ditch, having had his arse kicked by an enraged Connor. Not that I seriously thought Con would ever thump him, it would be too much like hitting a girl.

Ryan had taken me to an Italian restaurant in Middleton, a small picturesque village near Pickering.

The venue was romantic and was decorated authentically, making you believe you could indeed be sitting in a restaurant in the heart of Italy. The décor was fairly contemporary and the tables were dressed with white cloths and were candle lit. Hanging from the beams on the ceiling, there was an assortment of fake vines which were twisted around several wooden panels. Plastic olives of both the green and black varieties were also dotted around the space. It looked rustic. It was also fairly quiet, it being mid-week

The story to my parents was that Tom was with Harlow at The Crown, and I was going out for a meal with Natalie.

My mother, who didn't work and spent most of the time with her nose buried in other people's shit had unfortunately heard about the party this year. Due to what had happened with the Police in previous years and the 'elbow in the face' incident, she'd said outright that I couldn't go, setting a curfew of nine o'clock. Yes, nine o'clock; the bedtime of a twelve-year-old. Her stupid rule had only given me three *measly* hours with Ryan, and now my big brother was crapping all over that time too.

It was just after eight and we'd just finished our main courses.

"Creep?" Ryan questioned with a quirk of his head.

A smile tugged at the corner of my mouth before I explained, "Yes, my ringtone for Tom."

Having finished his steak, he settled his cutlery and pushed his plate away. He appeared amused by my reply.

"Bit harsh," he remarked, arching an eyebrow.

"What can I say, he's both a creep and a weirdo, it suits him," I returned drily.

Ryan leaned back in his seat and regarded me thoughtfully, the light flickering from the candle on our table highlighting part of his face. He was so mouth-wateringly good-looking.

"What ringtone do you have for me?" he queried with a teasing look.

OMG, Ryan's ringtone was way too embarrassing to share and so thinking on my feet I shot out, "Respect, by Aretha?"

Ryan grimaced.

I raised my eyebrows. "What? Even putting the lyrics to one side, it's more your era," I embellished with a cheeky smile.

His eyes creased. "Nice."

I pulled my phone from my borrowed clutch bag. I had chosen to wear a black fitted suit my mother had bought me for my uncle's funeral last year and I added one of her pale blue blouses. It was a restaurant after all, I couldn't very well have worn jeans and a hoodie. Ryan looked super fit in black trousers and an open neck grey coloured shirt without a tie, so fucking edible. He could have been the dessert as far as my palate was concerned. I tried to keep my looks of adoration to a minimum.

"Call him back," Ryan began, his tone encouraging which was an improvement from his initial annoyance. He *hated* mobile phones and only had one for work purposes. To be honest, he wasn't a fan of devices in general. He said that excessive phone usage led to stress, anxiety, sleep deprivation and generally disturbed the quality of real life. He had a point, when you went to the pub, there were always couples not talking, sitting on their phones. Sad really.

"He took Harlow to your house tonight without asking Connor, so I'd better check he's OK. Sorry," I explained.

110

"Why would he have to ask Connor? Surely Mike would have been the one to ask," Ryan questioned.

"Connor's protective of her I think, something like that," I replied, glancing down at my phone and pressing the icon for missed calls. Tom's number appeared at the top in red and I felt another twinge of annoyance infused with a *hint* of concern. Only 'a hint' though. He'd actually called my phone nine times!

"Yes, she's not the only one he's protective of, considering his behaviour at the pool club."

I toyed with telling him that Connor knew about us, but batted it off, the timing wasn't quite right. "Yes, a bit too much at times, but there's nothing in it. Not with me anyway. He was really firm with the guys about Harlow though. Like proper threatening."

"So, Connor warned all the boys off her?"

I nodded.

Ryan's expression changed and he gave me a knowing look, his lips pursed thoughtfully. "Sure, he did."

I knew what he was alluding to as I'd had my own thoughts about that. I'd also suggested the same to Tom, but the stupid shit had still gone ahead and taken her out anyway. My worry for my brother's health suddenly shot up a notch. Had Connor had words?

I came to my feet quickly, now feeling genuinely concerned. Any type of altercation, be it verbal or physical would be severely tipped in Connor's favour if something had kicked off with Tom.

"I better call him now and check he's still breathing," I half-joked.

Ryan's expression changed as his eyes searched my face. "Do you want me to call the house? Maybe it's something to do with the party?"

"No, I better do it."

"Or I could speak with Tom if you'd like?"

His suggestion almost gave me a stroke but before I could speak, he raised a hand to stop me.

"I wasn't going to call from your phone, so you can lose the horrified expression. I could call Tom to ask if he's with Nathan, say my brother isn't answering his phone."

Thank Christ for small mercies.

Ryan shot me a look, his deep eyes drilling into me with sincerity.

"Tell me what you want me to do and I'll do it. You're worried and I don't like it."

My heart leaped, genuine concern for my emotional state of mind laced his words. He was my crutch to lean on and at that moment I so needed it.

I focused on Ryan's flawless face. His jaw was jutted out at an angle, showing he was tense.

Shaking my head, I replied, "It's fine. I'll just give him a quick call. I won't be long." I needed to deal with Tom myself.

Surely Connor wouldn't hurt him; yes, he had a screw loose but he wasn't overly aggressive with his friends. Just a sarcastic sod most days.

Ryan nodded his understanding and slid out his own phone to check for possible messages. I knew he'd have none as he always had his phone on for work purposes, and the ringtone was *extremely* loud; a song from a band I had never heard of and hated. Mainly because of the number of times the bloody thing interrupted us.

I smiled my thanks for his words of support and twisted away from the table, heading over toward the ladies' room. Luckily it was empty and my phone had a full signal. I swiped the screen and hit the button for Tom.

He picked up pretty quickly.

"This had better be good A-hole," I blasted hotly.

"At last, where are you, I've called you about fifty times?" As usual, a total exaggeration. Annoyance continued to chew into me at his 'where are you' comment. Who did he think he was, my fucking keeper?

"None of your business shithead. What's up?"

I was still annoyed by his question, I never kept tabs on his arse.

"So, Connor turned up at the party and almost punched Nathan in the face again. He found out Harlow was there," he put in miserably.

"You're joking?" A thousand scenarios swam around my head, none of them good. "But he didn't hit him? Are *you* OK?"

"Yes, fine, and no it didn't get physical thank God. Just more squaring up and mouthing off, but Connor took off with Harlow, he wasn't impressed with me as you can imagine. Proper shit myself."

I bet you did, at least my conscience was clear, I had warned the idiot.

"He was so angry sis, fucking seething"

I imagined Connor must have been, as my brother only swore when absolutely necessary.

I swallowed, shifting the phone closer to my ear. "But you're OK I take it?"

"Yes, I'm fine. To be honest, Harlow bore the brunt of it. He literally dragged her from the house; *everyone's* talking about it." Tom's voice was rapid, he was obviously worried about her.

'*Everyone's* talking about it', oh dear, Connor would *not* like that.

I thought about how Harlow would have reacted if Connor had chewed her out in front of everyone at the party. Would she have burst into tears; she didn't look like the tough type. Who knew, maybe it was for the best and she deserved a few home truths. Going to a party with a bunch of fucking strangers when you'd been told not to, clearly wasn't the best of ideas. And I knew *exactly* why Connor would have warned her away, having been to several of Nathan's shindigs before. Let's face it, they were far from salubrious.

I had no concerns that Connor would physically harm her, after what had happened with his dad, he'd never touch a female in that way. Tear them a new one with his words yes, but physically lashing out; not in a million years.

There was an eerie silence on the phone and as if reading my thoughts Tom commented, "Ella, you don't think Connor would—"

"Categorically no. How the *hell* could you think that? Your mouth seems to run ahead of your brain Tom," I snapped back, thoroughly annoyed that he could *ever* contemplate such madness.

I heard Tom's breath of relief hiss through the phone. At the end of the day, my brother didn't know Connor like I did, or his past. Not yet. I pondered that thought, he needed to know really. Then he'd understand what he was dealing with.

"You should have seen his face El. He was *livid* and you did say something about the 'darkness' and all that shit. It's the most unhinged I've seen him in a long time. He's definitely not taking that medication."

I waited a beat or two before replying in a calming tone. "Look, you've nothing to worry about. I'll message Connor and check everything's OK? Would that get you to chill your tits and let me get on with my evening?"

I flicked a glance at my watch, it was now well past eight and my curfew was nine. I still had a mountain of profiteroles to get through.

Tom released another sigh of relief before saying. "Thanks, Ella, sorry to have interrupted—where did you say you were?"

I cleared my throat, nice try big brother. "I didn't," my reply was flat.

"Fine, whatever."

My thoughts suddenly shifted to Nathan who would no doubt be drowning his sorrows after I'd let him down. He'd probably held off texting me thinking I'd be at the party. Either that or he had finally got the message.

"Was Nate OK when you left?" I asked.

There was a beat of silence before Tom replied.

"He seemed all right. He was in the middle of getting a lap dance from Angela Smith when I left ten minutes ago."

Nice, thanks for the Intel bro. "Sorry," he added, possibly for damage control, which was of course *totally* unnecessary.

I raised my eyes to the ceiling. God give me strength, I totally didn't care if Angela had been sat on Nathan's face.

"I'll text Connor. Now piss off. I'll be home around nine."

I clicked the phone off before he could say goodbye and pushed it back into my pocket, washing my hands in one of the white basins.

I checked my reflection in the mirror, I had bags under my eyes but my face was thankfully free from sauce.

I continued to eye my reflection, the girl staring back looked tired. FFS. If it wasn't one thing, it was another. Wasn't life in the country supposed to be easy-going instead of majorly stressful like the rat race of the city? In my case, that was a big fat no.

After drying my hands, I went back out to our table, my mum's borrowed heels clicking against the marble flooring.

Ryan's frown intensified as he watched me approach and it worried me.

"What's wrong?" I asked as I sat down and picked up my fork. Dessert had arrived and it looked amazing.

My hand stilled, Ryan's phone was on the table and I glanced at it fleetingly. Did he know something I didn't? I felt like a spy without any of the answers.

"Noah Savvas sent me a text to say it's getting out of hand at our house, so I've asked for the bill."

My spirits sank as disappointment pumped into me. This was now the end of our evening.

Our meal together had been amazing, we'd shared starters and pretty much put the world to rights, the conversation had just flowed so well. We'd steered away from the subject of labelling 'us', and our chats had been pleasant and interesting with a few flirty turns along the way. I could be myself with this guy. I had considered dropping something in there about Nate to cushion the blow for when the news finally went viral, but decided I wasn't ready to spoil the mood. That conversation was certainly not going to be easy.

Now Nathan had unknowingly cut short my fantastic time. I buried the grudge. I already carried too many of those. Especially ones directed at that particular pain in my arse.

We left the dessert, Ryan paid for our meal and we exited the restaurant and made our way through the car park.

The jacket of my suit was quite thin and I shivered against the night air, it was fairly dark for a summer night and there was a definite nip in the breeze.

Warmth enveloped my torso as Ryan draped his jacket over my shoulders and I drew in his scent from a lapel.

"Thank you."

"You're welcome. Don't want my date to freeze."

I lit up like a match. There it was, that word, 'date' and again, this had come from Ryan's lips. Hope soared in my chest and I grinned back at him.

He rolled his eyes and took my hand, holding it as we approached his car.

"Yes, OK. Another date. Happy now?"

My smile widened and I looked up at him from beneath my lashes. God, I fancied this guy.

As we got to his car, he opened the door for me like a proper gentleman and I slid inside, still wearing his jacket. If he took it away too soon, it would have felt like I'd lost my security blanket.

Ryan joined me and we both buckled our seat belts. As he started the car, I explained that I needed to text Connor. Knowing the guy's opinions on phones, I didn't want to start texting without saying anything and appear rude.

"It's fine. So, I take it Tom also called to say things were getting messy?" Ryan asked as he steered out of the car park.

I shook my head whilst retrieving my phone. "No, not really. Just that Connor had turned up and dragged his stepsister out by the hair. Figuratively speaking of course."

The car growled out into the oncoming traffic. The main road was quite busy considering the lateness of the hour and I glanced at the clock on the dashboard. There was still enough time to get to my house before nine. I didn't want any uncomfortable questions from my parents when I got in. As far as they knew, I'd gone out to eat with Natalie and that was it.

"Is Nate OK?" Ryan suddenly questioned, his brow furrowed with concern for his brother.

"Yes, he's fine. He and Connor had an argument but it didn't get physical," I reassured him, swiping to find Connor's number in my phone.

"What else is new? I'm surprised they still talk. They obviously can't stand each other. It's like you're the glue holding them together. They're both unhinged if you ask me."

I cast him a sideways glance, my eyes resting warmly on the side of his face as he concentrated on the road. "Connor is much worse than Nathan, Ryan. In respect of temperament *and* unpredictable behaviour I mean."

Ryan nodded in agreement before casting me a look, saying, "I know, that's why I don't like you being too involved with Connor. I especially didn't care for what he did to my brother's face, even if Nate did deserve it." Ryan paused as he overtook the car in front of us. "If he ever does anything like that again, I may have to get involved," Ryan quipped gravely, siding with his brother.

He exhaled noisily. "In fact, Connor has been acting weird around me. His behaviour was odd at the pool club, irrespective of the protective thing."

A pang of something familiar kicked in.

"We think he's off his medication again, that could be why?" I put in, probably a bit too quickly. Of course, Connor didn't approve of me seeing Ryan, which was the real reason for the 'off' behaviour.

Ryan pressed a couple of buttons on the dash, and warm air started to circulate around me. "Medication for what?"

I cast him a curious glance. "To calm him down, keep him grounded. I'm sure I've told you before."

"No, I don't think so. I would have remembered something like that."

Those gory details of Connor's past, I had shared with no one, but I thought everyone was aware that the guy took medication and why. Maybe I hadn't told Ryan. He didn't move in the same circles as most people our age and so there was a chance he wouldn't be aware.

"If he has to take pills to deal with his temper, I most certainly don't want you near him," Ryan replied, shooting me a dark look.

Swallowing that lump that developed automatically when Connor and his past came up, I asked. "Are you warning me off seeing Connor?" Watching him through narrowed eyes as he checked his mirrors.

"No. Not as long as you're happy and he doesn't become a pain in my arse. But I don't like the fact that he's on mood-controlling drugs."

He paused as if choosing his words carefully. He obviously didn't want to appear to be dictating whom I could and couldn't see. To be honest, the thought of this particular man doing that, caused my tummy to fizz.

Ryan rolled his broad shoulders, his focus remaining on the road.

"At the end of the day, Ella it's your choice who you see. I wouldn't come between you and your friends. Unless I had to, of course. Why do you think I don't say anything about you and Nathan?"

I wrinkled my nose, confused as to his point, "What do you mean?"

He shot me a glance, his hands firm on the steering wheel.

"Your friendship with my brother. It doesn't bother me at the minute. I don't feel jealous but he's also been behaving strangely: like something's eating him.

That's why I was going to take you to my place that day in the car, to see how he reacted."

Digesting his words, I wasn't sure whether to panic or to come clean. I mentally chewed on the thought but again, decided it wasn't the right time.

"I don't know what you mean. We're friends. We've been friends for years," I returned drily.

He pursed his lips before replying, "I know that, but he's still a guy. As long as Nathan continues to see you as just a friend, there won't be an issue. If that were to change, however, there would be."

My heartbeat went from canter to gallop in a split second and the tone of my voice increased a decibel or two. "Well, I don't think you have anything to worry about. Nathan knows all I'll ever want from him is friendship. That's the same with all of my friends, I'm 'one of the boys' at the end of the day."

Ryan shifted slightly in his seat before he said, "As I said, as long as it stays that way, I don't have a problem."

There was a moment's pause before he added, "As far as my brother goes. You just need to keep an eye on it," he explained.

A sick feeling lodged in my stomach and I needed to do some damage control. Say something that couldn't be thrown back in my face when I did tell Ryan about Nathan.

"Look, you've nothing to worry about Ryan. We've been friends for years. I have only ever seen him as a friend and I've always been honest with him," I informed him gruffly.

"I know that. But if he ever gets out of line with you, I want to know about it." His tone was firm and commanding and I *loved* it, but God if only he knew.

A whoosh of pleasure shot through me along with a dart of something else. The dart had probably been sent from that stubborn part of my mind where I didn't allow *anyone* to tell me what to do. The two conflicting emotions were interesting. Anyone other than this man speaking me to this way would have been given a mouthful by now.

"Well, thanks for that dad," I put out there to lighten the mood and switched the radio on. The atmosphere was suddenly way too serious.

118

Ryan shot me a lopsided smile, amused by my snappy comeback. "If that were the case, the thoughts I have about you would be totally unacceptable not to mention downright vulgar."

I raised my eyebrows with a cheeky grin.

I turned back to my phone as we drove in silence with the music on low and keyed in my message to Connor.

Tom texted me. Is Harlow still alive or are you in the process of digging a shallow grave? If Connor was still seething, he probably wouldn't reply. He wasn't that keen on phones and electrical shit either to be honest, but he did have a phone.

The dots to signal he was typing appeared.

She'll live. I think she got the message. Tom is also in one piece and I didn't lay a finger on Nathan, if you're with Ryan.

The dots were joining together. I pulled my phone further toward my chest in case Ryan saw Connor's message which would have revealed he knew about us.

Did you open up all kinds of scary on the poor girl?

His reply. **She got away lightly, as did your fucking brother. Who obviously didn't listen. They all came sniffing around here this morning, I should have known.**

Wowzer, the length of his text surprised me. Connor was usually a one or two word replier and he hardly ever sent any emojis. That would be too human of course.

I shut down the conversation, only too aware of Ryan beside me. **Well, don't be too hard on her, we were all sixteen once.**

My reply was a tiny bit patronising really, considering Connor was only shy of twenty-two and me eighteen. To read it back, you'd think I was thirty.

Speaking of age differences, I turned in my seat to view the side of Ryan's strong profile. A picture of masculine, adult, perfection, and I started to bring him up to speed as he turned the radio off.

"So, it's all fine. Sounds like Connor had a few strong words to say to Harlow, but that was it and no he didn't touch Nathan."

Ryan turned to shoot me a glance, acknowledging the update with a nod of his dark head.

"Good. God knows what I'll find when I get back to the house. Is Tom still there?" Ryan questioned. He sounded exasperated as if he too was at the end of his tether with Nate's annual bashes, where police were called and people got elbowed in the face.

"No, he'll be on his way home I imagine, no doubt waiting to spill the rest of the gossip. You know, he actually burst into my room today," I informed him in an incredulous tone' remembering how the cheeky sod had just barged in.

Ryan grimaced and he shot me a dry smile. "Really? If Nathan came into mine without permission, I'd physically remove him."

His words were thought-provoking as they suggested a loss of control which would be so unlike Ryan.

"Whatever," I began in a playful voice. "I can't imagine you going ape-shit over anything. You're too calm and controlled for that type of uncivilised behaviour."

A hint of something I couldn't describe filtered between our two bodies. Ryan indicated and turned the car onto the A-road that led to my house.

He was silent for a moment longer before saying in a low voice. "That's where you're wrong Ella. I'm not always calm and in control. I'm human. Everyone is capable of losing it once in a while," he pointed out in a low, intimidating voice like he was warning me not to underestimate him in some way.

I savoured his words. It was the first time I'd seen a hint of something darker in him and I quite liked it. Yes, he could be icy and reserved, but he usually got his own way. I suppose I had to consider what it would look like when he didn't.

"OK, is that your way of telling me you have it in you to go all Fifty Shades on me?" I put out there in a joking voice.

Did his hands tighten on the steering wheel briefly at my words or was I imagining it?

His next comment surprised me more, as I didn't actually think he'd actually know what Fifty Shades of Grey was.

"You're obsessed with that book," he replied with a twist to his lips, his attention remaining on the road. "I'm just making the point that *no one* is perfect and you'd be recklessly naïve if you thought that was the case with me. We all have our demons, Ella," Ryan delivered softly.

I decided to inject a bit of sweet back into the tone of our conversation, not wanting to end the evening on a dark note.

My almost nineteen-year-old mind didn't really fully comprehend what he meant, but if we kept seeing each other, I would no doubt find out. And I so hoped so. It appeared there was a bit of recklessness in me as he had suggested.

"OK, I take your warning. We all have our ups and downs, good and bad points. I wouldn't ever take you for granted Ryan."

His reply certainly knocked me down a peg or two.

"I wouldn't let you." His blunt response forced a provocative shiver to rush through my limbs.

I decided against overthinking his reply, I was already way too paranoid.

We pulled up to the curb in the lane where he usually dropped me off and Ryan, pulled the hand-break on.

He then unclipped his belt, before leaning over to release me from mine, his body crowding me, in a good way of course. We were nose-to-nose, mouth-to-mouth, and my eyes closed, waiting for him to kiss me. I could have made the first move but felt uneasy with his earlier comment and I preferred him to take the lead anyway really. He was so much more experienced than me.

A wave of pleasure surged up my spine as his mouth took mine in a brief, passionate kiss. It felt like he was claiming me; his tongue sliding into my mouth. I was so turned on, there was something different there, a hidden warning of something, the kiss brief but even more intense than the one at the beach.

He pulled back slightly, his deep eyes on mine, looking into the windows to my soul, stealing my secrets.

"Believe me, control is one of the things I don't feel when I'm around you."

I smiled up at him shyly, realising that I was totally out of my element with him, this wasn't a boy who I could manipulate or second guess. This was a flesh and blood man. And one I wanted above all the others.

I placed my hand against his face in a loving gesture, hoping he didn't pull away. If anything, he leaned into my hand, his jaw flexing under my fingers and my tummy danced.

"I'll remember that," I whispered.

Ryan moved back into his own seat before sliding his phone out of his pocket.

"Just a minute, I need to check something."

My brow knitted, wondering what he was doing and I watched as Ryan keyed in his pin before he started swiping through his phone. Was he looking for something?

Suddenly my own phone started to ring and a bubble of embarrassed adrenaline snaked up my spine. The song Sex Bomb by Tom Jones burst from my bag. Busted.

Ryan shot me a look of pure sin. He'd called my phone on purpose to check the song I had assigned as his. I wanted the seat to swallow me up.

"You, Ella Wade, are a liar. Respect indeed," he grinned. At least he found my mortification amusing.

I nodded to the phone in his hand. "OK, OK, you can end the call now. Otherwise, you might hear my voicemail message, which is even *more* embarrassing."

His grin widened and he raised interested eyebrows before ending the call and re-pocketing his phone.

"Its fine, you don't have to change it. I quite like that song." he prodded with a cheeky quirk of his head.

"Whatever, it's not for discussion. I imagine your ego is even bigger now," I scoffed, unable to hide my own smile.

"I'll message you tomorrow," Ryan promised. His dark eyes roaming over my features. "Your face is flushed."

"I can imagine. Laters Sex Bomb."

And with those parting words and one last sultry smile, I opened the car door and slid out into the night.

Our eyes met briefly thought the window, a silent moment of understanding between us before Ryan's mouth parted in a full wolfish smile. He drew back into his seat, pulled off the break and steered the car out into the road.

I stood there and watched him drive away until I could no longer see the rear lights.

It hit me at that moment that Ryan Lane had my heart in his hand and I had given him free rein to do what the hell he wanted with it.

And there was *nothing* I could do about that.

Nine

I walked into the house just after nine and in spite of my mother's insanely early curfew, both she and my father were still out. Typical. Tom was in the main living room with the TV blaring to itself, sitting alone at our obnoxiously huge dining table. He appeared to be studying and was surrounded by books. Bit of an odd time really, considering he couldn't have been back from the party that long. He was such a nerd. His phone was beside him on the table, it was one of the earlier iPhones and it sat there with its cracked screen, looking like an ancient relic.

He glanced up as I approached; he looked tired. Probably from the stress. Tom did not handle conflict well.

"You're back early," he muttered, leafing through the large textbook in front of him.

My eyes narrowed as I pulled out one of the heavy dining chairs and dropped into it.

"I said I'd be back around nine. I'm just surprised you are. And why the hell are you working at this time?"

There was a beat of silence as he finished off what he had been reading.

"You didn't stay long then?" I asked, trying to get comfy on what had to be one of the most uncomfortable chairs in history.

He closed the book and gave me a daunting look. "It all got a bit awkward when Harlow left. You totally made the right decision by not going. It was a bag of crap and now I feel like my first date with Harlow was a complete failure," he sighed, before powering on, "I doubt she'll want to go out with me again and to be honest, I don't think I'd have the guts to ask her," Tom murmured solemnly. He reeked of desperation; the guy so needed to get laid. "Connor shot me a look of disgust and disappointment as they drove off. To think Connor Barratt actually made *me* feel irresponsible."

A chuckle escaped between my lips, "I know. What is the world coming to?" Purely for dramatic effect of course.

Tom released a sigh of frustration, dashing a hand across his jaw.

"I totally get it now. She's only sixteen, barely out of high school and I take her to a party where there's drugs and shit and people shagging in the bedrooms!"

Tom paused, his face a full-on grimace and his shoulders drooped in shame. "What a great idea for a first date, what a gentleman I am," he muttered.

I snorted, I wasn't used to seeing my brother looking so guilty and intense. The self-pitying expression needled me. "Hardly a date Tom and what did you expect, as you said, you took her to a fucking deadbeat party. You should have just gone to the pub. Simple but sweet."

I knew it was a bit cruel to go down the 'I told you so' route, but the git did it to me all the time. Back at you, brother.

His mouth twisted thoughtfully and I powered on, keen to know more about what had happened.

"So, why did Connor pick a fight with Nate when *you* were the one to escort the princess to the ball?"

He pursed his plump lips; I'd always thought them a bit big for a guy but hey ho.

"Nathan was all over her when Connor got there, stroking her arm and shit. Connor stormed into the party like the devil, face like murder," he explained in a quiet voice. "Nathan did that goading thing he does. Said something about how he was going to take Harlow upstairs and did Connor want to join them. I thought he was screwed at that point. Anyway, it didn't kick off in a physical sense but it was touch and go for a while."

"So, I take it Nate backed down and was left licking his self-inflicted wounds?"

Tom moved the book and gave me his full attention. "I think he was just pissed off that Connor showed him up in front of everyone. Once they left, he smashed some shit in the kitchen and then started to have a go at Natalie's brother. Of all the people to try and take on. Noah just laughed in his face. Nate's like a psycho at times but of course, nowhere as extreme as Connor. With Nate, it's like calculated, controlled bad behaviour. With Connor, it's unhinged, unpredictable chaos. He must have scared Harlow to death."

I smiled, nibbling my thumbnail before saying breezily. "That's Connor for you. I did text him by the way, and I think he just put her in her place. Made her see sense. Anyway, it doesn't matter, no one will give a shit about it tomorrow, *especially* if it's as messy as you say, booze numbs the memory. I take it, it's still going on now?"

Tom nodded before placing his hands behind his head and stretching. A hint of cigarette smoke teased my nostrils, evidence that he'd been to a party. Mum would probably shit it if she noticed. His alibi was the pub, where smoking was banned, so where had Tom really been? My mother was like Columo, *nothing* got by her. I toyed with the idea of mentioning it but decided not to, no doubt the prince wouldn't be asked to explain himself anyway.

I too stretched in my seat before resting my elbows on the table and steepling my fingers.

"I think where Harlow is concerned, you better prepare yourself for rejection. No offence, but if Connor is interested in her romantically, you've got no fucking chance." I know it probably wasn't nice to hear but it needed to be said. "And if he isn't interested in shagging her, he blatantly put the message out that he won't allow anyone else to."

His face creased as my words hit home. Tom wasn't stupid, Connor was an extremely virile, good-looking man. He had most of the girls and mums who lived in the village panting after him. There was also that rumour that he was hung like a stallion and amazing in bed, which of course would have added to the appeal.

"I get it. I'm not sure I'm ready to throw the towel in just yet though. Although I'll think twice about hiding my intentions. Maybe I'll go and speak to him. It's not like I'm just after one thing with her, I do actually like Harlow."

There was a moment's silence before Tom carried on, "I just hope the police don't get involved again, it was pretty rowdy when I left and it will probably go on into the early hours. God knows where Nathan's brother was."

Watching Tom thoughtfully over the surface of the table I advised, "Ryan's on his way back to break things up, Noah contacted him."

My brother frowned and dropped his arms to the table.

Even partway through speaking the words, I wanted to suck them back in, but there was *nothing* I could do except helplessly watch Tom's face slowly digest that information.

"How do you know that?" he questioned; his brow creased.

Heat flooded my face as I attempted to formulate the correct explanation as to why the hell I would know that Nathan's *brother* was on his way back home.

Tom pinned me with an assessing stare, swiftly changing to full-on interrogation mode. Why not just shine a light in my eyes bruv?

Fuck. Come on Ella, this was fixable surely. Think, think!

"Ryan texted me. I think he thought I was at the party." What the actual hell, the words spilled from my mouth like the most mortifying blob of verbal diarrhoea *ever.* They were totally unbelievable.

Tom shot up straight. "*Ryan* texted *you*? I didn't think you were that close."

I bounced back, a little too sharply. "It was only a text Tom, chill the fuck out."

A weird silence fell between us and I almost lost the ability to talk. My tongue suddenly felt twice the size in my mouth.

Tom's head shifted to one side as he regarded me; his eyes roaming over my shoulders as if looking for clues. I suddenly felt like I was draped in Ryan. And of course, I kind of was, which I only realised as he said, "Whose jacket is that?" nodding his head at me.

I peered down. Double fuck!

The guarded expression I must have been wearing was smashed away and there now was no way out. I felt like I was sinking into quicksand, *emotional* quicksand.

"What?" I blurted indignantly. Didn't they say the best line of defence was offence?

Tom slid swiftly to his feet, a mixture of feelings flashing behind his eyes, *none* of them in my best interests. Great, now was the time for my brother to suddenly become Mr. Observant. What the hell? Most of the time he walked around with his head in the clouds. Shit, this was now so *not* fixable.

"Ella?" Tom prompted; his forehead full of grooves of confusion. How I wished I'd just gone to my room, either that or given Ryan his fucking jacket back. Damn it!

I chewed the inside of my cheek, also rising to my feet and pulled the offending item further around my body; suddenly feeling exposed. I stepped away from the table with unsteady legs.

"It's mine," I almost choked out. Sweat prickled the back of my neck.

It's mine! I would have laughed out loud had it been any other scenario. My comeback was severely implausible, the jacket was about three sizes too large.

Tom moved his lanky frame away from his chair to get a better view and I took a step back, suddenly feeling unsettled. It wasn't a feeling I relished and had never felt it with Tom before. The whole situation was way too intense, I was like a naughty little girl having to explain herself to an angry, older sibling.

"Ella, it's a *guy's* jacket. I'm not that fucking stupid."

Tom hardly *ever* swore. I was toast, literally. The air around us crackled and buzzed with tension.

"It's Ryan's jacket, isn't it?" Tom stated as he tugged the lapel back, studying the material like he found it offensive; those sharp eyes now missing nothing. His face was scrunched up and he looked at me like I'd just told him the worst news ever when I hadn't even spoken.

I tugged the material from his hand and took another step back, my cheeks were on fire.

"So?"

Tom also moved back a step and I half hoped he'd back the hell off, but he just stood there and slowly raised a hand to cover his mouth.

"Why the hell are you wearing Nathan's brother's jacket," he questioned, almost to himself before starting to pace. He then stopped and turned back to me. "What are doing?"

I shifted, continuing to feel uncomfortable as his gaze lashed my senses. "What do you mean?" I must have been bright fucking purple!

My heart was literally thumping in my chest so hard I could feel it and I dropped my hands to my sides. Why the hell hadn't I taken it off in the car?

Tom took another step forward, back into my space. He now looked angry, again not something you saw often from someone who was usually so placid.

"You *know* what I mean. Are you fucking mental? *Where* were you tonight?" The questions fired out of his mouth like gunfire.

"None of your bloody business Thomas, don't think you can start to play dad," I bit back. The desperation slowly being tramped down by temper. I wasn't the coolest of cucumbers in these types of scenarios.

"You were with Ryan, weren't you? *That's* why you know about the call from Noah. Oh my God, I think I'm going to throw up."

I rolled my eyes.

"Are you for real? What the hell Tom? So what? I don't actually see what it's got to do with you anyway."

"What the hell are you doing with Ryan Lane, Ella? He's a fucking adult!" Tom shouted.

I shot a worried look to the door half expecting to see both my parents in the doorway with their hands on their hips. I didn't thank God, they were still out. I cautioned him anyway, he was suddenly really loud and all up in my face and I didn't like it one bit.

"Keep your voice down and what the hell, he's twenty-six; he's not *that* much older than me." My anger came roaring back to save me.

He started pacing again, his confused face looking like it was struggling to find an answer to the biggest question in history.

Thankfully, he stopped and faced me. "He's a Lane Ella, if mom finds out she'll go ballistic."

I exhaled noisily, feeling thoroughly exasperated. "And how the hell *would* she find out, unless *you* tell her? Which I know you won't do." I must admit, at that point, I wasn't totally sure that would be the case.

Tom dashed a hand through his curls. "I can't believe this. I'm actually lost for words."

Yeah, chance would be a fine thing. "Doesn't sound like it to me. Although I wish you fucking were."

His eyes creased. "Ryan Lane, as in Nathan's brother? Oh my God. Fuck my life."

His 'fuck my life' comment wound me up. "You do realise you're quoting me *to* me? Chill out, it's no big deal," I shot back, hoping he'd calm down. It really wasn't *that* big a deal, was it?

Tom started to gesticulate whilst glaring at me with wide eyes. "No big deal? I take it Nate doesn't know?"

I sucked in a breath at the mention of Nate. "Of course not, and it's none of his business anyway, or yours," I pointed out.

Tom's next question almost caused my legs to give out as my limbs started to tremble.

"Are you fucking him?"

These words made me flinch before my temper shot to the forefront. My hands curled into fists, nails digging into my palms as I physically restrained myself from hitting him. "You're over the line, that's *none* of your business!" I couldn't believe I managed to control my voice, which was surely on the edge of cracking.

Tom didn't care for my outburst and almost spoke over me. "You are aren't you? Oh, my days, this is some messed up shit. I can't believe it, what on *earth* are you thinking? Are things not complicated enough with Nathan that you have to mess around with his brother too?"

This conversation wasn't happening and I felt like I was drowning under the full force of Tom's contempt. I wanted to run to my room like I used to when I was little and Tom was being a dick to me. He used to torment me all the time but as I got older, our roles reversed and I got my own back. Ten-fold.

I shifted my focus back to the nightmare playing out in front of me. "You're overreacting Tom and we're not *actually* seeing each other. Not properly anyway. We're taking it slow, seeing how it goes." Why the hell I was explaining myself to the little shit was anyone's guess.

"Oh, I can tell you how it's going to go when it goes public. Does shit storm mean anything to you?"

And, my patience *snapped*. "I've had enough of this, it's none of your *fucking* business who I see! I don't question *your* actions. Way to go being a supportive brother," I snarled. Anger burned, slow and dangerous, how dare he attempt to dictate to me? He had no right, no fucking right at all.

Guilt flooded his features and he moved toward me. "Ella, I..."

I was ready to burst into tears, could feel them threatening. I shot Tom one last look of disdain, so he'd know how shitty he'd made me feel.

"I'm going to bed and if you tell *anyone* about this, I'll *never* speak to you again."

As I moved across the room, I could smell Ryan's scent from his jacket and for once, it didn't reassure me.

When I got to my room, I shrugged the jacket off and dropped it over a chair before heading to the bathroom.

Flinging open the door, I scanned the area. I longed to hit something, there was nothing civilised about the torrid emotions spinning inside me. I felt crazy and out of control.

I needed to wash the conversation I'd had with Tom from my skin, if that were possible. The shock that he also now knew had torn a massive hole in my usual composure. In respect of my secret, the cracks were well and truly starting to show.

What had started off as a beautiful evening, had turned into a complicated farce and my head was a shed of confused thoughts and cataclysmic regrets.

After I showered and changed into shorty PJs, I sat on my bed and texted Ryan to say we needed to talk. I now had no choice. I would have to tell him that Tom now knew about us so he was prepared; just in case. I seriously didn't think my brother would blab, but this was a unique situation and it was imperative to cover all bases. When I told him about Tom, I'd also drop in that Connor had also known for a while. Kill two birds and all that.

Sounds ominous. Ryan's reply came back.

My parents must have returned home whilst I was in the shower, but my mother didn't come to check I was home. Tom would have told her I was back, if she'd even asked. As long as the prince was safe, that was all that truly mattered.

I thumbed in my reply to Ryan, toning it down. I didn't want him to think I needed to speak to him about our relationship or any heavy shit and him not want to see me. I sighed, hating how insecure I still felt.

It's nothing major, just need a chat. I added a kiss blowing emoji. He didn't reply back. Typical boy.

As I placed my phone on my bedside table, there was a soft knock on the door. I'd calmed down but my emotions were still like a storm inside me. I paused, narrowing my eyes at the oak surface. Wishing I had ex-ray vision. Again, another soft knock. In all honesty, I knew it would be Tom. The softness of the tap was like the knock of shame. At least he'd taken my advice from last time about barging in. I told him to come in and he popped his head in through the gap. His expression one of truce.

Sliding into the room, he closed the door softly behind him. I remained sat on my bed but shuffled back to allow him space to sit beside me. Pulling my legs up to my chest, I flicked a piece of lint from my shorts. Tom and I used to hang out in my room all the time when we were little, it's amazing what growing up does, the distance it can put between you and those you were closest to. The thought made me feel sad.

"Mum and dad have gone to bed," Tom whispered. He didn't really need to be quiet as our parents room was in the opposite wing of our house. I appreciated that he'd at least took it down a notch from earlier.

I remained silent, not really knowing what to say but ready to accept his olive branch and maybe give him a leaf from my own. But just one leaf, the dude had severely overreacted and that's all he bloody well deserved.

The bed dipped under his weight. He was still fully dressed, his eyes shadowed. He obviously felt bad and I was glad.

"I'm sorry. I was a dick. It was just such a shock. I had no idea."

My mouth twisted in the semblance of a smile. I was still annoyed but partly pleased he was there. I hated going to sleep on an argument. That used to be the case regularly when Nate and I were fighting. I think the negativity after a fight eats away at you as you sleep and you always feel so much worse in the morning.

My forehead started to itch and I rubbed at it with my fingers. "It's fine. Look, I understand why you'd be shocked, but you have nothing to worry about," I reassured him. I knew his reaction was out of concern for me and nothing else. "I'm handling it. We're being careful so that no one gets hurt, mom and dad included."

He listened intently. My brother had such wise eyes. We always used to share our secrets. I felt more of a closed book than ever lately, the weight of information I carried pushing down on my shoulders like real pressure; a rucksack of problems almost.

As we sat there, bound by blood, I decided to share the burdens I had been holding onto for so long. Me and Nate, Ryan and I, even the darkest shit about Connor. I needed to offload. Carrying all those secrets hadn't been easy and I was a total believer of a 'problem shared' and all that.

I leaned further back against the headboard and Tom flipped around and joined me, climbing fully onto the bed and stretching out his long wiry legs.

He listened quietly, occasionally chipping in for clarity on certain aspects. I didn't go into major detail about what I had done with Nate as it felt too personal, but I did explain that the guy had become quite obsessive. Tom already knew part of that story after Nate had turned up at the house that night. I also told him about how I'd ran into Ryan at the train station and how we'd hit it off, saying how I'd always had a crush on him.

Tom listened with a pained expression as I told him about the abuse Connor had suffered during his childhood. I had worn that same expression at the beach that night when Connor had first told me.

We must have sat talking for the best part of an hour. It really did feel like a weight had been lifted.

As Tom left, I replayed his suggestions in my head as I climbed into bed. Part of me knew he was right, but I just couldn't bare it.

"You need to cool it down with Ryan until Nathan has had time to process the rejection. You don't want a scenario where he thinks you've been seeing his brother behind his back. That would feel like the ultimate betrayal and imagine what that would do to his relationship with his brother," he'd said.

I really did hate it when my brother was right. Ryan and I would have to hold off, for a little while anyway. Let things settle.

I needed to see Nathan again, clear the air. Maybe the best way to do that would be at the pub with the others? Try to get the group mentality on track again.

As I closed my eyes, I made my plan of action. I would meet with Ryan to try and cool things down, not permanently or for long, I couldn't face that. I would then make more effort with my friends and smooth things over with Nate as much as possible. Then when the time was right, Ryan and I could finally make a go of it, without all the hiding and see if there actually was *something* there worth saving. It certainly felt that way for me.

And that was it right there, the huge problem, glaring me back in the face. I didn't know where I stood with Ryan or how he really felt about me. But I knew my own mind, I was gradually falling for him and without any way of stopping myself.

And let's face it, I didn't really want to.

The guy had unlocked something in me that day at the station and whatever that was, it certainly didn't want to be trapped again.

Ten

"Why don't you just put it in the local paper Ella?"

These were the words that Ryan used a few days later when I revealed the fact that Tom now knew about us. His reaction should have annoyed me but I couldn't really blame him.

My eyes searched his perfect features, hating that he was displeased. The scowl he wore still didn't take away from the beauty of the man.

"I know—and I'm sorry. I didn't actually *tell* Tom, he *guessed,* and then I didn't have time to deny it. To be honest, part of me didn't *want* to deny it. I hate all this sneaking around shit."

It was a sunny day and we were in Ryan's car in The Downe Arms pub car park with the air con on full. I'd worn denim cut-offs and a button-down tee and Ryan looked major league hot in denim jeans and a tight black top. You could see the bumps of his six-pack through the material.

I watched as he leaned his head back against the leather headrest and closed his eyes. It gave me the opportunity to visually eat him alive. He was *gorgeous*, like a male model, sleek and sophisticated.

Knowing that I was there to suggest cooling things down appeared to be making me want him more.

"I've also something else to tell you," I whispered in a quiet voice. His eyes shot open and he twisted his head toward me with a penetrative expression.

I actually swallow, and gulped, almost like they do in those cartoons. My nerves were alive with an electric-type current that zipped up from my stomach and into my chest cavity.

Just say it, Ella! My conscience screamed at me.

"What?" Ryan put forth in a dark voice, his nostrils flaring. I hadn't heard him use that tone before and it made my tummy do a sneaky somersault.

I turned to face him, noting that his gaze flicked briefly over my bare legs. Ryan was also a leg man and let's face it, legs was all I'd got really.

"Connor."

Absolute fucking silence as Ryan digested my words, his eyes narrowing dangerously.

"What about him?" His sharp eyes were focused on mine.

Realisation that this wasn't going to go down well chewed into me and I felt my shoulders tighten. I batted off the decision to tell him *everything* and went for the watered-down version like the *pussy* I was. News about my night with Nathan would have to wait. Baby steps and all that.

"Ella," he bit out in a demanding, 'answer me' tone, his jaw ticking. The harshness of his tone cut through me.

"Connor knows."

To be honest, I was surprised he'd never noticed anything until he delivered his next words.

"I knew it!" Ryan literally shouted and he slammed his hand against the steering wheel of the car which sounded the horn. The noise was like a burst of temper and it echoed around the empty car park.

"How long?" he questioned, angling his large body towards me whilst placing an arm around the back of my seat.

Ryan pushed his face towards mine. "How long Ella?"

A thick black cloud slammed into my chest and I leaned back; Ryan's breath was still like a caress against my skin.

"Ages ago, Connor and I were at the beach and he shared his shit with me, I couldn't really not do the same. At that point I only told him I liked you though, we weren't seeing each other then."

There was an intensity in the air surrounding us and it was so thick you could almost taste it.

"And now he knows everything?"

I nodded. "After the first few times I'd seen you, he guessed and again, I couldn't really deny it."

I opened and closed my lips, my throat suddenly drying up. Ryan's reaction was so not what I was expecting. How the hell would he react when he found out that I'd had sex with his brother? I felt like bursting into tears. I had to fix it and quick but he started speaking again before I could think of what to say.

"I knew something was off with Connor. You should have told me sooner and how can you trust he won't tell everyone else? The guy has no restraint at the best of times," he complained, leaning back slightly, his eyes roaming my face.

I worried my lip, knowing he was right.

"I honestly don't think he would, we're friends, tuned into each other. He knows how much it would hurt me if he did."

Ryan carried on as if he hadn't heard me. "I know you've always been close to him, but you do realise that the weird vibe he puts out there could mean something else."

My face scrunched at what he was alluding to. "No, not that. Not with Connor, he doesn't see me that way," I announced, astonished at his suggestion. He was so barking up the wrong tree there. Connor just didn't agree with me seeing Ryan, especially when I hadn't resolved things with Nate.

"How do you know? It would certainly explain his animosity toward me. Especially if he's known all this time. To be honest, I'd put it down to him being a moody sod but now I'm not so sure."

There was a pregnant pause before he quietly imparted, almost to himself, "Maybe you should be with Connor—he's nearer your age?"

A hairline crack appeared across my heart. "He's like a brother to me. I can't think of anything worse. I don't *want* to be with Connor, it's you I lov—" the word thankfully froze in my throat, but Ryan heard it, even though it remained unspoken. He ducked, his eyes drilling into mine with a quirk of his head.

Slowly he repeated my words. "It's you I? You I, *what* Ella?"

My body erupted into full-on panic-mode, my breath coming in rapid gasps as I said with discomfort. "*Nothing*, I was going to say that you're the one I want." The music from that show Grease perversely sounded in my head.

It was useless, that half-spoken word of 'love' sat between us like the largest of elephants in the room, more like a fucking dinosaur.

Turning to look out of the window, I was no longer able to take the hardness of that glare. I jumped as Ryan's fingers slid over my face and he shifted my head back to face him, gripping my chin quite forcefully.

"What were you really going to say Ella?" he prompted with alarming softness, that cool stare roaming over me.

My tongue had fainted, and I couldn't speak.

Ryan released my chin and leaned back again before he twisted and started the car suddenly. "We need time out," he whispered in a gruff voice.

All earlier thoughts of cooling things down shot out of the window at the thought of him ditching me. It stung my insides like I'd been drinking bleach. "What are you doing?"

After turning on the ignition, the car growled to life and Ryan shifted towards me, his strong arm rubbing against my breast as he tugged my belt on. He then buckled his own and started to reverse the car, glancing out of the back window with one arm around the back of my seat.

"I'm taking you home."

This wasn't right, we weren't done talking. I had to do something, *say* something. Was this Ryan ending things with me because I got all heavy too soon? Shit, shit shit! My heart was pounding so much that it could surely break at any minute.

"Wait, don't you think we need to talk about this?" I shot in, thoroughly pissed off at myself. I'd revealed too much too soon and had now scared him off.

"There's nothing more to say, Ella. I need time to think?"

He must have been able to sense my uncertainty. "To think about what?"

He exhaled. "To think about what's going on between us. Both Tom and Connor knowing also puts us at risk."

I sat back in my seat; my legs suddenly cold as the air conditioning skittered over my bare knees. We drove most of the way to my house in silence, before I put out there in a quiet voice.

"It's just so unfair," I muttered in a despair-ridden tone as I nibbled my thumb.

"Life's unfair Ella. When you get a little older—you'll understand that," Ryan replied in a flat tone and my temper flared. It was on the tip of my tongue to tell him to go fuck himself.

"I can't believe you've just thrown *that* in my face." Hating him at that split second for bringing the age thing up.

Ryan stopped the car pretty much level with my driveway. "I just mean, maybe you should experiment with someone your own age. You said it yourself, you've never had a serious boyfriend. By the time I was nineteen I had been seeing a girl for three years."

Bully for you! I thought, I so didn't want know about his past fucking lovers at that point. I searched my thoughts for a great comeback and went with. "Not having had a serious boyfriend does not necessarily equate to me being a virgin, Ryan."

His face flickered with shock but he remained silent.

"Is that it then?" I jabbered, my lips wobbling as I undid my seatbelt. Ryan was gripping the steering wheel so tightly his knuckles were white. He remained facing the front, refusing to meet my gaze. His jaw was tight, the taunt muscle flexing.

I should have been given a medal for keeping back the tears when he said.

"I just need some time. I can't see any other way. We need to stop seeing each other for a while." Considering that's what I had been there to say originally, I didn't seem to be taking it too well. My intuition was messing with my head, it felt more like he was finishing things than putting them on pause.

My heart shattered into a thousand pieces and I struggled with myself, partly wanting to hit him, the other part wanting to throw myself against him.

"For how long?"

He cast me a brief glance. "I don't know. Please, get out of the car Ella. Before someone see's us." He was back to being Mr. Cloak and Dagger. I hated it as he'd been so open at the beach. That was the Ryan I wanted not this distant one that seemed to be floating away as each second passed.

I sobbed my laugh thinking back to his earlier comment about being with Connor. "You warn me off other guys, like Mr. Possessive, and then throw them back at me? Talk about mixed messages Ryan. I should hate you," I declared miserably, totally not meaning it of course.

"Maybe you should."

I forced my face not to crumble at his words and pushed open the door of his car, stumbling out into the angry sunshine. I severely needed time to salvage my pride.

Making my way up my driveway, the gravel crunching against my feet, I allowed the tears to pour down my face. His words just repeated time and time again in my head, like a never-ending headache.

A cocktail of emotions pumped through me. Pain, loneliness, uncertainty. Immense sadness.

Luckily my parents were nowhere to be seen when I entered the house and retreated to my bedroom. Tom would have been on his rounds and so I wasn't worried about bumping into him either. Not that I gave two shits about any of that bullshit really. I just wanted Ryan. Wished he'd have followed me up to the house and pulled me into his arms or something.

I so needed the safety and warmth of his body. The sadness I felt was almost like physical pain. Now I knew why they called it broken-hearted.

As I sat on the floor with my back pushed against my closed bedroom door, I drew my knees up to my chest, silently counting the moles on my legs, like a proper sad case.

My iPhone buzzed and I picked it up from the carpet, a sliver of hope that it was Ryan saying sorry.

I'm sorry. The words were right but the sender was wrong. They were from Nathan. My head almost exploded. Of all the fucking times.

If anyone were to ever ask my opinion on getting involved with the Lane boys in the future, I would tell them to run for their lives. Don't do it! Save yourself, I'd scream in warning.

I bumped the back of my head against the surface of the door behind me, hoping to knock some sense into myself.

Why had those buried words risen to the surface at that point? The timing couldn't have been worse. Deep down I knew they were true. Had always known how I'd felt about Ryan ever since I'd seen him all those years ago. He'd lit a fire in me then and although it had been in the distance, it had always burned bright. Love, at first sight, did exist, for me anyway.

And now it was over before it ever officially started. I attempted to bat down another wave of sickness that loomed, eyeing the screen of my phone until my eyeballs ached.

I was partly angry at Nathan and I knew I shouldn't be. I was the one who had fucked things up, *not* him. He'd been a pawn in what had to be one of the most depraved games of chess ever. Not that I had done this consciously. I wasn't that big a bitch, but over the last couple of years, I realised that I'd become closer with Nathan to get to Ryan, I knew that now.

The whole situation was truly starting to screw with my head.

Releasing a sigh of frustration, I texted my reply to Nathan; he didn't deserve the silent treatment.

Me too. Friends?

His reply was immediate, almost as if he'd typed it before I had hit send.

Yes, friends.

Maybe things ending between Ryan and I was a good thing? It was of course my head that had this thought; my heart was screaming no, no, no right up at it. The two were totally detached.

I must have sat there staring up at the ceiling for most of an hour, my head feeling full, yet being empty of thought until my gaze came to rest on Ryan's jacket where I'd draped it over the chair.

It now looked so out of place, almost making a 'look at what you could have won' statement.

I pushed to my feet and shoved my phone into the pocket of my shorts, padding over to it. A wave of desire swept through me as I lifted the garment and inhaled him. Ryan. It was like he was in my room. It was ironic really as he was now even further away than ever.

I toyed with the idea of texting Connor but then decided against it, he had his own issues. This then led me to think about texting his stepsister, Harlow. My fingers hovered over the send button before I deleted the message. I couldn't really send her a 'do you want to meet up for a chat so I can offload my boy drama' when I'd met the girl once.

I spent the next hour, pottering around my bedroom, feeling thoroughly miserable and looking like shit, hoping that Ryan would text me. It was difficult, but I managed to refrain from messaging him like a complete loser. I had to be strong.

As I unpacked a case that was still left full after my last trip to America, I started hatching a plan.

It didn't have to be over, surely? I could start to smooth things over with Nathan, without worrying about anyone else, and find my way back to Ryan.

He couldn't have lost all interest in me just because I'd been about to confess my feelings for him. At the end of the day, if that did put him off, then was he really the guy for me? I'd fallen for him because he was more mature and he didn't play those kinds of games that younger guys did with girls. That whole, annoying hot and cold thing.

I looked around my now tidy bedroom, trying to remember what they said about a tidy home and a tidy mind.

My spirits slowly started to lift and I pulled open my wardrobe and rummaged inside. My friend Natalie always told me that after any type of boy drama, that a makeover always boosted self-confidence. She'd spent many a night on the phone crying her body weight in tears over Connor.

I'd need every shred of confidence I was cable of feeling if I was going to win Ryan back somehow.

The next few days went by without anything unexpected occurring. I was working in Mr. and Mrs. Haunch's gardens, planting some marigolds when my phone vibrated from the back pocket of my dungarees. They were such a lovely couple and had kept their garden immaculate but now they were older and their ailments were kicking in; they found it hard to keep on top of it.

The Haunch's owned a rustic cottage on the edge of Pickering and they were such a cute couple; still touchy-feely, even though they were ancient.

After planting the last flower, I teethed off one of my gardening gloves and removed the other with my fingers.

Withdrawing my phone, I positioned my thumb to unlock it and accessed the screen. I had a text from Nathan to say a group of friends were going into Scarborough clubbing this weekend and did I want to go. I had to think long and hard, the music in Josephine's was usually loud enough to burst your eardrums. I usually spent the majority of the next day battling off tinnitus, as well the usual hangover.

I was about to re-pocket my phone, not sure that it would be such a good idea. Nathan and I were back to texting but we hadn't seen each other in person since that day at Martha's.

After a few minutes more, another message fell beneath the last.

I'll behave, I promise. I've got the message. Friends only. Please come.

Packing the garden tools into a storage box, I walked over to the greenhouse and started to tidy everything away.

As if on cue Mr. Haunch appeared, he was always dressed in shorts, all year round come rain or shine and he had the knobbiest knees you'd ever seen.

"All done sweetheart?" he began, riffling in his wallet.

I smiled and nodded, rubbing my sweaty hands down the front of my dungarees. "Yes, are you happy?"

Mr. Haunch directed a contented look over at the work I had done. "Super. Absolutely stunning, the Mrs will get a nice shock when she gets back from Emily's."

Such a lovely guy; the flowers were a surprise for his wife; the plants that used to grow there were destroyed by Mrs. Haunch's daughter's dog when they'd been dog-sitting.

The pair had a lovely home and I really enjoyed working there. They also had a hot tub which I'd been invited to use whenever I wanted. It was funny really as the thought of them sitting in it half-naked didn't concern me as much as it should. But I suppose everyone gets old and wrinkly one day.

After thanking him for the work and accepting his overly generous payment, I pocketed the money and set off down the driveway in order to walk down the road toward my house. It was only half a mile at the most.

I pulled out my phone, texting and walking (I know not a good thing) and I thumbed in my reply to Nate.

Yes, OK. I'll ask Tom too.

He replied with a fist bump and a thumbs up.

Coincidentally, Tom's Volvo pulled up to the curb beside me with the offer of a lift and I climbed in.

"How's it going?" he put out breezily. The car reeked of wet dogs and there was hair everywhere. We didn't even own a dog but of course, he'd been on duty shadowing Marcus, an experienced vet and close friend of my dad.

"Good. Just had a text from Nate," I began, clipping on my seat belt. Tom pulled the car away from the curb and shot me a brief glance.

"Really? As in, everything's cool between you?" he asked hopefully. Tom had been my rock over the last few days.

"Yes, it's fine. He's got it at last I think. Anyway, a few of us are going into Scarborough for the usual on Friday, you up for it?" I wasn't sure if Tom would come, he didn't always. Too much of a square and I don't think I had ever seen him dance.

He indicated and drove in through the gates to our house.

"Maybe," he replied blandly, non-committal at first but then a thought brightened his features. "Could I ask Harlow, would you mind, like an attempt for a second date?"

I did mind but knew I couldn't really say no, especially after the support he'd shown with the Ryan and Nathan situation.

"OK, cool. I'm fine with that. What about Connor though?"

He pulled the car into the garage and turned the engine off before turning toward me.

"I've spoken to him about it and he's kind of given in. I know he wasn't that happy, but he did give me the green light. Threatened to break my fingers if I hurt her."

I was surprised, maybe I had misread things between Connor and Harlow. I certainly had with Ryan so who knew?

"Go for it, what have you got to lose, it will also give me the chance to get to know her better. I can see if I think she is sister-in-law material," I joked. Tom's face ignited with pleasure.

Once back in my room, I decided to text Connor. He rarely responded but it was worth a shot. I hadn't seen much of him since the appearance of Harlow which again, added more weight to the idea that something was going on there.

I sat on my bed and pursed my lips as I thought about what to put. I wasn't about to cry my heart out about Ryan to Connor as he wouldn't have given a shit.

Are you good?

My eyes bulged as his reply was immediate. **Yeah, why?**

I decided to wind him up. **Just haven't heard from you. How's life, living with little sister?**

Fuck off. He shot back.

Tom had mentioned something about it having been Harlow's birthday recently, which gave me the opportunity to remain on that topic. Do some digging.

Heard she turned seventeen, did you buy her a pressie?

The 'Con is Typing' icon appeared and after a few seconds he responded with, **Mike bought her enough for both of us so no, I didn't.**

I smiled. **What did he get her, a pony?**

Connor had made out that she was spoiled and so it wouldn't surprise me if Mike had bought her something so extravagant. His reply was actually worse.

No, a fucking new car. She doesn't even have her license. Who does that?

My smile widened as it wasn't that unbelievable considering our friends. **Dur, Nathan's parents?**

Yes, and look how he turned out. Connor had a point of course.

Tapping my phone against my chin I decided to ask him outright if he liked her. **Do you like her? You can tell me you know, I'd never say anything to the others?**

Waiting for the icon to appear to say he was responding never came, which didn't surprise me. There were two ticks below my message though, so I knew he'd read it. Secretive fucker. Absolute radio silence, no denial, nothing.

I rolled that one around my head for a moment longer before switching my thoughts to what to wear to Scarborough. Maybe I'd meet someone and could use them to make Ryan jealous? Such a lame thing to do but I was running out of options. Ryan certainly wouldn't be clubbing. The thought was as insane as imagining Connor there.

My mind raced with thoughts of Harlow and Connor; they were both so perfect looking; they'd look like a celebrity couple if they ever did get together. Although, if Connor did want Harlow and went for it, she was in for a whole heap of trouble. To say the guy was damaged goods was a huge understatement. Part of me felt sorry for her. If there was one guy who would be hard to love, it would be Connor. Was he even capable of giving it back in return? He wasn't overly loving to his mother. I'd seen how his body would tense on the rare occasion she drew him in for an awkward hug. Mind you, she too had been starved of affection herself.

At the end of the day, village folk were tough. They had to be.

Life in the country was very different from city life and the conditions shaped a certain type of individual. Boys were allowed to be just that. They worked with their hands, were rough, and at times borderline uncivilised. Rural living was remote and cut off and mental health issues in farming and those industries connected to it were rife. Unfortunately, it went on without being addressed. We knew it happened; we just didn't talk about it. Discussing it would show weakness.

Village boys were men's men; dad would say. Connor and Nathan had issues for different reasons, but both were unpredictable and at times too hot to handle. Natalie's brother Noah had also been a bit of a head-case growing up and then there was Ryan, who was in a league of his own, calm, collected, and usually *always* in control. That day in the car was the most animated I had seen him; temperament-wise anyway.

Kyle and Max were probably the most normal guys I knew, but they were originally from the city and their parents were power-sellers on Amazon; so *they* had no connection to farming. And Tom was, well… just Tom.

I pushed myself back against the covers of my bed and closed my eyes, pushing the thoughts of stupid boys and that combustible village mentality far from my mind.

Eleven

Friday night appeared and I still hadn't heard from Ryan. The less stubborn half of me was *desperate* to message him, but I'd managed to fight the urge, distracting myself with the mundane task of re-organising my wardrobe. I needed to do something different, take my mind off the situation to stop myself from spiralling into depression. The misery continued to whip through my chest like gale-force winds. Being with Ryan put the sun in my sky. Without him, everything seemed so dull.

For the first time in years, I stood in my house wearing a dress. Yes, an *actual* dress. It was the clingy, black lace number that my mother had bought me a few Christmases ago. The material was unfamiliarly tight against my body, but it wasn't overly uncomfortable. The main thing that gave me pause was the hemline, as it was quite high, sitting just below my bum cheeks.

I narrowed my eyes at the amount of flesh on show. The last time I'd worn a skirt had been three years ago for school; part of my horrendous uniform.

Staring back at myself in my mother's full-length mirror, I felt totally different. Grown-up and feminine were alien concepts to me, but I didn't feel as repulsive as I'd thought I would. Why not wear it, and give it a go? I knew I needed to step outside of myself to establish if there was anything I was missing.

Mum came into the room as I was internally debating whether or not I had the balls to wear it in front of my friends.

"Ella! You look stunning," she gushed with a mixture of shock and delight. I felt like shielding my body with my hands. Mum saw my embarrassment and shook her head violently, meeting my gaze in the mirror.

Her next words struck a chord inside of me.

"Don't. Not for *one* second are you to change your mind. You were born to wear that dress. You have the body of a runway model, Ella, I've always thought so," she praised quite breathlessly. "Embrace it and enjoy it whilst it lasts," she bubbled through misty eyes. For the love of God, I put on a dress and the sight causes my mother to bawl her fricking eyes out. Possibly not the reaction I was going for.

Watching my reflection in the mirror, I pulled at the hem of the dress to cover my thighs but my mother stopped me.

"Leave it, it's the perfect length, you have great legs. You don't realise how lucky you are. You should show yourself off more."

Surely her words should have been considered strange coming from a mother. Weren't moms supposed to encourage their daughters to cover up?

"Honestly Ella, you look beautiful *and* classy."

"I just don't want to show too much off and end up feeling uncomfortable all night," I replied with a woeful look.

"Don't be silly, you're clubbing. Anything goes, I used to wear hot pants." The thought of my mother in hot pants almost made my eyes water.

I shook off those feelings of inadequacy as mum carried on showering me with compliments.

"You've always been a natural beauty with an earth-real figure; like a woodland sprite, or a pixie. God knows why you hide away under that awful shapeless clothing. You've got it in spades."

It felt a bit strange, mum giving me so much attention all of a sudden and I smiled shyly back at her.

For the first time in years, it was like my mother actually saw me, like I'd stepped out from behind my brother and she got me for a change. My heart squeezed; her words and positive energy were all I needed to fuel the courage to go for it. Fuck it, you only live once and all that. God knows what the others would say. I just hoped I didn't feel horribly out of place.

Mum grinned and asked Alexa to play some kick-ass dance music; blathering about how it would get me in the mood for some serious dancing. She'd obviously noticed that I wasn't myself over the last few days and knew I needed to have a good time.

She popped the usual, 'I was eighteen once' comment out there too, which of course she must have been, but I still found that almost *impossible* to imagine. I'd seen old photographs, mum looked younger now than she did back then. Probably a fashion thing.

The more I looked at myself, the more I liked what I saw. I'd even put on make-up and styled my hair. It had grown quickly and was now almost to my chin. It fell in soft chestnut waves and for the first time ever, I felt comfortable in my own skin.

As I grabbed the clutch bag I borrowed from mum, I wondered what Ryan would say if he could see me dressed like this. Would he be attracted to me this way; I knew he dug my usual look. I shook off the thought and went to find Tom.

Dad dropped me and my brother off in town and we were told to stick together and catch a cab back. Tom explained that Harlow's dad was dropping her off and picking her up, which was understandable considering she was still underage. To be honest, I was surprised Mike had let her come at all and my mind was boggled at what Connor would think about it.

When we arrived, Nate, the twins, and Natalie were already there and had luckily found an empty booth at the back of the pub. Nathan waved to acknowledge our arrival as we went to the bar.

About ten minutes later, we approached the table clutching our beers and everyone's eyes lit up as they saw me. I felt a mixture of pleasure and cringe; especially toward Nathan whose mouth fell open like a proper cliché.

"Shit sister. You should do girl more often. You look fricking amazing," Natalie complimented kindly, pulling me in for a proper girl hug.

I smoothed my dress down and moved into the booth, noticing the twins were staring too, which hardly *ever* happened.

"What did you do with Ella?" Max puffed out, looking toward the entrance of the pub with a toothy grin. Warmth at his comment bloomed in my chest and I almost blushed. Almost.

I darted them all a, 'behave yourselves' look, full of fake confidence. If I showed any weakness they'd pounce. Like wolves picking off the weak members of the herd.

"Yes, I'm wearing a dress, big deal," I remarked between tight lips, not hating the attention but not loving it either. "Get your fill now as it may never happen again."

Nathan's eyes searched my face, digging deep before he leaned over the table and briefly touched my hand. It was quick, the others not noticing as they were shuffling in their seats and moving their drinks to accommodate us.

"You're beautiful Ella, but I've always known it." I managed not to cringe.

The hint of sadness in his voice dug up old demons, but I cracked a shy smile. It was a lovely thing to hear, I just wished it were Ryan sat there saying it.

Natalie shuffled further over so I could sit beside her. She looked stunning as always, like a proper femme-fatale. She wore an outrageously colourful blouse; it wasn't my sort of thing, but really suited her. She was like a vamp with her long black hair, which fell down her back in perfectly sculptured waves. The girl wore that much hairspray that it hardly ever moved. You certainly wouldn't want to sit close if you were a smoker. Her whole head would probably explode like a bomb.

As the conversation flowed, Tom kept glancing toward the main doorway, impatiently waiting for Harlow to show. The constant bouncing of his head started to grate on my nerves.

"For fucks sake Tom, you could at least attempt to be cool. Girls don't like guys that are all over them, you know," I explained, purposefully not making eye contact with Nate, who was still like my own personal rash that no cream could irradicate.

"Who are we waiting for?" Natalie questioned with a glance towards the doors.

"Harlow," Tom supplied, managing to tear his eyes from the entrance. His reply injected a bit more life into those at the table and everyone sat up in their seats.

Narrowing her eyes, Natalie took in the varying expressions of each individual boy.

"Harlow, as in Connor's stepsister?" she glowered, asking for clarification.

She already knew the answer, but her face still sank at my words.

"Yes, Tom invited her; as his date."

My reply still didn't reassure her and why would it? It's not like Tom would distract her attention away from Connor. Connor was sex-personified and my brother had about as much sex appeal as a toilet roll.

"So, I assume she's shagging Connor then?" she remarked with a twist of bitterness. This of course changed the conversation to Harlow (again). My grand entrance was now well and truly forgotten it appeared.

"Probably. Especially after the shit that went down at yours Nate," Kyle replied.

Nathan's face scrunched as his mouth curled at one side in a sneer. "Connor showing up like a possessive freak you mean?"

"Absolutely, talk about aggressive, sexual tension, and all that. That shit was bouncing off him."

Tom suddenly piped up which was interesting. "I didn't read it as possessive. He was just pissed off she was there."

We all exchanged glances before Nate painfully put in. "You're in denial mate."

"So, you all think they're doing it?" Natalie peevishly repeated.

There was a beat of silence before Nathan replied.

"My money would be on yes. You have seen the girl right Nat and you know Connor's sex drive? I doubt the guy could go a week," he pointed out.

Natalie smoothed her hair back, obviously ruffled by his words.

"You don't know that. Maybe he's getting it somewhere else," she puffed.

"Well, we know he isn't getting it from you anymore," Kyle put in with a cheeky grin.

Natalie's smile slipped and she stuck out her impressively large chest indignantly. "And how would you know that? Connor doesn't kiss and tell," she sniped.

"Nope, but your face says it all. You're like an open book Natalie, and not a very good one at that," Nathan baited, locking playful eyes on mine.

To some, the banter may have been considered cruel, but you had to be thick-skinned if you were friends with any of us. The caveat to this was that if you could dish it out, you should be prepared to take it, and we were all usually capable of both. Apart from Connor of course, who played by his own rules and pretty much-expected everyone else to. He was a toe-the-line or I will fucking strangle you with it, kind of guy.

"To be honest, I haven't a clue what's going on with him. I haven't seen him for ages either," I revealed in reflection.

"If I lived under the same roof with a bird as fit as Harlow, I'd never leave the house," Kyle added with a dirty smile. Both brothers were *massive* players and had slept with quite a few girls in the village; one at the same time, I had heard. The idea of threesomes was totally gross, especially if one of them was your own brother. Did they close their eyes when taking turns? I wasn't even sure how that worked. The bottom line; the twins put the D in STD.

"As if you'd stand a chance with someone who looks like that you frigger. Especially next to the masculine glory that is Connor Barratt," Max tittered.

Kyle flipped him the finger and necked his beer.

"Fuck me, Max. You do realise that you've just admitted you've got a boner for another dude?" Nate retorted with an uncomfortable expression.

"What? All I'm saying is that he's hot shit to the ladies. I know when I'm beaten. Although I've got more than Connor in other departments," Max chuckled.

"Not brains that's for sure," Kyle volleyed back, coughing out a laugh.

Max looked mildly offended. "I meant a sense of humour dickhead. I make people laugh and girls eat that shit up. *Especially* one's like Harlow."

My smile remained intact, even though I was slightly annoyed by the Harlow Williams fucking appreciation society sitting before me. I could see from her expression that Natalie was definitely not in Harlow's corner either at that point.

Natalie Savvas was a guarded individual. She put on a tough, conceited sex siren front, but she was actually quite insecure. She dropped her guard with me at times, not for long, but I had seen who she really was and it was very different from what she projected. I also knew she'd had proper feelings for Connor, when all it had been for him was sex. Natalie admitted that he'd been clear with her from the start, but that she'd fallen hard anyway. I had been the one to pick up the pieces. Her shithead of a brother had been little help at the time. Like most twenty-something boys around here, Noah was too wrapped up in his own crap.

All the boys, apart from Tom, started flirting with the girls on the table behind us. Nathan was over-egging it a bit, but I suppose he was trying to show me that we were now back to being just friends and I was cool with that. I could see behind his façade that he wasn't totally over it. Don't they say time is the healer in broken heart types of scenarios?

After around half an hour, Tom's face lit up and I turned to see Harlow walking toward us. Most guys in the bar stopped what they were doing. Even the ones who were with girls.

She literally glided in like she had wheels; a tiny, beautiful blonde, like a breath of fresh air sent from heaven. How the hell did she do that? Look so angelic in a shit-hole like The Swan?

The dress she wore was stunning, a deep red lace number with a sweetheart neckline that showed off a fair amount of her cleavage. Let's face it, the girl was a walking hard-on. I noted with envy how her long hair swished provocatively as she walked, drawing everyone's attention in our direction.

My brother was almost panting like a dog and I felt a wave of pity, she was way out of Tom's league.

Harlow approached our table with a sweet smile, but I could see a trace of apprehension in her eyes. I moved out of the booth so she could sit in between Natalie and me, so she wasn't on the end. I wanted to make her feel welcome as I knew how it felt to feel out of place. She looked incredibly young and was lucky the bouncers had even let her in. The girl had probably unknowingly mind-controlled their dicks and the doors had miraculously opened by themselves.

After Tom introduced her to Natalie, she settled in her seat and he went to the bar to fetch her a drink.

Conversation flowed with a snarky Natalie directing Connor infused questions at Harlow. She dealt with them quite well, giving nothing away, and only flinched once.

"He's a tough nut to crack," Nat pointed out with a flash of fire in her tone, I could feel the jealousy radiating from her like the fallout from Chernobyl. She really did need to rein it in again.

"But well worth the wait."

At her suggestive words, Nathan's eyes locked with mine and he joked. "He's not the only one." Blatantly directing this toward me, recapturing my attention.

I rolled my eyes, kicking him under the table. "Don't start," I shot across at him, annoyed by the smirk he wore. That was the best comeback I could come up with, it appeared my cocky-meter wasn't at its best. I gritted my teeth so I wouldn't say anything else that I'd later regret. Nate could be such a wanker and I turned away and listened to what Harlow was saying about her plans to become a teacher. Her voice was high-pitched, a little on the squeaky side but still sweet. I probably sounded like a tenor in comparison.

After only allowing Harlow to get halfway through her explanation, Natalie interrupted rudely by suggesting that she didn't need to work as she could sponge off her rich daddy. Nat was in full-on bitch mode it appeared.

I partly switched off as the discussion split off into smaller conversations and Natalie and Nathan started verbally sparing; Nate said something about how she'd probably end up as a hairdresser like her mother, which wasn't actually accurate anymore. Elena Savvas now sold products to hair salons, a bit of a difference but again, I didn't jump to anyone's defence. Nat's lips were twisted into a flat smile without a shred of pleasure. Nope, tonight I was on 'fence mode', as in, that's where I was sitting and would remain for the rest of the night.

The word Golden Boy shook me out of my half-comatose state. That was the name Natalie would use to describe Ryan, purposefully to wind Nathan up and make him feel like a worthless piece of shit.

Tom and I exchanged a look, which Nate *must* have seen as his eyes narrowed and I took a sip of my drink and then stood, faking a trip to the toilet. Harlow offered to come with me. She obviously didn't know that out here, the whole 'girls go to the toilets in twos' thing didn't exist. Country girls were tough and independent and didn't need that 'safety in numbers' shite.

I slipped away and entered the bathroom, purely to wash my hands and reapply my lipstick. I checked my phone to see if I had a missed call from Ryan but again nothing.

When I went back to the table, everyone was finishing their beers and I was told we were moving on to The Brewers Tap.

It was rather uneventful in next place and after a few more bars, everyone was well on the way.

Just as we were finishing off drinks ready to head to the club, Harlow got up to go to the bathroom and I decided I needed a bit of fresh air myself and an opportunity to check my phone.

I'd only had a few beers but as I hadn't eaten much that day, the alcohol had already started to loosen me up. I left through the back door, knowing I didn't have long before we moved on.

Fuck it. The hefty battle I'd waged with myself to not make the first move was lost as I decided to message Ryan. I knew nothing good would come of it and that I'd regret it later, but my restraint went with my last mouthful of Budweiser. If I had to describe my mood at that point, I'd go for mellow.

I scrunched my nose, looking down at my last message to Ryan which had been sent when we were still seeing each other. It raised pleasing memories but also cruelly reminded me of what I had lost. A sliver of annoyance shot up my spine that he was now fucking ghosting me.

My mind started to calculate what to say. **In case you're interested, I took your advice. I'm out in town tonight getting blotto and being a teenager.**

I held my breath as I thumbed the send button, I didn't even wait to re-read it. I needed validation that he still liked me but admitting that to myself made me cringe.

Two ticks appeared to show it had been delivered and around a minute passed by with no reply. I started to regret what I'd typed. Reading it again, I bit my lip at how pathetic it sounded. The message reeked of an overenthusiastic girl attempting to make the boy she liked jealous. Shit. I could feel an 'I'm a twat' realisation being kneaded into me, like heavy fingers against the wateriest dough. Why the hell didn't I stay home and deal with our break-up in the traditional way, with ice cream and weepy movies and all that?

Stopping myself from jumping the gun and sending another embarrassing message, I moved to put my phone away but it buzzed to say I had a reply. I drew in a breath, almost paralysed with fear of reading it.

Slowly turning the phone over, I swiped the screen. Emotion like galloping horses charging inside me.

What does that mean?

WTF! That was it? What a *shit* reply. Annoyance flared in my chest that he was making me spell it out.

Swallowing that feeling of regret I had felt moments before, I ploughed on like a fucking farmer on speed.

You're not that dumb Ryan. I responded without shame, carefully evading sending a straightforward reply and knowing that he would hate that. 'Infantile evasions' he'd call that tactic.

So, you're messaging me to tell me you're on the pull? Does that about sum it up?

I continued with my line of attack, again not giving him a straight answer. I'd never managed to get Ryan to lose it completely, he was far too controlled for that, but I knew how to push *some* of his buttons.

I'm surprised you know the lingo, considering how ancient you are. I typed back, now enjoying myself. He'd thrown the age card at me in the car and so it was only fair to deal it back.

I would suggest you don't do anything you're going to regret, purely to spite me, Ella. It will only end badly for you. He replied.

Another thread of my temper snapped and there weren't many of those left. I needed to shut this down or it would end up ruining my evening. At least I had given him something to think about, even if his response suggested that he wasn't that fazed by what I had said. Had he ever given a shit about me?

I thumbed my reply. **I suppose we'll see. Night night x.** I knew it wasn't a good idea, but I left it at that.

As I walked back into the pub through the rear exit, Kyle, Max and Tom were hovering by the entrance. Harlow suddenly appeared out of the bathroom with Natalie just behind her and I moved forward toward them. Harlow's body language suggested she wasn't happy and must have been in the bathroom with Natalie. Not the best person to visit the loo with as a two.

I surmised that some damage control was required and I upped my pace to join her.

It was obvious that Natalie had been a bitch to her and I felt bad for having left them sitting together. It was bound to have been awkward, them being strangers, as well as the fact that Natalie was Connor's ex Fuck Buddy. Tom would have been at the table but of course, he couldn't have gone to the bathroom with her. I felt like such an unsupportive bitch and told myself I had to do better.

My eyebrows started to inch toward my hairline.

"Harlow, hang on, are you OK?" I asked softly as I found her side. "You look upset? What's she said?"

She tried to hide it with her hair, but I spotted the hurt in her eyes. My heart went out to her. She suddenly looked so fragile and vulnerable.

Harlow cleared her throat as we slowly made our way toward the others. Natalie had now joined Tom and the twins and was cackling about something. Nathan was nowhere to be seen.

In a firm voice, Harlow confessed. "She was just telling me how good my stepbrother is in bed," she announced, the steel in her tone surprising me.

I slid an arm around her shoulders, suddenly feeling protective, she was so much shorter than everyone else.

In a clear truthful voice, I threw my other friend (who could take care of herself) under the bus.

"Ignore her, she's jealous of you because you're hotter than her and you have Connor's attention." Her shoulders stiffened at the mention of Connor's name. "She's been after him for years."

She inhaled and pursed her lips, stopping just before we got to the others and turning to say. "Why are you friends with someone like that Ella?" Her perfect eyebrows were almost threaded in the middle. She was clearly confused and as I digested her words fully, I accepted that she had a point. Natalie hadn't exactly been the best of friends, what with the active listening and it always being about her, but what other options did I have? I was and had always been one of the guys. Now I was out in town; feeling all female and heartbroken, and yet I actually still had no one to share my problems with. No one that would really want to listen anyway. And I couldn't count my brother either.

Harlow was looking up at me, inspecting my face, trying to understand my silence.

It felt awkward and I realised that she was right. I had no fucking idea why I tolerated Natalie Savvas. Desperation? She certainly wasn't the type of girl you could bare your soul to.

"I don't know. Maybe because there aren't many girls to share stuff with in the village. Most of my friends are boys."

Her face dropped and she looked like she regretted her words. Worried that she'd offended me. The girl was probably the sweetest person I had ever met and at that moment, I hated the ugliness inside me. That snap judgement I'd made after what Connor had said that this girl would be as dull as shit. She was the polar opposite of that, she lit up a room with her looks *and* her personality; her *everything*. To be honest, Harlow was even too good for Connor.

I smiled back but something unreadable skittered across her pretty features. She looked sad and drained.

"So, she isn't lying?" Her words came out more of a statement to herself than a question, but I answered her anyway. I felt it only right that she knew the truth.

"No, they were definitely shagging at one point, but it wasn't serious. Just a bit of fun," I highlighted slowly, before adding a word of warning in respect of Connor. Words this girl definitely needed to hear. "Connor is too messed up to hold down a proper relationship."

I told her this as I didn't want her going through what I was with Ryan, the girl's shoulders were certainly not broad enough to deal with that amount of torture.

She shot me a look that I couldn't determine and I questioned her outright. "Are you sure you don't have something going with Connor?"

A spark of temper flared in her gaze and I realised that I may have misjudged this tiny package. There was a fire inside her.

"Are you sure *you* don't?" she shot back and I was just about to respond but Nate appeared and slid his arms around us, herding us toward the others.

"What the actual fuck, how long do you need to take a piss?"

He could be such an obnoxious twat and Harlow and I shot each other a look that said exactly that. Talk about a mood killer.

"Nathan you're giving me the ick. You shouldn't question ladies about such things," I complained, balling him out, no trace of humour in my tone. He of course totally didn't give a shit.

"If I see some, I'll make sure I watch what I say. Were you discussing the size of my cock?" Nathan questioned crudely with a smirk as we regrouped with the others. It was only partway through the evening and he was already well on the way. Alarm bells started to sound in my head. His comment could have fucked me over big time if anyone had been sober.

"You're such a dick," I mumbled.

He grinned at me, and Harlow and I raised our not-impressed eyebrows. "And if you get any more shit-faced, I'm going home," I added with a serious edge.

"You love it," Nathan announced with a grin, shooting me his version of a sexy look. I couldn't hide the small smile. He was incorrigible. I just hoped this was as far as he went.

"I mean it Nathan, save it," I replied, my tone now serious.

If Harlow sensed there was anything going on between us, she didn't show it as she trotted ahead of us.

I pulled away from Nathan and he trailed behind me like a kicked puppy.

As we approached the queue outside Josephine's Nightclub, I noted Noah's friend Jaxon was on the door, a possible opportunity to get in for free. I was all about the freebies.

My phone went off in my clutch and I checked it, I'd put it on silent and it vibrated to say someone was calling me. I glanced down and my heart raced. *Ryan* was calling me. My warning of getting off with someone must have worked, otherwise, why would he be ringing rather than texting?

Excitement jetted into me. He *did* care, he *had* to. I was already quite merry due to the booze and after that, I felt excited to get into the club and let my hair down. I could have done a victory dance on the spot.

We all huddled towards the front of the queue and I attempted to capture Jaxon's eye. Natalie and Harlow were being hit on by two guys, one of whom was openly leering at Harlow, whilst Natalie was lighting his cigarette. Jaxon was also checking her out and as I moved toward her, he noticed me and beckoned us all forwards.

People in the queue all moaned and shouted as we passed them and I grabbed Harlow's hand and pulled her along up the stairs and through the glass doors

"We got to go guys, sorry places to be, please to see!" I shouted, outrageously blowing off those in the queue.

We sailed past Jaxon into the club and after checking in our jackets in the cloakroom, I half dragged Harlow towards the bar and told her it was happy hour.

Buy one get one free only lasted during the first hour and I liked to get my money's worth. I ordered a couple of Vodka Red Bulls and Harlow went for two non-alcoholic drinks. I needed the booze as I was so stoked about Ryan calling. I thought about how he would be feeling, not knowing if I was with someone else or not. Making him suffer, just like I had during his silence. I knew it was juvenile but I was past caring.

Once we had our drinks, we found some seats together and Kyle and Max went to the bar to get more drinks. The rest of us set out our base for the night.

I slid into my seat and watched Tom attempting to impress Harlow by pretending to be cool. He was such a twat, the guy used words like 'poppycock' and 'super' for fucks sake as if he could ever be deemed 'street', the silly bint.

Tom leaned further toward Harlow, almost falling down the front of her dress and I suggested he back the hell off. He was such a sad case.

The others came back from the bar and we all sat together, drinking and laughing and moving in our seats to the music.

Harlow kept searching the room blatantly looking for someone, possibly Connor I imagined. I decided to test that theory.

"You won't see him you know," I put in over the music. The others were too busy talking about football.

She shrugged, defeated. "I'm that easy to read," she replied quietly. Glancing briefly at the others who were still none the wiser.

I finished my first Vodka Red Bull and said gently. Not wanting to sound unkind.

"Maybe not to the others, but I've seen that look before."

Kyle and Max started to argue about the off-side rule like the silly buggers they were and Harlow's eyes met mine as she leaned over to squeeze my knee.

A silent message passed between us, an understanding that we were both dealing with some boy-related shit.

A bit later after more booze and speaking solid shit for an hour, we all went dancing. My feet were literally killing me until eventually, the slow tracks came

160

on and I went to take a seat, hoping to check my phone again without Nate seeing. He was absolutely wankered and was dogging my every move. Harlow said she was thirsty and went to the bar as Nathan and I found our seats.

"I do love you. You know that don't you," Nathan slurred as he dropped down next to me on the sofa and I took his beer off him. Holding it out of his way when he went to take it back. He was such a lout.

"I think you've had enough."

He relented quickly, dropping his hand. "You're not the boss of me, kidding, you are totally the boss of me." He replied with a glazed expression, leaning his head on my shoulder.

His next words were fairly vague, but I didn't want to allow him to continue in case Harlow came back.

"I have something to tell you. Ella, about that night," Nathan slurred, dredging up our night together, but I shut him down.

I felt a flare of temper. "No, Nate. You promised." I reminded him but the sigh he released at my words was heavy. Maybe I should have given him a chance to explain himself. I just didn't want to go down that road again, re-hashing what we'd done.

I sat there for ages. Natalie had gone off with a guy called Mark whom she'd been grinding herself against for most of the night.

I scanned the room of the club we were in. Harlow was still not back from the bar and Kyle and Max were chatting to a guy on the other sofas. Probably sport-related crap. God, I hated sports.

Gradually Nathan's head became quite heavy and I realised he had fallen asleep on me. He was literally drooling drown my dress. So gross.

Whilst he was unconscious, I pulled my phone out to see I had five missed calls all from Ryan, and a couple of texts, I also had a message from Tom, apologising and saying he'd gone home early. Typical twat leaving me to get a cab by myself. I should have known he'd not last the night. He probably turned into a fucking pumpkin or something if he stayed out after midnight. Such a lightweight. I swiped to read the messages from Ryan, thoughts of Tom forgotten.

Answer your fucking phone! Was the first text and my tummy flipped-flopped. Ryan rarely swore in person or by phone. I could almost hear his voice as I read it. He was pissed off, which was *exactly* what I had wanted. His last message stated. **WHERE ARE YOU?**

I was surprised he wouldn't have guessed where I was considering Nathan would have told him he was going to town. Or maybe he hadn't, maybe Ryan was away?

I re-pocketed the phone, feeling too tipsy to respond now. Let him stew I thought, see how he liked it.

I swirled the liquid around the bottle of Nathan's beer and took a swig. It was flat and I raised my eyes to glance out at the crowd, feeling sad again and a bit childish in how I had dealt with the Ryan thing. Nathan was now half draped against me and he was snoring, fucking snoring like a pig FFS.

My eyes widened as they suddenly landed on Connor and Harlow who were walking toward me from one of the back rooms. What the actual fuck? Connor had come to the club? This surely meant there must have been something going on there. Unless Mike had sent Connor to collect Harlow in his place? That too was an option.

They approached us.

Connor was in full take-control mode as Harlow watched him from beneath her lashes, completely in awe of him. Kyle and Max had a taxi waiting and I followed Connor's instructions and woke Nathan up, telling him to go with the twins.

I was so relieved the night was over. I was tired in every area of my body.

My eyes searched for Natalie as I'd not seen her for ages. She usually took herself off and didn't always text me to let me know where she was, but I sent her a quick text to check she was OK.

Harlow and Connor waited in the lobby whilst I collected our jackets and we exited the club and walked over to where Conor's Ford Ranger was parked. I climbed in the back, pleased to be out of the loud nightclub.

As Connor drove with Harlow sitting beside him, there was a strange vibe in the cab. I raised the subject of boys in general, keeping my chat totally neutral and finding it difficult not to say Ryan's name. Partway through our journey,

162

Noah Savvas texted me to say Natalie was home and I read the text out to see the reaction of both Harlow and Connor, him having shagged her and Harlow now knowing that. Her shoulders stiffened and that was it really. She was tougher than I first thought.

As we pulled up to my house, I thanked them both for the lift and climbed out of the back.

My buzz had faded away and I just felt tired. A bit lightheaded but not overly drunk. I'd been stuck in my seat in the club for the past hour with Nathan's heavy assed head weighing me down and therefore stopping me from going to the bar. In reflection, that was a good thing as the effects of alcohol had slowly started to fade away.

I stomped over to the front door of my house and searched for my keys.

Twelve

As I fumbled in my bag, the hairs on the back of my necked prickled and the house keys fell out of my fingers, jangling to the floor. Bending to retrieve them, I saw a flash of movement from the corner of my eye and a pair of polished shoes appeared beside me. Shooting back up in alarm I almost plastered myself against the door as a pair of strong arms grabbed me. My heart raced in my chest as Ryan held me against his solid hard frame, supporting my weight. His scent was crisp, masculine, and heady and the skin tingled on my upper arms where he held me, the warmth from his steely frame flooding through my dress. My mouth literally dropped open in shock and my heart thundered in my chest.

I wouldn't usually use a phrase like 'knock me down with a feather' but at that point, it seemed the perfect way to describe how I was feeling. Overwhelmed didn't cut it. The variety of emotions pumping through me were mixed, chaotic and at war with each other; *excitement* and fear of the unexpected both fought for supremacy.

Ryan was here at last, and he wasn't overly happy from the look on his face. The time of reckoning had come, would I like the monster I had created?

"Ryan—you scared me," I shot out somewhat breathlessly, my heart skipping a beat. It almost physically hurt to look at him.

His head twisted down at me with an expression I couldn't decode. "My apologies, that wasn't my intention." He then shot a quick glance around the deserted yard before turning back and gently setting me away from him. I slapped a hand against my heart to stop it from leaping from my chest.

"Maybe think twice before jumping me from behind next time," I scolded, semi-playfully, my heart was still galloping like wild horses.

Ryan quirked an eyebrow and then motioned with his hand. "Give me your keys," he ordered firmly, his shoulders tense. He was magnificent, bathed in the glow of the security light. I raised the entire bunch and he plucked them from my shaking hands and immediately placed the correct key into the lock. Pushing open the door, he took the initiative swiftly and then stepped back, encouraging me to go inside with a sweep of his arm. There was a caginess about his actions and uncertainty continued to course through me.

He wore a dark sweater that fit snugly over his muscled chest and light denim jeans. The guy looked even sexier than he usually did. He followed me inside and closed the door softly. I was surprised he came in but wasn't overly worried about my parents or Tom. They slept like the dead.

Tom had left the standing light on in the hallway and I moved through the dimly lit area toward the kitchen, Ryan shadowing silently behind me. As we entered the room, I turned the downlights on which were dotted underneath each wall unit, so the light wouldn't be overly blinding. I then turned to face him, still struggling to rein in the commotion in my head whilst preparing myself for a looming altercation.

Ryan folded his arms across his chest and leaned sideways against the doorway, his whole frame was rigid as his eyes roamed over my body.

He was angry, you could tell by every aggressive angle. The text exchange from earlier came flooding back. He remained silent as his eyes slowly appraised me, missing nothing; his assessing gaze like fingertips touching my skin. His gorgeous face made my breath hitch.

"You really went all out I see," Ryan drawled in a smoky voice.

I cleared my throat nervously. "What does that mean?" I replied with a frown, not really deciphering his code.

He motioned towards me with a flick of his head. "The way you're dressed, for your night out, what did you call it, on the pull?" Antagonism lit his features and his dark attitude almost knocked me off guard.

I pulled a face, glancing briefly at my clothing before waving the white flag. "They were your words, not mine and you're wrong, I didn't dress this way for that reason. As for my text, you'd pissed me off and I was winding you up." Where was my backbone all of a sudden?

He cocked a brow. "Well done, it worked," Ryan confessed flatly.

"Really?" My heart leapt at his words and I bit my lip as I awaited his reply.

He paused momentarily before pointing out in a gruff voice. "I'm *here*, aren't I?"

I couldn't control my blush and the alcohol in my system appeared to be suggesting that I throw myself at him and press my body against his. Luckily my sanity prevailed. Thank God I'd had time during the ride back in Connor's car to sober up a bit. Our eyes remained locked as they clashed together over the dining table. It was all that separated us and I peeled my jacket off and placed it on the back of a chair with awkward movements.

Ryan continued to watch me in silence and I stepped backwards to lean against the kitchen counter; the edge pushing into the bottom of my back. I needed to appear calm, unfazed and not let on that his presence was doing crazy things to my insides.

He looked me up and down. "Very nice," he drawled in a deep voice as he was hit with the full effects of my outfit. I felt exhilarated that he liked what he saw. How could he not really, he was a guy and you could pretty much see every curve of my body. I was on the slim side but I was still all female.

My blood heated as he unfolded his arms, shoved off the door, and took a couple of steps toward me, leaning over the table and resting his palms flat against it. I watched him silently. His upper body was tilted forward and I could see anger and arousal fencing with each other, but he still appeared to be in control. At that moment, I wanted to smash that away; see him lose his calm. Let him experience the chaos his very presence caused my emotional being.

"I've never seen you dressed this way before: I think I like it," he murmured with a wicked grin.

I smiled suggestively. "You should see what I've got on underneath it," I whispered, feeling totally in my element for a change: the booze obviously feeding my courage. Ryan's shrewd eyes darkened, giving him that edge of danger and I felt warmth pool between my legs. I was so turned on, my eyes darting to where his firm hands touched the table, his fingers splayed and I desperately wanted them on my body.

His smouldering gaze followed my focus fleetingly, before he suddenly pushed off the table and moved toward me, masculine intent plain in his eyes. I regarded him quietly from my stance against the unit, refusing to back down.

Ryan cupped my chin and lifted it forcing my head up, my eyes wide as they took in his masculine beauty. The guy oozed sex appeal.

"You can lose the alcohol-infused vision of me taking you hard on the dining table because it's *not* going to happen. Not tonight anyway," he assured me in a deep voice. My legs suddenly felt like jelly at his words, but I remained upright thank God. It was almost like someone had removed my bones and replaced them with string.

I sucked in a breath. "No? Spoilsport," I replied in a disappointed voice.

His eyes narrowed further before he declared with promise, "I have much more finesse than that Ella," he warned in a delightfully sensual tone. The chemistry between us was off the charts, and potent.

My eyes widened as he released his grip on my chin, those fingers circling my upper arms and he hoisted me against him; closing the gap between our two bodies. My breasts were crushed against his chest and the movement dragged me up onto my tip toes. Delight ran through me at the impact and my head fell backward. His verbal retaliation came in the form of a devastating kiss.

I lit up like a rocket as his head lowered and he ground his mouth against my own, his lips were hard and demanding, almost a punishment but I drank in the experience, savouring it as his tongue drove into my mouth, stroking inside. Ryan's hands were still holding my arms as he drew me even tighter against him. I wanted to put my arms around his neck but my hands were trapped against his biceps which flexed with the pressure he was exerting.

He kissed me as if I belonged to him; with frenzied passion. Stamping his ownership almost. I wanted his hands all over my body and his legs pressed me against the counter; I could feel how aroused he was against my stomach. The thought that I had made that happen forced me to groan against his mouth, the noise like a cry of victory, and a primitive thrill shot up my spine. Ryan's scent was purely masculine, musky, and altogether too appealing. It enveloped me and a frenzied buzz quivered up my spine.

How I had missed him; this mouth, his body; that scent, *everything*. I didn't care that his kiss wasn't overly gentle, to be honest, I fucking rejoiced in it. *This* was what I needed; it was hot, hard and aggressive; his control well and truly gone. He took my mouth as if he had every right. It was almost as if the full extent of our passion for each other had been caged, but was now free and there would be no going back. I wanted him to touch me where I burned the

167

most and my legs parted, allowing him to move in closer between them. Wedging himself. He was literally pinning me against the kitchen unit and he growled as my own tongue matched his technique and we devoured each other. The kiss was hot enough to turn the ocean into lava.

After a few more moments of exquisite pleasure, Ryan slowly lifted his head, looking down into my eyes again which must have been glazed with desire, his grip on my arms loosening and he slanted his head and drew my bottom lip into his mouth, biting it gently. The pain was slight but delicious. He then pulled away slowly and stepped back, retaining eye contact as if we were still connected in some way. I was almost breathless with desire and my legs felt wobbly.

Ryan regarded me in silence as my chest rose and fell with uneven breaths. I was literally panting but his face was unreadable again, having successfully pulled the mask of control back in place. But it didn't matter, I had seen him uncaged at last, been on the receiving end of pure unadulterated pleasure, a heat that was well and truly stoked. I now wanted, no *needed* everything he had to give as pleasure soared within me.

"If you ever provoke me again with talk of other men, I'll put more than just my tongue inside you," his silky threat was pure erotica and another sexual charge of lust jetted through me.

I was literally speechless and *dripping* wet. This whole scenario had hugely increased my heart rate and it raced against my chest. We were both breathing fairly heavily.

Ryan glanced at my breasts, taking in how my nipples had hardened further at his words. My belly fluttered as I realised the truth that this man fucking *owned* me.

"When the time is right, your every orgasm will belong to me. Now, go to bed Ella, you need to sleep off the alcohol. We'll speak tomorrow when I get back from London."

The word orgasm crackled in the air between us and another jet of heat darted into me. His sexy, seductive voice made me think of rumpled bed sheets and hot bodies, damp from sex.

Running my hands over my hair, I shook my head and pulled back some control. I certainly didn't intend to let him be the boss of me all the time. I needed to show him that I too could be a strong confident woman (yeah right).

"I'm not *that* wasted Ryan, I didn't drink that much," I declared in a throaty voice before crossing my arms over my chest to hide my arousal. I now felt like he was telling me off and I didn't totally hate it but I wasn't about to let him get away with everything. I did have a backbone in there somewhere.

"You look like a pixie with anger management problems," he smiled, his eyes roaming over the way I was stood.

I gave him my best sassy look. "I'm just saying, I only had a couple of cocktails and that was right at the start of the night." I struggled to keep the quiver of nerves from my voice.

Ryan shot me a pointed look. "You shouldn't be drinking at all. You put yourself at risk tonight and I'll be having words as to why Connor didn't drop you at the door. It's well after midnight, anyone could have been hanging around."

Pursing my lips as I digested his words, I replied. "I was fine and anyway, I can take care of myself," I part whispered unconvincingly, my voice trembling slightly.

The look he shot me was pure authoritarian. "If I didn't have to leave, I'd been inclined to prove to you how very wrong you are about that."

Visions of sexual punishments danced before my eyes. When the hell had I become so horny? My pulse spiked.

"You're lucky, I have to be in London in a few hours and I have quite the drive ahead of me, thanks to your little stunt," he stated, pushing his hands into the pockets of his jeans.

I rolled my eyes, suddenly struggling to speak. It was like my tongue was attached to the roof of my mouth. "I'm sorry, it—"

Ryan held up one tanned hand to cut me off. "Save it for tomorrow night," he instructed firmly, his 'take charge' attitude kicking in again. "I'll text you when I know when I'll be back, but it will be late. Now I suggest you get to bed and I'll see you tomorrow."

And with those parting words, he drew away and left the house, closing the door gently as he exited. Ryan took all the charged energy from the room with him. How I didn't puddle into a heap on the floor was a miracle. I felt almost giddy with pleasure.

After managing to find my bed without too much noise, I laid there, staring up at the ceiling, thinking of Ryan and our encounter in the kitchen, visions of where it could have led dancing in my head like a silent promise of things to come.

The next day, I woke up around lunchtime to an annoying Tom banging on my door telling me to get my lazy arse up. I checked my phone to see I had a message from Nathan and I swiped the screen. He was probably a bit woolly-headed about his behaviour in the club and wanted to check that he hadn't made a nuisance of himself; which of course he hadn't really, apart from drooling down my dress.

His text came as a surprise and I re-read it a few times.

You want a contract? Mum and dad are on about hiring a landscape gardener to re-do all their shit flower beds and I suggested you. They've seen what you've done at the Haunch's cottage and mum was well impressed. What do you think?

I almost broke out into a full-on dance. Not only did I need the work and experience; this would give me more of an excuse to see Ryan.

I messaged him a thumbs up and a thank you and he shot back. **Get your arse sorted, and I'll pick you up in twenty. You might want to take a look and hear what Sally has to say before you give a definite answer. There is quite a lot to do.**

K, I thumbed in, still not able to bat away that suspicious feeling that there was something in this for him.

I peeled off my underwear and took a quick shower before dressing in my signature dungarees which I wore for work. They were ultra-baggy but extremely comfortable.

As promised, Nathan collected me in his abomination of a car and drove me to his parent's house. I knew I wouldn't see Ryan but I asked about him anyway.

"Ryan away again then?" I questioned.

Nathan nodded and explained what I already knew about Ryan being in London. His next words, however, confused me.

"It's for the best that he's out of the way, to be honest as he thinks mum should hire a professional gardener."

My brow threaded. "And what am I? Playing at it?" I shot out feeling slightly offended.

"I think he just thinks it's too much work for one person. I don't think it was anything personal," he deflected, I still took his words like a punch to the stomach. What the actual fuck?

My temper simmered. "Doesn't he think I can do the job?" I scanned his features and he shrugged his shoulders as he changed gear. "Not sure, he was well against it though. I was surprised as I thought you two got on OK."

OMG, if only he knew. I pursed my lips as he pulled the car in through the gates. His dad was painting the fence at the side of the house.

Whilst Nathan parked the car, his mother came out.

"Look don't worry about Ryan, he's a moody twat but he isn't here that often. When you've finished with my mom, pop up to mine. I need to speak to you, and not about heavy shit or anything. I just have some stuff I need to say."

To be honest I ignored part of what Nathan's was saying as annoyance pulsated through me. I didn't understand why Ryan thought I wasn't up to the job. He'd always been so supportive before. Pushing the negative thoughts aside, I admitted that he probably didn't want me there in case one of us let something slip about whatever it was that was going on between us.

Sally was really welcoming and chelped on about her vision for the gardens. They had quite a bit of land and she took me to a section of garden near the decking that led from their huge kitchen at the back of the house. I felt really comfortable in her company, considering I'd had one of her son's tongues in my mouth earlier that morning and of course my past with the other one. Something I had willed myself to forget about. Maybe if Nathan had come to terms with the fact that there was no 'us', I could just forget about it and never have to tell Ryan. Of course, in the back of my mind, I knew that wasn't the right decision. The truth always came out, I knew that.

Sally liked my ideas and explained that I'd got the gig. I almost punched the air.

Luckily, I wasn't given the opportunity to visit Nathan in his room as Sally called him down and told him to take me home.

On the way back in the car, I received a call from my dad asking if I could help out in a few weeks at his practice on Reception. This fortunately stopped Nathan from being able to air the 'stuff he had to say'.

As I hung up, Nathan explained that he was due to meet Ryan at the pub for a drink when he came back from London. He asked if I'd like to join them which was weird. The thought of being sat between the two of them under the circumstances almost made me break out in a full-on rash. My skin was constantly itching during the rest of the journey home. I was puzzled that Ryan had arranged to meet Nate, considering he was due to see me later. Maybe he meant much later after the pub? I shelved the thought. I didn't care what time he came over as long as I saw him.

Nate dropped me back home and I spent the rest of that afternoon sketching my ideas for the Lane's flower beds and googling all the different complementary colours for blooms and shrubs.

Glancing at the time, I wondered how Harlow and Connor were and decided to walk around to Mike's to break up the evening, still assuming Ryan intended meeting me after dark.

When I got to Mike's farm, it was quiet and his car wasn't there which suggested he was out.

Connor's Ranger was parked up and so I went in through the open door and called his name. He immediately appeared from his mother's study, looking slightly sheepish.

"What the fuck do you want?" he put in moodily.

"That's a greeting for you," I batted back with a roll of my eyes.

The power of his personality almost pinned me to the spot. "Harlow's not here, she's fucked off to the pub with Tom," his voice was steely.

"I know, it's quiz night. Nate and Ryan are going. You not fancy it?"

His eyes darkened further. It so wasn't the right thing to say.

"You know I hate quiz night."

I gave him a toothy grin. "You've never even been to quiz night. You should try it. You might like it or are you scared you'll get all the answers wrong? You'd do OK, you're not Max."

His twisted his lips, suddenly lost in thought. "Connor?" I questioned, feeling concerned.

"I don't seem to have the answers for anything at the minute. Fuck," he bit out before turning his back on me and walking into the study. OK, there was definitely something going on there.

"What are you on about?" I questioned, following him with a grimace.

He threw himself into one of the floral chairs, looking extremely out of place against the feminine flounce that was his mother's taste.

"I just feel all over the place at the minute," Connor muttered quietly. I thought about the text from Tom and Connor's behaviour at Nate's party.

"That'll be withdrawal Connor. Tom told me you're not taking your meds."

I planted myself on the opposite sofa and gave him a fixed look. "Well?"

"I can't be doing with that shit anymore, it does fuck all. I just feel half asleep all the time."

I exhaled sharply, not really knowing what to say.

"If the Doctor says you need them, you should be taking them," I replied, keeping my tone even.

"The Doctor is a dick. They do *nothing* apart from make me as numb as fuck and I'm fed up of feeling that way. Doing what I do for a living, I can't afford to be dozing off, especially if I'm operating machinery and shit."

I frowned, wondering if he'd had any near misses. "Are you saying you fell asleep at the wheel or something?"

He shook his head and flexed the muscles in his shoulders. "No, but I can't concentrate. It's hard enough focusing with Harlow here."

"Well, maybe you need something else. A milder dose if they're confusing you."

"They're *not* what's confusing me, Ella?" he rasped, rubbing his face.

"You're talking in riddles," I puffed out in frustration. Conversations with this guy were never straightforward.

Connor sighed, looking worn out and he closed his eyes, leaning his head back against the chair.

"She's driving me *insane*," he suddenly whispered into the silence.

Understanding bloomed in my head. Ah ha. "I take it you mean Harlow?"

"Yes, *fucking* Harlow. I wished she'd never come here. She's seriously messing with my head."

I pursed my lips thoughtfully. "So, Nate was right all along, you do like her?"

"Who gives a shit what that blow-job said. It's more than that, so much more and I don't know what to do about it."

I leaned forward in my seat and placed a hand on his knee in support before suggesting. "Why don't you speak to her, sort things out if she's that much of a pain in your arse?"

"You don't get it. Just go away. Talking to you is adding to my fucking headache."

"You're your own worst enemy Connor Barratt. If you close yourself off, people won't be able to help you?" I advised, pulling my hand back.

Connor opened one eye and peered at me with an unimpressed look. "The fuck I care? You can talk, you've got more fucking baggage than me with your fucking triangle shit."

I stretched against the sofa, shooting him a glare, my patience evaporating. "It isn't a fucking love triangle shithead, and what the fuck would you know anyway?"

Either off or on his meds this guy was clever, always managing to turn the tables on a discussion. Taking himself off the menu.

"So what's going on with you and shit for brains?" he successfully deflected again.

"I'll assume you mean Nathan and so nothing." I bounced back and stood up to walk toward the window, giving him my back.

"He's behaving himself but the Ryan thing is still complicated. I don't know what to do really."

"You know what you need to do, Ryan has a right to know Ella. It was one fucked up night and if he really wants you, he won't give a shit. Well, at first, he might but he'll get over it."

I seriously had my doubts about that one. A thought suddenly occurred to me as I turned with folded arms, shooting him a pinned expression.

"How would *you* react if Harlow had slept with your brother, even on a 'one fucked up night' scenario?"

"I can't answer that as I don't have a brother," he pointed out flatly with a lopsided smile. Now looking extremely relaxed and sure of himself. Talk about hot and cold.

"Let's say for arguments sake that you did?"

He snorted with attitude and gave my question a moment of thought.

"Easy, I'd break his fucking nose and make his life a living hell."

I exhaled loudly and dropped my arms to my sides.

"And there you go, it's going to get messy no matter what I do," I sighed, nibbling one of my finger nails.

We spoke for around another half an hour before I decided to head off and leave him to his misery. He didn't say it, but I could tell he was pissed that Harlow and Tom had gone to the quiz, they were probably all cosied up next to Nate and Ryan, playing happy families.

As I left the house and headed down the driveway, I heard the throaty roar of Mike's car.

As it motored closer toward me; I saw it that wasn't Mike, it was a beat-up van and I didn't recognise the driver. Probably one of the farm hands? It passed me and I set off jogging, realising the time.

I needed to change my clothes into something a bit more feminine for Ryan. I really had started to embrace the girly stuff. His reaction to me in my dress had given me that boost of confidence I needed. I really had started to feel more confident in my own skin.

Thirteen

I'm on my way, meet you outside yours in ten.

The text came just as I was pulling on my clothes. I'd chosen a tight black tee instead of my signature hoodie and a pair of pale blue skinny jeans. After what my mother had said about my body and Ryan's reaction to me in a dress, I felt a bit more confident about my appearance. It's funny really that it had taken me so long to realise that looking nice, made you feel nice.

Thankfully, I had the chance to get ready without interruptions from annoying parents or brothers. Saturday was 'date night' for my parents and so I didn't need to make any excuses as to where I was going. Tom was probably still at the quiz with Harlow, or at least on his way back, and so without having to sneak around, I exited the gates of our property and made my way toward Ryan's car.

As I opened the door Ryan greeted me with, "I take it you didn't see my last text?"

I slid as gracefully as my tight jeans would allow into the car and pulled the door closed, my brow threaded at his question.

"No what?"

"I asked you to bring my jacket," he replied coolly.

Ah yes, of course. I still had his jacket in my room. "Oh, that one. Sorry, no can do—I cut the sleeves off when you blew me off," I declared with a grin, fastening my seatbelt.

He shot me an unimpressed look. Of course, he knew I was joking. "You cut the sleeves off the jacket of a fifteen-hundred-pound suit? And you expect me to believe such madness?"

"Mad is *exactly* what you are if you spend that much on clothes, that's obscene," I pointed out with a look of my own.

"You wouldn't understand when you blatantly spend little to nothing on yours," he bit back cheekily. Excitement thrummed through me at our verbal sparring.

"You didn't seem to think that my clothes were that offensive last night," I pointed out with a sultry edge.

His eyes darkened. "That was different. I've thought about nothing else for most of the day to be honest. Although it wasn't the dress I was thinking about, it was more about what was beneath it. You recall I know exactly what *that* looks like."

Heat pumped through me again at the thought of Ryan watching me through my window.

"Ah yes, your stalker moment. Bit sick and twisted of you. I didn't have you down as the voyeuristic type Mr Lane."

"I didn't have you down as a sexy underwear type either. So it appears we both have secrets."

As he delivered those particular words, it was like all the air in the car had been sucked out.

I cleared my throat nervously, it felt like there was a boulder in there and Ryan shot me a look, his own features switching to concern.

"You, OK?"

I recovered quickly. I had no option. Ryan had just hit the nail right on its huge regretful head.

"Yeah, sorry. Just got a frog in my throat for a minute. Anyway, if you'd stuck around last night; you could have had another peek," I put in quickly. I wasn't feeling it now but I needed to push past Ryan's comment about 'secrets'.

If he noticed anything was off, he didn't show it and I watched as he pushed back in his seat and turned toward me. The black leather jacket he wore made him look swarthy.

"Not like that, not when you've been drinking," he replied drily.

His words instantly wound me up. "For fucks-sake Ryan, you make it sound like I was hammered."

His face twisted and he cocked his head at me. "You'd been out all evening and I could tell from your gutsy texts that you must have been fairly tipsy. You're not usually that daring Ella."

His words of warning would usually have lit a fire in me but I suddenly felt uncomfortable. The comment about secrets still circling me like a rabid dog.

I smoothed my hair back off my forehead and crossed my jean-clad legs. "Maybe I have more of a backbone than you give me credit for?" I pointed out, thinking how ironic that thought was, bearing in mind I was too much of a pussy to tell him about Nate. How I hated that particular secret.

I channelled my best 'what the fuck' expression and changed the subject. "And what the hell is your problem with my gardening work all of a sudden?"

He looked puzzled and shrugged his huge leather-clad shoulders.

"I don't have a problem with your gardening work, why would I?" His tone was even and I powered on.

"Bad-mouthing me to your parents ring any bells? Nathan told me."

Realisation bled into him. "Ah, the contract," he snorted, shaking his head, his mouth quirked in a knowing, unapologetic smile.

My eyes narrowed. I wasn't sure why he thought it amusing. "Yes, the fucking contract. What's so funny? You know I need the work," I pointed out.

He pursed his lips. He had such a sinfully attractive mouth. "Yes, Nathan explained you'd got the gig. Well done. Oh, and I met Harlow tonight."

I almost shot back, don't change the subject but his comment about Harlow batted that away. Here we go.

I raised my eyebrows and shot him a frosty look. "Yes, she went to the Quiz with Tom. And?"

My insides twisted at the thought of him saying anything nice about her. If he found her attractive, forget my nails, I'd probably chew an entire finger off.

Annoyingly, Ryan did that, 'I have no idea what you mean' thing that boys did when they were trying to piss you off. "And what?"

I rolled my eyes so hard it hurt. "Well, she's gorgeous, isn't she? Did your limbs start to melt on the spot?"

I puffed out a jet of hot angry air at his evasion and he chuckled, he could probably taste the jealousy bouncing off me. "Bit on the small side for me really."

I blew out a breath. "Whatever." I bit back.

"To be honest, I'm not even sure how that would work," Ryan sang with a playful twist of his lips. I wasn't amused.

"Stop trying to wind me up."

He gave me a pointed look. "In plain terms, no Ella. She doesn't interest me at all. I prefer women who can look into my eyes without needing a step ladder for a start."

My eyebrows shot up into my hairline in a 'whatever' motion but I moved that shit on for my own sanity, my irritation fading.

"Anyway, don't change the subject," I put in quickly. Totally not wanting to speak about other insanely attractive girls with him.

He laughed, "You were the one who wanted to know if I got the rock-on for the new girl," he remarked balefully.

"Please don't say rock-on when you're speaking about another girl," I retorted, now officially peed off. His mouth curled in a smile at my sour expression.

"I think I quite like the idea of you jealous," he grunted with a sly smile. I wanted to punch him in his firm, jean-clad thigh. His stance was relaxed and he looked so sexy in his casual clothes, relaxed back against the seat of the car. Desire stabbed through my body.

I switched the topic back. "So, spill it. Why did you feel the need to slag my gardening services off?"

My eyes narrowed as he circled his shoulders and shifted in his seat. "I wasn't slagging anything off. I just don't want you working at our house."

My frown deepened further as he point-blank admitted it. "And why the hell not?" I shot out, suddenly feeling cross.

He raised his sexy eyebrows and looked at me like I was a moron. "Self-preservation," he pointed out with a twist of his perfect mouth.

I snorted and it wasn't a lady-like sound. "What does that mean?"

He released a pent-up sigh of frustration before shooting me a knowing look. "You know what self-preservation is?"

Thoughts raced through my mind, none that I particularly liked either. "Because you're still trying to ignore this thing between us?" I suggested, the guy had lost me.

He bit out a laugh, I was obviously on the wrong track.

He leaned toward me, his eyes roaming over my features. "Because I don't want to have to deal with the sight of you bending over the flower beds and not being able to do anything about it."

And BOOM. His reply took the edge off my temper and stirred up a variety of other emotions.

My mouth made an Oh shape, but no sound came out.

Ryan saw it and spoke the words for me, as understanding snaked into my mind. "Yes Oh."

There was a beat or two of silence before I shot him a shy smile.

"Sorry, I jumped to the wrong conclusions," I admitted frankly.

Ryan shot me, a 'you don't say' look. "I know, you did that after our last discussion in the car. I hadn't had you pegged as a drama queen type."

I rolled his words around my head before pointing out. "Well, you can't blame me. You gave me the silent treatment pretty quickly."

"You know I don't use my phone that much and I was working away. What did you expect?"

I managed to stop myself from pouting like a little girl. "You could have checked in with me at least," I replied moodily. "I'd thought that we were done for good." I didn't reveal the full extent of how upset I'd felt during the cold shoulder period. I felt worried that it would give him too much power. I still needed to play a little hard to get.

Ryan placed his hand on my leg, now deep in thought.

"I want you, Ella, you *know* that. But as I said before, we need to take it slow."

I knew what he was saying was right but I was so fed up of feeling so much uncertainty. I realised that things were already clouded by the Nathan thing but why couldn't I just have a normal relationship with this guy? *Because you got pissed and shagged his brother!* Yet again, the unhelpful part of my conscience chipped in. Like a fucking Gremlin on my shoulder that I couldn't flick away. I closed down the thought as Ryan was still speaking. His deep voice resonated in the car.

"Maybe after your birthday, we can go public and you can tell your friends, well, *the rest* of your friends. I'll have a chat with your dad. Your parents will be the ones to freak out the most I imagine," Ryan put in lightly.

Wow, I hadn't expected his comment about speaking to my dad like he was going to fucking propose. I bit my tongue before blurting out anything embarrassing.

"Can you give us some more time, Ella?" Ryan questioned in a throaty voice, as he ran his fingers up and down my leg. It was such a tender move and at that point I would have done anything he said.

My mind was still scrambled with thoughts of the unknown but I knew what he was suggesting made sense. I actually needed the time he had asked for to deliver my own news. I toyed with the idea of saying it there and then, the mood was right. Then it would be out there, my silly mistake with Nathan.

As I wasn't really sure about what *had* happened, I could play it down and suggest it was more of a fumble. I swallowed, knowing that the right thing to do was to be fully honest.

Taking a deep breath, I decided it was now or never.

"I have something to tell you, it's nothing major and it happened in the past." I paused briefly as Ryan cocked his head and twisted his body so he fully faced me. His face was clouded and a strange sensation prickled my skin.

It was dark outside now and I jumped suddenly as a hand banged on the window of the car.

Shit! Both me and Ryan jumped in our seats.

It was Tom. I shook my head at Ryan who scowled. "It's Tom," I told him, before turning to push the door open.

"What the hell Tom, are you trying to give me a fucking stroke?" I admonished as he glanced into the car, seeing Ryan and giving him as 'what's up man' look.

"Nope, but you're about to give mum one. She just texted to say they're on their way back. I just passed you in the car when I dropped Harlow off. Thought you'd appreciate the warning."

I nodded and shot Ryan a look, mum would shit a brick if she caught me in his car at this time. I wanted to kiss him goodbye but Tom still stood there, lingering like a bad smell. Take the hint dickhead and piss off.

"I'll be out in a sec, go away," I grumbled and pulled the door closed to block out his annoying, melon-shaped head.

Once he had scuttled off and I twisted back to Ryan, realising that I now didn't have time to tell him about Nate.

"I better go. When will I see you?" I asked, my voice paper-thin at the thought of having to wait to see him again properly, a few stolen moments in the car together, just wasn't enough for me.

"Probably mid-week, I'll text you."

I smiled, hiding my misery. "OK, don't forget I'll be working on your garden and so don't be surprised to see me there," I pointed out.

Ryan nodded before stating. "But no *fucking* signals Ella, no blatant come-ons, we can't let anyone know just yet. We also need to figure out how to deal with Nate. You may not have noticed, but there is *something* there, he's been acting weird ever since you got back."

Alarm bells started to peel again. Shit, Ryan *had* noticed Nathan's weird behaviour? This revelation made me realise that I was running out of time to tell him about what happened, otherwise the situation would become unfixable. Especially if Nate got in there first, any future plans for me and Ryan would probably be done for good.

I leaned over the gear stick and he met me halfway, our kiss was tame but nice, very different from the one during the early hours in my kitchen. The feel of his mouth against mine caused liquid fire-like desire to hum through my torso. Our chemistry was so evenly matched.

He lifted his dark head and cast me a wicked smile.

"Later," he drawled, light dancing in his eyes. I must have been wearing one of those ear-to-ear grins.

As I left the car, I started to hatch my plan. The next time I saw Ryan, I would tell him about my silly mistake. I would then break the news to Nathan.

Rubbing my arms against the cool breeze, my thoughts raced. Nathan Lane, the ticking time-bomb of the century. He wouldn't take the news well.

Watching Ryan drive off, I turned and made my way up the driveway toward our house. As I entered the living room, Tom was sat with this study books again. It was Saturday, did the guy ever rest?

"So how was the pub I questioned?" plonking myself in front of him.

He closed the book and looked across at me, shrugging nonchalantly.

"It was OK, we lost though. There was also a weird atmosphere when your name came up, but I suppose I should have expected it. I take it Ryan still doesn't know about Nate and vice versa yet?"

I nodded, leaning forward on the table. "Not yet, but we've spoken about where things are going a bit more. Ryan wants us to wait until after my birthday before we say anything."

Tom scratched his jaw, looking thoughtful.

"How about you and Harlow? How did it go?" I asked, unable to sift out the dubious element to my tone.

He looked sad and my heart swelled, I didn't like to see him upset. Tom had never had much luck with girls. Nice guys rarely did.

"She just friend-zoned me," he revealed, palming the back of his neck.

I offered him a friendly understanding sister smile. He didn't get them often and so I hoped he appreciated it.

To be honest, I'd never thought he'd have a chance with Harlow anyway. There was too much going on with her and Connor. Maybe it was time to see her again, I could do with a girl's view on things.

The noise of dad's car revving up the driveway dragged our gazes away and Tom's brow creased as he pushed to his feet. Dad drove like an old lady usually.

Something was off. We both approached the door as my parents climbed out of their car.

They made their way toward us with varying expressions, dad was texting and mum looked worried.

"What's wrong?" Tom questioned our father as he walked past us into the house, completely blanking us. Mum approached me; her face strained.

"Mum, what's up?" I repeated Tom's words, wondering what the hell was wrong, my brows scrunched together.

"Come in the house, both of you," she replied, motioning for us to go into the kitchen.

As we went into the room, my mother lowered herself onto one of the chairs, and then dad came back in.

"Anything?" she questioned him with a frown, but he shook his head. "I'm just wondering whether to drive around and see if everything's OK?"

What the actual fuck? They were talking in code and it was starting to piss me off. From the expression on their faces, they were confused and anxious.

"Will one of you tell us what the fuck is going on?" I snapped out. My mum actually flinched like it was the first time she'd heard me swear and dad left the kitchen with a harassed look; his phone to his ear.

Mum's lips were pursed in thought and she scratched her brow before saying, "There were police cars at Mike's place. Your dad's trying to get hold of him to find out if everything's OK?"

Police cars? Everything had been fine when I'd left Connor earlier that evening. What the hell?

Panic flared in my chest at the thought of someone being hurt.

"Was there an ambulance or anything?"

Mum shook her head. "I don't know, you could just see flashing lights. I think just police cars. Maybe there was a break-in?"

I moved to the other side of my mother and looked down at her. "I only left there an hour or so ago and Connor was in. Everything was fine."

Tom joined in with, "And I only dropped Harlow off about 20 minutes ago. Shit, you don't think something's happened to her?" he shot out hastily.

"We should go over there now," he suggested starting to pace.

"Slow down," my dad shouted from the doorway of the kitchen. "No one is going anywhere. We don't want to jump to conclusions or get in the way. I've left Mike a voicemail to ask him to let us know if he needs anything."

"Yes, let's not make ourselves busybodies just yet. It could be something straightforward," Mum added.

I literally spent most of that night awake. I texted Connor, begging him to call me to let me know everything was OK. I really didn't have a clue what had happened. Was Harlow hurt in some way? Had there been a break-in like mum had suggested? Maybe one of the animals had gotten out?

I also texted Ryan.

Something has happened at Mike's place. I've texted Connor but no reply. Have you heard anything?

He actually texted me back pretty quickly which I was relieved about. I needed his calming strength.

No, I've not heard a thing. How do you know? He messaged.

Mum and dad drove by and there were police cars at the house.

He fired back. **I'm sure it's nothing to worry about.**

In the morning, when I went down to breakfast, the atmosphere in the kitchen was sombre. It was like someone had died and my heart raced behind my ribs. Praying for Connor to be OK.

It was then that my parents told Tom and me that Connor's psycho father had found him and his mother and that Connor had been attacked. Nastily beaten. He was OK but in bad shape and my heart squeezed at the thought of my friend in pain. I hazily remembered seeing that van drive past me when I left Connor's, maybe that had been his father? Shit, if only I'd known, I could have raised the alarm.

From what my dad said, Connor put up quite the fight and his dad was now back in custody.

The whole thing was a shit-storm and it put my problems into perspective.

I left the house and messaged Nathan, Kyle and Max to let them know what had happened. I then sent a separate text to Nate to say that we needed to talk.

His reply was. **I agree. We do need to talk.** And I wasn't sure how I felt about that.

The time had come to deal with my demons in an adult, calm way. My head was clear, I knew what needed to be done. Compared to Connor's problems, mine were tiny. So, I'd had drunken sex one night at a party. At the time, Ryan and I hadn't even been a thing. He'd been out of reach, a girlish crush. I'd only ever dreamt of being able to get close to him. I'd been such an insecure person at that time, I had never believed that something could have happened between Ryan and I. He'd been so grown up, mature next to my awkward little girl.

It was the past, and I needed to secure a future.

Fourteen

Mum reported that Rachel didn't want any visitors for the first few days, to allow Connor time to rest. He had busted ribs and was on the strongest of painkillers and from the sounds of things, wasn't in the best of moods. No shock there then. I decided to leave it a couple of days before heading over there.

On the day I visited, Connor was still in bed, propped up against the headboard, looking like he'd gone a few rounds in a boxing ring. He was properly mashed; split lip, swelling, and purple angry bruises covered his face. It was not nice to see and the fact that it was his dad that had put those marks there, made it so much worse.

Clive, one of the farm hands had told Nathan that Connor had leathered his father to the point where Carter couldn't stand. The saying, 'I'd hate to see the other guy' didn't apply to me, as I would have appreciated seeing the lowlife beaten to a pulp. Carter Barratt could rot in hell for all I cared. Hopefully, now that his son had bested him, he would be out of the picture for good.

On Thursday morning, dad dropped me off at the Lanes' estate on his way to the surgery. It was a bright sunny day and perfect weather to start what would be my third official gardening job.

I walked up the driveway, towards the huge house. Nathan's car was parked in front of one of the garages at an awkward angle, the paintwork glowing like a toxic spill. He really didn't give a shit, did he? I wondered how long the Porsche would last before he wrapped that one around a tree.

I noticed Ryan's car was also there but the curtains to the annex where he slept were closed. It was only eight in the morning and so he'd probably still be in bed. He'd texted me to say he had been on his way back from a show in Edinburgh and so no doubt he'd be exhausted. I thought fleetingly about how he'd look when he was sleeping. Probably peaceful and mouth-wateringly tasty. I couldn't wait to share a bed with him, not necessarily do anything major too soon, but to wake up in his arms would surely feel amazing.

The smell of cut grass and fresh air teased my nostrils as I made my way toward the back garden where Sally wanted me to start. She had already pointed out the shed where there were gardening utensils I could use, which of course was better than lugging my own stuff around. I reminded myself again how much I needed to pass my driving test.

It took me around an hour to turn over the soil in the first bed and remove the weeds. As I was breaking up the larger bits of soil, Ryan's voice washed over me.

I was on my knees working with the trowel and twisted my head to peer over my shoulder. Excitement coursed through me.

"See, this is *exactly* what I was hoping to avoid," he began, motioning to my backside as I was leaning over the bed on all fours. He looked like he'd literally just rolled out of bed, in loose-fitting jogging bottoms and a baggy tee. His hair was mussed and I longed to run my fingers through it. I pushed myself up onto my knees and then stood, turning to face him.

I released an unsteady breath. "Hey you," I greeted with a smile, moving towards him, shielding my eyes from the sun with my hand. It was quite strong and I was already hot and sweaty from working but I didn't care how I looked, Ryan was here and talking to me. An added plus.

Ryan's mouth curled as he watched me approach, pushing his hands into the pockets of his joggers, drawing my gaze to that area. I couldn't stop the dirty thoughts from circulating. I imagined he'd be pretty big, the rest of him was. I batted away my pervy thoughts. It appeared I also needed to get laid, not that I could remember what that actually felt like. My one time with Nathan being hazy, to say the least.

Ryan watched me down his straight nose and rocked back on his heels. Everything the guy did was cool. If I'd have attempted that type of move, I'd probably be on my arse about now.

"Nice outfit," he stated, flicking his head toward my attire. My dungarees were probably the most unattractive clothes I owned but again, I didn't care, I knew this guy liked what was in them.

I shrugged, my eyebrows shooting up towards my hairline. "What do you expect? I'm working, my little black number has no place here," I replied, casting him my best sexy look.

I stopped before him and peered up into his gorgeous face, drinking him in. How I so wanted that simple pleasure of just being able to spend time together, without hiding. To be able to walk over to him and thread my arms around his neck. Push my chest into his, like normal boyfriend and girlfriend stuff.

"I quite like the rustic you and of course, I know what you have on underneath them. You like the lace against your skin," he whispered, his eyes now hooded.

His words sent a frisson shooting up my spine and I cocked my head to one side, loving the fact that he'd come to see me. After his words of warning about how I was to act in his company, I thought he'd ignore me. Had prepared myself for that. But this was just so much better.

I grinned and placed my hands on my hips, giving him a schoolmarm look. "Are you sure you're supposed to be fraternising with the staff?" I joked with a twist of my lips.

He shot a glance over his shoulder and then stepped towards me; our two bodies were almost flush. "That's the problem, Ella, I want to do more than fraternise," Ryan announced roughly, his watchful gaze immensely alluring. I was the bee to his honey and I so wanted to touch him, I didn't care that anyone could see. We were outside, but his male scent still enveloped me. His nearness was causing havoc with my pulse rate.

I tutted and continued with my teacher talking to a pupil tone. "Mr. Lane, I thought there was to be no flirting or 'making eyes' at each other. Surely for such a controlled individual, you aren't *already* breaking the rules."

His eyes roamed over my face like he was desperate to get into my head and steal my secrets. "Maybe I decided to fuck the rules," he drawled, lifting his hand and pushing a lock of my hair behind my ear. I felt a stab of satisfaction.

"You have such neat little ears," he commented wistfully.

I suppose 'neat little ears' were better than the cauliflower type.

My smile was automatic, the guy made me feel dainty even though I was almost five foot eight. At school, I'd towered over quite a few of the boys my age, another fact that had added to that feeling of inadequacy I had battled during childhood.

The expression on his face changed from pensive to serious. "It's only been a few days and I've really missed you."

His words dragged my thoughts to Nate who said the same thing the other week. Unease bubbled in me. Whenever I had amazing thoughts about this guy, his brother was always there lurking in the background. Spoiling things.

There was movement behind Ryan's shoulder and I leaned to look behind him. As I was fucking saying, the source of my exasperation materialised. He was standing in the open doorway of the conservatory like he'd heard my fucking thoughts. He had shorts on, his chest was bare and he had a serious case of bedhead. His ripped body was fairly magnificent, but he was nowhere near as stacked as his brother. Ryan was taller, broader, and more *everything* to be honest.

Ryan's eyes narrowed as he watched my movement and he shot another glance over his shoulder to where Nathan was standing there, watching us. When he turned back to face me, he looked annoyed and rolled his eyes. That was not something he usually did and I wondered if we were actually starting to turn a corner.

I shifted nervously from foot to foot suddenly feeling guilty, like we'd been doing something other than talking.

"I hope you're not distracting the help Ry," Nathan bit out with a cocky undertone.

Ryan's eyes were on mine and I looked away, pretending to rub away an invisible patch of mud from my palm.

Nathan pushed off the door and came to stand next to Ryan. Side by side you could totally see the difference in their build. In *everything* really. Ryan's skin, hair, and eyes, although similar to his brothers were also slightly darker. He was just so much more, in *every* way possible.

Both brothers stood before me now and it felt a bit surreal, the formation of our bodies actually spread out in a triangle. Oh, the joy.

Ryan did something that he didn't usually do, he surprised me as he cocked a look at Nathan. His expression was slightly mutinous.

"It's the other way around brother, she was distracting me," Ryan drawled out, his eyes skirting back to mine and a hint of something strange lit the air between our bodies. Nathan frowned and he watched his brother with a curious edge.

"I should get back to work really," I put in quickly with a nervous smile, wanting to keep things neutral. My voice sounded like it was coming from somewhere in the distance.

"And how's she doing that? You trying to talk yourself into a hard-on Ryan," Nathan chimed in with a trace of amusement before moving closer toward me.

Don't answer, please don't answer I thought. What the actual fuck was happening here. Ryan appeared to be throwing caution to the wind which was causing chaos to channel through my brain. I sensed a pissing contest coming on.

"Maybe. Who wouldn't notice her? Must be the work clothes," Ryan slid back and motioned toward me with a flick of his Rolex-encased wrist. I dropped my hands to my sides, unsure what to say.

I glanced down at my unfeminine baggy clothes and wondered if he was being sarcastic to put Nate off the scent but his tone was much too suggestive. Would Nathan pick up on that?

Abso-fucking-lutely!

"I can safely say I've been noticing Ella for quite some time now. My question is when the fuck did *you* open your eyes?" Nathan's voice was now quite firm. Not overly angry, I'd heard him speak to Ryan like this before.

I cleared my throat as Ryan turned to face his brother and it was suddenly like I wasn't there. They eyed each other with varying expressions. Shit, this was majorly messed up.

"Oh, I noticed." The impact of his dominance was like a stamp across my skin suddenly.

Nathan unfolded his arms and he shot a glance at me, before turning back to his brother, his eyebrows almost met in the middle his frown was that deep.

I decided I needed to put an end to whatever the hell they were doing.

"As I said, guys, I need to get back to it so you can take your big dick contest somewhere else please."

They both turned to look at me as I glanced between them.

"There's no competition there Ella," Nathan put out, grabbing his junk. Ryan's eyes narrowed at the gesture. He wasn't impressed by his brother's childish reaction.

Ryan shook his head, his face showing amusement but it didn't reach his eyes. Nathan's actions were so juvenile, I almost felt embarrassed for him. Almost.

"I'll leave you to it Ella and please don't let dickless here put you off," Ryan suggested with a definite tone, not rising to the bait.

I moved back to the flower bed as Ryan walked off, leaving Nathan just stood there, I clocked the strange expression he wore before turning away. Like he was contemplating something. Oh dear. Fuck my life.

"What's up? I need to get on Nate," I commented in a dismissive voice. Get the message fucker!

I could feel his eyes burning into my back as I pulled the trowel out and frantically starting to break up more dirt. Thank God I had something to do with my hands as they were shaking.

I heard Nathan moving beside me as he came close. He stood there like a tower as I carried on working, watching him from the corner of my eye. His next words totally unwelcome.

"What were you guys talking about?" he threw down at me and I stopped digging and pushed myself to my knees, shooting him my best bland look.

I attempted to force reason and logic into my voice. "Nothing really, just talking about work and stuff," I lied. My tongue felt twice its usual size as I almost lisped the words out.

Nathan put his hands on his hips as he stared down at me with a semi-disbelieving look. Suddenly feeling vulnerable on my knees before him I pushed to my feet and slapped the mud off my hands, regarding him pensively.

Before I could answer, he dropped his hands to his sides and snorted, "Please tell me my fucking brother wasn't hitting on you?" his tone dropped to a growl. Shit.

My eyebrows creased in surprise. I so hadn't expected him to say that. I shook my head, mentally coaching my reply. "Why would you think that?"

Nathan pushed one hand into the pockets of his shorts. The muscles of his stomach rippling and he scratched his chest with the other.

"Just wondered why he's sniffing around out here? Now he says you're a distraction. What the fuck does *that* mean?"

I dropped the trowel, meeting his unwavering gaze. "He was probably being sarcastic Nathan, I'm covered in mud, look at the state of me. He's probably winding you up," I pointed out, folding my arms across my chest.

He exhaled sharply. The guy was miffed all right. "Yeah, well it worked, the fucking cock." He shot a look at the empty doorway where Ryan had made his exit.

I paused, thinking about the best way to reply, and decided that I just needed to go for it. Every little step forward in this nightmare would ensure that when the time came, it wouldn't be as much of a shock or as painful; for *everyone* I hoped.

"You'd tell me if he said or did anything to upset you, wouldn't you?"

I pursed my lips and thought about my answer. "Probably not," I added truthfully.

"What the fuck does *that* mean?" There was a storm brewing, but I powered on regardless.

"I can fight my own battles, Nathan."

He grimaced and scratched a hand over his chin.

"Well, you didn't seem to be fighting. I saw him touch your hair. What the fuck was that about?" Nathan rallied and my eyes flared.

"We were *talking* Nathan; I can't even recall him touching my bloody hair. Stop doing what you always do," I complained, lying about the hair thing.

"And what's that?" His nose scrunched up. It wasn't attractive. Neither was the possessive boyfriend act.

"Freaking out over nothing," I puffed, starting to get annoyed.

"So, *nothing's* going on?"

"We've had this conversation, Nathan. You're not my boyfriend, you don't get to dictate what I do or who I do it with?"

He didn't like that. He took a step back and shot an agitated look toward the doorway again.

"What the fuck Ella? Is that your way of telling me that you're into my *brother*?" He snapped with a red face, his eyes narrowing dangerously.

I took a step toward him and poked him in the chest, hard. I was at the end of my tether with it all, the guy was starting to make my life a misery.

"I am pointing out that I can do who and what the fuck I want, you are not the boss of me and it's time you accept that."

"And *Ryan* is? When the fuck did *that* happen?"

I puffed out a frustrated breath and ran a hand through my curls.

"I'm not saying that. Stop twisting my words," I responded breathlessly.

So many different expressions were mirrored in his eyes at that point and I knew I had to take myself out of the equation before the situation became any more toxic.

"Go put a shirt on and get out of my face Nathan," I shot out angrily as I moved to start tidying the tools away.

He just stood there, watching me moodily. Like a man-sized mardy fucking baby.

"Either that or *help* me," I pointed out as I lifted the spade.

"Thought you didn't need my help," he replied in a pathetic voice, appearing to have backed down. For all that is Holy.

I paced over to the shed and started putting everything away.

Maybe my working there hadn't been such a good idea.

Nathan did help by gathering up my gardening gloves and passing them to me. That was about it though. Fucking useless piece of shit. He was the laziest person I knew.

"I'm sorry," he suddenly responded in what I would describe as a small voice.

I exhaled noisily. "You seem to put yourself in a position where you have to say that to me a lot."

"I know."

"And you need to stop."

I pulled my phone out, ready to text my father, but Nate held up his hand and stopped me. "I'm going over to see Connor if you want to come?"

My eyes searched his features and I digested his words, I'd seen Connor recently but maybe I could kill two birds and all that. I needed help and at that moment the only person I felt I could talk to was Harlow. I needed a girl's point of view.

I reluctantly accepted Nathan's offer of a lift to Mike's farm.

The whole situation with Nathan and Ryan was so screwed up and I felt like I had no one to turn to. Every decision I made seemed to be the wrong one, like fate was trying to punish me for my actions. That one silly inebriated mistake.

Although we didn't know each other *that* well, I needed a woman's perspective and the only one I trusted enough to help me was Connor's stepsister.

Having changed into black jeans and a dark tee, Nathan came out of the front as I stood waiting by his car. He actually opened my door for me which was odd but I thanked him and climbed in.

As he joined me, I saw him shoot a glance towards Ryan's bedroom window and I followed his gaze as he climbed into the Porsche.

Whilst he reversed the car, my eyes locked onto Ryan who was stood looking out of the window of his bedroom. He had a mug in his hand and was watching the car with a thoughtful expression.

He knew. The hairs on my arms stood to attention.

That look said it all, he knew there had been more between Nate and me and my pulse went off like a rocket.

I was fucked.

After giving myself a silent telling off for possibly overreacting, by the time we reached Two Oaks, I was ready for some serious girl time. I'd removed my baggy dungarees as I had tight jeans on underneath which were at least clean.

Nathan pulled the car up to the house next to Connor's Ranger and I thanked him for the ride and climbed out, leaving him texting on his phone. And yes, he had been texting whilst he was driving, the reckless twat.

I was still hovering in the yard waiting for Nathan to finish messaging when Harlow came out of the front door, looking stunning as usual. She made Victoria's Secret models look less than average.

She automatically assumed I'd come to see Connor but I corrected her. "I came to see *you* actually."

Harlow was surprised, her perfectly shaped eyebrows lifting as she watched me. She explained that she was going for a walk which I immediately jumped on. It would take us away from the house and give me a perfect opportunity to offload. I so needed her opinion on my current situation.

If I dared that was, after seeing her, I started to get nervous about laying myself open.

To break the ice, I went with. "So how is the patient today?"

Harlow winkled her cute nose and I pushed my hands into my pockets to stop them shaking. "Not too bad, although he did injure himself yesterday after going against advice to rest."

Her words came as no shock. Connor preferred being on the go, didn't like too much thinking time. "They're making one of the outbuildings into a gym. I heard several 'F' words and stayed well away."

I grinned as I followed beside her. If there was one other person who gave me a run for my money with bad language, it would be Connor.

"Yes, forever the hothead," I replied. "At least it gives him something to focus on. Connor with too much thinking time is not a good thing."

At my words, Harlow's shoulders drooped and she shot me a sad look. Now what had I said? I was about to question her but she recovered quickly and replied, half to herself. "I just hope he doesn't overdo it."

BOOM! This girl had it bad. From what I had heard about her, Connor should consider himself a lucky guy. She was probably exactly what he needed. A sweet, innocent, pure, nice girl to drag him out of that darkness that shrouded his life.

Harlow led me up a small pathway that I didn't know existed. The girl must have explored the area as she knew exactly where she was going.

Silence enveloped us. All you could hear was a slight breeze rustling the leaves surrounding us and farm vehicles in the distance.

I worried my lip, wondering how to broach the subject as I was so unused to girl talk.

As we walked, I noticed from her body language that Harlow didn't look especially comfortable herself. I thought we'd broken the ice at the club but apparently not. I decided to keep Connor in the conversation as when his name was mentioned, the girl lit up.

"I hear you and Connor are getting along?"

She flicked a glance towards me, replying. "Yes, things are good." What a fucking bland reply. I had hoped she'd give me a bit more than that. It would be the perfect taster to allow me to add my own bit of boy drama in there.

Fuck it. "Just good?" I questioned with a suggestive eyebrow.

Harlow's face darkened. Oh dear, I'd hit a sore nerve and my comment backfired as she shot out. "Stop fishing Ella. As you said yourself, it's complicated,"

I cleared my throat nervously as she blatantly drew the attention back to me. She knew there was something I needed to get off my chest. The fact of this should have made it easier but it didn't. I kicked a stone with my foot, frustration bubbling in my gut.

"That's guys for you, I guess. Fucking unsolvable puzzles, the lot of them," I replied ignoring her tetchy comment.

We turned the corner near a large tree and were met with some of Mike's sheep. Frolicking with their young in the field before us.

I moved to stand by Harlow who had positioned herself at the fence and was staring out at the lambs with a contented expression.

There was a beat of silence before she turned back towards me and then hiding became impossible.

"What about you? You have anything 'complicated' you want to talk about?"

I twisted towards her with a vacant smile. The time to fess up had come.

"Ella?" she questioned again, her eyebrows sky high and the verbal diarrhoea I'd been holding in, erupted like lava.

I told her *everything,* all about the situation between me, Nate, and Ryan, the party, the sex, the bumping into each other in Pickering and sharing the cab.

She made a few strange observations along the way. She'd actually believed the whole pregnancy rumour for some strange reason. She also thought I'd been interested in Connor, which totally grossed me out. The girl had beauty but was obviously not that astute.

Of course, Harlow didn't give me answers to my problems but just being able to offload was a huge relief. She also made me feel less guilty about sleeping with Nate, saying how it was one silly drunken mistake and that these things happen and that I wasn't to overthink it.

The advice she did give was brief. She suggested I tell Ryan about Nate as soon as possible. Especially after the recent animosity between them. Plus, Nathan would probably tell his version of events, with me being the instigator and all that. Which I still wasn't sure I believed. Nope, that certainly left a bad taste in my mouth.

I left there feeling much happier than when I had arrived and knew at that point that I had met a friend in Harlow, even if she was only there temporarily. But who knew right, maybe Connor would convince her to stay?

Fifteen

Over the following week, I worked flat out at Ryan and Nathan's house, wanting to impress their parents and make Ryan see how good I was at my job. Even though he'd said he didn't want me there due to the distraction I'd cause, I had a feeling he still thought the work was too much for me; yes, I was slim, but I was stronger than I looked. The need to prove him wrong drove me on.

I'd thought about what Harlow had advised and was so at the point of taking each boy to one side, but shit just got in the way. Bad weather kicked in which was annoying considering it was still summer, it made a mud bath of one of the flower beds I'd prepared and I almost had to start from scratch.

Ryan and I hadn't been able to see each other much due to his work schedule being borderline slave-driving. If I hadn't been working for his parents, I would probably have gone an entire week without seeing him.

On the days he came back when I was working in the garden, he'd come and see me and we'd chat here and there, but of course strictly no touching. Especially after the hair-touching incident which hadn't gone unnoticed by Nathan.

I'd caught Nate watching us a couple of times with a half-puzzled half annoyed expression, as if he was scrutinising our body language but tried to ignore him. Maybe it was a good thing that he could see Ryan and me getting along. It may soften the blow when the time came to reveal all.

During the moments Nathan spoke to me or brought me some of his mother's homemade lemonade, my heart sank at the fact that he was the wrong brother.

Late one evening, just before it started to get dark, I'd finished all of the weeding of bed one and had planted some beautiful flowers, well bulbs that would eventually *become* flowers. I just had the larger bed to weed and I'd almost finished with the first phase of the project.

I'd felt a sinking feeling at the thought of not working there for a while, as it would take me away from Ryan again.

I did try to ask when I'd see him, but was always shot down with a warning look. I texted him but never got a definite reply. The end of the summer was approaching and that would mean that Ryan would be even busier.

After putting the equipment away in the shed, I wiped my fingers on a rag, my dungarees were well and truly mucky and my cheeks must have been stained with dirt. My face would itch when it came into contact with soil so I knew I'd look a mess.

I walked around the side of the house onto the front and was greeted by both Nathan and Ryan's cars. I smiled at how different the brother's tastes were. Ryan's wheels were black, sleek, and sexy. Whereas, Nathan's car looked like a large glowing bogey.

As I was about to message my dad to say I was ready to be picked up, I heard scuffling and noise, like voices but I wasn't sure.

Thinking it may be Sally, I shuffled around the front of the house towards an alcove which sat in-between the main house and Ryan's annex. The sun was setting, and there was a slight red glow like it was angry almost. I didn't realise that it mirrored what was about to unfurl.

Someone mentioned my name and as I rounded the corner, I recognised Nathan and Ryan's voices. My shoulders scrunched and I pushed my back against the wall to hide. I wasn't ready to show myself just yet; the boys were talking about me and I needed to establish a context. Their voices were slightly raised which I found more than a little worrying, but I still remained concealed for the time being.

Ryan's tone was incredibly firm. "I think you need to accept that she isn't interested in you, not that way. You've been friends for years, so why fuck it up now, obsessing about what it's not."

"How would you fucking know? It's not like we ever talk about shit like this," Nathan shot back in an annoyed voice. Oh, dear.

I held my breath, waiting for Ryan's reply, alarm bells whirring in my head.

Ryan released a bark of laughter; incredulous I would go for. "Why on earth would you suddenly decide to make a move? If it's to get back at me, you can save it, not *everything* has to be a competition, Nathan."

Those words seemed to resonate in the air and the atmosphere became incredibly frigid.

I almost choked on my tongue, how much of this conversation had I missed? Should I break it up or leave them to it, there was just no way of knowing what the best course of action was. Either way, I was starting to panic. They were talking about me in a relationship type of way. This wasn't the way it was supposed to go. I should have got in there first. Shit.

It was eerily quiet before the breeze rustled the bushes next to me, almost drowning out Nathan's next words.

"The way I feel about her has *nothing* to do with you. Our relationship changed last year, not that it's any of your fucking business, but we've done stuff, OK?"

Fuck my life! Nathan was about to blurt out our secret to Ryan. It was over. Nate had gotten to him first, I felt like someone had punched me full-on in the stomach. Adrenalin whooshed inside me like a fucking tornado.

"What are you on about, what *stuff*?" Ryan questioned sharply. I could hear the thread of steel in his voice.

Taking a deep breath, I pushed off the wall and moved around the side of the house. It was time to man up and come clean, to all parties.

The boys stood in a faced-off stance, in touching distance. A shiver of what I interpreted as fear clawed up my spine. The muscles of Ryan's back were bunched together and he twisted at the sound of my footsteps as if he'd sensed me. I could see his face was lined with tension as was Nathan's. It was about to kick off. Damn, testosterone-fuelled idiots!

I cleared my throat and moved towards them. "What's going on?"

Nathan inclined his head as I approached and Ryan glanced at me briefly before he dragged his attention back toward his brother. They hardly even acknowledged me which was rich, considering I was the highlight of their fucking conversation.

I walked over to stand beside them both as they stared each other down. Ryan's eyes bore into Nathan's, it was like I wasn't even there. It was a stand-off, like what boxers did in the ring before the first punch was thrown.

Ferocity blazed between them.

"Guys," I prompted. "What's wrong?"

Nathan cut his gaze from Ryan and turned to look down at me with an unimpressed glower. He then flicked his head towards the other man. "Big brother here's suddenly got the hots for you. Which is about as wrong as you can get, I'd say."

The violence of my emotions created a sick feeling to pool into my stomach.

I shot a wary look between them and said quietly in my best soothing voice. "Right, OK. So what—what do…"

Nathan watched me struggling to form a sentence before he rudely cut in.

"—did you hear what I said? Ry here seems to have an Ella fascination?"

My face must have been riddled with guilt and I failed to pry my tongue from the roof of my mouth. "Nathan, I think we need to talk," I whispered gently.

Nathan's eyes ran over my face, taking in my expression, which at that moment, was anyone's guess as to what it was doing. His eyes narrowed further, a dangerous fire lurking in there.

"Why are you looking at me like that?" he bit out and took a step back, possibly in order to improve his view of me. On impulse, I leaned closer to Ryan, I didn't even realise I was doing it until Nate's curious expression intensified. He watched my body language with all-seeing eyes.

I didn't know how to reply, my mouth hung open and my eyes searched the side of Ryan's face, hoping for some support. Silence thrummed in my ears and it felt like someone's hands were slowly wrapping around my throat, cutting off my voice.

Nathan's mouth was now a thin, tight line and he cast a look between us, realisation hitting him like a physical slap. I felt a chill run down my back and my pulse skittered as anxiety took hold.

"What the fuck is going on?"

"You need to calm down Nate," I advised, my eyes wide.

There is only one way of describing it, Nathan menaced, moving towards me, his hand raised as though he was going to grab my arm, but Ryan slid his body sideways, blocking his path.

Nathan stopped, glancing up at his brother with confusion.

"Don't Nathan," Ryan warned in a cold voice.

Feeling small and insignificant, I stepped to the side so I could still see Nathan and the chaos of emotions that were zooming at one hundred miles per hour around his face.

201

He took a step back and folded his large arms across his chest. "Get the fuck out of my way Ryan, this is between Ella and me," he demanded in a gruff voice, eyeballing his brother grimly.

Ryan shook his head. "You're wrong and you need to back the hell up."

Nathan's grimace became much meatier as he shot back. "I'm wrong, am I? What the hell are you on about?" Nate bit out with a sneer, rolling his shoulders before relinking his arms. His biceps bulged.

He arched a questioning eyebrow, his gaze bouncing between us before he said in a low, deep voice. "I knew it! You *are* you fucking her."

Nathan's words echoed like a gunshot around the alcove as he lowered his arms to his sides. Both men's hands were now curled into fists and their bodies were moulded into a fighting stance.

Ryan cleared his throat and shot me a quick look before turning back to his brother. Dragging a hand down his face, his entire body throbbed with pent-up something, aggression, despair, shock?

"I'm not going to gratify that with a response. Not everything is about sex you fucking child."

Nathan laughed, but there was no humour in it and he sniffed the air as if he could smell something foul.

"Bullshit, I should have trusted my fucking instincts," he bit back before adding. "And as for not everything being about sex big brother. With El and me, that's *exactly* what it was about."

Grooves appeared along Ryan's forehead as he shot a look between me and Nate. Oh God no. My heart continued to pound.

"What are you rambling about?" he questioned rapidly, his brows threaded angrily.

Nathan's mouth curled unpleasantly and he goaded his brother. "Me and Ella, surely she told you we've been sleeping together."

At that moment, I wanted to die.

Nate's tone was purposeful, intended to wound and ridicule. Every blow from the past where Ryan had always come out on top and Nathan the loser was plied into that sentence. The feeling that this wasn't just about me sifted into the chaos that was my thoughts. There was more to this. Years of fucking resentment. The jealousy of one younger guy and his older, much more impressive brother, who just got it right without even having to try.

I knew Ryan was shocked by his brother's revelation, but he masked it quickly and I shot in. "We are *not* sleeping together," I corrected, using my strongest tone. I would certainly set the record straight. God this was awful. Ryan's jaw was clenched. "Stop *lying* Nathan."

"So, you never fucked me?" Nathan roared back in a challenge, his eyes piercing mine.

My forehead was so scrunched up, it was painful. "*Once.* That's it—we did it once when we were both drunk at your party last year. I don't think that counts as us sleeping together," I pointed out in a God-give-me-strength tone. "It was a *mistake* and has *never* been repeated," I shouted, trying to sift out the hysterical element which was raging in my head. "You know that and it's *never* going to happen again."

Nathan scratched his jaw as he turned back to his brother who said nothing, his mask of control now fully back in place.

Ryan just stood there, looking larger than life and expressionless. I so wanted to pull him to the side and tell him the whole story. Force him to understand. Why the hell had I left it so long?

"So, it's never going to happen again, and why not, when you enjoyed it so fucking much?" Nate sneered, disbelievingly, now looking at me like he wanted to throttle me.

"I've told you a thousand times that there is *nothing* between us! You just can't seem to get that into your thick head."

I now didn't give a shit if my words provoked the monster in him, I was sick of him ruining my life.

There was a beat of silence before Ryan drawled out from the side of me in a calm, steady voice which I totally wasn't buying. His huge frame was tense, coiled like a spring and I could see a vein at his temple pulse. "You've slept with Nathan?" He directed the question at me but his gaze remained on his brother.

I turned to him, despair in every part of my being. Praying that he'd look at me. "It was one night Ryan, *before* you and I got together and I've regretted it ever since. I was waiting for the right time to tell you," I replied miserably. The whole thing has been like dealing with my own personal hell. The only slight hint of reprieve had been when I told Connor and confided in Harlow.

"When?"

I sucked in a breath, trying to make sense of Ryan's question. "What do you mean when? When was I going to tell you or when did it happen?"

"When did you fuck my brother Ella?" His voice was almost sinister, his jaw clenching. He still didn't look at me, which made it feel so much worse. Was I being dismissed? I felt like a cast-off.

Needing to be strong, I told myself that it wasn't my fault. Shit happens and I replied. "I told you, it was way before anything happened with us. In the past."

Nathan came back to life then and suddenly appeared much larger, he turned to blast at me.

"So, you and Ryan? You've been seeing each other behind my fucking back all this time?" he bit out, looking back and forth between us.

"No, it wasn't *like* that," I was almost begging him to listen to reason, this was so unfixable.

Ryan was silent again. His hooded gaze still directed at this brother. I could see he was struggling to control himself. That tell-tale muscle in his jaw started to tick again.

Nathan's voice suddenly increased in volume as he boomed.

"Really, then what was it like Ella?" Possessive aggression poured from him in waves.

Ryan suddenly exhaled noisily, his nostrils flaring as he came to life and shot out at Nate.

"I suggest you leave the grown-ups to talk Nathan and fuck off."

Nathan didn't like that and I was invisible again. It was just the two of them and they shifted on their feet, almost mirroring each other's movements. We were back to those squaring-up manoeuvres. The boxers in the ring scenario. Christ.

"You're the one who needs to fuck off, making a move on my girlfriend behind my back, some brother you are!" the younger guy shouted, as they slowly startled to circle each other. The guy was fucking delusional.

The evening was getting darker around us, making the situation feel more sinister and dangerous. How I wished their parents would come home, and put a stop to the madness.

Nate was angry but Ryan was now *furious*. I had never seen him this mad, I was used to his cold calmness most of the time. His fists were clenched and his chest started heaving.

"Please, stop. Both of you. This is insane. Nathan, you know you're not my boyfriend. Please don't make this any worse than it already is. Ryan, please?"

I just wished the situation would dissolve immediately, either that or I could wind back time and just confess the shit I had done to Ryan *before* it got to this. As Harlow said, I could have played it down. Nathan was blowing the whole thing out of proportion for his own selfish purposes and at the same time wrecking what I could have had with Ryan. I felt like screaming into the sky.

The bodies of both brothers were tight with tension.

As I eyed Nathan warily, I was furious that he could do this to me after saying he accepted us as just friends and everything that had happened over the past few weeks. But as I said, it wasn't just about me. This was about one up-man ship and the younger brother trying to come out on top for a change. A proper big dick contest between two grown men. I knew this was harder for Nathan, he had probably been jealous of Ryan his entire life.

Watching their movements, the boys were about to dance and I don't mean the fun kind. The nasty type where contact will be made and where there would be no going back.

I reattempted to force Nathan to admit his lie. "Tell, Ryan you're not my boyfriend Nate, have never been. Tell him the truth."

He shook his head, throwing me a fleeting look. So not ready to play ball. "It makes no difference, boyfriend or not, I know what you fucking taste like," Nathan sneered toward his brother in a goading voice.

A red mist rose up between them. Ryan made no allowances for the fact that Nathan was shorter and the gloves were off. One strong hand shot out, grabbing Nathan by the throat, squeezing, shoving him a few steps back against the rough stone surface of the side of their house. Nate's hands clawed at his brother's arm to escape but it was futile. The breath had whooshed from his body as his back impacted the stone.

My lips must have been clamped together in horror and so I had no idea where the scream came from. My head felt like someone had poured anti-freeze in there and I shot forward, my hand on Ryan's shoulder, shaking it, pleading with him to let go. Nathan was slowly turning blue and looked like he could pass out at any minute.

"Ryan, please let him go," I begged and he shot me a sideways glance, his eyes vacant like he didn't recognise me. A jet of helpless pain shot through me. Now I knew what Ryan meant when he'd spoken about control and how everyone had their breaking point.

After a few more seconds, Ryan's vision seemed to focus and he stepped back, and dropped his brother who fell to his knees choking and clutching his throat for air.

Ryan's body was tight with tension and after a brief glance down at Nate's crumpled body, he turned away, looking down at me with questioning eyes full of anguish and pain. Negative emotions that I had put there.

Then the real bomb exploded. The next developments appeared to happen in slow motion. Ryan had his back to Nathan and he was staring down at me, his mouth parted, almost as if he intended to speak. I could see a blurry, swaying Nate behind him as he slowly pushed to his feet. He then addressed his bother in a low assertive voice. "That's it, turn your back on me like the pussy you are."

Ryan's face contorted and he spun around and slammed his fist into his brother's face, catching him directly on the jaw. The younger guy fell back against the house, briefly dazed before he drew himself back up, spat some blood on the floor, and hurled his weight at his brother, his shoulders hitting Ryan in the stomach in a rugby-type of tackle. I lunged backward to safety, to stop myself from being knocked to the floor.

They pushed against each other backward and forwards for a minute, before Ryan shoved his brother off him and Nate fell back a step.

Nathan slowly lifted his hand to touch his mouth, his fingers coming away smeared with blood. He glanced away with disgust before redirecting a look of pure hatred at the man who had delivered the damage.

The wound on Nathan's mouth where Ryan had hit him started to bleed, but the damage caused by that first contact was minor, suggesting that the older and much bigger man must have pulled his punch. I noticed a section of Nathan's face slowly turning red.

Unfortunately, what was vocalised next made the situation even worse. "Just one more thing *brother*. When you get between her legs, remember I was there first," Nathan spat out between battered lips.

The second punch hit its intended target full force, and the sound of bone contacting bone reverberated as Ryan's fist smashed into his brothers' nose.

All hell then broke loose as the two men went at each other like snarling animals. A full-on fight erupted, with wrestling, grabbing of tops, shoving, punches flying, ribs being hit, some blows connecting, others hitting the air. At one point both men fell to the floor and rolled around on top of each other, both struggling for supremacy. Grunts, swearing, crunching and thudding erupted and my yells sounded like they were coming from a mile away. Under any other circumstances it would have been comical, the fight wasn't like those you see in the movies, where it is pretty much choreographed; this was real and raw. This was behaviour like I had never experienced and could never have imagined. It made that ruckus with Moses Wallis look so tame in comparison, even the elbow in the face.

With shaking hands, I found my phone and searched for Connor's number. He was the only one who could break this up before they killed each other. I had never felt so helpless. There was no way I could come between them physically or I'd end up with more than an elbow.

Connor's phone was ringing out, and I prayed he'd pick up. I turned briefly back toward the two men who were still going hell-for-leather on the ground, before Nathan wobbled to his feet and aimed a kick at his brother's ribs.

Ryan rolled over and uncurled his large body, coming to his feet again, towering over his brother.

"You fight like a bitch," Ryan spat, with a sneer. His face was fairly free of damage, whereas Nate looked like he'd gone a round with Tyson.

I turned away again, not being able to properly process what I was seeing. Anxiety at the situation was pumping thought every vein under my skin.

"Ella?" Connor's voice suddenly rang out in my ear and I shot down the phone in a semi-hysterical voice. I can't imagine I made much sense.

"Calm down, what's wrong? Where are you?" he put in quickly, his voice raised.

I took a breath and tried to explain again but he got it. His reply was what I wanted to hear, I just hoped he got there quickly. I was petrified the guys would kill each other.

The words were stuck in my throat but I managed to choke out. "I'm at Nathan's, they're fighting. They know."

"I'm with Noah, we're on our way."

He ended the call and I turned toward the two brawling men who were once again circling each other, trading insults. Like twenty odd years of shit left unsaid was now being aired. This wasn't just about me. Realisation dawned on me that there really was unfinished business between these two. I'd never really noticed much of an atmosphere between them. Maybe from Nate towards Ryan but not the other way around.

As they appeared to be at a temporary impasse, I pleaded with them, moving a step closer. "Please both of you stop, Connor is coming. Please enough now," I almost cried out. The tears of shock at the situation and how violent it felt was like acid running down my face, but I welcomed the sting. I deserved it.

This was my fault. I was responsible for breaking up this family. How would they ever recover from this? Ryan's face was also starting to swell but he looked much healthier than Nathan, whose right eye, the one with the scar was almost swollen shut.

Both men ignored me and Nathan carried on with his annoying provocative comments as they circled each other again. Ryan's shirt was ripped.

"So, you haven't had a chance to see her naked yet? It's pretty fucking amazing," Nathan sneered again as they watched each other through dark hooded expressions. His words were pure filth, there was now no off button, no filter. The only thing that would stop Nathan from saying things so extreme they could never be taken back, would be for Ryan to knock him out cold.

I shook off the thought. "Ryan, ignore him. He's winding you up on purpose. He knows exactly what buttons to press," I bit out, moving even closer toward them, though ensuring I was a safe enough distance in case it kicked off again. God only knew it could at any minute.

"You heard that Ry, those are Ella's words. I know what buttons to press," he mocked, still wearing that sneer. His suggestive tone must have pushed Ryan over the edge. The older man had had, enough.

Ryan surged forward again, aiming his shoulder at Nathan's stomach and knocking him to the ground.

Nathan landed on his back, with Ryan pretty much straddling him, and raining punches into his fallen brother's face.

Stop, he needed to stop, Nathan's nose was bloodied and I guessed it may be broken. I thought I was going to vomit. I moved to Ryan, hitting his back with the palm of my hand, and begging him to stop.

Ryan seemed to come to his senses and he stopped, drawing back but remaining on his knees. He was breathing heavily.

Suddenly everything went so fast, I felt like I was on one of those spinning rides at a theme park.

The noise of Connor's car crashed into my ears and both he and Noah appeared, both grabbing one of Ryan's arms and dragging him back off Nathan, physically restraining him, telling him to 'cool it' and to 'calm the fuck down'. Casting a glance between the two battered men, I moved to the one who needed me most, Nathan. He was still on the floor and he wasn't moving, his hands were over his face, in a shielding position.

I ran my fingers up Nathan's chest, moving his hands away to inspect the damage. I needed him to be OK.

He coughed and his good eye opened. Defeat lined his face, Defeat and something else. Peace, relief almost, it was an odd combination.

"I'm sorry," he whispered through a blood bubble and my heart tore into two. I was totally to blame for this nightmare.

After seeing he was OK, just mashed up a bit, I pushed to my knees and turned to see Ryan behind me. He was still being held by the arms by Noah and Connor although he'd calmed down. He looked almost glassy-eyed, like he was looking through me.

His eyes narrowed as he took in my position beside his battered brother and he shrugged out of Connor and Noah's grasp, raising his hands to say he was good.

Ryan dragged the back of his hand across his mouth. There was a fire still ranging in him, he looked wild and savage.

I stood on wobbling legs and moved toward him, but he took a step away from me and shook his head. One hand held out flat, warding me off. My face creased at his reaction.

Ryan had a bruise on the side of his face and I so wanted to soothe it, kiss it away.

His next words tore me apart.

He looked between his brother and me, before saying in a low, harsh voice. "You've made your choice." The sharpness of his voice sliced straight to the bone.

My mouth dropped open and I furiously shook my head, desperate to explain, to scream and say he'd got the wrong impression.

As I made another move toward him, he shoved away, shooting me a look of contempt, brushing past me and striding over to his car. Should he even be driving in that state? Could he even, see?

I was numb, my legs like jelly as I attempted to go after him, but he had already started his car and it growled to life almost angrily. A hot ball of stress burned in my chest.

Ryan set off out of the yard spraying pebbles, the car speeding towards the gates and I ran after him, screaming his name.

He only just cleared the gate post and despair exploded in my chest.

I had lost him. Lost the man I now knew with absolute certainty that I was in love with.

A hand on my shoulder made me jump as Connor noted from behind me, "He needs time to cool off Ella. You all do."

I weakly nodded my head, knowing he was right.

"Give me a minute to get Nate inside and I'll drive you home."

My arms came up to automatically rub at the gooseflesh created by the sudden chill in the air and I felt the most miserable I have ever in my entire life.

My past mistakes swirled around my head like a Tsunami.

Almost sinking to the ground, Connor helped me over to one of the benches which sat in front of the house. My face must have been marked by tears of despair and I suddenly felt grubby. I wanted to disappear, and fold myself up small so that no one would ever see me.

I sat and Connor pushed my head down between my knees and told me to stay put. My limbs had well and truly stopped working and my body went exactly where he wanted it to go.

I was dazed. As Noah and Connor helped Nathan into the house, our eyes met briefly. I knew he was sorry as guilt and pain were etched into every bruise on his face.

I didn't smile, didn't say anything, I felt numb. I just looked back at him feeling nothing. Owing him nothing.

The hiding was over, but at what cost?

The next question; was there a chance of recovery and by this I didn't mean of the body, I meant of the mind.

At that point, misery started to spread through my body like a virus. I couldn't process any coherent thought apart from...

Fuck my life.

Sixteen

The farce was over, but I didn't feel any joy or relief.

The journey over to mine in the car was a blur, Connor and Noah dropped me home and I went into my house like I was sleepwalking; bitterness and regret thumping through me.

It was late and everyone appeared to be in different areas of the house. Thankfully, I managed to get to my room without any unwelcome questions. I must have looked a state; my eyes were stinging and my face, gritty as hell.

I sat in the bath and also put the shower on, welcoming the water pounding down on me for a good half hour, until my fingers started to prune. I'd purposefully doubled up on my method of bathing, desperate to remove that *nasty* feeling off my skin.

The sense of gloom I felt radiated around the bathroom. I hadn't even put the light on and had sat there, surrounded by lukewarm water in part darkness.

After climbing into bed, without thinking twice, I'd texted Ryan, *desperate* to know where he was and that he was OK. I didn't try to call him as I feared my throat would close up and there'd be no sound.

During that first hour in bed, I was restless; the events of the night replaying in my head like a horror movie, and I cradled my phone to my chest, as if it were a lifeline to Ryan. I needed his drugging warmth. Deep down I *knew* he wouldn't reply.

'You've made your choice.' The impact of that statement had been like taking a bullet and had hit me hard. A strange breathlessness had caught my chest.

At one point during the night, I went to the window and looked out, hoping I'd see his car there, but of course there was *nothing*, just an empty road; cruelling reflecting the way I was feeling. I left my curtains open on purpose, allowing the moonlight to highlight sections of my bedroom.

Nathan's jacket was still draped over the chair and part of me wanted to put it on, sleep in it, feel it against my skin.

Just after midnight, I listened to an old voicemail from Ryan, drinking in the sound of his voice like a proper sad case. My attempt to steer away from pathetic behaviour being an epic fail.

Clenching my eyes, I eventually fell asleep and had dreams of several types of scenarios during what was probably the worst night ever.

Around a week went by and I heard *nothing* from Ryan. He could have put his car in a ditch for all I knew. I spent most of the time in our garden or my bedroom and kept myself to myself. My parents knew something was off but they didn't ask me outright about it.

I had spoken to Tom briefly. He had heard about the fight and he was supportive, saying he was there if I needed to talk. I appreciated the gesture, but he was probably the *last* person I wanted to talk to. Sister and brother relationships were hardly ever straightforward, especially ours, considering the unbalanced way our parents treated us both. My brother was also super-hyped about the new girl at the surgery. He was so quick to jump from one girl to the next and that fickleness started to grate on my nerves.

My level of tolerance was at an all-time low and I was a firm believer in the 'if you can't say anything nice, don't say anything at all' quote. I, therefore, kept my distance from everyone.

Connor messaged me a couple of times, but he wasn't at his best. Harlow had gone back to London, and he was struggling. He didn't ask for help of course, Connor being Connor.

I hadn't heard anything from Natalie but Connor explained that Noah mentioned something about her being in Spain with a new guy (I imagined this would be Mark from the club, but she never messaged me about it).

There had been no contact from Nate. Although I'd thought about it, I hadn't been able to bring myself to message him either, my emotions toward him were so mixed, switching from anger to understanding and then finally, guilt. It was majorly messed up.

Eventually that constant anxious feeling and the nervous knots in my stomach unravelled, and I was left with a hollowness. I embraced the emptiness, as 'feeling nothing' was easier to cope with.

The weather over the weekend had been forecast as sunny and I still had to complete the first phase of the gardening project at Mr. and Mrs. Lane's house.

I didn't want to go, of course not. I didn't feel ready yet, but I knew the rules about being professional and sticking to your deadlines.

When my dad dropped me off at their estate, I could still smell sweat, blood and despair as I walked up the drive way. Apart from a few scuff marks in the grass, you would never have known what had happened in that alcove.

My nerves were doing crazing things to my insides and I knocked on the door with my heart in my throat, not really knowing how to behave. Would Nate and Ryan's parents know that I was partly the reason for their fight? Would the boys have made up or would they still be at daggers drawn? Maybe Ryan hadn't been back to the house at all. I was clueless.

If I was asked anything about it, I decided being honest was the best course of action.

As Sally answered the door, she smiled and immediately put my mind at rest. Maybe she didn't know it had anything to do with me? Her expression suggested that she didn't.

She opened the door wide and invited me in and I smiled shyly and lumbered through the hallway, still feeling awkward. Sally followed me into the kitchen, her expression now fairly bland.

"Have you come to carry on the work or to visit the wounded?" she questioned in an even voice.

I knew I needed to see Nathan and check he was OK, but was I ready to do that there and then? I was still so angry with him.

Deciding to bite the bullet I replied, "The wounded first and then I'll carry on weeding if that's OK?"

Sally's nodded with a smile and motioned for me to head up the stairs to Nathan's room. If she knew anything, she didn't let on.

Before she walked away, I asked her in a quiet voice.

"Have you seen Ryan?"

She turned back and looked down at me with a creased brow. "No, he's gone away for a few days, to calm down. You know how the boys get when they've had a fall out," she put in.

My mouth almost dropped open in shock, she talked about it as if it wasn't a big deal. Her comment also suggested that Nathan and Ryan had fought before. Like it was a usual occurrence. I had never heard anything like that before.

Neither brother had ever said their relationship had come to blows. Yes, there was that weird atmosphere between them but I'd put that down to the usual sibling rivalry, like what Tom and I had.

"So they've done this before, you know, the physical stuff?" I questioned before I could stop myself, jamming my hands into the pockets of my dungarees.

Sally dashed a hand through her hair, her clear eyes, bright and honest.

"Yes, *unfortunately*. Not often—but they're brothers, there has always been that competition thing between them. When they were teenagers, they used to fight all the time. They're both hot heads, although Ryan controls his temper much better than Nathan does. We always put it down to an age thing."

I took a step toward her, feeling a slither of reassurance wash through me. So they had fought in the past. This gave me hope, maybe I hadn't ruined their relationship irreparably.

"Boys will be boys," Sally grinned.

I wasn't sure whether to feel pleased or disgusted by this revelation. Surely a fight which resulted in physical damage, shouldn't be batted off as a 'boys will be boy's' scenario. I decided to take myself away from her, not sure I agreed with that logic.

My heart now felt like a boulder in my throat as I made my way to Nathan's bedroom, the same room where I had shared his bed. I still felt so ashamed.

I fanned my hair to ensure it didn't appear too wild and knocked on Nathan's door.

After a moment or two he called me in and I pushed the door open and slid inside.

The room was dark, but the TV was on. I ignored the boy smell.

Nathan was sat in his gaming chair in the middle of a video game. He threw the gaming controller onto the bed before spinning in the chair, giving me his full attention. His face was still a mess but the swelling had gone down.

His expression was fairly unreadable apart from a hint of surprise.

215

Neither of us spoke, we just stared at each other.

His mouth curled in a half smile and mine did something similar. The ice most definitely needed breaking and at the point, I wasn't sure how to go about doing that.

I turned away, gathering my thoughts and pushed his door closed before twisting back. Nathan rocked back in the chair, viewing me through half squinted eyes.

I pulled out his wheeled office chair which was slotted under his computer desk, and lowered myself into the leather, bringing us both to a similar level. We watched each other from across the room. It was a fairly small bedroom, considering how wealthy the family were and how many bedrooms the house actually had.

Clearing my throat which felt like the bloody desert, I offered him my peace-keeper face before saying. "How are you?"

He cocked his head as his eyes ran over my face. "I don't know, how do I look? Fuck-ugly I imagine?"

I snorted. "Well you don't look your best," I replied in a calm voice. Now I was actually in his company, some of the apprehension I'd felt at the thought of seeing him started to drain away.

Nathan gave me a slight smile and shrugged before saying in a quiet voice. "I'm surprised you're here to be honest." His teeth clicked.

I pursed my lips, dipping my eyes and nodded my understanding.

"I know and I'm sorry it came to this. I should have mentioned something sooner, about Ryan I mean."

An unreadable expression flittered across his features but he remained silent, watching me. I took this as a signal that I should try and explain. "The thing with Ryan, was just one of those things. It started off slowly and just seemed to snow ball."

Nathan inhaled and blinked rapidly before saying. "I so *don't* want to talk about Ryan right now."

I chewed the inside of my lip, totally understanding that, but surely, we couldn't ignore what was actually a major factor in this drama?

"I get that, but I think it's only fair if you know everything."

Nate rubbed the back of his neck, obviously uncomfortable. "I don't *want* to know *everything*," he snapped, before reining himself back in.

There was a beat of silence before he released a whistle of air through his teeth. "Look, I'm coming to terms with it, but it isn't easy. Just thinking about the two of you, is... Let's just talk about us."

He must have seen the swell of horror on my face before he cut in again, "And I don't mean 'us' like that, so you can stop shitting yourself. I mean our friendship. If there is one now that is."

To be honest, I was amazed at how well I was holding out this particular olive branch. The guy had behaved *atrociously*, to the point where he'd probably have to spend the rest of his life apologising to me, but I couldn't help but feel sorry for him. He looked horrendous and from his expression, he appeared to be feeling sorry enough for the both of us.

The heavy thumping in my heart must surely be visible through my top.

I opened my mouth to continue, but he moved a hand from his neck to ward off what I was going to say.

"Stop Ella. Give *me* a chance to explain. As usual. I'm the one who fucked up."

His face was screwed up like he felt physical pain and my eyes widened as he dashed a hand through his hair before saying, "I had no right saying those things to you, *or* Ryan. Though as I said, I don't want to talk about him just now, not yet."

Once again, I almost swallowed my tongue. Nathan Lane was apologising.

"What I will say is that... from that day when I saw you and Ryan in the garden, I *knew* something was going on. It was the body language and the way you looked at him. You've *never* looked at me that way."

Nathan's eyes were searching my face, as if hoping to behold my expression when I'd looked at Ryan that day.

He closed his eyes for a moment and took a deep breath before opening them and pinning me with a hard, resentful stare.

"I just saw red."

I frowned. "Why didn't you ask me about it? If we'd talked about it, it may have stopped this from ever happening."

"I get that, but you didn't say anything either," he pointed out.

"I know. I just didn't know how to break it to you, you were so determined that something was happening between us."

I paused, deep in my thoughts. "I should have told you," I said quietly.

He flexed his shoulders with a grimace and shook his head. "No, I get why you didn't. I've behaved like a possessive freak ever since you got back. Even I would have been worried about speaking to me. I've been a dick and it's taken an arse-kicking from my fucking brother to put things into perspective, and not just about you. About myself too."

I welcomed his words. It appeared that he accepted that the angst inside him was not all about me.

"That message I got from you about us needing to talk, the night Connor got attacked. I think that's when I knew it wasn't going to go anywhere, with us I mean. Everything was turning to crap and I knew I had to get my shit together. My parents were getting pissed off about the weird atmosphere between me and Ryan and so we'd agreed to meet at the pub, you know, to talk about stuff. Deal with our shit, but the *fucking* quiz was on and Harlow and Tom were there so we didn't have the chance to clear the air. I just knew something was off but I wasn't sure what it was. When I saw you together at the house it just really pissed me off," he confessed in a strained voice.

My brows threaded. "Then what happened?"

"You know the rest. The night of the fight, *before* you showed up, Ryan was in a foul mood and balled me out for the way I'd behaved in front of you. I just felt sick of him telling me off all the time, like he's our fucking dad and then the argument got even *more* personal."

I pursed my lips and folded my arms, watching him with renewed interest. Nathan Lane was actually offloading. Something he should have done years ago from the sound of things.

"So, *have* you heard from Ryan?"

He shook his head. "No, and I don't expect to for a while. He always takes himself off and out of the way when shit like this happens."

"So, you've had fights before?"

"Of course, although not so much over the last few years. When we were younger, they'd get *really* ugly. Our parents always thought it was the age difference. Him being older than me, but not by enough to not stop us from rubbing each other up the wrong way. Ryan likes to give orders and I have an issue with authority. It's a fucked up combination really."

"So it wasn't *just* about me then?" I put in hopefully, the puzzle coming together.

"No. Not all of it I suppose, I think I just used you as a catalyst to provoke him. Over the last two years Ryan has become exceptionally good at controlling his emotions. It used to annoy me, as it's like *he's* the grown up, calm and controlled and I'm the fucking wayward kid."

"I do kind of know how that feels like Nathan," I said, my relationship with my own brother, a perfect example.

"How would you know what *that* feels like?" Nathan was genuinely puzzled.

"Next to Tom. The soon to be Vet, I feel like a constant failure, so the kid from your example," I pointed out, unfolding my arms and resting my hands on my thighs.

Nate shrugged his large shoulders, not buying it. "So, what, he's smart. But there's nothing special about him; he's about as interesting as a turd."

I smiled. "Not to my parents. They worship the ground he walks on and I don't get a look in."

He really had no clue. But of course, he didn't, he spent most of our past conversations talking about himself and not seeing what was going on around him.

His voice dipped. "I'm sorry, I had no idea. You always seem so much more confident when you're around him."

"Nope. It's a front. Just like the one you put on Nathan. I use laughter and confidence to hide my insecurity and you use rage."

I now didn't care that I was baring my soul to this boy. He was doing the same. Isn't that what true friends do?

"Honestly, you'd never know. If anything, you would think you're the one on top with Tom in the shadows, not the other way around."

"What can I say? I'm a great actress."

He grinned and looked like a cheeky little boy suddenly. "Sounds like we both are."

I smiled back and raised a brow, "What, you're a great actress too?"

He rolled his eyes, "You know what I mean."

"So, Ryan then?" I prompted, refusing to be side-tracked.

"Look, I meant what I said. I don't want to talk about Ryan. Not to you. I can see you have feelings for him and that's your choice. I know we're not together, not really. In fact, not at all," Nathan revealed, his eyes now quite watchful on my face. "You do what you need to do. It's not my business really. But I can't be the friend you talk about it to."

The colour suddenly seemed to fade from his face, his cheeks sallow. Like he'd just thought of something that made him feel ill.

"I'm sorry about what I said to Ryan, about us sleeping together."

I leaned back in my seat, casting him an arched brow.

"Yes, our night of sin which I instigated," I puffed out with a slightly embarrassed look.

His expression became even more serious and he swallowed; his Adam's apple bobbing with the movement.

Nate released what I would call a sigh and part groan of frustration. An interesting combination and my hackles rose slightly.

"What?" I questioned, unsure why the sudden change in atmosphere. Had I given him the memory of what could never be? I mentally kicked myself.

Nathan jammed a hand through his mussed hair again, before leaning forward in the gaming chair.

He gave me a pointed look, the type that penetrated deep into your bones. Our eyes were tangled and my forehead scrunched up in question. What the heck was he going to say now? The boy was still totally unpredictable. If he started to go into details of 'that night' I'd die from embarrassment.

His next words weren't a total shock, at first.

"I lied Ella."

My tongue licked against my teeth as I absorbed this information before saying, "About what?" I had an idea of what he was going to say. At least I thought I did. He was going to fess up that *he* was the one who came on to me that night, not the other way around. I knew it would have been way too out of character, I was such an insecure person, even plastered.

He shoved back in his seat, looking thoroughly uncomfortable.

I tried to put him out of his misery. "I know Nate. I was a virgin, totally inexperienced. I knew I wouldn't have made the first move. You seduced me, not the other way around."

I swallowed, still hoping he didn't go into detail.

Nathan's expression plummeted further.

Now what?

I gritted my teeth. "Nate, what they hell is up with you? I've never known you to be tongue tied. It doesn't matter now, it's in the past."

"That's just it Ella, it's *not* in the past. It *never* happened."

My head started to swim with confused thoughts, past and present as Nathan pushed to his feet.

I watched as he started to pace like a caged animal before stopping in front of me and squatting down so our eyes were almost level. He placed a hand on one of mine which was folded in my lap.

I wrinkled my nose, not comprehending his words or maybe it was my brain refusing to. "What do you mean?" My voice was grave. It was then like being hit in the face with a sledgehammer.

"We *never* slept together. Well, we slept, but we didn't have sex. You're *still* a virgin Ella. "

And BOOM! The bombshell exploded and it was so intense that actual pain shot through my temple.

A thousand questions all jumped all over each other in the race to put themselves out there. *What the actual fuck!?*

I shot to my feet and he almost fell over, my eyes narrowed into slits as he uncurled himself to stand again. Nathan regained his balance and then moved back a step, giving me more space.

My breath felt like it was clogged in my chest and I released a heavy breath, not able to comprehend his words.

Searching his expression in confusion, it then hit me that I'd known. Somewhere deep, down inside of me I think I'd always known.

Guilt doesn't even come close to describe the emotion etched into every line on Nathan's face, each one highlighted by the bruising.

"Just repeat what you've just said?" I spat; my tone harsh but guarded. Curiosity morphed into desperation.

Nathan Lane had lied to me. He was a liar. We'd *never* had sex.

All those months of guilt, all the madness and worry it caused me. The brakes it had put on things with Ryan and me. The list was fucking endless.

"Say it," I almost screamed, my eyes wide. His shoulders slumped and he pushed his hands into the pockets of his jogging bottoms.

"We never had sex that night, I made it up," his voice was low and dripping with regret.

I felt like he had suddenly injected me with a drug, part dizzy, part enraged. I stamped out the weaker feeling and went for the throat.

"What the hell Nate? *How could you fucking lie about something like that?* And what about how we woke up, I was fucking naked, and yet what, we did *nothing*?"

His own voice raised to match mine but his was full of regret. My voice was full on tiger time.

"I made the whole fucking thing up and I can't tell you how much I regret it now. It started off as just a joke, something to wind you up, I was going to come clean a day or two after, but then the joke went too far and I couldn't take it back. And I'd started to like you. I know it's stupid, but I thought if you believed we'd been intimate you might see me differently. As more than a fucking friend."

I took every word in but it sounded like his explanation was coming from miles away. He was now rambling and I'd lost my ability to speak. I hung on everything, like each word could be added as evidence on this trial for the death sentence.

"I'm sorry. I became obsessed with it, with you, us."

I shook my head whilst pacing, totally not agreeing with what he was saying. "I was always straight with you about there being no us Nathan!"

"I know that now and I fucked up. What do you want me to say?"

I stopped and turned back to him. "You did more than that. And what about the naked thing? You *must* have undressed me or something?"

His head dipped and he sighed, "You undressed yourself Ella, you wanted to go skinny dipping in our pool, but you pretty much passed out on the bed."

"And you what, did *nothing* to me?" I bit out, tears now threatening to bust from my eyeballs.

"Of course not! For fucks sake, I'm not a *fucking* rapist. I didn't touch you. I would *never* have touched you, even if you hadn't passed out. You were smashed out of your head and not in your right mind. You were also at your most vulnerable I remember. I may be a prick in every other way of life, but I wouldn't force myself on someone who couldn't say yes or no. *Especially not you. I love you dammit*! You were one of my friends, my *best* friend. Someone I wanted to be closer to."

Full on meltdown mode was approaching like a race car.

"I can't believe this. Do you know how I've felt over the last year Nathan, do you have any clue? I felt like a failure, a slut. Guilty for *ruining* our friendship. Hating myself for what we had done."

His expression became pained and knowing. "I know and if I could take it back I would. I'm sorry Ella, I truly am."

I dashed a shaking hand through my hair, shooting him a glare. I didn't point out about what damage he had done to my chances with Ryan, my throat felt too dry at that stage.

There was a weird silence as Nathan took a step toward me, his arms by his sides. I could see from his body language that he was uncertain what to do.

He moved closer and I held up a hand to ward him off, turning my back on him, unable to look him in the eye.

"It fucking kills me to say this but you can tell Ryan the truth now. Tell him it was all a lie."

My hands were balled into fists, I was terrified of lashing out. The guy was already black and blue. I didn't welcome his suggestion about Ryan on iota.

There was another moment's pause before he said, in a small voice. "Or, I can tell him. Come clean, say how I messed up. Tell me what you want me to

223

do and I'll do it Ella. To see you guys together will be hard, but I'll deal with it. If you really do care about him."

That numbness that had been smashed away after his revelation of the fucking century started to bleed back in. "Why would he believe either of us," I said slowly, my voice only just above a whisper.

"I can speak to him, say I lied to spite him. I've done it before. He'll probably kill me though, finish the job. But I'd do it, do it for you."

I massaged a temple with my finger, feeling the tell-tale sign of a headache before turning and pinning him with a stare.

"No, I don't want you doing me any more favours Nathan. Stay out of my business and in fact, stay out of my life," and with these words I slammed out of his room, almost knocking Sally over in the hallway. She was carrying laundry.

"Oh, are you ready to start on the garden?" Sally questioned in a part surprised voice.

"No, I quit."

And with those parting words, I took the stairs two at a time and started the long walk back home. A mountain of angry emotion building inside me.

It was Monday morning and I was sat in my room feeling thoroughly sorry for myself. Tom knocked and asked if dad had spoken to me about filling in at the surgery and I said I'd already agreed to help. I hated the idea of working indoors, but there was no way I was in the zone for gardening. My body ached and I wasn't sleeping. I felt emotionally exhausted and physically drained.

Everyone at home continued to give me a wide berth, which suited me fine. Connor tried to call me a couple of times, but I didn't accept the call. I just needed space from *everyone*. Tom attempted to corner me in my room, but I told him to piss off, in a not-so-nice way. I was suffering and the mean Ella roared like a beast inside me.

Dad dropped me off at the surgery, giving me a quick reminder of how the phones worked before heading off on his rounds. There were only two appointments in the diary and they were due during the afternoon, which at least gave me *some* time to find my feet.

The next day was a long day with loads of animals being brought into the surgery. Mainly dogs by random people; strays that had been found by the side of the road.

There were also several calls-out to farms around the village and so it was quite busy.

I wasn't as bored shitless as I thought I'd be as I stood on receptionist. At least it took my mind off my troubles.

After a full-on day on my feet, I checked my phone for what felt like the one-hundredth time. Still no reply from Ryan. It was only as I was about to lock up at the end of that day, that he appeared. My heart swelled in my chest. Thank God, at last.

His expression was deeply troubled but he looked amazing, the slight bruising on his face giving him a dangerous edge. I turned the key of the surgery and pulled the door open to allow him in, my face alive as I moved toward him. He shot me down by warding me off with one hand.

He wore a black jumper that had seen better days and black jeans, his expression was dark and I could only pray that hadn't come to fight. I was desperate to save things, move on in some way and of course, I still had the matter of Nathan's lie to deal with. Did I tell him so we could move on? Part of me didn't feel that I should have to. It happened, or should I say, 'didn't happen' in the past.

My breath whooshed out in a hot wave of relief. To be honest at that point, I was just happy he was there, although how he knew I'd been covering at the surgery was anyone's guess. I decided to use this question as an ice breaker.

"How did you know where I was?"

He turned and pushed the doors closed behind him. "Tom said that you'd been covering on reception when I called over to your house."

I smiled thinly. "You did, that's gutsy."

He leaned back on the door and folded his arms over his chest, looking down at me with a guarded stare. "To be fair your mother was fine, not a shotgun in sight."

There was a beat of awkward silence between us.

"I guess she doesn't need one now," I put in quietly, testing the water. Worrying that he was there to officially end things.

He ignored my words.

"So, how's it been, working here? Looks like you've been busy."

I ignored him and went straight in for the kill.

"Why have you been ignoring my texts?" I accused with a raised brow.

Unfolding his arms, he dashed a hand across the rough stubble of his jaw, he hadn't shaved in days. It made him appear more virile. His eyes were locked to mine. "I didn't want to answer them in the wrong frame of mind and say something I couldn't take back." His excuse didn't matter, his rejection still hurt in the corner of my heart.

I forced myself to take a slow, calming breath.

"I see, and now you feel able to look me in the face, after everything you know."

He exhaled, his nostrils flaring. I so didn't like the strained feeling between us.

Ryan tilted his head as his eyes probed mine. "I wouldn't have had a problem looking you in the face before Ella. You've done nothing wrong—not really. But it is complicated isn't it. Not the norm."

I wasn't sure how I should feel. Did he mean it or was he setting me up for a fall? I felt so out of my element and struggled with my reply.

"I agree with it not being the norm but I don't agree with the doing nothing wrong comment, I messed everything up?" I part whispered miserably.

He pushed off the door and took a step toward me, his arms now unfolded, his hands fisted at his sides. His expression was serious, but not unkind or hateful thank God.

"You behaved like a teenage girl Ella. You went to a party, and let your hair down. There's nothing wrong with that. It's part of growing up. Boys do it all the time. Yet girls are judged when they do the same. And I don't judge Ella."

I felt my hopes lift a bit but only slightly as I knew there was a 'but' coming on.

"So—you've forgiven me then?" I questioned, feeling thoroughly hopeless.

Ryan raised a hand and pushed a wayward curl of my hair behind my ear. The gesture would usually have felt loving, but it didn't at that moment. He shook his head slowly as he dropped his hand suddenly; as if my hair had burnt his fingers. "It's not really about forgiveness Ella—it's not as easy as that."

I sighed, feeling too weak to carry on the conversation. It felt like my legs were about to give out.

"I don't know what you mean Ryan. You just said that these things happen and I explained it was in the past, *before* us," I gestured between our two bodies with my hand. "It's not like I cheated."

He smiled coolly before saying, "I know that."

My pulse twitched. "Then why are you being so cold and distant?"

He pinned me with an apologetic look. "I'm sorry, I didn't think I was. We're just having a conversation, saying what needs to be said."

I moved away and walked back to the reception desk and propped my back against it, I needed some support, so I didn't slump in front of him like a total weakling. I knew I needed to keep a lid on the stress and resentment I was now feeling.

"Are you speaking to Nathan yet?" I questioned, changing the subject.

He moved toward me to close the space which I had put there. "We've spoken briefly. What happened won't come between us permanently, so you have nothing to worry about there—we're brothers—blood. We used to fight all the time when we were younger."

I raised an eyebrow at that one, I couldn't imagine they'd fought to that extent. "Really, I doubt that. You were both unhinged—like animals, I thought you were going to kill him at one point."

He tried to hide it, but I saw the flash of shame cross his features.

"And I wished you hadn't been there to see it—to see me like that. I'm not proud of myself, but I did warn you, everyone has the ability to lose control. We all do, it's what makes us human."

Yes, that and the ability to be a big fat liar, I thought, thinking of his dick of a brother. I toyed with the idea of telling him the truth at that point but decided to hold off a little longer. There was still that part of me that felt that I shouldn't *have* to explain myself.

"So, we've established we are all capable of losing it and making mistakes, so where do we go from here, what happens to us?" I asked tightly. I suddenly felt quite adult in my skin at that point. Everything that had happened over the past few weeks, appeared to have shaped a more confident me. If I hadn't been so upset, I would have embraced the change.

That aura of power still pulsed around him and I longed for him to grab me and pull me into his arms.

Ryan watched me with a guarded look, totally silent for a few beats. The air was thick in the room and one of the dogs from the back, an overnighter barked loudly, making me jump.

He then delivered the gargantuan blow. I felt it like a punch worse than an elbow, worse than anything, but I had to be strong.

"That's just it. There can be no us from here."

Pain continued to lance through me as my heart cracked down the centre at this rejection. Don't do this, don't bail on me, I wanted to yell. It was a mistake, what do you want from me?

I swallowed. "I'm confused, you just said—", I literally choked out.

He cut me off, his voice gruff, "—I know and I meant it, I don't want you to feel guilty about *anything*."

Several thoughts circled the conscious bit of my brain, did he think I wanted Nathan and was attempting to give me an easy way out?

Clearing my throat, I went in for the kill, "You accused me of choosing Nathan over you after the fight. Do you remember?"

He reared back slightly and pinned me with a confused look. "To be honest, I can't remember much from that night, but you did run to him first I recall."

I released a sigh of exasperation before pointing out. "He wasn't moving Ryan and he was in bad shape. That's the *only* reason. He's my friend, I care about him, God even love the nightmare, but not in the way you think."

"Are you sure you know the difference, you're still so young."

The need to punch him in the face, soaring up into my chest and I clenched my fists.

"Don't do that, don't *patronise* me. I know what I *feel* Ryan!"

"*And what is that, Ella?*" he almost snarled, his head lowered in a calculated slant.

"I'm in *love* with you Ryan, you *must* know that. I think I've always felt that way. Even before that time in the car that day, although you certainly weren't ready to hear it from the way you reacted."

He glanced to the ceiling briefly, before drilling me with a look, stating, "I was *shocked* Ella, things were going too fast and I needed it to slow the hell down."

I shrugged moodily. "Well, your response wasn't what I'd expected. You come across so mature all the time, yet you acted like a school boy running for the hills after the girl he likes gets too fucking heavy." I couldn't believe how grown up I sounded, considering the adolescent reaction, which was desperate to smack its way out there.

His expression was lined with barefaced regret and his shoulders sank. "I know and I'm sorry."

I hesitated a moment before repeating, "So where do we go from here?"

He rocked back on his heels again before placing his hands into the pockets of his jeans.

"I don't know," he sighed, his tone tortured, "I can't get the thought of you and Nathan out of my head."

I rolled my shoulders, they suddenly felt so still. "And?" I returned drily, the threat of tears right there.

He stepped toward me, closing the space between our bodies, staring down into my face. "I just think that there's too much stacked against us. Wanting us to fail."

I closed the distance between our bodies and placed a hand on his arm. He moved his head to watch my fingers against his sleeve.

"But surely now that everything is out in the open, we can have a go at an actual relationship, like normal people. There are no secrets now."

He drew back so my hand dropped away from him and I felt like I was drowning.

"There shouldn't have been any to start with Ella. And that's the problem. Look, I know it was before, but he's my *brother*. It's too hard Ella. We live together for fucks sake. He's always there. I just can't get the image out of my head and it makes me want to lose my shit. That's not something I ever want you to see again. I care about you too much."

229

He cared about me but he didn't want to be with me? How fucked up was that?

"I don't know what to do. The only way this situation can be controlled is by us not seeing each other."

At those words I realised that this guy *was* human. He *didn't* have all the answers. Yes, he was more experienced than me, generally more mature and grown up, but he too, didn't get it or know how to handle this situation. His conclusion therefore, was to walk away. The easier way out. The fucking coward's route.

I'd had enough, I felt numb and tired. The events of the last week had taken their toll emotionally. "Please just cut to the chase Ryan. You're finished with me." I sighed, feeling drained.

There was another moment of silence.

"Yes, it's over, it has to be. The thought… the image of you and my brother like that, it's just too much. I can't imagine *ever* touching you now."

I felt like I was slowly dying inside, and said in a vacant voice.

"So, I'm damaged goods after just one night—or are you disappointed that you won't be getting a virgin?" I knew my words were ridiculous and old fashioned but I was lost. I wasn't even aware of what my brain was telling my mouth to say. I was still a fucking virgin.

"It's none of those things *damn it*. Surely you see how messed up it is. You were with my brother, a guy nearer your age, probably more suitable for you."

"I think you need to get over yourself and stop telling me what I want."

"It just brings me back to my point about our ages. We are not talking about a year or two Ella, the difference is significant. We are at different points in our lives."

I reiterated my earlier words.

"I don't care about Nathan. I want *you*, Ryan. Nathan is a friend and has only ever been a friend." Tell him, tell him, my heart screamed but my head blocked it. No, he should have been able to move past it.

"So, you don't want to be with me because I was with Nathan first and I'm young. Even though I have said how sorry I am and that I don't care about the age gap. You still don't care about me enough to move past those things and try and work at it?" I paused upon reflection, adding, "Maybe you're not the man I thought you were. The type to stay and fight when things get hard. Maybe you're giving me an easy escape." Frustration twisted my insides. I so didn't mean it.

It was all talk, brave words but I needed to salvage some self-respect. I wasn't about to beg this guy. I would never beg anyone.

"Maybe you're right. Maybe that pedestal you put me on was just too high," he replied flatly, his voice now devoid of emotion and there it was that, super human control back in place again. Only a flicker of something that resembled pain, or uncertainty lingered at the back of his eyes.

I took a step back and purposefully narrowed my eyes at him. "So, this really is it then?"

His shoulders dropped, the fight leaving his body.

"I've already made my decision. Yes. It's over Ella and it may not feel that way now, but this is the best, for both of us."

"If you say so Ryan, you always seem to have all the answers," I pointed out miserably. I now just needed him to go before I bawled my eyes out in front of him.

There was a split second where I thought about telling him the truth about me and Nate but then buried it. I didn't want him on those terms. "You can't forgive me for Nathan?"

He scratched his jaw, contemplating his answer.

"It's not really about you, personally. I can't forgive the situation. It's not right, or fair on any of us. Some things just aren't meant to be Ella."

My next words could have been considered spiteful but I was heading toward woman scorned as I said, "The constant reminder that Nathan got in there first. That's the real problem."

"I just don't know how to get past it and I'm sorry. I don't like that feeling of the unknown. I'm a controlling bastard, I find it hard to let go at the best of times and that isn't fair on you, as I said, it isn't fair on any of us."

"Fine. Have a nice life Ryan," I put out numbly as I pushed past him and opened the door, standing there with my back straight as I waited for him to leave.

He went to move past me before stopping and turning to face me one last time, "Ella," he began, trying to appeal to me in some way. How the hell did he think we could leave this situation on neutral ground? It was like that's what he was aiming for with is 'Ella'.

His lips twisted as he walked through the door and then turned back.

"It hurts now but in the longer term, you'll accept that I was right."

"Goodbye Ryan," I murmured miserably, only just managing to keep the tears at bay.

He released a sigh of exasperation before he said softly, so softly I almost didn't hear the words. "I'm sorry."

"Me too." All the fight whooshed out of me as bone-deep despair flooded my body at full force.

As I closed the door, my misty eyes met his through the glass, and that hairline crack across my heart split it into two.

Seventeen

The week that followed my official split with Ryan was shit, I'm not going to lie. I couldn't seem to swallow that bubble of panic and loneliness. I was losing weight, having totally lost my appetite and I wasn't sleeping well. I'd wake up during the night in one of those cold sweats, replaying the fight between Ryan and Nathan over and over. That memory of Ryan's face through the glass doors of the surgery still choked me up. I couldn't get my head around the fact that we were done, even before we'd actually started.

Disappointment felt like fingers consistently tightening around my throat. Ryan had been so quick to shut things down that it made me wonder if he had ever *truly* cared for me. Of course, I blamed myself the most. I should have told him about Nate sooner instead of letting him find out in the worse possible way; no wonder he'd fucked off without a backward glance.

The fact that I was still a virgin, having never slept with Nathan was still a huge relief, but I still didn't feel capable of bringing myself to tell Ryan. He should have forgiven me, at least tried to get past it. Of course, I understood why he'd be grossed out at the thought of me having sex with his brother. The whole mess was a shit show, no matter which way you sliced it.

By the end of that week, I'd made up my mind. I knew it was the coward's way out, but I had to get away again. I needed to give my mind time to heal from the memories that just kept slapping me in the face.

I was going back to America and there I would give myself time to get my head right. My heart needed major repair work and I had to overcome that sickening sadness that just wouldn't go away. Would I ever be truly happy again? Didn't I deserve to be happy?

To say my goodbyes and not just disappear off the grid, I decided to gate crash the pub the following Tuesday, having already packed a case and booked my flight to JFK. My aunt was overcome with excitement when I called her and I was really looking to spending Thanks Giving in the USA, an American holiday I had never experienced.

My parents were not happy that I was to be away at Christmas time, but mum understood why I wanted to go. I didn't go into details, but she knew I'd had some boy drama. She'd also guessed it was with one of the Lane boys as talk of the fight had been rife in the village.

I wasn't sure how much of a shock my going away would be to my friends and to be frank, I didn't really give a shit at that point. I hadn't even confided in Connor.

Tom and I drove in silence to the pub to meet the others. It was the first time I'd see Nate again in person since the fight. Yes, he'd sent the occasional text here and there but to be honest, I felt so numb. I had fortunately managed to boot away the huge grudge I'd felt, although only over the last couple of days. We had a history at the end of the day. Six years. I couldn't keep hating him, it didn't seem right. And didn't they say that pent-up ill feelings had the power to decay the soul?

As Tom and I entered the pub, Connor and Noah were there, looking as scruffy as fuck, having obviously come straight from work.

Noah was a mechanic by trade but had started working with Connor on his gym project. They were in the process of refurbishing one of Mike's outbuildings. Noah himself was an avid gym goer and knew pretty much everything there was to know about training equipment and fitness programs.

Having a gym handy would also provide Connor with an onsite outlet to release any stored-up aggression. At the end of the day, the guy had been through more shit than anyone could relate to, so you didn't judge. He also missed his girlfriend Harlow. They'd spent October half term together at her house in Surrey and he'd been a different person when he'd first returned back. A certain skip in his step. I didn't ask for details that's for sure. He was now counting the days until she came back up North for Christmas.

As Tom and I moved to the bar, Nathan appeared wearing a crooked grin.

The guy's fist bumped and I smiled my hello, this time not feeling that punch of anxiety. Now I knew Nathan and I *hadn't* slept together I didn't have that constant niggle on my mind about what had actually happened that night. I still couldn't believe that he'd managed to keep the lie going for over *a year*. I suppose that's what happens when a prank backfires. I still wasn't amused that I was the one it had backfired on. All those months of feeling embarrassed and mortified at the thought of us having sex. And yet, it had *never* actually happened. It was like I'd grown my virginity back rather than never having lost it.

We got our drinks and walked toward Connor and Noah who were sat at our usual table. It was funny, as *neither* boy moved to make space which forced us to slot in awkwardly between them. Noah possessed a similar attitude to Connor, neither gave a fuck about social niceties. They were like night... and later that night.

I placed my beer on the table and plopped down into a chair as Tom and Nathan did the same. Nate's bruises from the fight were almost non-existent now.

He'd messaged one day to say that his relationship with Ryan was strained, but that they were talking again. Blood is thicker than water and all that shit. I hadn't heard a thing from Ryan.

I thought about at which point to share my news as the conversation started to flow around the table.

I was due to fly in a couple of days and would have left sooner but dad had asked me to provide a hand-over to the new girl at his work. Luckily it hadn't taken long and she was a fast learner thank goodness.

The girl was called Lucy and was a timid little thing. She also scurried, like a mouse, with bright carrot-coloured hair and an alarming number of freckles on her face. She had pretty eyes though, really wide and a bright startling blue.

Tom had spent the morning buzzing around the surgery when he should have been on his rounds. Very much the smitten kitten *again*, and to be honest, this time they'd probably be quite well matched; her seeming like the less adventurous type. Buttoned up, I would say. And well, Tom was Tom, he wasn't exactly Mr. Excitement.

"What were you guys talking about?" I threw across the table, flicking a glance between Connor and Noah. They were both still slouched in their seats, staring into their drinks. At my comment Noah raised his head, his hair was so black it almost glistened blue. He was also naturally tanned due to his Cypriot heritage on his father's side. Both Connor and Noah were of a similar build, but Noah was slightly taller and his muscles looked more manufactured, honed by workouts at the gym. Connor's build was more natural from farm work and knocking the shit out of stuff of course. I imagined both boys had a history of violent tendencies.

"This bitch thinks he can bench more than me. Two hundred and ninety pounds to beat motherfucker. Your lady arms would snap at that weight," Noah drawled with a baiting grin.

Connor snorted and took a slug of beer, before placing the bottle on the table and cocking him an eyebrow. "When you're ready to test the theory Princess, let me know," he replied absently and then followed this up with a playful wink. The pissing contest was all tongue in cheek of course, and fun to watch. It cheered me up, if only slightly. How I would miss this banter.

"Challenge accepted. Tell you what, to even the playing field, I'll give you a couple of weeks' head start on your training, just to make it fair, me being over a foot taller than you," Noah offered with a grin.

Connor snorted. "Fuck off are you a foot taller. Sticking your hair up like a bitch doesn't count as extra height pussy. That's just plain of fashioned cheating man."

Noah cleared his throat and took another swig of beer, a challenge glittering in his eyes. "Whatever you say, short-arse."

Connor grinned at that one. Being over six feet, the insult lacked any real weight. The banter continued to flow and I embraced it, it was so refreshing.

"Maybe I'll join you and start training, it'll give me something to do," Nathan put swiftly.

Both Connor and Noah turned slowly to look at him with doubtful expressions.

"You could try getting a job Nathan, make an honest man of yourself," I suggested with a grin.

He shot me a lopsided smile. "Where's the fun in that? Besides, maybe I can be the judge in this competition of yours," he suggested, shuffling back into his seat as he motioned toward Connor and Noah.

"There is no competition," Connor replied smoothly.

Nate nodded his understanding. Both he and Connor had thankfully sorted out their differences ever since Carter's attack on Connor. They had found a middle ground. It was nice to see them more at peace. They still took the piss out of each other, but gone were the unpleasant undertones.

"So—how's it going with Harlow?" Nate asked, shooting a semi-guilty look toward Tom who had of course worshiped the girl.

Connor chewed his lip thoughtfully before he grabbed his beer and cradled it against his chest.

"It's *going*, I think that's all you need to know," he replied in a flat voice. The guy still didn't give anything away, not to these idiots anyway.

I had a go at coaxing some gossip from him but he shut me down just as quickly. "So, you been to first base yet?" I put out there, knocking back my own beer. "I imagine the lady prefers ribbed for her pleasure?"

My comment backfired straight away.

"You don't want to hear about my love life Ella—it'll just remind you of your non-existent one," he replied smugly. He could be such a mean twat.

To be honest he was right. I was jealous. Jealous that he had a girlfriend whom he adored and even though it was long distance, it was going really well from the bits of things he'd told me.

Connor then did what he did best and turned the tables on me.

"So, Ella about that? Anything going on with you that you wish to share," he voiced, shooting a cocky glance around the table.

His expression was one of pure challenge and it felt like all the air had suddenly been sucked from the room. Nathan sat at the table like the huge elephant in the room. I batted off my annoyed reaction as without realising, Connor had given me the perfect opportunity to spill my news.

"Well, there's nothing to report there. But there might be, who knows? I'll let you know when I'm back."

Connor's eyes narrowed and echoed. "When you're back?"

Nathan, who totally misunderstood where I was going with my words, chimed in. "Good luck with that. Finding anything decent in Scarborough is up there with winning the lottery."

Noah also jumped on board. "Yes, or Tom getting laid."

"You do know I'm sitting right here?" my brother put in, actually jumping to his own defence (which was a nice surprise). He was usually such a kiss-ass. "I've met someone actually and we're going out on Saturday," Tom threw in there. A murmur of doubt erupted around the table. The twats had now skated over the point I was about to raise. I sat back and listened, waiting for my next opportunity.

Tom cut in through the murmurs. "What? I've actually got a date this time and there are no psycho members of the family to warn me off," Tom raced on, shooting an accusing glance at Connor who shuffled in his seat. "No offence," he added.

Con shot him a lazy, amused look, "None taken."

All ears at the table pricked up and everyone sat upright.

"Well fuck me sideways, I stand corrected big lad, who is she?" Noah replied unfazed.

My brow wrinkled until I realised who he meant, the new girl Lucy at the surgery. Here we go again. I knew he liked her but boy was he quick, she literally just started that morning. Aren't you supposed to let the dust settle? Fools rush in and all that. Of course, Tom was a huge fool and so I shouldn't have been surprised really.

"She's probably only agreed to go out with you because you're the boss's son Tom," I pointed out, knowing it was mean but enjoying winding him up about it.

He shrugged with a shit-eating grin. "Don't really care, she said yes—is the main thing."

Nathan grinned. "Does she have one of those white sticks?"

Everyone, even Connor laughed around the table.

Tom just rolled his eyes. "You guys are such wankers."

People cleared throats and composed themselves quickly as Tom shuffled in his seat with a wounded expression.

"Go on, we're only messing, tell us about her?" Nathan coaxed, putting away his smile and trying to appear genuinely interested. My eyes assessed his averted gaze, he was doing that, not making eye contact thing with me and I was grateful, to be honest. He'd finally got the message. I imagined Ryan had helped with that task. I still felt a smidge of resentment toward him but hopefully that would die with time.

Tom took ages to answer and so I replied for him, placing my drink on the table, aware that I still had my news to share and they were all still oblivious, although Connor kept looking at me with a wondering expression.

"Her name is Lucy Meadows and she's the new receptionist at dad's surgery. I must applaud you, Tom, you were quick to get in there but I must warn you, you know what they say about redheads," I commented with a smile, reining in my inner bitch, just because I was a lonely miserable cow, didn't make it OK to drag Tom down with me. I wouldn't give him any glory either though. That would be too nice of me.

At the word redhead, Noah's eyes narrowed, his gaze flickering between me and Tom.

"Did you say *Lucy* Meadows?" he repeated, sitting up in his seat, pretty much casting a shadow over the entire table.

Tom nodded and shot a shy glance around. Connor pursed his lips as he turned away from me to peer at Noah with a questioned look.

"She a pintsized ginger thing?" Noah asked curiously and Tom's puzzled expression increased in intensity.

"Yes why?" he puffed out.

Noah slouched back and rolled his eyes, shooting Tom a look of sympathy. "Good luck with that one bro, fucking thorn in your side if there was ever one."

Tom sat forward and placed his glass down so hard that some of the liquid sloshed onto the table.

"You *know* her?" I couldn't tell whether Tom was happy about the possibility of that or not. More shocked. Lucy had only *just* moved back to the village and so I was surprised that Noah knew her.

Said giant flexed his massive arms by rolling his huge shoulders and deposited his empty beer bottle on the table before folding them over his chest. There was no way Connor would be able to bench more than Noah, the guy was fricking huge. All corded bronze muscle. He'd be smoking hot if he wasn't so rough looking. His hair was also way too long and he always had beard growth on his face. Like he only shaved when he felt like it. He was a mechanic by trade and so was regularly covered in oil too, not the prettiest of pictures. Not like... I stopped myself from going there. It was still way too painful.

"I know her," he declared nonchalantly like he couldn't give a shit. I saw something flicker in his eyes though, call it women's intuition and all that. The guy was guarded and I wondered in what capacity he knew this Lucy. I certainly couldn't imagine it would be in a romantic capacity. It would be like a stallion trying to get it on with My Little Pony. The girl would be minuscule next to Noah. How would that even work? She was probably the same weight as one of his legs.

My trip was suddenly forgotten as I watched the scene playing out before me.

"How do you know her? What's she like? She seems really nice," Tom babbled, desperate for further information. The guy was starting to allow his hormones to predict his every move. He came over as more than desperate with each word.

"It's the nice girls you have to watch Tom. I remember her from school, she was in the year below me. She's part of the church or used to be. Her dad and brother live in the parsonage behind All Saints Church in Sinnington. Her dad used to be a Pastor there. Fucking strange family. She went away to Uni. Fuck knows why she'd want to come back here."

That would explain the crucifix necklace she'd been wearing when I saw her earlier, so I was right with my buttoned-up assessment.

I smiled, it appeared Noah knew an awful lot about her.

"That's quite a bit of information Noah, you know her bra size too?" I taunted. I needed to be the playful Ella, keep that mask in place.

He shot me a 'wouldn't you like to know' look. Interesting, Oh dear, poor Tom, it appeared he may have competition, *again*.

Tom appeared to be in a daze as he sat watching Noah in silence before he said, "Y-You sound like you remember her quite well?" he stuttered, basically repeating what I had said. He looked flustered like his hopes of something with this girl had been dashed away. As far as sex appeal was concerned, my brother had about as much as a fly next to Noah.

"It's the hair man, you'd never forget the hair, like liquid fire," Noah replied as he caressed his bottom lip with his thumb, his eyes on Tom.

I decided to chip in, I didn't want to see my brother involved in what appeared to be a big dick contest with Noah Savvas, it was way too uneven.

I still didn't really think that anything major would have happened between them, my God, the girl would probably fit in his fucking pocket she was that small. She made Harlow look well-built.

"Anyway, sorry to interrupt your guy-shit, but back to my news please," I put in, glancing around the table my eyes falling on Nathan.

Connor's knowing look remained in place, the guy had had my measure all along and had just waited 'quietly' until the topic turned back to me. I used the word quietly instead of 'patiently'. Patience was an alien concept to Connor.

"So, this is the part where you tell us you're fucking off again." He drawled, raising an eyebrow.

Boom, there it was said. The news didn't come from my lips but at least it was out there.

I nodded and shot them all a bland look as if to say, 'it's none of your business really'.

Connor snorted before unhelpfully saying. "So, running away again instead of facing the music. Will you ever stop being a pussy, Ella?"

"I've faced the music Connor and I've decided I'm not happy with the fucking tune," I replied without glancing at Nathan. I didn't want to give the guy a complex that I was leaving because of him.

His words had riled me but before I could carry on, Nathan pushed in with, "Where you off to? The states again I take it?" He distracted Connor's comment which amazed me, it was so the nice thing to do. To stop me from having to deal with difficult questions. We didn't talk about it openly but everyone now knew about Ryan and me. Fuck me, even Noah knew being the one to drag Ryan off Nathan.

It sat there unsaid floating in the air between us before Nathan asked in a small voice. "Does Ryan know?"

An uncomfortable silence wafted around the table, there was a cough or two and Tom necked his beer, dribbling some down his chin.

"I think the cat is well and truly out of the bag now guys and no, I haven't told Ryan, there's no point. We aren't together, I don't think we ever were really. Anyway, it's complicated. Yes, Connor, I'm going away because it's what I need to do for my sanity. OK?" Complicated, that fucking word again!

I eyed my friends who all just sat there like a human chain of disappointment, my decision being the cause. They all wore the same expression. After around a minute of silence, Connor shifted in his seat before stating, "Do what you

241

need to do. When you've cleared your head once and for all, get your arse back home and plan your next move."

His 'fight for what you want' message was threaded in with his surprisingly nice words.

Clear my head, come home and make things right with Ryan was how I deciphered his code. I could see what he was saying but I couldn't see a way back into that situation and I didn't know if I wanted it now. Feeling like shit for the last two weeks had been the hardest thing I'd ever gone through. Did I want to put myself in that position again? The whole, it is 'better to have loved and lost shyte' could do one. At the moment, my answer was a big fat fucking no thanks.

I pushed to my feet and Tom made a move to stand but I warded him off.

"I'm off. Enjoy your drinks guys. I'll miss you all when I'm out at parties every night with really cool fun American people, but I'll Facebook you and so please try to restrain your jealousy."

"When do you leave?" Nathan asked quietly as I came to my feet. I could see he didn't welcome the information.

"The day after tomorrow. My flight is at ten from Leeds Bradford."

"Do you need a lift to the airport?" Nate questioned.

"I don't think that's a good idea, Nathan," I replied flatly, no longer hiding. The cards were well and truly on the table now.

He nodded his head as if he was agreeing with me.

"Tom is taking me."

"How long are you going for this time?" Connor asked, still focused on his beer.

"I don't know, a few months."

My answer didn't sit well with anyone as they all slowly pushed to their feet, apart from my Tom of course who was still reeling from Noah's revelation that he knew his intended honey.

I hugged Connor and he instructed me to stay in touch and to follow his 'wrap it before you tap it' guidance and not get the clap. I hugged Nate too, it was awkward but we survived. Noah and I just kind of patted each other's shoulders. He looked uncomfortable which of course he would, to me he was just Natalie's brother.

I told Tom I was going to walk home: it was only around a mile. I needed some clear headspace time.

As I pushed open the double doors of The Crown and walked out into the carpark, I heard a sound behind me but kept on walking. I was done with my village friends and needed to embrace the new me.

"Ella," Nate's voice called from behind me, him having followed me out.

I stopped and took a deep breath before turning to face him. Cocking my head to the side, I delivered my 'what' eyebrows.

He sauntered over slowly: his face unreadable.

"For what it's worth, I just wanted to say sorry again."

I smiled, water under the bridge and all that.

I was just about to turn away but his words stopped me. "I'm guessing by the fact that I am still walking and breathing that you didn't tell Ryan that I'd lied," he went on, his voice husky.

He looked down at me, again like he was seeing me for the first time but I didn't feel uncomfortable.

I chewed the inside of my lip and then replied. "No, I didn't see the point."

Nathan released a puff of frustration before saying in a small voice. "He misses you. You must know that. I've *never* seen him like this. Working like a demon, says little when he's home. Locks himself away. The guys a fucking shell, Ella."

My tummy flipped at his words, I hated that he too was struggling but what could I do.

"And what do you want me to do about that Nathan," I said, a little too sharply.

He looked like a kicked puppy again. "Sorry," I apologised. I didn't want us to leave on bad terms.

"I just thought you should know," he whispered sadly,

"He was the one who walked away."

"But you haven't told him the truth, if you told him that, things would be different. You could make a go of it, I'm sure. Why I am fucking saying this I don't know."

I exhaled, letting his words wash over me. This scenario was extremely odd, it was like a coin had been flipped.

"You trying to set me back up with your brother is all a bit weird Nathan, I mean after everything that's happened." I pointed out flatly.

He went quiet for a moment and jammed his hands into the pockets of his jeans. He looked at me through a fringe of hair. His locks had grown quite long and he looked even more rugged. Once the guy sorted his shit out, he'd probably make someone a great boyfriend. He'd certainly look after a girl, maybe a little too much, being so obsessive.

"You should tell him, *please.*"

I slowly shook my head, the misery I had experienced since Ryan had walked away started to pump through my chest again and I knew I needed to shut this shit down.

"No Nate, it's over. He couldn't forgive me for being with you, couldn't get past it and I can't forgive *him* for that."

"So, it really is over."

"Yes, over before it even began."

Another level of sadness entered his eyes and he whispered under his breath. "I hate myself for what I've done to you. I hate that I've come between you and..."

I jumped in as my temper flared. "...between me and your brother?"

"No," he began. "Between you and your happiness," he stated, now quite firmly.

I cleared my throat before leaving him my parting words.

"Don't beat yourself up Nathan. If it was meant to be we would have got through the shit about you and me. We obviously weren't in the place I thought we were."

"You're wrong." He responded with conviction.

I gave him one last lingering look and then replied sadly.

"I guess we'll never know. Take care, Nate. Text me, although not every day stalker boy."

He grinned but it didn't reach his eyes.

I walked out of that car park with a hole the size of a small country in my heart.

The violence of my emotions shocked me. I could almost hear my heart splitting in two (again).

Eighteen

Tom was fairly animated in the car as he drove me to the airport. Thankfully the conversation didn't include either of the Lane boys or *anything* that had been said recently.

The new receptionist Lucy, at dad's surgery was the main direction of the discussion. Tom regurgitated the same spiel he had that night at the pub when he'd gushed over Harlow's arrival. It had never taken him long to pick himself up and dust himself down again. Part of me wondered if Tom would *ever* get a girlfriend. Where girls were concerned, he acted as dumb as a brick half the time. It was an odd one, as he wasn't totally unfortunate looking and he was intelligent. After he paid his student loan off and starting making proper money, he also had a pretty impressive career mapped out.

Lucy would settle well at dad's practice and in Tom's opinion, they had loads in common. Even though they had known each other for a matter of hours. My thoughts darted to Noah's reaction that she had returned to the village. Tom may have a problem there but I had everything crossed for him. The girl seemed nice, as I said before, a bit on the shy side, but that would probably suit Tom to the ground.

As we pulled into the airport, Tom dragged me in for a hug, telling me to enjoy myself, let my hair down and fuck the past. I didn't miss the toned-down suggestion that I should consider giving other guys a chance. Sow some wild oats and all that. Coming from my brother, that should have been a no-go conversation, but it still made me smile.

I thanked him again and wished him luck in his pursuit of the Lucy girl and dragged my case into the terminal. It was busy and the check-in desks for my flight had just opened.

As I joined the back of the queue, I began replaying the past couple of months in my head whilst checking I had my paperwork for the fortieth time.

That ache of not being with Ryan was still there, the wound stubbornly throbbing, but the last couple of days had been easier. I'd stopped checking my phone for messages and had concentrated on packing for my trip back to my aunts.

Not everything in life was about boys, at least that's what I'd tried to convince myself of. It was tough, but I knew I needed to embrace being on my own. Life had been so complicated recently, like a proper whirlwind. Yes, relationships were hard, but should the right one feel *that* draining? Of course, I accepted that there were extraneous circumstances in my situation with Ryan.

At the end of the day, if he didn't want to be with me and couldn't get past the Nathan thing, maybe he wasn't the man thought he was. If he loved me, we would have dealt with it together, one day at a time. Not just shut down what we had and not even *attempt* to make it right. I felt another knot of anxiety tighten in my stomach. Who was I kidding, I cared about the guy that much, that my bones were hurting. My head and my heart were still in two totally different queues.

Talking of queues, the check-in one had started to fill up behind me and I dragged my case further forward. There were three desks and so hopefully it wouldn't be long until I had checked-in and could move through security. I *hated* security. I was always fearful of someone stealing my phone after I'd placed it in one of those boxes for the scanner. What can I say? Paranoia must have been my middle name.

I was surrounded by people from all different walks of life, some families, others holding hands, and the occasional loner. I felt a lump rise in my throat as a boy in the queue ahead of me, turned and pecked his girlfriend on the cheek. They must have been so excited to be going away together. How *amazing* it would have felt to travel to America with Ryan, sitting together on the flight and making exciting decisions about where we wanted to go and what to see. God, I hated pipe dreams.

The man behind me ushered me forward as the queue moved up. I had been briefly checking my phone. Connor had sent me a message to wish me a safe trip which was refreshing. After swiping the screen, I pocketed it and closed the gap before getting a mouthful from Mr. Impatient behind me.

I was almost at the front desk, with just two families in front of me when a ruckus kicked off toward the back of the queue, dragging my attention around. People appeared to be moving to the side, maybe they were being sent to another queue?

I squinted my eyes, trying to establish what was going on. I now faced the back of Mr Inpatient's head, who had also turned to look.

Shuffling forward again and turning back to the front, I now had one family left before I could check my hold bag in and I started to search in my bag for my passport and boarding pass.

What happened next caused an abundance of emotions to race through my brain.

I heard my name being called, but it sounded like it was coming from the other end of the airport. My mind almost stalled as I turned around, searching for the source of the sound.

The queue of people behind me parted to let someone through and as I saw that someone, my pulse took off.

Ryan.

My mouth fell open as Mr. Impatient moved to allow the much larger, more determined man through. Ryan stalked toward me, his perfect face swimming before my eyes and I felt my gaze feast on his masculine beauty. He owned the area around him and offered no apology for barging through everyone.

I couldn't compute why he was there; my headspace didn't have the capacity at that moment, I just remained silent and looked up into his penetrating stare. The lump in my throat felt like my heartbeat.

His look was one of relief, I would say.

"Ella," he began in a throaty voice and a shudder reverberated down my spine. Every inch of my skin prickled at his sudden nearness. A fog which was warm and comforting wrapped like a blanket around me.

The people in the queue had split away and were watching us with varying expressions, some annoyed, some inquisitive.

"Don't go," Ryan put in. His deep voice resonating around us.

My knees knocked together at the sound of that rich timber. "I have to Ryan. I can't stay here like this."

My head was such a scramble of thoughts and I didn't really comprehend what he was asking me.

"You *need* to stay."

"What do you mean?" I questioned, my brow wrinkled as I released my hold luggage and stepped toward him. We were face to face in the mix of a bunch of strangers, a couple of whom tutted and one that rudely moved around me and took my place in the queue.

"I don't care that you slept with Nathan."

And BOOM. We now had the attention of everyone in earshot, including a security guard and a lady from Jet2.

An excited murmur, possibly at the thought of some meaty drama whizzed around us.

"You don't care?" I questioned, not sure I believed what I was hearing. My eyes roamed over him, he wore his signature suit, his shoulders stretching the tailored fabric.

His gaze remained steady. "Well—I care, but not enough for us to be apart," he half whispered in a husky voice, staring down into my upturned face. He looked at me like he hadn't seen me for weeks and his hair was messy. He didn't look like the usual pristine Ryan.

I heard someone question who Nathan was, under any other circumstances, it would have been quite comical.

His hand touched my face and my heart leapt in my chest. He was here to stop me leaving, *wanted* to be with me in spite of everything. That must have been why he was there.

If that was the case, this was the real Ryan, this was the man I wanted him to be.

"But he's your brother—how can we ever put it behind us?" I questioned, causing our audience to prick up their ears even more. I saw the security guy and the Jet2 woman mouth the word 'brother' to each other in shock.

I held back telling him the truth about Nathan and me for a moment, needing to see how hard he intended to fight for us. I had to know he would have forgiven me if it had happened in the past. I accepted that it would have been strange at first, but we should have been strong enough to move past it. That's what I'd hoped anyway.

"Look—hear me out," he began, stepping close to speak directly into my upturned face. He glanced around and then lowered his voice, having realised our audience now regarded us as their own personal soap opera.

"I fucked up. My reaction was wrong. You slept with Nate, it was a mistake and I know that now. I was just so jealous, and angry. I couldn't move past it, but I was wrong. I can and I will. I won't allow it to come between us. And I promise, I will never hold it against you. You or Nathan."

I took in his words, purposefully not wrapping my arms around his neck and kissing him stupidly. How I had so wanted to hear those words of regret. How he'd really felt. It was new to me, seeing Ryan with his heart on his sleeve and I relished everything about that moment. Being in the airport also suddenly felt quite romantic, although I wasn't sure about the bystanders. No one seemed to care about checking-in at that point and people just continued to gather around us.

"But how are you going to feel about me and Nate as friends? He really has managed to move on now, I think. But he's part of both our lives."

He pursed his lips, drinking in that thought for a moment before replying in a half-tortured voice. "It's going to be hard. I'm not going to lie. But I will do whatever it takes Ella. I *need* you."

I was sure I heard a sigh from the crowd at that one. And someone asked 'is Nate the brother?'

I attempted to ignore the buzz around us and focus on Ryan.

"Stay, please stay with me," he ordered firmly, his voice gentle but commanding.

I exhaled, so torn. Happy but so unsure. I'd felt so hurt.

That shred of doubt was then ripped out of the scenario as Ryan closed the small gap between our bodies and he took my face in his hands. Our eyes tangled and warmth bloomed in my stomach.

"I *love* you, Ella."

I couldn't stop the sob of delight which burst from my chest and Mr. Impatient told our audience in an 'I knew that' type of tone. 'Told you, he *loves* her.'

Nods and a few claps erupted.

"You love me?"

I must have looked like a dazed animal between the headlights of a car.

He smiled warmly as he stared down, his eyes full of longing. The truth of his feelings exposed on every corner of his face and my chest swelled with joy.

"I love you, have done for months, I don't know maybe longer. Please stay. Stay with me. *Be* with me."

Need pumped through me and I could almost hear my heart beating against my chest. I wrapped my arms around his neck.

"Well, you know I still love you too, right?" I replied, feeling the mist of tears, allowing my gaze to drift over him.

He closed his eyes in a thank God expression, before opening them and looking directly into my soul.

Again, a burst of oohs from our audience and one guy shouted. "Kiss her then!"

Assorted laughter kicked off around us. It was like a scene from a movie and I grinned, darting a look around the crowd.

Ryan's smile lit up his face and his eyes creased. He also cast a glance around. My awareness of him at that point was off the chart, my skin was literally tingling.

"Better do as I'm told," he drawled with a quirk of his head.

Ryan Lane, my one and only true first love, pulled my face toward him, lowered his head, meeting me half way and kissed me to an eruption of applause. Before his mouth met mine, I saw the security chap and Jet2 woman come together with a high five.

Raising up onto my tiptoes, I opened my mouth and welcomed the sweet invasion of his tongue. That familiar hot wave of lust rocked my core and we were alone, no one else existed. The eyes that were feasted our way, gone.

The kiss went on and on and I pushed my body against him, revelling in the fact that this boy loved me. I was loved at last. What happened in the past was the past and I didn't have to hide anymore. The contact of lips was insistent and I gathered his taste like I had been starved of affection for months, years even.

Someone tapped Ryan on the shoulder and he reluctantly pulled away, his eyes swimming with desire.

We both turned, startled at the interruption as Ryan gripped my wrists, gently lowering them from around his neck.

The security chap stood, staring at us both with a cheesy satisfied smile. His eyebrows raised.

"As much as this has made my day lad, I think you and the lady need to go somewhere a bit more private," he suggested with a wink.

We shot a glance at our audience, some of whom beamed back, others resuming their positions ahead of me in the queue.

"Yes sir," Ryan replied as he grabbed my case.

Jet2, unclipped the cordon tape of the queue so we could slide out and whispered. "He's a keeper."

I grinned back and pulled my hand luggage further into my shoulder, fleetingly checking my passport and boarding pass were back in my bag.

Ryan's strong fingers curled around mine as we made our way through the airport together as a couple. I kept glancing up at him with the meatiest of smiles.

"Come on, I'm parked outside. If I haven't been towed that is."

We left through the sliding doors of the airport. Ryan's sleek car was there and a tow truck and was just in the process of backing up to take it away.

"Stay here," Ryan whispered gruffly, taking control. He popped a kiss on my head and left me with my luggage as he walked toward the tow truck guy.

I sat on my suitcase and stared at him, attempting to read his lips as he spoke at length with what was at first, a moody put-out man. The guy's face eventually softened and he shot a look toward me. I gave him a finger-tipped wave and he grinned. Ryan had obviously told him some of our story.

And what an amazing beginning to our story. I certainly wouldn't see it as an end. We had so much to look forward to. Yes, it wouldn't be easy but things were about to become a whole lot better. I would tell Ryan the truth about Nathan.

After Ryan settled the misunderstanding with the tow truck guy, he helped me into the car like a proper gentleman and secured my case and hand luggage in the boot.

Joining me in the car, he fired up the engine.

"I think there is still stuff to say, but I better move the car before that guy comes back again. He gave me two minutes before either towing or clamping."

I nodded and settled back into the familiar seat of his car feeling on top of the world.

On the drive back to Yorkshire, we didn't talk too much about 'us'. Ryan explained that Nathan had been the one to tell him about my intention to leave and how he'd pretty much had a go at Ryan for potentially losing something so special. His about-face was a surprise. He said when he'd found out I was leaving the country, he'd panicked, feeling like his heart was being ripped from his chest. He said it was then that he knew how he really felt.

As he drove his car in through the gates to my house, Tom was just climbing out of his car, having just arrived back. He saw us both and his mouth widened in a huge smile, his face lighting up. He stopped and grinned but didn't approach the car, obviously understanding that we had some stuff to say to each other first.

Ryan parked his car bang in front of our house, for all to see. We were no longer hiding. Sneaking around like what we were doing was wrong. That was over and now the world would see us; together.

"So, I thought we'd have a chat to your parents first, get them used to the idea that I'll be dating their daughter. What do you think?" Ryan announced smoothly and my heart skipped a beat. The level of happiness was so extreme, I was surprised I managed to contained myself. I wanted to scream and clap my hands with glee.

"I think that sounds great. But before we do. There's something else you should know," I began, my voice suddenly shaky.

He undid his belt, his brow furrowed and he pinned me with a look that said, I don't care. *Nothing* you say will make me feel anything else or change my mind, which was another relief.

"I didn't sleep with Nathan."

His mouth fell open as confusion swamped his gorgeous face. He shook his head.

"I don't care Ella, it doesn't matter. It's in the past."

I smiled, pushing a curl of hair behind my ear, undoing my belt.

"It isn't in the past, because it *never* happened. I *never* slept with him. I've never been with anyone in fact."

At my words, I saw relief and confusion crash into his expression, but he was trying to hold it back, almost as if he didn't believe my words. Too good to be true and all that.

"I don't understand," he whispered, lowering his head, trying to see into my thoughts.

"Nathan lied."

His eyes flared dangerously. He was angry now and he had every right to be, but now was not the time.

"Lied, He fucking lied about it? What the hell?"

I held up a hand to stop him from saying anything else, anything to rock the boat between him and his brother. I saw his fists were clenched white against his thighs.

"It never happened. We got drunk, I wanted to swim, got undressed and then passed out. Nathan did the same. He explained that there's no way he was in a state to do anything and wouldn't have anyway as we were friends. And of course, it wouldn't have been right."

"It absolutely would not have been right!" Ryan half yelled before lowering his voice. "Sorry, go on. Where is that famous control of mine," he half joked. He was struggling to control his temper.

"We woke up half naked together and that was it. He made up the sex part as a wind-up. It started out as a joke but then when he didn't come clean soon enough, it got out of hand and he couldn't bring himself to tell me. By that time he'd also started to develop feelings for me and so he left the lie out there, thinking that if I thought we'd been intimate, I may give it a go to see if there could be something romantic between us."

"That little bastard," he bit out, partly to himself.

I put my hand on his thigh and he placed his fingers over it. "Look I know he was wrong, but we do silly things when we want something"

Ryan gave me a thoughtful look. "But what if he still wants you now?"

"Even if he does, he knows I want to be with you. The fact that he was the one to tell you to come after me proves that."

He nodded slowly. "You're right, I think. But let's keep an eye on that anyway, just in case and let's not rub his nose in it."

"I agree," I smiled.

Ryan's fingers curled around my wrist and he pulled me toward him so I was leaning across the gear stick. "Come here."

Both hands gripped my upper arms and he kissed me to the point where I was almost breathless.

Our journey was just beginning. It was time to tell the world that we were together. A thought suddenly occurred to me.

"Ryan," I questioned, pulling my mouth away from his.

"Yes," he muttered, part-dazed with passion.

"Are you going to make this official and ask me out?" I asked in a breathy voice.

His mouth curled in a sexy, suggestive smile. "Abso-fucking-lutely. Ella Wade…"

"Yes," I replied with a hiccup.

"Will you be my girlfriend?"

BOOM!

"I thought you'd never ask." And our next kiss, sealed the deal.

Grinning like a Cheshire cat, me and my new boyfriend entered my house in a contented daze, hand in hand.

We were together *at last*, no hiding. We would take 'us' one day at a time. Relationships were hard and had to be worked on at.

Over the last few months, irrespective of what I now had with Ryan, I had found myself. I was a fighter; I'd dealt with such vast and differing levels of emotional torture and had come out on top. I hadn't let things beat me down, if Ryan hadn't have come for me, I do believe I would have been strong enough to move on, *eventually.*

Relationships do not mould us into who we are. We do that ourselves, learn by our mistakes and develop as people. Life is full of hidden challenges and we all will at some point in our lives have to deal with regretting something we have done.

Life is short, we need to live life to the fullest, and embrace everything it throws at us; the good and the bad.

I knew from that point forward that I would spend no more energy holding onto …regrets.

THE END

Meet Harlow and Connor, and Ella and Ryan in
Lucy and Noah's story, FIERCE

Excerpt

Noah's finger traced the skin on my bare shoulder. My whole body suddenly leaped to life. He too cocked his head to one side with an expression full of lustful intentions.

"Nice suit. Do you have these all over your body?" he questioned; his deep voice thick with an emotion I didn't recognise.

I glanced back toward where he touched a small cluster of freckles on my shoulder.

"Yes," I breathed out in a soft voice. My control was severely starting to fray around the edges. Let's face it, the guy was lethally attractive and had probably been breaking hearts from his cot.

His own breath was warm against my neck and I lifted my head further, allowing our gazes to tangle; his eyes dark and heavy; full of silent promise. The woodsy scent of his skin with the slight twinge of chlorine lingered between us.

"One day," he drawled slowly, his forehead dipping to mine, "one day I am going to count every single one of them."

https://mjtennant.weebly.com/

Printed in Great Britain
by Amazon

32907194R00145